"ENGROSSING."
— Senator John Glenn

"A GEM OF A THRILLER."
— *Publishers Weekly*

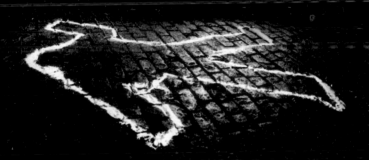

"A MURDER
OF HONOR

takes us deep within the Washington scene—political,
human, and criminal. It is everything you hoped it would
be. An elegant and wonderful book."
—*New York Times* bestselling author Robert B. Parker

Also by Robert Andrews

CENTER GAME
LAST SPY OUT
DEATH IN A PROMISED LAND
THE TOWERS

A MURDER OF HONOR

ROBERT ANDREWS

BERKLEY BOOKS, NEW YORK

This is a work of fiction. Names, characters, places, and incidents either are the product of the author's imagination or are used fictitiously, and any resemblance to actual persons, living or dead, business establishments, events, or locales is entirely coincidental.

A MURDER OF HONOR

A Berkley Book / published by arrangement with
the author

PRINTING HISTORY
Marian Wood hardcover edition / February 2001
Berkley mass-market edition / January 2002

All rights reserved.
Copyright © 2001 by Robert Andrews.
Excerpt from *A Murder of Promise* copyright © 2002 by Robert Andrews.
Cover photograph of crime-scene tape by Kaluzny/Thatcher/Tony Stone.
Cover photograph of chalk outline by Edward Holub/Tony Stone.
Cover design by Thomas Tafuri.

This book, or parts thereof, may not be reproduced
in any form without permission.
For information address: The Berkley Publishing Group,
a division of Penguin Putnam Inc.,
375 Hudson Street, New York, New York 10014.

Visit our website at
www.penguinputnam.com

ISBN: 0-425-18302-5

BERKLEY®
Berkley Books are published by The Berkley Publishing Group,
a division of Penguin Putnam Inc.,
375 Hudson Street, New York, New York 10014.
BERKLEY and the "B" design
are trademarks belonging to Penguin Putnam Inc.

PRINTED IN THE UNITED STATES OF AMERICA

10 9 8 7 6 5 4 3 2 1

THANKS TO FOUR WHO READ THE EARLY DRAFTS UNder exceptional circumstances: my daughter, Elizabeth Andrews, and my son-in-law, Brett Wilson, coping with a first pregnancy and back-to-back flights to Rio, Paris, and London; George Weigel, between fortnightly trips to the Vatican; and John Kester, while packing for the North Pole.

And thanks also to Chuck Babcock, who kicked this off over lunch, and Pete Dantuono and George Ward for their professional advice. Any departures from police procedure are mine.

Honor is like an island, rugged and without a beach;
once we have left it, we can never return.

—Nicolas Boileau-Despréaux

For B.J.

A MURDER
OF HONOR

THE *WASHINGTON POST* LEAD STORY ON JANUARY 3, 2000, IS the murder of Father Robert J. O'Brien. Under a headline reading "Community Activist Slain in Drive-by Shooting," two photos, taken thirty-one years apart, emblazon the front page. In the first, police stuff a slender priest into a paddy wagon. An angry crowd of ragged men and women, black and white, surround the cops. The caption says "1969 arrest of Rev. O'Brien in civil rights protest." In the second photo, a body lies on the sidewalk, arms and legs splayed in the improbable angles of death. It is a night picture. The Capitol dome floats white in the background. The caption says simply: "Murder scene, Pennsylvania Avenue."

In the same edition, on the front of the Metro section, the *Post* carries a story with the banner "Murder Suspect Killed Resisting Arrest." A photographer has caught Franklin Delano Kearney and Josephus Adams Phelps watching an attendant load a body bag into the back of an ambulance. Frank carries a nasty-looking military assault rifle. José holds a ten-gauge riot gun. Both men are in their fifties; Frank is the rangy, lean white guy, José the heavyset black one. You could get the idea from the photo that both men have been around the block. You'd be right. Between the two of them, they have more than fifty years on the D.C. force, partners all the way.

That Monday morning, a "get your ass down here" call from Randolph Emerson woke Frank Kearney early. He didn't have time to read the *Post*. He didn't know about the O'Brien murder. That would come forty-five minutes later.

ONE

MORNING SHIFT WAS coming on, and Frank wearily pushed through the crowded station house toward Emerson's office. The hallway noise and grab-assing made him jumpy and irritable.

Frank Kearney had become a cop indirectly. His road map started zigzagging in his sophomore year at the University of Maryland, when he decided his sociology major wouldn't get him a job. Nobody ever *did* sociology, Frank realized, except the professors who taught it, and he didn't see himself playing faculty politics to get tenure so ivy could grow on him until he retired at sixty-five. So he dropped out, intending to drift across the country for six months, maybe a year. See what was going on in Haight Ashbury.

But Frank's draft board was faster than he was, and instead of Haight Ashbury, he found out what was going on in the Iron Triangle as a grunt in the First Infantry Division. Like the rest of his squad, he ricocheted between ironic humor and scorching outrage at the cosmic joke that had stuck him with the nasty end of a very short stick. And like the rest of his squad, he cursed the relentlessly tedious stupidity of the Army by day, and by night the savage cruelty of the Vietcong.

Frank came out of Vietnam with a Combat Infantry Badge, a Bronze Star, and a Purple Heart. He also came out with the realization that he liked keeping bad things from happening to good people. He liked that more than he disliked uniforms. And so when he got back to College Park with the GI Bill, he went into law enforcement and from there made it into the DCMPD, the District of Columbia Metropolitan Police Department.

Now, outside Emerson's office, Frank's stomach flared. With one hand he pushed the door open, and with the other he fished in his jacket pocket for a Maalox tablet.

Frank had known Emerson twenty years, and he'd never known him anywhere but behind a desk.

"Took your time," Emerson said. He sat at his desk, wearing his suit jacket.

Frank took the jacket as a bad sign. Emerson normally worked in shirtsleeves. He wore a jacket only when he was kissing up or kicking down. Frank guessed that it wasn't going to be a kissing-up morning. His stomach was now searing. Half the trouble in the world happened because somebody like Emerson wanted to feel important.

His hand still in his pocket, Frank finally worked the Maalox tablet loose and palmed it.

"I had a booking," he said, trying not to sound defensive.

Emerson had the *Post* on his desk. He looked down at it.

Frank casually brought his hand out of his pocket and slipped the Maalox into his mouth.

Emerson looked up just as Frank was bringing his hand down. "You and Phelps are regular stars. Metro coverage. Even pictures." He tapped the photo of Frank and José. "You guys have an agent?"

"We took down a bad guy. It happens in this line of work."

"Happens a lot with you two."

"Maybe the rest of the department ought to be doing more, Randolph."

Emerson sighed. "We all did like you and Phelps, we wouldn't have any taxpayers left."

"Taxpayers?" Frank's eyes narrowed. He leaned for-

ward and with an index finger jabbed the body bag in the *Post* photograph. "Jimmy Foxworth? A taxpayer? In his whole life he never paid tax once. He was supposed to be doing life for raping and murdering a schoolteacher. He served twenty-three *months*. He goes up before the parole board, does a born-again song-and-dance. They buy it and turn him loose. He was out two days when he shot an old broad in a 7-Eleven." Frank drew a breath. "Courts keep the Jimmys in jail where they belong, we won't have to work so hard on the street."

Emerson wasn't listening. "And then there's the Johnny Sam lawsuit. ACLU's all over our asses."

"Johnny Sam killed two cops, Randolph."

"Manhandling suspects is against regulation. Whether they're jaywalking or killing cops. And Frank, I don't know how to tell you this, but we need *evidence* to convict."

"We had the son of a bitch. Two eyewitnesses. One just got on the wrong end of a hit-and-run and the other's flown."

Emerson tilted back in his chair and eyed Frank up and down. "You know what the talk is?"

"I know all kinds of talk. What brand you got in mind?"

"The talk is that we need some new faces in Homicide."

"Oh?" Frank raised his eyebrows. "You getting reassigned?"

Emerson shook his head as if he'd heard an old joke badly told. "The talk is that you and Phelps are cherry-picking. The talk's that you're retired on the job. Keeping your score up by going after pissants."

"Murder's murder, Randolph."

"But all murderers aren't the same, Frank. Some of them have 'Here I am' signs hung all over them. Like Jimmy Foxworth. A pissant. You and Phelps seem to be bagging more than your share of pissants. And the Johnny Sams of this city sue because you guys give away knuckle sandwiches."

Frank felt a sour acid burn. The Maalox wasn't working. He thrust forward across the desk, bringing his face close to Emerson's.

"Just a damn minute, Randolph," he said. "Eleven-thirty last night, José and I are getting shot at. Six-thirty, we get off shift. I'm in the rack for all of an hour, I get a call from you to get my butt down here. What for? To rehash Johnny Sam? Or discuss that rat Foxworth's virtues? Or debate the degree of difficulty of our case load?"

The outburst momentarily rocked Emerson back. He took a deep breath, then put on a glare. "You're right, Detective Kearney," he said in a low voice. "I didn't call you down here for any of that." He thrust the front page of the *Post* at Frank. "You and your pal read the rest of the paper? Or just the parts you're in?"

"WE GOTTA *WHAT*?"

José stood in his living room. He wore a pair of baggy white boxer shorts that hung beneath a heavy gut. With the gut and the cross frown and the thick ridges of scar tissue over his eyes, he looked like a grizzly disturbed in hibernation.

José had grown up in Washington, the oldest of five boys. His father, a lay preacher, managed a garage six days of the week and on Sundays regularly brought down your basic hellfire and brimstone at Bethel AME. His mother taught seventh-grade math at Browne, out on Benning Road.

José went to Howard to major in accounting and get into professional football. He made the varsity team, but never as a starter. He wasn't big enough for the line or fast enough for the backfield. In his junior year, he said to hell with it and tried boxing.

The moment he stepped into the ring, he felt at home. At two hundred six pounds, with a thirty-eight-inch reach and a rock-hard belly, he survived the early matches with more experienced fighters until he found his own style. José's fighting was straightforward enough: Take the offensive and never let up. Crowd, push, punch. If an opponent lands one or cuts you, never show you're hurt. Get back up on your toes, bore in. Crowd, push, punch.

Though tempted to turn pro, José stayed in college. He was big, he was hard, but it didn't bother him to admit his mother and father scared the shit out of him. And Mama and Daddy said stay in school.

Afterward, he realized, Mama and Daddy'd been right. His ring career following graduation lasted just eleven months. That's all it took for him to realize that a pretty good college boxer didn't go very far against pros who'd been in the game since they were nine.

He'd been living at home only two weeks when his father waved the classifieds at him and told him two things: one, get a job, and two, get out. Three weeks later, José answered a Metropolitan Police Department ad. Two weeks after that, he moved in with another recruit, who had stuck an index card on the bulletin board advertising for a roommate. A white guy named Frank Kearney.

After leaving Emerson's office, Frank drove to José's home in Washington Heights. He leaned on the doorbell until José opened the door.

"Here." Frank handed the *Post* to José, who scowled at the front page for a moment before lumbering over to a desk, where he found a pair of glasses. He scanned the paper, then, still scowling, looked up at Frank.

"So?"

"So, Hoser, we gotta take over the O'Brien case," Frank repeated.

"From who?"

"Milton and a rookie."

"Well, why aren't Milton and his rookie working it?"

"Emerson says we're cherry-picking."

José looked down at the picture of the dead priest and then at Frank. "A fucking drive-by," he muttered.

Frank walked over to his chair, the one he sat in when he and José watched the Redskins. He sat down, threw a leg over one arm of the chair and waited. He and José had been over the hurdles together. Frank figured he'd gotten the better deal in the relationship. It'd been José who'd seen him through the divorce, the self-pity, the booze, and helped him out the other side.

José shook his head. "Fucking drive-by," he repeated.

Frank nodded. Drive-bys you solved by luck. And mostly, the luck ran against you. Usually, shooters in drive-bys didn't know who it was they'd shot. Didn't care before, didn't care after. Seen all the flicks, done a little crack, had yourself a woman—what else to do on a Saturday night when all you had left was a Glock and a stolen set of wheels?

"You know what the king of cops is trying to do, don't you?"

"Put us in a trick bag," Frank said. "Milton's too junior. Emerson wants two names to throw to the wolves if he has to."

"Emerson's basic one-time good deal," José said. "We're lucky and get the shooter, Emerson gets the credit. We fuck up—"

"—we fuck up and Emerson gets us," Frank finished.

TWO

FORTY-FIVE MINUTES LATER, José motioned through the windshield. "There they are."

Two blue-and-whites, light bars blazing, parked in front of the National Archives. The January wind fluttered the yellow police-line tape marking off a section of the sidewalk.

Frank pulled in behind the patrol cars. He and José got out and walked to the small knot of uniformed officers and plainclothes. Milton was sipping coffee from a foam cup and talking with a uniformed officer Frank didn't recognize.

Milton, a slender white guy in his thirties, recognized Frank and waved. "Headquarters said you're taking over," he said.

"Yeah," Frank said. Early-morning pedestrians slowed to gawk, then hurried on.

Milton drew himself up slightly. "*I* didn't ask for any help."

"I know, Milt."

"Emerson fucking benched me."

"Don't make it anything big." Frank looked around. "Where was he? O'Brien?"

"Here." Milton held out an eight-by-ten glossy at arm's

length. A body sprawled on the sidewalk inside a ring of bystanders' shoes. Milton pointed toward the sidewalk.

Frank took the photo, eyed it, then the sidewalk where O'Brien's body had been. "Notification?" he asked, as he fished in his coat pocket.

Milton opened a pocket notebook.

Frank pulled out his own notebook and began recording the basics as Milton read them off. A 911 call at one-thirteen. From a pay phone, Milton added, answering Frank's question before he could ask it. Sanchez had been the first officer there, arriving at one-nineteen. Sanchez reported having successfully secured the scene. Milton had gotten there at one thirty-seven. Weather had been fair, pavement dry, temperature nineteen Fahrenheit.

"The nine-one-one?" José asked.

"Nothing," Milton said. "No name. And nobody here when Sanchez got here."

"And O'Brien was dead?"

"As they get. Looks like he took it in the chest."

"Emerson said a drive-by. How do we know without witnesses?"

"That's what the nine-one-one said. Drive-by, drive-by. Like that."

Frank made a note to check the recording.

"Nobody touched anything?"

"Nothing to touch, except O'Brien."

Frank turned to José. "You got anything?"

José shook his head.

Frank turned to Milton. "He's at the M.E.? O'Brien is?"

"Meat wagon removed the deceased at four fifty-two. Area's been closed off since then."

"Residence?" Frank asked.

Milton looked in his notebook. "Four hundred D Northwest. Sent two uniforms over to seal the place."

Frank knew the building. O'Brien's halfway house for the homeless and the hopeless. A block from City Hall, a spare, utilitarian building. For years, O'Brien had campaigned out of that building. Antiwar marches, sit-ins at City Hall, pickets at the White House. Something happened, it always seemed to come back to O'Brien and the ugly building on D Street.

Frank looked at the uniformed cops who had kept the area secured and imagined they were as tired as he. Milton was holding out the 601.

"Okay," Frank said, taking the form and putting it in his notebook, "it's ours." He held the notebook out as if weighing it. Milton seemed pissed, and so Frank told the young detective, "Don't let this bug you."

Milton's eyes held a little glimmer of sympathy. He crumpled the foam cup and tossed it into a nearby trashcan. "I already forgot, Frank." He started to turn, then paused and looked back. "Thanks. Watch your ass."

"Yeah." Frank sighed. "Thanks." He remembered when he was Milton's age, and found himself thinking, You're young, you're bulletproof. The older you get, the more your ass means to you. That it was so pissed him off. That he thought about it at all pissed him off more. Then his eyes met José's, and Frank knew that José was reading his mind, and that pissed him off even more.

"Match," Frank said, pulling a quarter from his pocket. "Evens you get the search warrant." Frank flipped. José pulled a dime from his pocket and held it in his palm, heads up. Frank's quarter landed heads.

THE DISTRICT MEDICAL EXAMINER'S OFFICE IS ON MASS-achusetts Avenue Northeast. In Washington, the compass means a lot. You go up Mass Avenue Northwest and you go up St. Alban's Hill, past the Vice-President's House and on to the National Cathedral. You pass embassies and chancelleries with immaculate sidewalks, exquisitely sculpted landscapes, ancient sheltering oaks.

Northeast Mass wasn't embassy Washington. Instead of boxwood hedges, you got beer cans and broken glass and weeds, rows of parking meters beheaded for their quarters, and a vandalized newspaper vending rack hanging crazily from its mooring to a lamppost.

Inside the M.E.'s office, Frank signed in. "Morning,

Grace," he said to the gray-haired woman behind the counter.

"Frank," she acknowledged. "You ain't retired yet?"

"I'm *tired*"—Frank did a playback with their old joke—"but not *re*-tired."

Grace laughed. "Guess you're here for the preacher."

"Who's cutting?"

"Dr. Tony." Grace pointed her pencil over her shoulder toward a set of double doors.

Frank pushed through. Cardboard cartons and chemical drums crowded the narrow corridor. The scent of denatured alcohol cut the air like a delicate blade. Under the alcohol lay a thicker layer of formalin, sweet and clinging with the overripe essence Frank associated with death.

Halfway down the hall, Anthony Upton, the M.E., a slender, middle-aged black man, stood at a doorway in a long rubberized apron, sipping coffee. He watched as Frank approached.

"Hello, Tony," Frank said.

Wordlessly, Tony Upton nodded, then turned and stepped into the dissecting suite. Frank followed, his footsteps echoing off the tile floor. The body locker, a massive refrigerator in gleaming white enamel with polished chrome handles, stretched along one wall.

Ten evenly spaced tables filled the room, shiny stainless steel with drains, tubing, and blood gutters. Above each table, a microphone and a hanging scale with a polished chrome bowl. Nine were empty. At the tenth, a man, Upton's assistant—the diener—waited with a gurney and its cargo, a white plastic body bag.

"There," Upton said, pointing to the table.

An arctic blast of air from the overhead vents chilled Frank. He stared at the body bag and imagined he could feel the refrigerated cold radiating from it.

From a wall rack, Upton took a clear plastic face shield. Frank found one, slipped it on. Dark spots of dried blood were encrusted across the plastic. He found himself wondering whom the blood had come from.

Snapping on rubber gloves, Upton pointed toward the

gurney. The diener unzipped the body bag and with a prac-
ticed, efficient motion slid O'Brien's naked corpse out of it
and onto the dissection table.

Upton reached above the table, flicked a switch on the
microphone, and checked the red On light. Then he
reached for the yellow toe tag and examined it. "O'Brien,
Robert," he said for the microphone.

O'Brien's skin was waxy, the mouth partially opened as
if frozen while trying to talk. In the center of the chest, two
small wounds less than an inch apart, one a clean circular
puncture, the other elongated and ragged.

Upton measured the wounds, and with long stainless-
steel probes resembling knitting needles estimated the angles of entry. He noted his results for the microphone. That
done, he turned to Frank.

"I'm cutting now," he announced, as though in warning.
Frank nodded.

Upton plunged the scalpel deep into O'Brien's left
shoulder. He cut quickly across and down to the bottom of
the breastbone, then up, to finish at the right shoulder.
Without pausing he made the second cut, this one from the
center of the chest to the pubis. As Upton cut, the incision
furrowed open behind the scalpel. Now Frank could see
the meaty red and white of the exposed rib cage and the
packed tangle of intestines and organs of the abdomen.

Homicide autopsies all hit Frank the same way. He'd
long since gotten over the nausea part, but what never left
him was a sense of profound sadness at seeing a human being carved up like a side of beef. He let his eyes unfocus
into a thousand-yard stare and stepped into another place
and time. He only dimly heard the grating sound as Upton
chopped through ribs and cartilage. From a distance, he
heard him report the weighing of heart and lungs.

"What?" Frank realized Upton had turned away from
the dissecting table and was saying something to him.

"The bullets," Upton repeated. He handed Frank a
porcelain pan flecked with blood.

With a pair of pick-ups from a nearby tray, Frank examined one of the slugs. It resembled a small silver-gray

mushroom. The bullet's nose had been flattened by its impact with O'Brien's body, the stem engraved with the spiraling lands and grooves of the weapon that had fired it. He heard Upton dictating his findings.

"The cause of death was two twenty-two-caliber gunshot wounds to the chest," Upton said into the microphone. "The mechanism of death was loss of blood and shock secondary to traumatic hemorrhage of the lung. The manner of death was homicide."

"Thanks, Tony."

Upton looked surprised, disappointed, like a host whose guest was leaving the party early. "There's more," he offered. "The abdomen. The brain?"

Frank looked at the eviscerated body, then at the two tiny slugs. He rolled them back and forth, a prospector panning for ore, and shook his head. "No," he told Upton. "That's all I need for now."

THREE

FRANK LEFT THE M.E. and drove to the shelter on D Northwest. A neatly lettered sheet-metal sign over the main door outside said "St. Francis Center." Three stories, battleship gray. A grim, tight-jawed, no-nonsense building. Also the only building on the block with no graffiti, no broken windows, no trash on the sidewalk. Frank nodded to the uniformed cop who stood in the shelter of the doorway to keep out of the wind.

"Third floor," the cop said, stepping forward and pointing up to a corner window.

ONCE INSIDE THE BARE ENTRYWAY, FRANK CAME FACE-to-face with a young priest. "I'm Father Timothy Dash," he said. He made no move to shake hands.

Frank introduced himself and handed Dash a contact card.

The priest glanced at the card, then at Frank. "Father O'Brien's room has been sealed off. Why?" Dash had the close-cropped intensity of a soldier or a long-distance runner.

"Procedure," Frank explained.

"It's not the crime scene."

Frank took a deep breath. "It's procedure, Father. We'll be careful, but it's something we've got to do."

Dash said nothing.

Frank tried a smile. "Look, Father, I won't do your masses if you don't do my investigations."

The priest's expression didn't change.

Frank dropped the smile. "The stairs?" he asked.

Dash pointed.

ON THE THIRD FLOOR, SPUTTERING FLUORESCENT LIGHTS drained the color from the hallway and made it look a million miles long. At the far end, José sat in a chair, reading a magazine. In another chair, a uniformed cop leaned against the wall. When he saw Frank, the cop tilted forward and simultaneously reached for a clipboard at his feet. José stood, and from his inner coat pocket pulled out a legal-size envelope, which he wagged at Frank.

Frank glanced at the seals on the door as he took the clipboard. He wrote his name and badge number on the access form and handed the clipboard to José. The uniformed cop held out two pair of rubber gloves and plastic booties.

While José was signing, Frank pulled on the gloves and booties.

"You meet O'Brien's number two?" José asked.

"Yeah. Probably gives sourdough at communion." Frank nodded to the cop. "Let's open up."

"Anything at the M.E.?" José asked, watching the cop unseal the door.

"Two slugs in the chest."

"Oh."

"Close together."

José turned to Frank. "Close?"

"Coulda covered them both with a quarter."

José didn't say anything, but looked intently at Frank.

"Something else."

"Yeah?"

"Twenty-two long rifle."

"So?"

"Twenty-two's small for a street piece."

José laughed. "Hell, Frank. This's Murder City, USA. We seen shooters use swords, bricks, and Civil War muzzle loaders, for God's sake! They'd use an atom bomb if they had one." He shrugged. "Punk has a twenty-two, punk uses a twenty-two."

The uniform stood waiting, the door to O'Brien's room open.

"After you," José said.

Frank stood in the doorway. Except for the books, it could have been in a barracks. Ten feet square, white plaster walls, a worn but highly buffed linoleum tile floor. Basic furniture: an unfinished wood desk and chair, a pair of institutional gray metal file cabinets, a couple of metal folding chairs, a narrow bunk bed. Over the bunk, a crucifix, and on the wall over the desk, two framed photographs.

Frank gave the pictures a closer look. In one, O'Brien had a wrist lock on a riot policeman. The cop, baton raised, was about to club a man down on his knees. It was one of those black-and-white photos from the sixties, taken in what looked like a southern city, complete with cops in helmets and dark glasses, and leashed police dogs. In the other, Frank guessed, O'Brien was at the Vatican, because the guy O'Brien was talking to was the pope. O'Brien looked like he was lecturing. In the background, junior clerics wore shocked expressions, but the pope looked bemused and intrigued.

Bookshelves covered an entire wall. More books, the overflow from the shelves, had been stacked neatly on the floor. Forensics would have a job, going over the place for prints. Frank scanned the titles. Alinsky's *Rules for Radicals* and Sandburg's *Abraham Lincoln*. Lenin next to Jefferson. Voltaire's *Candide,* Webb's *Fields of Fire.* Don't tell me what a man's like, Frank thought. Just show me what he reads.

"You want to start?"

You work with somebody for twenty-five years and you come to unspoken agreements about a lot of things. Like how you drink your coffee, who drives in crappy weather.

Who's first to get to the office, and who's first to leave. And so it was automatic that Frank began searching the room around to his right, and José started to the left.

The two men worked thoroughly and carefully.

Frank started with the closet. Four worn black suits, vestments, a dark green nylon ski jacket, four pair of black shoes. On the closet shelf, a black fedora and one of those woolly-bear hats you used to see commies wearing when there were still commies in Russia.

Frank was just getting into eyeballing the closet good when José broke the silence.

"Look here."

José stood by one of the file cabinets. He had on his half-frame reading glasses and he held a manila file folder.

Frank stepped over and looked in. "Clippings."

"Yeah—see what?"

Frank opened the folder wide. He held it out at arm's length.

"Here."

Frank took José's reading glasses. "Classifieds."

"Yeah?" José prompted.

"Hunh," Frank said. *"The Blade."* He thumbed through a sheaf of personal ads from the District's gay newspaper. They ran the gamut—from self-descriptions of tops and bottoms, of the well-hung and the submissive, to searches for others who wanted their sex French or Greek, to ads for leather bars and bathhouses.

Frank got a hollow feeling, and the room suddenly seemed far away. "There's more of them," he heard José say.

He felt his stomach churn. He shook his head. "Here." Frank handed the folder back to José, along with the glasses. "We got all we're going to get. Let's see what we can find out from *The Blade.*"

THE NEWSPAPER PUBLISHED OUT OF AN OLD TOWNHOUSE near the waterfront. Stacks of yellowing back issues covered every flat surface in the cramped, overheated room that served as the business office.

"I can't help, gentlemen." *The Blade*'s business manager, a short, stocky man named Raskin, shook his head. "I can't tell you if anyone answered one of our personals or put one in."

José put on his "I can't believe this shit" look.

Before he could say anything, Raskin held up two fingers. "First, there's confidentiality. If it ever got out that we gave that kind of information to the police, we'd be shut down." Raskin looked back and forth between José and Frank sitting on a sofa facing his desk. "I suppose the courts could order us to, but we'd fight it all the way to the Supremes.

"Second, there's process—how we do things here. We accept cash or money orders for ads and for response-box rentals. Over ninety percent of our ads and boxes are paid for that way. If your man sends a letter to a personals box"—Raskin motioned with his hands—"we pass it directly to that box. We don't know where it came from. We don't know where it's going."

José GOT INTO HIS SEAT, AND BEFORE FRANK COULD start the car said, "That bothered you."

"What?" Frank asked, knowing he already knew.

"You don't like it." José touched a knuckle on the folder with the clippings.

Frank thought about it. "No. No, I don't." He started the car and glanced around at the traffic.

"Drive-by," José said, "they don't give a shit if he's a priest or if he's gay or if he's a rhinoceros."

"Yeah. If it was a drive-by."

"*If* it was a drive-by? You saying something, or just thinking?"

Frank eased out into the street. "I don't know. Maybe just thinking, Hoser."

"Fucking drive-by."

"Yeah." Frank knew what José was thinking. In a drive-by, access and motive didn't mean squat, because the shooter was going after anybody. You could investigate the victim's background until hell froze over and come up empty.

Instead, you went looking for witnesses and you pumped your snitches. A witness to ID the car or the driver. Drive-by shooters did it for kicks. Anybody stupid enough or crazy enough to drive around shooting people for kicks also got kicks talking about it. And so you worked the snitches.

That's the way you went after drive-bys. Still . . .

"We make the rounds in the morning?" José half asked, half suggested.

"Yeah. Fine with me."

"You don't sound like it's fine with you, Frank."

"Yeah. Maybe . . . hell, I just don't know. I got some bothers."

"What?"

"Nothing solid. A feeling. Just a feeling."

"Feelings got reasons."

"Okay. The slugs. Twenty-two's not a drive-by piece. A priest with clippings of fag personals. Sure, you can explain it all away. But put it together, and it's out-of-place stuff. Stuff that doesn't fit."

"What's that you say about hoofbeats?"

What Frank said about hoofbeats was from his procedures lectures at the academy. Don't overcomplicate an investigation, he'd tell the rookies. Stick with the basics. When you hear hoofbeats, look for horses, not zebras.

Frank sighed. "Humor me, Hoser, humor me. We don't find any zebras, we'll look for horses."

FOUR

FRANK LIVED ON Olive Street in Georgetown. Built in Grover Cleveland's first presidency, the small two-story rowhouse had been in terminal disintegration when Frank bought it, all he could afford after the divorce. At the time he intended to stay only until he'd gotten Tom and Francie through college.

His first mistake had been to refinish the oak floors. Then, in the living room, he discovered burled walnut paneling hidden beneath layers of paint. He spent three months of night and weekend work stripping, sanding, and staining. From then on, what had been a simple fix-up grew into a restoration project, and the house on Olive Street had become a home. Now, fifteen years later, Tom was a lawyer in Louisville, Francie was a molecular biologist in San Francisco, and Frank was still living on Olive Street and worrying about a new roof.

A light snow had just started falling when Frank locked his car and made for the house, half a block away.

He switched off the security alarm and opened the door, then paused in the doorway, taking in the reassuring comfort of the old house: the aroma of wood, leather, and a faint hint of cigar smoke. He felt the tension ease between his shoulders.

After hanging his coat, he turned on the lights and made his way down the long hall to the kitchen. This was Frank's favorite room. He had expanded the original narrow galley by opening an exterior wall and glassing in what had been the back porch. Five years earlier, he had found an almost new chef's range, all industrial black iron and polished stainless steel, above which he'd hung a mismatched collection of copper pots and skillets.

He'd been in the kitchen less than a minute when a large gray cat squeezed through the flap he had set in the door to the backyard.

"Here, Monty," Frank said, picking up the cat. "You get into any trouble today?" With his hands he explored the animal. Satisfied that Monty had gotten through another day without an alleyway brawl, Frank put him down. He filled his dish with dry food and watched as the cat ate noisily.

The red light winked patiently on the answering machine. Frank pushed a button and heard Kate's voice. He listened to the message, glanced at his watch, then reached into the refrigerator for a beer, and began dinner.

FRANK ANSWERED THE DOORBELL A LITTLE AFTER SEVEN. Kate Dwyer, five-six, blonde, and forty-eight, kissed Frank on the cheek as she rushed by. A dusting of snow covered her coat and knit hat.

They had met three years earlier, in one of those coincidental ways in which many couples meet. Kate, a lawyer in the District's legal department, had been rushing to catch a cab. It was raining. She and Frank got to the only available cab at the same time. Frank opened the door for her. In her haste, she got in and shut the door. Then, as the cab pulled away, she looked back and saw him standing in the rain, right hand raised, middle finger extended. She'd had the cabby stop and back up.

Kate shook the snow off her hat. "Damn parking, Frank. You ought to get the city to reserve something out front for you."

"Park by the hydrant. I'll fix the ticket."

She laughed and handed him her coat and hat. "You're too straight even to fix a ticket."

"Not for you."

Kate kissed him again, longer this time. She pulled away. "I smell lasagna."

"Smell again. Cavatelli with sausage and garlic."

"You going to tell me all about the O'Brien thing?"

"After we eat. Cavatelli gets gummy, you let it sit."

KATE CORNERED THE RED SAUCE LEFT ON HER PLATE with a thick bread crust. Frank refilled their glasses.

"Okay," he said. "O'Brien." For the next ten minutes, he walked her through it, from the moment Emerson gave him the case to the autopsy.

"Then we searched his room."

"And?" Kate asked.

"José found a folder full of clippings. Personals. From *The Blade*."

"Oh," Kate said.

They sat in silence, looking at each other. Then Frank spoke. "I had a call slip waiting this afternoon. Some TV reporter's on our ass."

Kate said hesitantly, "You're in the middle of a serious flap."

"Really?" Frank smiled.

"Frank." Kate shook her head.

He saw she was worried.

"I mean *really* serious. Like you say, a grade-A, down-and-dirty shitstorm, Frank. The District's already number one in the country for homicides. Country? Did I say 'country'? In the whole damn world. Now a national figure gets blown away. Robert J. O'Brien. Saint of the streets. Scourge of the establishment. Uplifter of the downtrodden. Every gun-control organization with a letterhead has scheduled press conferences for tomorrow. Senate Judiciary Committee's cranking up special hearings."

"And the Mayor's Office?"

Kate sighed. "He's going up to the Hill tomorrow."

"Covering his ass? Ask Congress to come up with another feel-good law? Make it a federal crime to shoot priests?" Frank taunted. He grimaced. "Politics."

"You're shocked?"

"Yeah," he said, playing on the *Casablanca* line, "I'm shocked, shocked—politics in Washington."

"You aren't worried about yourself?"

Frank laughed. "Hoser and I are just hired help. We'll get by." He picked up a videocassette from the sideboard. "Mind some homework?" he asked.

"Movies?"

"The TV guy. The one who's on our case. He interviewed O'Brien. Six, seven months ago."

Kate waved her glass at the TV. "Roll 'em."

Frank fed the cassette into the VCR. The screen flashed; then the header blinked into focus.

"Inquiring Minds?" Kate exclaimed. "Oh God!"

Frank fast-forwarded past the introduction and commercials until a man appeared, sitting in an easy chair, hands and head moving in erratic gestures.

Frank flicked the remote.

Motion stopped. The man in the easy chair smiled out of the screen. Good teeth, silver hair, square chin. Just enough wrinkles for credibility.

"Hugh Worsham," Kate said. "How'd O'Brien ever agree to—"

Frank shrugged. He flicked the remote again, and Worsham came to life.

"America's homeless, a capital embarrassment," Worsham said to the camera. The voice was a rich baritone. Frank picked up a faint midwestern accent.

"What to do about it?" Worsham asked. "We compare and contrast two solutions. Solutions proposed by two very different men. And very different solutions. Last week, we saw homeless activist John Hennington . . ."

Worsham trailed off as the screen replayed part of an earlier program. The scene opened on a busy street. Frank recognized it as McPherson Square, less than half a mile from the White House. Hennington, a thin, sandy-haired man, stood beside a white van neatly painted with the sign "Loaves and Fishes." Stretching from the van was a line of ragged men—Frank judged there to be about thirty to forty of them. Hennington was passing out box lunches as someone inside the van handed them to him.

"Here," Worsham's voice-over explained, "is John Hennington feeding the homeless of our nation's capital. He started in 1972, over a quarter-century ago."

The camera switched to Hennington. "There's no end to it," he was saying. "The richer we become, the longer these lines." He gestured to the waiting men. "Our government spends more on weapons than on our weak."

The camera panned the square. A few men sat on benches, absorbed in eating. Others, finished, were walking away. The scene faded with a shot of abandonment—a close-up of discarded lunch containers blown by the wind, bumping crablike along broken sidewalks.

The screen came back to Worsham in his library. "And this week, Father Robert J. O'Brien. As we said, a very different man, a very different approach."

O'Brien's face filled the screen. It was a clip from an interview, an excerpt Worsham had chosen that would convey the essence of O'Brien to the television audience.

The camera came in close on O'Brien. So close Frank could see the pores in his skin. O'Brien had a bulldog look about him.

"Government handout programs," the priest said in a rasping voice, "just encourage the blight on our streets. We have very few who are truly homeless. Most of the wreckage we see lying in alleys aren't there because of the economy. They're mentally ill, they've got problems with drugs or alcohol, or both. And if they aren't crazies or addicts, they're bums."

Worsham's face appeared. The reporter wore a sad "I told you so" smile. "And as they say, that's just for starters. Join me as *Inquiring Minds* meets a very remarkable and very outspoken man."

Frank watched as the screen faded into the next scene.

O'Brien and Worsham walked through the shelter. The dormitory with its rows of bunks, their blankets taut with sharp hospital folds. The shower rooms with primitive but spotless plumbing and gleaming floors. The dining room with its long communal tables and benches, the busy kitchen. The same theme throughout: well used, often patched, but clean and serviceable.

Then a sequence of scenes showing how the shelter worked. The camera followed the progress of a middle-aged black man named Tom. The entry medical exam, the showers, barber, clothing issue. A steady diet of job training, physical conditioning, and religious instruction.

Another series of scenes followed O'Brien's graduates. No Fortune 500 executives, no Silicon Valley start-up millionaires. But men working, bringing a paycheck home to a wife, maybe even to a wife and kids. Short interviews with former addicts, alcoholics. One guy obviously under medication, but holding down a job, not screaming from a doorway or defecating in a gutter.

Finally the camera homed in on Worsham and O'Brien—Worsham's trademark, the windup interview. Frank recognized the setting: it was O'Brien's room. Worsham sat in one metal folding chair, O'Brien in the other.

Worsham glanced at the legal pad in his lap, then up to O'Brien. "Thank you, Father, for the tour. I must say, you come across as a man of contradictions."

O'Brien raised an eyebrow. "Contradictions?"

Worsham nodded. "A priest who fought in Vietnam?"

"It was before I was a priest."

"But Vietnam . . ." Good manners apparently kept Worsham from finishing.

"It was a just war."

Worsham waited for more, but O'Brien sat quietly, having said his piece. Worsham picked up: "Who then came back to America as a civil rights activist in the South?"

"Another just war."

"Who would reform Washington without government help?"

"I refuse handouts from the corrupt."

Worsham played interrogator. "Meaning Mayor Malcolm Burridge?"

"Meaning the corrupt."

Again, Worsham waited for more, but it wasn't coming. He glanced again at his legal pad and said, "Father O'Brien, you've shown us a very impressive operation. I'm certain our viewers want to know how successful you are."

O'Brien looked quizzically at Worsham. "Success?" O'Brien didn't seem to like the taste of the word. "Success?" he repeated. "How do you want to measure it? By the number of meals we serve?"

Worsham shared a sly grin with the camera and the audience beyond. "I'm sure you know the number of meals, Father. How about the number of souls?"

O'Brien laughed. It was a good laugh, Frank thought. From a man you'd spend time with over beers.

"Number of souls, Mr. Worsham, you'd better ask God about that." O'Brien shot him a stern look. "That is, if the two of you are on speaking terms."

Worsham laughed, but to Frank the laughter had a hollow ring. O'Brien's image faded. The next segment lead started. Frank clicked the remote to turn off the TV.

He stood and started cleaning off the table. "They won't wash themselves."

Kate smiled. "No dessert?"

"Didn't know you wanted any."

She leaned close and kissed his neck. "I do."

Frank took her hand. "Dishes'll wait."

Frank woke around two in the morning. One moment he was asleep, the next awake. No crazy dreams. No falling sensation. He just opened his eyes and there he was, awake. Dim light through the window threw angular shadows across the ceiling. Beside him, Kate breathed softly. He lay quietly. Her warmth was almost palpable, with a life of its own.

He reached for her. Then, before he touched her, the Worsham interview replayed in his mind. When it was over, he found himself standing at the window, looking out at the street below. The snow was still falling.

He watched it for what seemed like forever. And then he felt Kate beside him.

"Beautiful," she whispered, pressing her cheek against his shoulder. The snow had covered the street, the cars along the curb, and lay heavily on the boughs of the tall cedar that had been planted more than a hundred years before, when Frank's house had been built.

"A flake at a time," Frank said. "Damn good thing it doesn't come down all at once."

They were silent for a long time, standing together, watching the snow fall.

"O'Brien woke you up."

"Yeah."

"And?"

Frank shrugged, trying to pin it down. Then he found it. "He seemed . . . real." He paused, thought more.

"Trying to remember. I must have worked four, five hundred homicides. I remember names. I remember ages, sex, black, white, Asian, whatever." He turned to Kate. "I remember details, but I don't remember ever *knowing* them—how they'd been as people. And I never thought about what they could have been. What they could have done."

Kate rested her cheek on his shoulder and put an arm around him.

"And you know O'Brien."

Frank hesitated and watched the snow for a while. "Yeah," he said finally, "I think I do."

"And that will make a difference?"

"Yeah. I think so."

"A better difference? Or worse?"

FIVE

FRANK GOT INTO the precinct early and made his way to the third floor, past Emerson's office, then down the hall to Records and Modus Operandi. A light glowed behind the frosted-glass panel. He knocked softly and pushed the door open.

"Yes?"

The husky female voice came from behind a computer at a corner desk. The rest of the office was as yet empty. A wisp of blue smoke curled above the computer.

"Eleanor?"

"Who else?" A woman's face peered around the side of the computer. Eleanor had been in R&MO when Frank came on as a rookie. She was the department's institutional memory. There wasn't much about crime and punishment she didn't know. And what she didn't know, she could find out. She'd looked old then, but she didn't seem to have aged since. Short iron-gray hair, rimless glasses, cigarette hanging from the corner of her small mouth.

"No smoking in city offices, Eleanor."

"Those are duty-hour rules." She pushed her chair back to get a better look at Frank. "They want the work done, either they hire another ten people or they do it my way and put up with the smoke." She took a deep drag on the cigarette and followed the smoke toward the ceiling, then looked back at Frank. "What do you want?"

"What do you know about Hugh Worsham?"

"Reporters used to get the facts, then tell the story. Now they decide the story, then dig up the facts they want and disregard the rest. Easier that way."

"He's one of those kind?"

"A Geraldo wannabe. Anything to get top billing. Slap shots, back shots, cheap shots."

"Oh."

"High-profile case, Frank. Just your luck to get Worsham."

"Yeah. He got any contacts in the department?"

Eleanor gave him a "You should know better" smile. She looked toward Emerson's office, down the hall. "You can go a long way in this town, you know who to leak to."

Frank nodded. "You hear anything . . ."

"Yeah." Eleanor watched him as if taking a measurement. "That lady lawyer you been seeing—Dwyer?"

"Kate."

"First one I've seen put up with you for this long."

"Otherwise she's pretty smart."

"You ought to get smart yourself, Frank."

"You starting that again?"

Eleanor pulled on her cigarette and sent another plume of smoke toward the ceiling. "You and José have played cops and robbers long enough," she said. "Grow up. Take your retirement and get out. Get a real job."

"Like you?"

"My job doesn't get me shot at."

"I been lucky."

"I remember a couple of times you weren't. Luck's a sometime thing."

Frank turned to leave.

Eleanor scooted her chair sideways and disappeared behind the computer. "Have a good one," came her voice, along with a cloud of smoke.

* * *

IT WAS BEFORE NINE WHEN FRANK PULLED UP AT THE shelter.

The office was a small room off the street entry. Two wooden desks—one, Frank assumed, had been O'Brien's. An old computer on a rickety stand, three chairs, a file cabinet, and on the wall, a crucifix. High-sheen floors, polished windowpanes.

Father Dash stood by the window. "We can sit." He pointed to the chairs.

Frank had a theory that what you got from a subject depended on how you started the initial interview. Frank looked at the priest. A tight-wound man. All hard edges.

"Watched a tape last night," Frank said. *"Inquiring Minds."*

"The Worsham interview?"

"Father O'Brien came down heavy on discipline."

"First requirement to getting people off the street." Father Dash clipped his words.

"Used to be able to commit the crazies."

"Used to. But these are tolerant times," the priest replied with irony. "Now the courts defend their freedom to disintegrate in doorways."

"You don't?"

"We don't tolerate destructive behavior. Destructive of others, destructive of self. We aren't a democracy."

"And the people who stay here?"

"You accept our food, you accept our shelter, you accept our discipline. That's the deal. We don't subsidize street living." He gave Frank a long look. "But you aren't here to talk about the causes and cures of dereliction."

"No."

"A killing like that . . ." The priest raised his hands in a gesture of surrender and frustration. "How do you make sense out of something that is in itself senseless? How do you find evidence in randomness?"

"Random depends on how you look at something."

Frank studied the priest, then asked, "You understand God, Father?"

Dash looked puzzled.

"But you try, right?" Frank produced a notebook from a coat pocket. "You mind? Notes? I've got to try understanding random."

Dash gave a slight nod.

"Did he have a personal life?"

Dash blinked as though he hadn't expected that question. "Personal? We all have personal lives."

"I mean, relationships. That didn't involve this place. Personal relationships."

Frank watched the priest's eyes narrow. Whatever he was weighing, Frank told himself, it didn't come out to trust.

"His personal relationships were with God and the Church," Dash said carefully, his face tight.

"Any close human friends, Father?"

"Come on, Lieutenant."

"Come on?"

"You're asking that in a way that means more than what you're saying."

"Oh?"

"As if close human friends were something you keep secret."

"Okay. Did Father O'Brien have any contacts in the gay community?"

Dash looked stonily at Frank. "No more or less than any of us in the human race. We all have gay contacts. But you don't mean it that way, do you?"

Frank didn't say anything, just stared back at Dash.

"If you're asking if Father O'Brien was gay, or was violating his vow of celibacy, I'd tell you no."

"What was he doing out at one A.M.?"

"Walking."

"That's not what I meant."

"That's what you asked."

"Okay, Father. Do you know *why* he was walking at one A.M.? And please, don't tell me he was walking because he didn't have a car."

The priest stiffened, and shook his head in resignation. "Father O'Brien is . . . Father O'Brien *was* . . . a night person. Catnapped during the day, worked mostly at night. I'm the opposite. That way, we covered this place twenty-four hours a day. He'd regularly take a break around midnight and go for coffee over at the Crystal Palace. Must have been where he'd been when . . ."

Frank made a note, then looked up. "Okay, Father," he said, low and careful, "I'd like to get back to names."

"Names?"

"People he knew. People he dealt with."

"There're a lot."

Frank nodded. "Let's start."

FRANK PARKED ON M AT TWENTY-EIGHTH, TWO BLOCKS from Garrett's. The early lunch crowd was beginning to fill the sidewalk. In the press of bodies at the curb waiting to cross Twenty-ninth, he caught an elbow in his side, kidney level. It was hard enough that he knew it wasn't accidental. Frank dipped his right shoulder and spun a quarter-turn, and grabbed an upper arm just above the biceps. He pulled and came face to face with a big, bulky man, well over six feet tall. Thick eyebrows sheltered dark, close-set eyes.

"Excuse me, Detective," Johnny Sam said with an exaggerated formality. "I simply must watch where I'm walking."

Stifling the impulse to smash Sam's mouth, Frank whispered hoarsely, "Don't bother, Johnny—you won't be walking long."

Sam smiled. "I had hoped the department would teach its officers the value of manners."

Frank flashbacked to Mary Quinn, a new widow clutching a folded flag to her breast. The firing squad getting all too much practice, the inevitable bugler and taps.

"You killed a good cop, you bastard. And you're going to pay."

Sam widened his sneer. "The jury said I didn't kill anybody. And I think, Detective, the D.C. government's going to pay, and pay me well. But don't worry. I'll make a nice little donation to the police welfare fund."

Frank grabbed a handful of cashmere topcoat and wrenched Sam toward himself. As he drew his right fist back, he felt a sudden, massive pressure across his chest.

"Let him go, Frank," he heard José say in his ear. It seemed to come from a long way off, and he tried to swing his fist forward, but José tightened his grip. "Let. Him. Go."

And he did. And the rest of the street came back into focus, and he felt as if he'd been underwater. He pulled the cold winter air deep into his lungs.

"Let's go, Hoser," he managed to get out. As they entered Garrett's, Frank turned and saw Johnny Sam still standing there on the sidewalk, smiling.

JOSÉ FED THE JUKEBOX, STANLEY BROUGHT COFFEE, AND they sat for a long while at their table listening to the Elvis oldies, saying nothing. Finally Frank felt loose enough to ask, "What you got?"

"Everybody on the street knew the guy. Nobody on the street knows shit." José spooned sugar into his second cup of coffee. "Nothing about a car, shooter, driver. No bullshit talk going."

"Nobody pissed?"

José shrugged. "Just about everybody in City Hall. O'Brien was a quick man with the wire brush."

"Names?"

José shook his head. "Nobody in particular." He tested his coffee. "Just bureaucrats. The priest?"

"Stiff."

"Yeah?"

"Like he's got a cast-iron rod up his ass. But I got him started on associates. Got six pages' worth."

"What'd he say about the clippings?"

"I didn't ask him. Not directly." Frank felt a twist of uneasiness at not having worked Dash harder. He knew José would have laid out the clippings to the young priest.

José would have used the clippings.

Ordinarily, he would have, too. But this time he hadn't.

Why hadn't he? He looked up and saw the same question in José's eyes. You can lie to your woman, your boss, or even yourself. You never want to lie to your partner.

"I guess the priest stuff gets in my way, Hoser. Way I was raised and all, priests didn't even think—much less *do*—sex." Frank sipped his coffee and hurried on to cut his loss. "But I did ask him about gay contacts."

"And?"

Frank shook his head. "Dash denied it."

"Well. Like I say, drive-bys don't give a shit how you swing. Or if you swing at all. Answer to this is out on the street somewhere, Frank. Not in that shelter."

Frank got the image of O'Brien gut-open on Tony Upton's stainless-steel table, two mushroomed bullets rattling around in the blood-specked pan.

"Maybe you're right, Hoser."

"You don't sound like it. We still looking for zebras?"

Frank didn't answer.

"It was a drive-by, Frank." José frowned. "A drive-by. Doesn't matter what his background was."

"Look, nothing shows up in a week, we both work the snitches and the street."

José nodded with just a slight shaking of his head to go with it. A half-and-half answer.

Stanley brought the usual—two platters piled with the house special of smoked-pork-and-red-pepper sausages and a mound of hash browns covered with two eggs, sunny-side up.

Frank watched as José worked the ketchup.

"Lemme have some."

José looked up. "You always have Tabasco."

Frank reached for the ketchup. "Time to try something different."

SIX

FRANK PARKED IN front of the Crystal Palace a little after one in the morning. He sat for a moment, looking at the diner, its stainless steel and steamed-over windows. There used to be a lot of diners, he thought. One by one they'd closed, until in all of the District, only the Crystal Palace stood the night watches. Now they were making a comeback, diners were. At least out in the suburbs. Out in Arlington, Silver Spring, Chevy Chase. Maybe one day they'd make it back to the city, too. He got out, taking care to lock the car.

HAMILTON ADAIR, COUNTERMAN AND NIGHT MANAGER, brought coffee and stood surveying Frank.

"Cop?"

"Homicide."

Frank showed his credentials and badge. Adair glanced at them, then back to Frank's face. Frank was a big man, but Adair was bigger, and younger. A thin eggshell-white scar ran from the corner of his left eye down his cheek. Solid, chipped-off face. Muscular tattooed forearms. Squared hands, beefy, powerful fingers. A good man to be night manager anywhere.

"Wondered when you'd be in," Adair said.

"Me?"

Adair shrugged. "You, the cops," he explained, wiping his hands on his apron. "He was here that night, just before."

"O'Brien?"

"Father O'Brien. Yeah."

Frank pulled out his notebook. "You remember what time?"

"Same time as usual—midnight."

"Same time as usual?"

"Pretty much set your watch. I come on shift at eleven, an hour later . . ."

"Every night?"

"Oh no. Monday to Friday."

"You two talk?"

"Depends on the business. That time of night, it's usually not too busy."

"What'd you talk about?"

"All kinds of stuff. Redskins, shit going on in the street, politics. The Corps—"

"The Corps?" Then Frank made out one of Adair's tattoos, the Marine Corps globe and anchor.

Adair laughed. "Course, he was an officer—me, I was a grunt."

"Vietnam?"

"Yeah." Adair's reply was abrupt. "We were there different times—none of them good times."

Frank nodded, sipped his coffee. "How long did you know him?"

"Three years."

"He ever in here with anybody?"

"Sometimes somebody, sometimes by himself."

"Anybody in particular?"

"Once or twice Father Dash."

"Anybody else?"

"Last couple of months, he'd meet this kid here."

"Kid? Did he have a name?"

Adair rubbed his fingertips across his chin. "Not that I

know. White kid. Tall, skinny. Twenties . . . mid-twenties at most."

"Twenties," Frank echoed.

"Pimples," Adair said. "One of them greasy, ratty pony-tails. Glasses. Thick ones. You could hardly make out his eyes."

"You know where he came from?"

Adair shook his head and indicated a booth in the corner. "When O'Brien and him met, they sat over there. They'd talk, sometimes more than an hour. I never heard what they said."

"Nothing at all?"

"No. But I think a lot of it was . . . intellectual."

"How so?"

"Books—the kid would bring in papers, a book. Another time, the father would."

"But you didn't hear anything?"

"No. I mean, I'm not a book guy. I don't pay attention to that kind of stuff."

"You said they met the last couple of months. Not before that?"

"No. Well, not here, anyway."

"Last time you saw him with O'Brien?"

Adair paused. "Last time I saw him was the night the father was killed. They left together."

"Okay," Frank said, closing his notebook. He sipped his coffee. Adair was still standing there, so Frank asked, "What kind of man was he?"

Adair thought for a moment. "He was a good man."

Frank put his contact card on the counter.

"I want to send a sketch artist around. Get a picture of the kid. You hear anything . . ."

Adair took the card, looked at it, and then at Frank. "Yeah, sure."

Frank shouldered into his coat and was at the door when Adair called to him.

"Lieutenant?"

Frank turned.

"Lieutenant, you get the motherfucker who did it—"

"I'll try—"

"You *get* him," Adair finished, "you get him good. You understand? Get him good."

FROM THE DINER, FRANK WALKED WHAT HE GUESSED would have been O'Brien's path the night he'd been killed. At the scene, he found traces of the chalk outline where O'Brien's body had fallen. No blood on the sidewalk; twenty-two slugs didn't make much of a mess going in, and they didn't come out.

Frank looked toward where the car would have come from. He tried to imagine the moment: seeing headlights, hearing engine noise, the sound of tires, turning, getting shot. As he did so, the scar tissue and reset bones in his left shoulder twinged.

He wondered whether O'Brien knew he'd never see this place again.

The first time, Frank wasn't certain he'd heard it. Then it came again—the scuffling of a shoe on pavement. He spun toward the noise. Running footsteps sounded from a nearby alley.

Frank sprinted into the alley. Whoever was running was doing badly; a garbage can crashed against the pavement. Without breaking stride, Frank slipped his automatic from his shoulder holster, holding it high with the muzzle pointed skyward, his thumb ready to flick the safety off.

He rounded a corner and came to a full stop. No more sound of running feet. Frank whirled. Behind him and to his right, a figure burst from the shadows of a Dumpster and headed up the alley in the direction from which Frank had come.

Frank caught up in two steps, and in a diving tackle threw his left arm around the figure's shoulders. The two of them crashed to the littered ground of the alley.

Adrenaline rushing, Frank rolled and twisted on top. He pinned arms beneath his knees and rammed the muzzle of the automatic between a pair of wide-open eyes.

For an instant, he felt as if he'd reached into an alien

world and snagged something that resembled a human, but not quite. The red-rimmed eyes, the greasy strands of hair, the doughiness of the body beneath him, and above all the sour odor of urine and unwashed skin.

"God, mister, I didn't do nothin'."

Frank slumped in relief as the adrenaline evaporated. He got to his feet, pulling the man up with him.

"Mister," the man began, "I didn't do—"

"You sleep here?"

The man, eyes still on Frank's automatic, pointed vaguely toward the street.

"Heatin' grate by the Metro." He paused, then shifted his gaze to Frank. "Got any change, mister?"

Frank holstered the automatic. He clenched the derelict's wrist, turned and walked out of the alley, half dragging the stumbling man behind him. At the sidewalk he stopped. By the Metro stop, wisps of steam rose from a heating grate. Fifteen, twenty feet at most from the street.

"You see a shooting here the other night?"

The man began a palsied shaking. "Shootin'? Shootin'?" The quivery voice rose, skating toward hysteria. "I didn't see no shootin'. No! No!"

"Stop that!" Frank shook the man by his shoulders.

Still wide-eyed, the man swung his head back and forth. "Didn't see nothin'," he screeched. "Nothin'."

Frank's frustration exploded. He grabbed the front of the man's tattered jacket and the man started crying.

What the hell am I doing? As if a switch had tripped somewhere inside him, Frank froze. He dug in his pocket and came up with several bills.

"Sorry," he muttered to the derelict, stuffing the money into his filthy jacket.

The man pulled out the bills and looked vacantly at them, then at Frank.

"Man killed here." Frank gestured toward the street. "He meant something to me." Frank said it, then realized it was true. He suddenly felt tired and old and wanted nothing more than to be in bed. He started toward his car.

"Father O'Brien?" came the voice from behind him.

Frank stopped and turned. The derelict stood in the blue-silver cone of a streetlight. A ragged black-and-white character, something out of Charlie Chaplin.

"Father O'Brien?" the man asked again, cautiously. "You knew Father O'Brien?"

Frank walked back, slowly, carefully. "Yeah," he said. "I knew him. Sort of. My name's Frank." He stopped a few feet from the man. "What's yours?"

"Arthur."

"That your first or last name, Arthur?"

"Just Arthur. Never gave nobody no shit, Father O'Brien." He spoke in a bewildered voice, like that of a lost child. "Shot him." He looked at the chalk marks. "There. That's what they did. Shot him. Right there."

"You saw it?"

"Saw him." Arthur's child's voice picked up. "Car—"

Frank noticed the pay phone near the curb. "You called nine-one-one," he said, more to himself than to Arthur.

"Then him lyin' there, Father O'Brien. Stayed with him until I hear the ambulance, then I run." Arthur paused, then whined. "I didn't take anything a his, mister." He looked fearfully at Frank. "I swear! He—"

"I know, I know." Frank took it easy. "You see the car? You see the shooter?"

"We're talkin'. He's askin' me how I am. . . ."

"Then?" Frank prompted.

Arthur's eyes darted toward the street. "Car!" He pointed, suddenly all energy, waving his arm wildly. "Starts up. Lights!" The words came tumbling out. "Then the car! It comes! Car . . . lights . . . shots."

There was a long silence, and when he spoke again, Arthur slipped into a childish singsong. "Little shots. *Pooh. Pooh.* Like that. Then Father O'Brien falls. Father O'Brien falls."

Frank waited. When he sensed Arthur wasn't going to say any more, he asked, "Anybody with him?"

"Anybody?"

"Father O'Brien . . . was he alone?"

Arthur didn't say anything for a while. Then he shook his head. "Nobody. Just me and him." He stared back into that night. "Father O'Brien falls, Father O'Brien falls," he chanted.

"The car," Frank broke in. "It *started*?"

"Pooh. Pooh." Arthur made abrupt puffing noises, staring all the while past Frank to something more real. "Little shots like that. Then he falls. Father O'Brien falls."

Frank wanted to shake the man again, but he waited.

"Fast. Shots."

"The car, Arthur, the car," Frank said. "You say it started?"

Arthur's watery eyes focused jumpily on Frank. "Sittin' over there." He pointed. "Started. Lights. Shots."

"What kind of car? You know what kind of car?"

Arthur got a look of comprehension. "Oh, yes. I know," he said.

Frank felt a kick of excitement.

"Red."

"Red?" Frank forced himself to keep his voice even and soft. "Red? That all? Red?"

Arthur smiled proudly. "Red. That's what it was. Red car! Red!"

"Red car?" José turned from the one-way glass. "Red car. Shit, *that* is a big help."

In the interrogation room on the other side of the glass, Arthur sat at a wooden table, alone except for some foam cups and an empty box of Dunkin' Donuts.

By eleven, Frank and José had worked Arthur for almost three hours. By that time, the sketch artist had finished a drawing of the man Adair described having seen with O'Brien in the Crystal Palace diner the night of the shooting: thick glasses, ratty ponytail, thin pimply face. Arthur studied the drawing for a long moment before he shook his head—nothing.

The interrogation was over. All they had was the red car. The red car had started, its lights had come on. The car had driven by, there'd been two shots. And O'Brien had fallen. And that was that.

"ANYWHERE HERE'S GOOD." ARTHUR WAVED TO THE SIDE of Pennsylvania Avenue.

Frank pulled over.

Arthur got out without a word.

Expecting to hear the door slam, Frank turned when it didn't. Arthur stood on the sidewalk, bent over, looking in the car at Frank and José.

"I'm sorry."

"Yeah?"

"I mean, that I couldn't . . . couldn't do *better*. Red car isn't much."

"It's something. You did the best you could."

Arthur kept looking at Frank and José, perhaps trying to store the image somewhere in the tumbled attic of his mind. "You? What you goin' to do?"

"Do the best we can." Frank paused, then: "What about you, Arthur?"

"Me? You askin' about me?"

"Yeah. What are you going to do?"

Perplexed, Arthur stared wordlessly at Frank.

"You got choices, Arthur."

Arthur continued to stare. "Choices." He handled the word carefully, as if it might explode. He looked at Frank and José a moment longer, then shut the door.

They watched as he shambled away.

"What was all that about?" José asked.

"All about?"

"Choices?"

Frank was thinking about what O'Brien had said in the interview with Worsham. About souls being saved. The thought faded, and then he was in the car with José. "Don't know. Just something . . ." He turned to José. "Okay, how do you stack it now?"

"Car starting." José semi-nodded to himself. "Car was waiting. Maybe."

"And O'Brien with his Monday-through-Friday-coffee-like-clockwork," Frank added. He sat motionless, looking out at the spot where someone had murdered O'Brien. Glancing ever so slightly up and to his right, he caught his own eyes in the rearview mirror.

Okay, asked the eyes, *why's this different?*

I don't know, Frank answered.

Yes you do, the eyes insisted.

Frank replayed it. O'Brien and Arthur talking. Then the sound of an engine starting. Headlights. Screeching tires. Shots.

You've seen it before, the eyes reminded him.

Frank thought for a moment. Images of death from a nightmare that had followed him through the years. Single bodies—men, women, kids. Bodies in pairs. Bodies in cars and in the street. Bodies spread through a three-story crack house. And before the cop days, it'd been Vietnam and bodies stacked like cordwood.

Yeah. I've seen it. Good guys die facedown in the gutter. The bad ones just . . . just drive off.

You getting philosophical? asked the eyes.

No. Just frustrated. Sad. Nothing we've done's made a difference. José . . . me . . . all the cops in the world . . . nothing any of us have done has made a difference. We've still come to a place where some son of a bitch can shoot down a priest and drive off in the night.

So this's different because it's a priest?

Yeah, Frank told the eyes. Yeah. It is, precisely because it was a priest. You can't get worse than shooting a priest. I was growing up, even the worst scum would never have shot a priest. Now nobody cares. Nobody's afraid of hell. And because of that, nobody's safe anymore.

You haven't been in a church in over twenty years. And now you're worried about priests and hell.

All the same, Frank told the eyes, all the same.

"You there, Frank?"

Frank looked away from the mirror to José. "Yeah. Just thinking."

"You know you're right?"

"Right?"

"Zebras. We're looking for zebras."

It took him a second to connect. "Yeah. Zebras."

"Next?" José asked.

"We got three leads. Father Robert J. O'Brien, the kid in the diner, and a red car." Frank let his thoughts loose to see if they might settle on something. "We got the sketch guy over to the diner and Milton's working the car. Let's you and me go back to O'Brien's place."

"And when we get there?"

"Go over his room again."

"We did it once."

"Like the poet says, Hoser—that was then, this's now. Now we're looking for zebras."

SEVEN

FRANK CALLED AHEAD from the car, and they found Father Dash waiting for them at the shelter entrance. The priest wasn't happy.

"Your fingerprint people just left. You've already been through his room once. What do you expect to find this time?"

"I don't know."

"A fishing expedition?"

"Fishing?" Frank put on a smile. "Yeah, I guess so, Father. You don't fish, you don't catch anything."

The priest said nothing, just stood there blocking the doorway.

"We can get a warrant," José said in a matter-of-fact voice.

Dash looked at José, then Frank, then José again. "Well, I guess you're going to find what you want to find," he said with resignation. He stepped aside and pointed down the hall. "You know the way. Let me know when you leave." He turned and strode off in the direction of the office.

Frank watched, and shook his head. "Lost the chance to save two more souls."

"Don't think he was especially looking for the chance," José said. "Let's go."

FRANK STOOD IN THE DOORWAY OF O'BRIEN'S ROOM. Nothing was changed, yet everything seemed different. The room looked smaller. As if somebody had squeezed the last breath of life from it. Without comment, Frank started right, José left.

The same four suits hung in the closet, and the same fedora and commie woolly-bear hat sat on the shelf. Frank stared into the closet, trying to fasten on anything in particular. Forensics had dusted it: splashes of black fingerprint powder blossomed on the woodwork and floors.

He gave the closet a last look, then moved on to the first of the two file cabinets—the one where José had found the *Blade* clippings. An hour later, Frank had worked through most of it, and José, having worked around his side of the room, was going at the other one.

Frank rose slowly from the file cabinet, feeling his knees and back protest.

"Nothing here, Hoser."

José, too, had finished, and he shut his drawer. "Zip. Bills and accounts. No nut letters. No FedEx from the Unabomber."

"Yeah." Frank remembered the sinking feeling he'd had when José had found the *Blade* clippings file. He was relieved there wasn't anything more like that, but at the same time he found it odd there wasn't. A person who collects things like that ought to collect other things like that. He stretched his back and nudged the bottom drawer shut with the toe of his shoe, and made a note to have Auditing go over the stuff for financials.

Massaging his back, Frank stared absently at the room. From down deep, something picked at him. Like when you know there's something you meant to get at the Safeway but can't quite remember what.

"You ready to go?"

He heard José ask, but somehow it didn't seem that José was really talking to him. Frank walked slowly back to the closet, as if he might find there whatever it was that was nagging at him.

He opened the closet door and stood staring at the four suits and two hats. "Hunh," he muttered to himself.

José stepped over to his side. "Yeah?" José watched him. "What you looking for?"

"Don't know," Frank said. Something about the closet. Everything was ordinary, yet it wasn't. He kept looking inside. "Don't know," he absentmindedly whispered to himself. But even as he said it, the shapeless thing grew larger and began taking form.

He craned his neck, looking first at the upper part of the closet, then the lower. He looked more.

"What're you doing?" José asked.

From his jacket pocket, Frank had pulled a nasty-looking Austrian switchblade he'd taken off a pimp who'd used it early one Sunday morning to carve up his whore's face.

"Something funny. Shelf, here."

Saying it out loud made it clearer to him. Something *wasn't* quite right. Then it came to him: The back of the closet was closer above the shelf than below.

He pressed the hasp lever and felt the knife kick as it flicked open. He reached in and took the fedora and the woolly-bear hat from the shelf and handed them to José.

Frank jimmied the thin blade into the joint where the sides of the closet met the back wall. He pried. The blade bent. Then, with a creaking protest, the back gave way. A thin plywood panel clattered to the floor, followed by bills. A waterfall of hundreds mixed with a sprinkling of fifties and an occasional twenty.

FRANK SAT ON O'BRIEN'S BUNK, STARING AT THE MONEY.

"Working theory?" he finally asked. He didn't hear anything, so he turned to look at José, who was leaning his butt on O'Brien's desk. José was staring at the money, too.

A carpet of cash. Frank was about to ask again when José turned to him.

"Theory?" José said.

"Somebody did O'Brien because of the money."

"Pretty basic."

Frank thought for a long time. "It's a start."

"Okay. They killed him for the money." José shut his eyes and seemed to have drifted off, but Frank knew he was thinking. "Okay, they killed him for the money," he finally said.

"I heard you the first time."

"But don't you see, Frank? That means they *knew* he had it. And you don't kill somebody for the money until you know *where* they have the money. So if they killed him for the money, why didn't they take it? And why a driveby? You going to kill somebody, you don't have to take chances on a drive-by. I mean, shooting from a car takes skill. You want to be sure, you just walk up behind and blow them away."

Frank closed his eyes and thought about O'Brien. He knew he'd said the right thing without knowing exactly why he'd said it. Words came to him like that sometimes. The way you can sometimes pick a whisper out of a cheering crowd in a stadium. He took apart what he'd said, word for word. Then—it was like turning a corner—he came onto why he'd said it the way he had.

"I didn't say they killed him *for* the money."

"No? I thought you did."

"I said they killed him *because of* the money."

"Same thing."

"No, different."

"How different?"

"This way," Frank began. "They knew he had the money."

"That's what I said—"

"They knew he had the money, but they didn't necessarily want the *money*."

"Why?"

Frank thought about it for a few seconds. "What they wanted was O'Brien dead, because he knew something about *that* money." He was certain that he'd put the first pieces together. They fit just right. "They didn't want the money, or they'd have killed him when they knew where the money was. He'd be dead and we wouldn't have found any money."

"I still don't—"

"They killed him hoping two things," Frank said. "One, that we'd mark it off as a drive-by, and two, that we wouldn't find the money."

"But we did find the money."

"But they were willing to take that chance, as long as O'Brien was dead and couldn't tell us what he knew *about* the money."

"And so we—"

"So we find out what O'Brien knew about that money, and that tells us who did him."

"Next?"

Frank got up. "Next," he said, "we count the good father's stash."

EIGHT

THE GUSTING NORTH wind carried a nasty mix of rain and sleet, so Frank stepped into the Coach store on Wisconsin Avenue to wait for Kate. Located in an expensively renovated nineteenth-century building, the ground-floor shop was narrow but deep. A display counter ran the length of the store. Larger leather goods filled floor-to-ceiling shelves. Behind the counter, a lone salesclerk was waiting on three young men. Frank stood by the door, watching for Kate.

He turned to see the clerk haul down a large purse from the shelves behind her and lay it on the counter for the young men to inspect. He noticed she kept one hand close to the purse handle. As if scouting a potential battlefield, her eyes went to Frank, then to the door, then returned to the boys.

High school, Frank thought. Clean-cut. Close-cropped hair, two-hundred-dollar Nikes, pastel mint and white warmups. The three kids crowded at the counter, heads bobbing, hands darting, shoulders shifting, bodies weaving.

"How much's this bag?" It was a kid's voice, but with a chilling undertone of insolent confidence.

The woman said a price.

Frank winced, but the kid didn't blink.

He turned to his companions. "Ey, you guys want one a these for your mama?"

The three exchanged sly smiles. The clerk looked at Frank, then past him for reassurance.

"How much's three of these bags?"

The clerk worked a calculator, her free hand remaining near the bag on the counter. With tax, over thirteen hundred dollars.

She made as if to claim the bag, to return it to the safety of the shelf behind her.

The kid's hand beat her to it, pulling the bag across the counter to him.

Frank turned full-face toward the clerk and the kids, and stepped back to block the passage to the door. He slipped his hand inside his coat toward his shoulder holster.

The clerk's eyes widened in apprehension. One hand froze in the act of reaching for the purse. Her other arm crossed protectively over her breasts.

"We'll take three."

The kid smiled slowly, lazily to his buddies, then straight at Frank. He recognized it—the "Gotcha" smile of a boxer or basketball player who's just head-faked an opponent. The kid reached into his warmups and came out with a wad of bills. He counted off the crisp hundreds and made a nonchalant show of the still-thick wad before easing it back into his warm ups.

The three left, walking with an identical cocky jock-rolling of the hips, carrying Coach bags to their mothers.

Frank and the clerk exchanged looks. Then the clerk realized he was staring at the stack of hundreds in her hand. She dropped her eyes and put the money in the cash register without counting it. Frank turned away and watched the street for Kate.

"Five . . . how much?"

The steak stopped halfway to Kate's mouth.

"Five hundred thousand. And change."

"My God."

Frank eyed the steak on Kate's fork. Red center, black crust. And enough cholesterol to drop him in his tracks. He glanced at his own plate. Grilled salmon. He sighed.

Kate recovered quickly. "You're keeping it quiet—the money."

Frank nodded and took a pull at his beer. "The money means O'Brien wasn't a chance victim. I don't want his killer to know that we know that."

Kate looked suddenly at the steak, startled, as if she had no idea how it had gotten there. She put her fork down.

"Something bothering you?"

She leaned across the table, eyes narrowed. "Remember Worsham?"

"TV guy. And . . . ?"

Not sure of herself, Kate said, "Well, it might be something or it might be nothing at all."

"Let's try it."

"Charlie Simmons called the mayor about O'Brien."

"Simmons—the city treasurer?"

"Yes. And the mayor's campaign manager. Don't forget that."

"Why's he talking to Burridge?"

"Simmons got a call from Worsham. Worsham wants to interview him about O'Brien. Simmons wanted Burridge's okay."

"And?"

"I only heard the mayor's side of the conversation. Apparently Simmons didn't know exactly why Worsham was interested. There was a lot of chatter back and forth. Ended up with Simmons getting the go-ahead."

Frank sat back in the booth and looked around the crowded restaurant. Two tables away, a waiter presented a bottle of wine to a fat guy and his wife. The waiter cradled the bottle in the crook of his arm as if it were liquid gold. Well, it probably was. The money in O'Brien's closet, and the wine and the fat guy, and the kids in the Coach store drifted across Frank's mind. Not center stage, but in the background, hazy and fragmentary. He shifted his gaze to

Kate. He looked at his salmon again and pushed his plate aside. "Share some of your steak?" he asked.

THE NEXT MORNING, JOSÉ WAS ALREADY AT HIS DESK when Frank got in.

"What's that?"

"Artwork." José closed the folder and pushed it across to Frank's desk.

Frank opened it. "The Kid," he said. He studied the drawing, then marked a distribution form as "Possible witness," clipped it to the sketch, and tossed the folder in his out basket. The sketch would be distributed at the evening roll call, but Frank wasn't hopeful. For as long as he'd been on the force, he'd never gotten to where he could make an ID from a sketch. After, sure, you could find resemblances. But to pick a face out of a crowd on the basis of a drawing . . .

He looked at José. "District treasurer's getting media inquiries about O'Brien."

"Simmons?"

"Yeah."

"What the hell for?"

Frank reached for the phone. "Let's go see."

ONE HOUR LATER, FRANK AND JOSÉ SAT IN CHARLES Simmons's outer office.

A series of four framed photographs hung behind the secretary's desk, where guests couldn't help seeing them. Each featured Simmons with a president of the United States. Three were the standard White House reception shots: Simmons in black tie shaking hands in receiving lines with Jimmy Carter, with Ronald Reagan, with George Bush. In the fourth, however, Simmons sat beside Bill Clinton in a golf cart, the two of them yukking it up, looking for all the world like lifelong buddies.

José pointed to the Clinton photo. "Man in Washington

with a picture like that on his wall doesn't need a twelve-inch dick," he whispered.

Another minute or two passed before the secretary got up and opened the door to Simmons's office, ushering them in.

Frank scanned the treasurer's desk. Piles of computer printout sheets, a cup of yellow number-two Dixon pencils, an old-fashioned ledger book, and a small bronze plaque reading "The buck stops here." What you'd expect, Frank thought, of a bean counter.

But Simmons didn't quite fit Frank's picture of a bean counter. He looked like an aging offensive tackle who hadn't gone entirely soft. Thick eyebrows and a full mouth set off his round, beefy face. He tilted back in his chair and folded his hands in his lap. "Don't see many cops unless I'm getting a ticket," he said in a deep baritone.

"No tickets. A TV reporter—Worsham. We understand he wants to talk to you," Frank said.

Simmons frowned. "Where'd you hear that?"

"Around," Frank said.

"Around," Simmons repeated. He shook his head. "Can't belch in this town without somebody making a case about it."

"Worsham?" José asked.

Simmons nodded. "Yes. He wants to talk to me."

"About?" Frank asked.

"About the St. Francis Center." Simmons got an impatient look. "What business is it of yours, Lieutenant?"

Before Frank could answer, Simmons spoke. "That's right . . . the priest . . . the drive-by shooting!"

"Yes."

"I should have made the connection," Simmons said apologetically. "It's everywhere—the papers, TV, drive-time radio." He paused and looked at the two detectives. "The media. They are very good at throwing rocks. Never had a job themselves." He shook his head sympathetically, then tilted his chair forward and put his elbows on his desk. "Okay. You're Homicide. You're here about Worsham and the priest. So?"

"It might be useful to know why your office is investigating his operation."

" 'Investigating' isn't the word I'd use."

"What word would you use?" José asked.

" 'Review'," Simmons said with precision. "That's what it is. Investigation's when you suspect something. A review is a matter of course."

"Why're you reviewing the St. Francis Center?" Frank asked. "I didn't think O'Brien's operation got any money from the city."

Simmons looked glumly at Frank. "I've no choice. Father O'Brien didn't get city funds, but he ran a charity—a tax-exempt outfit. The law says you've got to justify your charter every year. And the law requires me to sign off on the justification."

"So it's routine," José said.

"It was, until now, until Worsham called and then you guys showed up," Simmons said. "So now you know what we do and why we do it. Do you still care?"

"We care," Frank said, "if you come up with something that might tell us who killed O'Brien."

Simmons pursed his lips in thought. "Certainly. But I wouldn't hold my breath if I were you. I thought it was a drive-by. Why should there be a financial aspect to this?"

"We've got to look at everything," Frank said.

Frank and José exchanged glances. José shook his head slightly. The two got up. Frank extended a hand to Simmons.

"You'll let us know if you do find anything irregular?"

Simmons took the hand. "Sure. And you'll do the same?"

Frank nodded. "Sure. Sure we will."

"You drive?" Frank asked.

José went around and got in the driver's side, but he didn't start the car. He sat quietly, then asked Frank: "Well, what about that?"

Frank gnawed at a fingernail and thought. Finally he said, "Worsham smells a story."

"So do you."

"I'm betting Worsham is going after a different story."

"Different?"

"Worsham could have O'Brien in his sights."

José started the car. "He's trying to do O'Brien in?"

"Maybe. Like Simmons said, guys like Worsham make their bones by throwing rocks."

"And we make ours by catching killers."

"Meaning . . ."

"I mean," José said, "our job's to get O'Brien's killer, not to save his reputation."

NINE

Frank got José's call at around six. He'd spent Thursday, the third day after the O'Brien murder, on paperwork, while José had been on the street, working snitches.

With the rain and evening traffic, it took Frank almost half an hour to get to the Bolling exit off the Southwest Freeway. Two miles past the air base, he saw the battered sign for MacKenzie Salvage hanging on an open chainlink gate. A uniformed patrolman waved him down at the entrance guard shack.

"Detective Phelps here?" Frank asked, holding up his credentials.

The patrolman checked the credentials, then searched Frank's face. He waved him into the salvage yard. Electric red and blue flashes lit the night sky over mountains of scrap.

Frank eased his car down a lane between piles of rusted metal. The flashing lights grew brighter. Another turn and the lane opened up. Police cruisers, an ambulance, and heavy-equipment vans filled a large clearing. A bank of portable floodlights cut the gloom.

Out of his car, Frank started for the floodlights.

"Frank!"

He turned. José, in a bright yellow department-issue

slicker, came toward him, carefully crossing the litter-strewn ground, holding a plastic coffee cup.

"What you got?" Frank asked.

José pointed toward the floodlights. The two made their way between an ambulance and a tow truck. In the clearing, Frank saw a mass of girders and hydraulic plumbing almost two stories high.

"Compactor." José pointed to the hulking structure. "Thing takes a lot of electricity. Cheaper rates late at night, and the yard only turns it on when they got a buncha cars to crush."

They walked toward the compactor. Intense flares of bluish-white light exploded in the shadowy interior of the web of girders, and Frank heard a popping sound like static.

". . . So they were going to crush some cars tonight. They come over here to the compactor to get it ready. They find somebody left a car here."

Rounding a corner of the compactor, Frank came to a ramp and the open maw of the machine. Inside the big steel box, two men in welder's helmets worked with oxyacetylene torches. Barely visible in thick clouds of glowing smoke, they looked like ghostly deep-sea divers.

José shouted something, and the welders stepped away from a cube of metal the size of a large desk. "Used to be a Beamer. Red." José aimed his flashlight up to the control deck. "Operator came on duty. Saw the Beamer already here in the compactor. *That* wasn't too unusual. But then he saw rats. That's what was unusual. He came down. Found this . . ."

José turned the flashlight beam into the compactor. Jutting from the top of the crushed car was a human skull. The skull strained upward, mouth open, as if frozen in a scream, begging for release. The rats had picked it clean, except for the scalp.

Frank walked around to what he guessed had been the front of the car. He flashed his light at the skull. Gold gleamed.

"Good dental work," Frank said. He looked at the car

and the head longer, then took his cell phone from his pocket.

"Who you calling?"

"Upton."

AN HOUR LATER, THE MEDICAL EXAMINER PULLED UP IN A dark gray Jaguar. Upton got out, glared at the rain, then at Frank and José. "What the hell is this, Frank?"

Frank pointed to the compactor. "Need some advice," he told Upton. Then he shouted to the welding crew. "Turn the lights on."

Generators labored as the floodlights bathed the crushed car and its grinning skull centerpiece.

"Sweet Jesus," muttered Upton. "But what do you want me for?"

"If the boys with the torches keep hacking away like they were, I'm worried they'll incinerate anything that might be inside the car. You know about bodies. Thought maybe you could honcho the cutting."

After he'd studied the cube of crushed metal, Upton nodded. "Shit," he said, "the things you do for friends." He left Frank and José, and made his way to the compactor. "Come on," he yelled to the welding crew, "we got some dissecting to do."

ANOTHER HOUR LATER, THE CUTTING TORCHES SNAPPED off.

"Must be finished," José said.

Upton was waving them over.

As he got closer, Frank caught the stomach-wrenching odor of rotting flesh. Upton, holding a portable floodlight, stood over the smoldering metal bale. Off to the side, one of the welders was doubled over, losing what was left of his dinner.

"Oh, shit," José murmured when they got close enough to see what Upton and the welders had freed. Bone, muscle, and intestines were laced among the twisted metal.

Frank pointed. "That a leg?"

Upton nodded.

"What now?" José said.

"I gotta sort this out back at the shop," Upton answered.

"Sort?"

"Look." Upton motioned to the side of the wreckage away from Frank and José.

They walked around. José saw it first. "What's that?" he asked

"Arm," Upton said.

An elbow and forearm protruded from the wrinkled sheet metal, as if someone inside were trying to get out.

"Jesus," said Frank.

"There were two people in the car," Upton explained. "One was probably on top of the car when they compacted it. The way the car folded up, it wrapped around everything except the head." Upton pointed to the arm. "And this one looks like he—she?—was in the trunk." Gore and chunks of tissue mingled with the remains of a spare tire and a jack handle. A large curved bone fragment, possibly part of a skull, gleamed bluish-white in the floodlights.

"Looks like it's been through a meat grinder," José said.

Upton shrugged. "Looks like a long night's work."

Frank rolled his head around, trying to ease the tightness that ran from his neck down to the small of his back. He nudged José with an elbow. "You for a beer and steam?"

José nodded. "Maybe two beers and steam."

FRANK GROANED INWARDLY AS HE FELT HIS MUSCLES RE-lax under the wet steam. Eyes closed, he tilted his head back against the steam cabinet's cushion. He drifted off, contentedly floating between waking and sleeping.

"Beats working," he heard José say. He opened an eye. José, in the next cabinet, was leaning back, too. Eyes closed.

Paulie's gym, open twenty-four hours a day, was a soot-stained two-story brick building near the projects. Paulie's wasn't an upscale fitness center. No NordicTracks or stair climbers or aerobics classes. You wore cotton shorts or gray sweats at Paulie's, and you went there for boxing, weights, or basketball. You could drink a few beers in the locker room, get a massage, then sweat it out in the sauna or the steam cabinets.

"Place gets more run-down every day," José mumbled.

"Part of Paulie's plan."

"How's that?"

"Keeps it guys only," Frank said. He floated along some more, feeling his pores open wider. "Ever notice how those health club ads never show people who really need to be there? You ever see anybody with a gut in one of those ads?"

"Just hard bodies."

"Yeah. Now if Paulie could restrict membership to ordinary women—the ones who need a few inches worked off here and there, that'd be all right. But the next thing you know, the hardbodies would show up. Non-hardbody women don't like the comparison. So they'd leave. Next thing you know, the hardbodies are bitching about no carpets and the locker room smell, and a guy won't be able to get a beer and steam. Keep it guys, keep it sweats and cotton shorts, and keep it run-down. The Paulie Plan."

"Good thing you weren't advising Lincoln," José gibed. "I'd still be choppin' cotton or whatever they did on the plantations."

"Not a black-white thing, Hoser," Frank said in a mock-serious tone. "It's a guy thing."

"Oh," José said. "Then it *is* something serious. Us guys gotta be on guard. No spandex at Paulie's."

"That's it." Frank grinned to himself. "Paulie's—a spandex-free zone." He drifted around for another moment or two before José brought him back to business.

"Think that was the car?" José asked.

"Might be, might not," Frank answered drowsily. He shut his eyes and listened as someone in the distance worked on a punching bag. He cracked an eye open and looked at José. He was looking up at the ceiling, and Frank

knew the wheels were turning. He shut his eyes and relaxed. José'd come up with another angle in ten, twenty
seconds, no more.

It took less than five.

"O'Brien's stash?"

Frank listened to the staccato rhythm of the punching
bag for another couple of seconds, then opened his eyes
and looked over at José. "Yeah?"

"Not too many places you get money like that."

"Yeah." Frank closed his eyes again and saw all the cash
he'd seen before. Cash in rolls, bundles, bags. Attaché
cases with neatly banded hundreds, car trunks that looked
as though the stuff had been shoveled in. Now cash in a
priest's closet. You didn't get that kind of money out of a
collection plate.

"You think—?" José began.

Frank cut him off. "Come on, Hoser."

"You don't know what I was goin' to say."

"You were going to ask was O'Brien maybe on the
wrong side."

"Well? I wasn't talking he *was,* I was just saying possi-
bilities."

Frank thought about it. He didn't want to say anything
right away, so he unlatched the steam cabinet, got up, and
padded over and drew a cup of water from the cooler. He
drank it and held the empty cup up to José. He nodded, so
Frank refilled the cup and took it to José's cabinet, holding
it to his partner's lips. José drained the cup, and Frank settled back into his cabinet.

After a minute or so, José asked, "Priest gets to you,
doesn't he?"

"Yeah. Yeah, he does."

"Why?"

"Don't know." Frank stared at the ceiling. He felt his
heart beating. "I just don't want it to be a world where you
can't trust a priest. If it's gotten like that, then you and I—
cops—are the only people left who can keep this from
turning into a jungle. If it's gotten like that, I'm out of

here. Take the retirement and try to talk Kate into taking off with me. Go someplace where we can leave our front door unlocked—"

"No places like that anymore, Frank."

Frank closed his eyes. Again, he picked up the sound of the punching bag. He kept listening, letting the rhythm take over his consciousness. Then whoever was working the bag stopped, and the spell snapped.

"No, Hoser," Frank admitted. "Guess not."

TEN

THE NEXT MORNING, Frank was hanging up his overcoat in the office when the desk sergeant's voice came over the intercom.

"Citizen outside here, wants to see you. Nicholas Pasco. *Doctor* Nicholas Pasco."

"Pasco?"

"Says it's about the O'Brien case."

Frank looked at his coat, dripping melted snow. "Give me five minutes," he told the voice. "Get him coffee and put him in one of the interview rooms."

FRANK GLANCED AT THE CONTROL PANEL ON THE DESK sergeant's console. A green light glowed under the monitor for the interview room where Pasco waited.

A table and four wooden chairs nearly filled the windowless interview room. Nicholas Pasco, a thin, intense man with silver-gray hair and gold wire-rim bifocals, sat in one of the chairs, an unopened coffee container in front of him.

Frank shut the door and introduced himself. Pasco's handshake was firm, decisive. The two men sat down opposite each other. Frank didn't take out his notebook. He would later. You did that first thing, and some people acted like you'd put a snake on the table in front of them. Besides, there was the recording equipment grinding away in the closet behind the desk sergeant.

"I guess the place to start is when Father O'Brien—" Pasco began.

Frank cut him off. "First, who are you?"

Pasco cocked his head as though he didn't understand Frank's question. Then he sat back in his chair and clasped his hands in his lap. "I am Dr. Nicholas Pasco. Georgetown University. Economics. Actually, I'm head of the department."

"Okay, Dr. Pasco. Now Father O'Brien."

Pasco leaned conspiratorially toward Frank. "I want to know . . . did it have anything to do with money?" Pasco made a rolling motion with a hand. "His murder, I mean—"

Frank put on what he thought of as his patient smile. "This will go better if I ask the questions, Professor."

Pasco got a startled look, mouth half open, eyes wide. It didn't last long. He sat back in his chair with a low laugh. "You're right. Ask away."

Frank worked through the preliminaries. Pasco had known of O'Brien by reputation only. Then, a little over two months ago, the end of October, Pasco had gotten a phone call from the priest. Could they get together?

They met two days later in Pasco's office.

"How'd you find him?" Frank asked.

"Find him?"

"What was he like?"

Pasco looked past Frank, then focused on him. "A man of honor."

"Honor?"

"It's a virtue people don't value much these days."

"Stiff-necked?"

Pasco shook his head. "Not at all. He had a dry, self-deprecating wit. After all, he was an Irishman. I got so I looked forward to his visits." Pasco stared off, tugging on more strands of his memory. "He was a good man. Good in a solid, dependable way you don't often see. I shall miss him. I was looking forward to knowing him better." Pasco smiled weakly. "As I get older, I find I meet fewer interesting people."

Frank sat quietly, reading unfeigned sadness in Pasco's eyes. "What did he want?"

Pasco sat up straighter and squared his shoulders. "Money. He wanted to know about money."

"Money. Like—how you make it? Banking? Loans? That kind of thing?"

"No. A different kind of thing." Pasco regarded Frank carefully, as if trying to figure out whether he was a serious student or not. "A different kind of thing," Pasco repeated. "Lieutenant, do you mind if I do my shtick?"

Frank settled back. "Do your shtick, Professor."

"In my classroom," Pasco began, "I teach that we live in a world of two different economies . . . what I call the Small Economy and the Big Economy. In the Small Economy, things are made—manufactured—and sold. The Big Economy, on the other hand, is a place where the things being traded are not goods like cars, toothbrushes, or ocean liners, but financial instruments."

"Like stocks?"

"Exactly. Bonds. Securities. Currency exchanges. And any form of debt." Pasco jabbed a finger at Frank. "You own a house?"

"Yes."

"You have a mortgage?"

"Sure."

"Chances are, over the life of your mortgage, it's been traded between banks."

"Couple of times."

"Just so." Pasco nodded. "Your mortgage is a chip in the Big Economy."

Guy's hitting his classroom stride, Frank thought.

"And that Big Economy," Pasco continued, "is somewhere between twenty and fifty times the size of the Small Economy."

"Where people buy and sell cars and toothbrushes," Frank interjected.

"Cars and toothbrushes—that's the Small Economy. Precisely. In the Small Economy, Lieutenant, money is a *thing,* a piece of stamped metal or a scrap of printed paper. Money in the Big Economy is a *system.* Money is electrons flowing through a worldwide network of hundreds of thousands of computers."

"So it was the Small Economy that O'Brien was interested in?"

Pasco shook his head. "No, Lieutenant. From the start, Father O'Brien wanted to know how the Big Economy worked."

"He was getting lessons on how Wall Street works?" José sliced through an over-easy egg draped on a mound of hash browns.

"It wasn't about investing, it was about how the stuff was handled. Electronic fund transfers between banks. Things like that."

"What makes you think O'Brien going to Pasco had anything to do with him ending up dead?"

Frank sipped his coffee and watched José scoop up egg and potatoes. "O'Brien's focus. According to Pasco, O'Brien got to be a regular nut on money. When he wasn't down at Georgetown with Pasco, he was reading everything in sight. He was still going full-bore, right up to the end. His last conversation with Pasco was on the afternoon before he died."

José wiped his lips with a paper napkin. "We got half a million in cash from the closet of a dead priest who was a Donald Trump wannabe. He was also a former Marine who kept a file of faggot personals. We got a couple of twenty-two slugs and a shrink-wrapped Beamer with body-parts stuffing."

Frank was suddenly hungry. He waved at Stanley. One over easy and a half-order of hash browns wouldn't do serious damage. "I don't know what the connection is, Hoser," Frank said, unwrapping the napkin from his silverware. "But dammit, I know there is one."

"Somewhere," José said.

Stanley came over to the booth.

"Somewhere," Frank said to José. And then said to hell with it, ordered two over easy and a full order of hash browns.

Frank and José walked into the office from Garrett's, and the phone started ringing. José answered, scribbled a note in the log, then hung up. "Mr. District Treasurer Charles D. Simmons's secretary," he announced with exaggerated formality. "Mr. District Treasurer Charles D. Simmons would like us to drop by."

"Just drop by, like that?"

"Well . . . no. Like three-fifteen."

"Ah. Precise."

"Yeah. Precise."

"I don't guess she said why."

José yawned. "Mr. District Treasurer's secretary just said three-fifteen."

Frank took the next call. It was Tony Upton. He was ready to see them right now.

Upton met Frank and José in his office. Frank breathed a sigh of relief. He didn't mind the dissecting room, but Upton's office was warmer and it didn't smell like alcohol, formalin, and cut-up meat.

He offered coffee. Both Frank and José declined. He waved the two detectives to chairs facing an X-ray light panel and a whiteboard.

The M.E. opened a manila folder, reviewed his notes until he found what he was looking for. "We had two bodies. A black male, age thirty to forty-five, and in the trunk a Caucasian male, no age estimate."

"Why's that?" José asked.

Upton looked up from his notes. "Why's what?"

"No age for the white male—the trunk man?"

Upton gave José a tired look. "I'll get to that." He took a

felt-tip marker and on the board drew a box with four wheels. "The black male was lying across the roof and hood when the compactor jaws closed in. The car wrapped around everything except the head."

"Nasty way to go," said Frank. "Death by compactor."

Upton shook his head. "He was dead first. Shot twice."

"Twice?"

Upton rewarded Frank with a smile. "You got it." He reached into the folder and came out with a small Ziploc bag. He handed it to Frank. "Familiar?"

Frank looked at the two mushroomed slugs, then handed the Ziploc to José.

"The cause of death was two twenty-two-caliber gunshot wounds to the heart."

"Like O'Brien," said José, giving the bag back to Upton.

"A difference." Upton replaced the bag in the folder. "Black guy—Beamer Boy—was shot in the back."

Frank stared at the whiteboard and the car Upton had drawn. "Guy takes two in the back and ends up on the roof of the car before it's compacted. Only one place he could have been." He got up, uncapped a marker, and sketched the girders of the compactor.

"Beamer Boy's up here." Frank drew a stick figure on the compactor platform above the car. "Zap. Zap. Somebody gives it to him in the back. He falls . . ." He dotted a trajectory from the platform onto the top of the car.

"And Trunkman—the white guy?" José asked.

"He was already in the car, wasn't he, Tony?" Frank said.

Upton nodded.

"Two twenty-twos in him?" José guessed.

Upton shook his head. "No. Cause of death, massive shock due to multiple fractures and third-degree burns to his feet and genitals."

"Tortured to death?" Frank said. "Jesus."

"Going to take a little longer to ID him than the black guy. No fingerprints."

"What?" José asked.

"While they were at it, they cut off his fingers."

* * *

FRANK AND JOSÉ GOT TO SIMMONS'S OFFICE AT THREE-ten. The secretary took their names, checked her computer screen, and pointed to a sofa.

Frank picked up an old *Newsweek*. The Indians, for God's sake, setting off nukes. He tossed the magazine back onto the coffee table. Next it'd be the Swedes. He gazed past the secretary and out the window, where, in the distance, you could make out the Washington Monument with its space-age scaffolding. He nodded off.

"It's three damn forty-five," he heard José complain.

Frank's head jerked up. He was starting to say something when the secretary motioned them into Simmons's office.

Simmons was on the phone. He waved the two detectives in and pointed to a sofa and cluster of chairs.

Frank surveyed the office, then switched to the phone conversation. He could tell from the tenor of Simmons's voice that the business part was over; he and whoever he was talking to were into the good-bye schmooze. Simmons sounded heartbroken. Like he was leaving his best buddy in the world. When he hung up, he stared at the phone.

"Asshole," he said, then looked at Frank and José and grinned. "Spend more time in this town massaging egos than doing honest work."

Simmons found a folder on his desk and went to take a chair facing Frank and José. He tossed off a brief apology for keeping them waiting, and opened the folder. He studied the contents, his lips compressed in concentration, and nodded as if recognizing something he'd seen before. He looked up at José, then to Frank.

"The good Father O'Brien might have been a saint, but he was a shitty bookkeeper." Simmons thumped the folder with the back of his hand. "Review of the Center's finances. Lotta money passed through, and a lotta money got spent, but only O'Brien and God can account for it."

"That bad?" Frank asked.

"That bad. Mayor's not going to like it." He had a worried expression. "Not going to like it at all."

"Oh? Why?" José asked.

Simmons looked at him as if he were a simpleton. "It opens Saint Robert O'Brien up to all kinds of conjecture."

"Like . . . ?" Frank said.

"Like embezzlement," Simmons answered.

"Embezzlement?" Frank realized the word had come out sharp and quick. He caught José cutting him a sidelong look.

Simmons shrugged. "Look, Detective, this guy wouldn't be the first holy-roller to betray the faithful. That Swaggart fellow, remember him? Remember his hookers? And that other one—Bakker? The one whose wife looked like a survivor from a Mary Kay explosion?" Simmons wiped his hands across his face. "All the makeup? Suzy Wong?"

"Tammy Faye," José offered.

"Yeah, sounds like." Simmons nodded. "Anyway, soul savers get a messiah complex. They get to thinking they make their own rules."

Frank studied Simmons and got nothing from it. "What about Worsham?" he asked.

Simmons looked as though he didn't know what Frank was talking about, then came onto it. "Oh. Yes. I see. Him . . ." He consulted his desk calendar. "Tomorrow. Tomorrow at three."

"And you're going to tell him?"

"Tell him? About what?"

"About your conjecture—embezzlement?"

"Guy asks, I'll tell him the facts. That O'Brien's books were so bollixed up we can't tell how he handled his money. If Worsham wants a conjecture, he can make his own."

"And you don't think he won't?" Frank asked.

"His business, not mine." Simmons waved a dismissive hand. "First Amendment. Freedom of speech."

IN THE HALLWAY, JOSÉ TURNED TO FRANK. "WELL?"

"Well what?"

"You weren't too happy with what Simmons was saying."

"Showed, did it?"

"Yeah." José shook his head. "You watch that shit, Frank. Nobody appointed you O'Brien's guardian angel."

ELEVEN

THE NEXT MORNING'S *Post* carried the story front-page: "Body in salvage yard connected to slaying of priest." Frank read it without surprise. And when he got to the station, it didn't surprise him, either, when José told him that Emerson wanted to see them.

At Emerson's door, José rolled an open hand. "After you."

"Thanks," Frank said, and entered without knocking.

The first thing he looked for was the suit jacket. Emerson was wearing it. Emerson also had the *Post* spread out on his green plate-glass desktop. Behind him, Frank heard José's underbreath "Aw, shit."

Emerson ignored them, apparently absorbed with the paper as they stood at semi-attention in front of his desk. As always, the name plate on it caught Frank's eye. An inmate in the Lorton metal shop had turned the stainless-steel nightstick, which rested in a walnut cradle on the thick glass desktop. Gold etching along the length of the nightstick said "Randolph Emerson." Frank studied the name plate and wondered as he usually did where the inmate who'd made it was now. Finally he figured Emerson had gone on with his act long enough.

"I see you're finished reading, Randolph," he said.

Emerson looked up, eyes narrowed, searching for the catch.

"Your lips stopped moving."

Emerson sat back in his chair and gave Frank and José an exasperated frown. "Instead of solutions, all I'm getting from you two is more problems." He tapped the *Post* with a manicured fingernail.

"Meaning what?" José asked.

Emerson picked up the paper and glared at it as though willing it to vanish in a puff of greasy smoke. "Meaning whoever's shooting and hacking their way through this city is bringing all kinds of shit down on us."

"Not to mention killing a bunch of people," Frank added.

Emerson had a tight, pinched look around his mouth. He tossed the paper on the desk and aimed a finger at Frank and José.

"We got that scumbag Worsham on our case. The next thing's Dan fucking Rather or Peter fucking Jennings. Network news. *Sixty* damn *Minutes*. White House's already pissing and moaning. Next it'll be those bastards on the Hill."

"Could be," Frank murmured in agreement.

"And they'll be calling for heads."

"Could be," José repeated.

Emerson slapped the desk with a sound like a shot.

"Could be, could be," Emerson mimicked. "Could be"—he leaned forward—"that I'm looking at two people who are damn sure going down before I do."

O'BRIEN'S FUNERAL WAS ON A GRAY MONDAY MORNING. The Georgetown graveyard's stone chapel was nearly filled as Frank and José took seats in a pew at the rear. Frank scanned the chapel. Mostly men, only a handful of women. Frank guessed that the men who weren't wearing collars were from the Center. Among them, he spotted the black guy named Tom who'd been in the Worsham TV report.

Dash said the mass in Latin. O'Brien would have liked

the Latin, Frank imagined, though several of the younger priests rolled their eyes.

After the service, Frank and José fell in behind the pall-bearers, who were carrying O'Brien's coffin out of the chapel. As they exited, Frank glanced across the street, where a telephone repair van was parked. Inside, he knew, a camera crew was training high-power lenses on each mourner. At both ends of the block, uniformed cops were directing traffic and, less obviously, recording license plate numbers.

A gravel path led the mourners to the grave, some twenty yards away near the top of a knoll.

The graveside ceremony was brief. Dash said a prayer and the pallbearers watched as the plain wooden box was lowered into the red earth. The priest sprinkled holy water, then a few clods of earth, which made hollow rattling sounds as they struck the casket. Then the men in black broke away in twos and threes, walking down the hill across winter-browned grass toward the gate.

Frank stared at the grave. Past and future, he thought, looking at the raw cut in the earth. He caught a movement in the corner of his eye. At the crest of the hill, three gravediggers stood silhouetted against the slate sky, motionless like sentinels.

José glanced at Frank. "See something?"

Frank continued to stare at the crest of the hill and the motionless men.

"Guess not," Frank whispered.

Overhead, hidden in the leaden clouds, a jet from Reagan National climbed to altitude, its sound rapidly vanishing as it passed. As he walked by the grave, he stooped, picked up a handful of dirt, and sprinkled it on O'Brien's coffin.

TWELVE

FRANK WAS AT JOSÉ'S just before seven. José let him in and went to the kitchen for beer and chips. Frank eased into his chair and fired the remote at the TV. He tuned to the evening traffic report. Remote cameras showed a snakelike trail of red taillights. Another bad night on New York Avenue. All you needed was one fender-bender and you had gridlock and several thousand dinners going cold. And several thousand cold dinners would mean a couple hundred domestic arguments. And out of those couple hundred arguments, there'd be one or two that would turn into fights, and those could get real nasty. At least there wasn't a full moon.

Frank didn't watch much TV because TV was generally garbage. Once, while recovering from a gunshot wound, he'd tried to kill time by watching wall-to-wall TV: the morning shows, soaps, game shows, early-evening news, the dumb-white-male sitcoms and brainless cop shows, topped off with Letterman or Leno. Two days of that and he decided he'd rather get shot again.

José brought in the beer just as Worsham came on the screen, in a dark topcoat and white silk scarf. The camera pulled in to frame him chest up, silver hair and sharp features. A cover for *GQ*. A recruiting poster for the Harvard faculty.

"Great hair," José said.

The camera cut away. Worsham stood on the sidewalk in front of the National Archives. It was nighttime. Cars sped by; headlights flashed, then disappeared. The Capitol dome glowed ice-white over his shoulder.

"It was here, a week ago," Worsham said solemnly, "that Father Robert J. O'Brien was gunned down."

The camera angled to show that Worsham was standing near the chalk outline of a sprawled body.

"Shit!" José exploded. "Those aren't our marks."

"Artistic license." Frank sipped his beer.

The camera pulled in closer, on Worsham's face. "Franz Kafka wrote that 'every death is a mystery,' " he intoned melodramatically. "The original mystery of Robert J. O'Brien's death is deepening. And as that mystery deepens, the questions multiply. Questions that weren't apparent at his death.

"There is the original question, of course: Who killed Father O'Brien? We know that someone in a car drove by this spot"—Worsham paused and pointed to the sidewalk and the chalk outline—"and fired two shots. That someone murdered a man revered by many as a saint of Washington's mean streets. Despite all-out efforts, the police are no closer to finding the killer."

Worsham started to walk again, engaging the viewer in an apparently personal conversation. Frank grudgingly had to hand it to Worsham—the man was good.

"At first, Father O'Brien's killing seemed like one more tragic act of senseless violence. A deranged gunman, the victim . . . anyone in the wrong place, at the wrong time."

Worsham walked a few more steps. "Then a man at a District salvage yard came to work and found this. . . ."

The screen abruptly darkened, then illuminated with a frightening angle on the skull. Close up and grinning, gold teeth and all. Another shot: The crushed BMW as it sat in the compactor's jaws, the skull smaller now but still morbidly visible.

"Where'd he get that?" José asked.

"Probably from some Evidence file clerk for a fifty," Frank answered, without taking his eyes from the screen. It was standard procedure: Surveillance filmed all suspected homicide scenes. It was also standard procedure that he and José would review the films. But they hadn't yet, and he got a queasiness in his stomach, seeing it first on TV. It was as if someone had crept up behind him without his realizing it.

". . . identity as yet unknown," Worsham was saying. "But the connection with Father O'Brien is this." He opened his hand and the camera showed two bullets in his outstretched palm.

"Fakes," José shouted at the screen.

"They're twenty-two slugs, Hoser."

"But they aren't the same ones!"

"Like I said. Artistic license."

The scene changed. Worsham now stood in front of the MacKenzie Salvage sign. "The same gun that killed Robert O'Brien also killed the unidentified person so gruesomely depicted in official police photography." Worsham paused and looked into the camera. He tilted his head as if to say, "And what about *that*?"

"Who talked to him? Who gave him that shit?" José asked.

Frank pulled at his beer. "You been around. You know there's no sense trying to find the leaks."

José nodded. "Still gives me a creepy feeling."

"Yeah. I know." Frank motioned toward the screen. "Here comes our boy Simmons."

The seal of the District of Columbia blossomed on screen, and beside it a brass plaque announcing that this was the office of the city treasurer. A flicker and the camera was inside Simmons's office. He sat behind his desk, wearing his suit coat. Worsham sat opposite him in an armchair, and twisted around to look into the camera.

"Robert O'Brien's murder reaches into improbable places," Worsham said. "Here, we discuss the killing with Charles Simmons, who for eighteen years has served as city treasurer."

Simmons smiled uncertainly at Worsham and the camera.

"Doesn't look like he's enjoying himself," José said.

"I've seen better faces on a broken clock."

Worsham turned to Simmons. A second camera profiled the two men as they faced each other across Simmons's desk.

"Mr. Simmons, can you tell us why the city treasurer's office is conducting an investigation into Father O'Brien's operations?"

"In-*ves*-ta-*ga*-shun?" José mimicked. "He's making it sound like a Brinks holdup."

Frank waved José off and leaned forward to catch Simmons's reply.

The treasurer worked his mouth soundlessly several times, then lurched into an answer. "Ah . . . *well* . . . I don't . . . we don't . . . call it an investigation, Mr. Worsham. We . . . ah . . . refer to such a . . . ah . . . *process* as . . . ah . . . as a review."

"Oh!" Worsham acted surprised. "A world-famous figure is murdered on the streets of the nation's capital, you and your department are going through his finances with a fine-tooth comb—and you call it a *review*?" Worsham smirked. "Please, Mr. Simmons!"

Simmons started to answer. Too slowly. Worsham interrupted. "All right, Mr. Simmons, we'll accept your definition. Now, why is your department inves—oh, sorry—why is your department *reviewing* Father O'Brien's financial records?"

Simmons started on the same answer he'd given Frank and José, about how the city had to review the records of charities even if the charities accepted no government funds. But as he got into his explanation, he stumbled, tripped over his words, fuzzed his definitions. What assurance he had begun with was quickly evaporating.

"He's running out of balls," José said.

"He's let Worsham get to him," Frank said.

Simmons's face was glistening despite the TV makeup. He knew he wasn't coming across well, Frank thought, and he knew that's what Worsham wanted. And knowing he was playing Worsham's game made Simmons even more nervous. He was no longer the self-assured senior civil servant with photographs of presidents on his office wall. Now he was a frightened government hack, his gut tied in knots. Frank pictured Simmons's paranoia taking over, creating legions of whistle-blowers in his office, dumping dirty laundry by the ton into Worsham's in box. Stuff that could destroy Simmons's credibility. Or worse—make him a laughingstock.

Worsham dragged Simmons from one whipping post to another. He beat up on him for conflicting accounts of previous reviews of the St. Francis Center. He relented with a couple of softball questions, then bored in on Simmons from a different, unexpected direction—the treasurer's official entertainment budget. Worsham dragged out expensive planning meetings in Puerto Rico, municipal fact-finding delegations to Paris and Rome. Standard stuff for the District government, but now the flop-sweat was drenching Simmons face.

"This is not a pleasant learning experience for our treasurer friend," Frank said, part of him enjoying Simmons's discomfort.

"Yeah," José agreed. "We hard-ass somebody in an interrogation like that, they'd lift our badges."

Worsham was now smiling pleasantly at Simmons. The city treasurer's shoulders dropped slightly as he relaxed. But Worsham wasn't through just yet. Almost casually, he asked, "Returning to your review of Father O'Brien's center . . . would you say, given the large sums of money from private donors, that there was the possibility of embezzlement?"

Simmons opened and closed his mouth like a beached fish. Worsham cut in before he could speak.

"You *did* say earlier"—Worsham consulted his notes—"that the Center's books were in such bad shape that, I quote, 'We couldn't do a professional audit.' End quote." Worsham pinned Simmons with a prosecutor's look. "You *did* say that, didn't you?"

Simmons, still working his mouth, struggled and finally nodded.

Worsham waited, seeming to want more.

"Yes," Simmons barely got out.

"Then let's go back to my original question, Mr. Simmons—is there the possibility, the opportunity, for large-scale embezzlement under such circumstances?"

"Don't answer it, you damn fool!" José, half out of his chair, shouted at the on-screen Simmons.

But Simmons, now desperate to throw the hook that Worsham had sunk in him, nodded, falling into the deeper trap set by Worsham's hypothetical question.

Again, Worsham did the "I'm waiting" routine.

And again, Simmons came through. "Yes," he whispered. "It's possible."

The camera closed in on Worsham and his frown. Abruptly the scene shifted, and the screen flashed a series of interior shots.

"The diner," Frank said.

There was Adair, the night manager, at work behind the counter, then a close-up of Worsham in a booth.

Worsham opened a folder and withdrew the composite drawing of what Frank had come to think of as the Kid. "This police sketch has been circulated to all law enforcement agencies in the metro area. The notice carries the annotation that the subject is wanted for questioning in the O'Brien case. This man's identity is unknown."

"This man"—Worsham looked somberly into the camera, letting a moment of silence build suspense—"sat in *this* booth with Robert J. O'Brien, just minutes before O'Brien walked out *that* door to his death." Worsham gestured to the exit. "This man"—he briefly held up the picture—"whose identity is unknown.

"And so the question: When Robert O'Brien walked from here, was it to a random death, or was he meeting an appointment with fate?"

The image faded and a pet food commercial came on. José turned the set off. Both men sat drinking the last of their beer.

"Well?" Frank asked.

"He's got Simmons running for cover," José answered.

"Other than that? All over the parking lot, nothing new."
José belched. "Isn't going to knock off Koppel that way."

Frank looked at the dark screen. "When I was a kid," he
began thoughtfully, "I liked those puzzles where you connected the dots."

"Yeah. And made a picture."

Frank nodded. "That's what Worsham was doing."

"Connecting dots?"

"No, not yet. Just putting the dots down. When he gets
enough dots, then he draws the picture."

José eyed Frank, then asked, "What kind of dots would
he have if he knew about the half-million and the *Blade*
personals?"

Frank got up and stretched the tightness out of the small
of his back. "Be the crap-hits-the-fan dots."

"A buck says Emerson's on our ass before roll call," José
said.

"We'll see," said Frank.

FRANK'S VOICE-MAIL LIGHT WAS ON WHEN HE GOT IN. HE
looked at the insistent light and with one hand reached for
the Maalox bottle while the other reached for the phone. He
listened to the brief message. The recorded voice sounded
like a man forcing himself to take deep breaths. Frank hung
up. He sighed heavily, and as he walked by José's desk, he
tossed a crumpled dollar bill onto the blotter.

FRANK KNOCKED ONCE AND ENTERED THE OFFICE. A
shirt-sleeved Emerson sat slumped behind his desk, his
chin on his chest. He looked up and took a second to register Frank. "Where's Phelps?" he asked, his voice tight.

"Hasn't gotten in yet. You want us both?"

"Yes." Emerson looked at his watch in a quick, nervous
manner. "No," he countermanded. "We'll go without him."

"Okay, Randolph," Frank said. "We'll go. Where is it
we're going?"

Emerson pushed himself out of his chair slowly, reluctant to leave its sanctuary. He reached for his jacket. "We're going to see the mayor."

THE FIRST THING FRANK NOTICED WHEN THE DOOR TO the mayor's office opened was Simmons. The city treasurer stood in front of a huge carved walnut desk. The mayor, Malcolm Burridge, sat behind the desk, absorbed in a file. He was a lean, handsome man, dark milk-chocolate skin, hair silvering at the temples. A young and very attractive woman stood attentively close to his chair.

As Frank and Emerson crossed the thick pile carpet to join him, Simmons rolled his eyes at Frank, then made a small turning-out motion with his hands: Nothing you can do but get ready for what isn't going to be fun.

Burridge continued to work on the file. Finally he signed a sheet of paper, closed the file, and handed it to the woman. He watched as she left the office and shut the door behind her.

"Nice ass," Burridge said wistfully. "A very . . . nice . . . ass."

Emerson laughed uneasily. Burridge jerked his head toward Emerson as if he'd just smelled something bad. Emerson's laugh cut off and his face turned red. Burridge examined the three men in front of his desk, his dark eyes tracking back and forth like oiled ball bearings.

Once he'd decided they weren't a bad dream and wouldn't go away, Burridge shook his head. He tilted back in his big leather chair, so Frank could get a good shot of his nostrils.

Turning his head to look straight at Frank, he said, "And I take it that you're the department's Dirty Harry."

Emerson did his nervous laugh again.

Frank said, "I'm Frank Kearney's Frank Kearney."

Emerson gave Frank a sidelong glance, waiting for lightning to hit. Instead, Burridge got a private smile on his face. Then he dropped it and leaned both elbows on his desk.

"I'm gonna give you boys a lesson in practical politics,"

he began, his voice like boulders grinding together. "Father Robert O'Brien was one big pain in my mayoral ass. He was antigovernment down to his rosary and his boxer shorts." Burridge paused to see if the three clowns standing in front of his desk were paying attention. Satisfied that they were, he continued, "But he was an international figure. Already there's talk of a posthumous Nobel Prize. And a special Congressional Medal. Hell"—Burridge waved a hand—"maybe they'll even carve his face on Mount Rushmore.

"Now, though, they're after my ass—big time they're after my ass."

Frank noticed Burridge was smiling. He imagined the mayor was enjoying the memories of narrow escapes he'd made from the jaws of political death. Like getting shot at without being hit.

"But I can take care of my ass. My *personal* ass, that is. I can have this lousy job as long's I want it. But do you know what else is at stake here?"

Burridge leaned further forward, looking for an answer from the three clowns. First Simmons, then Emerson, and finally the ball-bearing eyes came to rest on Frank.

Nobody said anything. Frank heard Emerson beside him breathing as if he'd been worked over in the ring.

Burridge tilted back, giving another nostril shot. "What's at stake, gentlemen, is the future of the District of Columbia." He paused. "Statehood," Burridge rolled slowly, his voice deepening reverently. "Statehood," he repeated even more solemnly as the vision possessed him.

Suddenly he crashed forward in his chair, whipping up both hands, pointing them like six-guns at the clowns in front of him. "And statehood means two senators in the U.S. goddamn Senate!" His voice boomed. "And voting rights in the House! And a state government! State courts!" Burridge jumped to his feet, lifted his gaze to heaven. His eyes widened and his body vibrated with cosmic energy, limitless and pure. His eyes fastened on Frank. Bored holes right through him, and Frank knew Burridge was looking beyond him. Way beyond.

Burridge's voice dropped low. Only its intensity made it audible. "Statehood, gentlemen, means . . . *pork!* It means we get fed dollars. Everybody talks about the turnaround in New York. Shit! You give me half the goddamn money that wop mayor's gotten from the feds and I'll build you a paradise in Anacostia!"

Burridge fell silent, and Frank imagined the mayor was seeing the Washington slums reborn.

Another quick change: Burridge the preacher disappeared; Burridge the mayor was back onstage. Vision time was over. Now it was time for the wire brush.

"What happens to statehood? O'Brien's shot down on my fucking Main Street! My cops can't find the killer! We look like some Third World country."

Frank thought he heard Emerson whimper.

"That's bad enough. Then my treasurer—my campaign manager, for God's sake—goes on TV and says O'Brien's a goddamn *embezzler!*"

Simmons stepped into the line of fire. "I didn't call him anything, Malcolm," he said, greasing out the mayor's name.

Burridge wasn't having any of it. "You might as well have, Charlie," he snapped. "Why the hell you ever went on that little weasel Worsham's show in the first place—"

"I—"

Burridge cut Simmons off with a chop of his hand. "No matter, Charlie. It's done. You screwed the pooch and you're not goin' to unscrew it." Burridge delivered a blistering look at the three men, this one a napalm run, then slowly, emphasizing each word: "I . . . don't . . . want . . . any . . . more . . . surprises." He paused to make certain this sank in.

Frank watched as Emerson's head bobbed vigorously and Simmons turned deathly pale.

"Now," Burridge continued, "do I know what there is to know? *All* there is to know? Because if I get any more surprises from you"—he stabbed a finger at Emerson—"I'll have your balls for a necklace."

Emerson trembled and looked as though he might collapse on the spot. Sensing his fear, Burridge thrust his head forward. "There is something!" He bent across his desk toward Emerson.

Emerson shot a desperate glance at Frank.

Frank kept what he hoped was his best poker face, but inside, he felt the elevator drop. Then he heard Emerson say, "There were clippings. O'Brien had some clippings."

"Clippings?"

Emerson struggled. "Ah . . . want ads."

"Want ads? You mean classifieds?"

"Ah . . . yes."

Burridge exploded. "Get fucking to it, Emerson!"

Emerson looked even sicker. He pointed to Frank. "Kearney found them."

Burridge's eyes clicked onto Frank.

"They were a file of clippings," Frank said. "From *The Blade*. Personals. Men looking for other men."

Burridge got Emerson's sick look. As if it were contagious. "Any evidence?" he asked in a stunned voice. "Any evidence he was gay?" He shut his eyes for the answer.

"No," said Frank.

Burridge massaged his forehead with his fingertips. He opened his eyes. "Anything else?" he asked.

Simmons shook his head. Emerson didn't. He stared at Burridge with the glazed, expectant expression of a rabbit hypnotized by a cobra.

Burridge's voice was now soft and menacing. "What else, Emerson? What else?"

Frank knew Emerson would either screw it up or pass it to him, so he jumped in before he could answer. "We found a bundle of cash in O'Brien's room."

Burridge turned to Frank. "Bundle?"

"Half a million."

Burridge's mouth opened. Then closed. Then he swallowed. "Half a million . . . *dollars*?"

Frank nodded. He and Burridge exchanged a long look, each man measuring the other.

"That's it?" Burridge spoke to Frank as if Simmons and Emerson weren't there. His voice was surprisingly calm. "That's the worst of it?"

"That's the worst that we know."

Something in Frank's voice made Burridge wait.

"That's the worst that we know . . . now," Frank added.

"HOW LONG?" KATE ASKED.

Frank stared into the flames. A good, steady fire of ash logs. Pine burned brighter, but pine sputtered a lot and didn't last very long. He shrugged, still staring into the flames. "Murphy's law of secrets," he finally answered. "The nastier the secret, the faster it gets out. If O'Brien had been running around at night healing lepers and turning water into wine, nobody'd ever know."

"The clippings and the money . . ." Kate said. "Think of all the egg on all the faces if—"

"—if it turns out that the politicians had been taken in by a gay priest who was a world-class crook?" Frank got up from the sofa and nudged a log closer to the fire's center with a poker.

He turned to face Kate. "That'd be bad. But it could be worse."

"How?"

"Suppose O'Brien was innocent? That there was some other explanation for the ads and the money?"

"How'd that be worse?"

"Because the way this town works—do you think Worsham would wait a second to go on the tube with the clippings and the money? Do you think he'd wait for an explanation—if there was one? Everybody watching Worsham would get the picture: Here's a gay priest on the take. Even if it came out later that O'Brien wasn't, you'd never get a retraction from Worsham and you'd never chase the whispers down."

"But . . . if there was another explanation . . . later . . ."

"The damage would already be done. I remember fifteen, twenty years ago, there was a guy, worked for Carter or Reagan. Treasury or Labor Department, someplace like that. Anyway, the rumor mill got working that he was crooked, mob connections, gambling, that kind of stuff. They dragged the poor bastard through all of it, the newspapers, talk shows, congressional hearings. The feds finally took him to court. Case against him fell apart. Jury found him innocent. And the poor bastard asked the judge, 'Now where do I go to get my reputation back?' "

Frank watched the firelight reflected across Kate's high cheekbones. He flashed back to the morgue and Upton's scalpel laying O'Brien's body open. "First they kill O'Brien, then they'd murder his honor—trash everything good that he did, everything worthwhile he stood for."

THE NEXT MORNING, FRANK HAD VOICE MAIL FROM Woody in Surveillance. The photos from O'Brien's funeral were ready for him anytime.

THIRTEEN

"Two hundred eight subjects at the service," Woody read from his notes. A panoramic color photo of the graveyard and chapel flashed on the large screen behind him. "Two-oh-nine if you count the deceased."

Woody snapped the remote, and Frank studied the screen. The surveillance van had been parked so Woody's long-lens cameras could catch each mourner entering the graveyard.

Frank turned his attention to Woody. Eight years before, Elias Woods had been hired away from the National Security Agency to organize the department's technical surveillance. Where most division chiefs jockeyed for publicity, Woody avoided it like a bad cold. His picture had never appeared in the papers, and few in the department even knew where he lived. It was the same with his division. His first move had been to take Surveillance deeper undercover. He had requisitioned a long-vacant dead-end corridor, which he sealed with a heavy vault door under twenty-four-hour guard. He'd bricked up the windows, installed an armored electrical system, and covered the walls with copper mesh to keep others from snooping on him the way he snooped on them.

"And you got two hundred eight full-faces for us."

Woody nodded.

"Got them ID'd?" José asked.

Woody put on a hurt look. "Give me half a break, Hoser. We got *most* ID'd. Give me another couple days, and I'll give you all two hundred eight names and their mommas' and daddies', too."

"How many unknowns?" Frank asked.

Woody ran a finger down the spreadsheet. "Sixteen."

"Let's see them."

Woody nodded and snapped the remote. The chapel photo morphed into a head-and-shoulders shot of a heavy-jawed white man wearing a dark topcoat and pale scarf.

Woody looked at Frank and José.

Both shook their heads.

Three more pictures—nothing.

The fourth got a nod from Frank. "Hamilton Adair," Frank recited. "Night manager, Crystal Palace, over on Tenth."

Woody made a note, then snapped the remote again. Frank and José ran through the rest of the faces without recognizing one.

"That does it," Woody said. "Give me a couple of days—"

"And you'll get the mommas and daddies," José finished.

Frank froze halfway out of his chair. "What's that?" He pointed to the screen. Another photo, this time of the graveyard.

Woody smiled. "Oh. That's you and Hoser—"

"No," Frank said. "There." He gestured to the hilltop above the grave.

"Well." Woody gave the screen a puzzled look. "Those? The gravediggers."

Frank stood up and walked to the screen and peered at it, remembering how his attention had been drawn to the hilltop that day. "Yeah. I saw them," he said, "but I saw three. Here"—he reached out and tapped the screen with his index finger—"here there's just two."

In the background, a phone rang once, twice; the projectionist motioned to Frank. He went to take the call, and moments later came back to his seat. "That was Upton," he told José. "Finally got some prints off Beamer Boy."

José nodded and glanced at his watch. "Three twenty-five. What you want to do?"

"Upton's sending the prints over to ID. They won't have anything today. Let's go visit a graveyard."

An hour later, Frank and José knocked on a door in Alexandria. Frank knew the area as Little Dixie, grimy brick rental units and ratty juke joints, their parking lots filled with pickup trucks decorated with Confederate flag decals. Just off I-95, Little Dixie was an enclave of southern mill hands who had moved to Virginia when their textile jobs had unaccountably flown to Singapore, Hong Kong, and Kuala Lumpur.

Frank knocked again.

"Yeah?" It came as a muffled shout from somewhere in the apartment.

Frank knocked louder and stepped to the side. "Police," he said. Silence for a moment, then hurried footsteps in an upstairs apartment, then a toilet flushing.

The doorknob moved. Frank stepped back slightly and opened his topcoat. The door opened, coming to a sudden stop against a heavy chain lock.

"Yeah?" The voice was hoarse and surly.

"Bobby Neal Turner?"

"Who're you?"

"Detectives Kearney and Phelps." Frank held out his badge and credentials. From where he was standing, he couldn't see the voice's owner.

"You're D.C. cops. This ain't D.C."

"Observant," José whispered to Frank.

"It's the end of a long day, Mr. Turner," Frank said, letting a little irritation show. "You can talk to us here or we can go down to the Alexandria station. No difference to us. Your choice."

The door shut. Frank heard the chain lock rattle; then the door opened. His first impression was dirty and big.

"You Bobby Neal Turner?" José asked.

"Yeah." Turner filled the doorway. Two twenty-five, two-fifty, Frank guessed. His grease-stained sweatshirt with a Marlboro logo topped a pair of black jeans tucked into scuffed biker boots.

"We come in?" Frank asked. When Turner hesitated, he said, "Or you want to talk out here in the hall?"

Turner stood aside.

The first thing Frank saw was the Harley in the living room. Turner had obviously been working on it. In contrast to the disorder visible in the rest of the apartment, pistons, valves, and smaller parts had been laid out around the Harley with military precision.

"Cemetery office gave us your name," Frank said.

Turner looked cautiously at Frank and José while he wiped his hands on a rag. "Yeah? So?"

"We're interested in a job you did."

Turner's jawline tightened.

"Gravedigging job," José said.

Turner relaxed noticeably.

"Cemetery office said you dug the grave for Robert O'Brien."

Turner nodded. "Yeah. The priest."

"Your helper was a Eugene Francis Feltner."

Turner looked disbelievingly at José. "Geno's middle name Francis?" He smiled. "Fran-cis," he teased out the name.

"Just the two of you?" José asked.

"Always just two. You do a grave by hand, no backhoe, you do two guys. No room for three unless one a them's the stiff."

"I looked up at the grave site," Frank said, "and I saw three of you up there waiting."

Turner's brow furrowed; he nodded. "Yeah. Me and Geno. An' the swish. He shows up, watches, then goes."

"A swish?"

Turner sneered. "Guy shows up, watches, then goes. Doesn't say nothing. Watches, goes."

"What makes you say he's a swish?"

"Just looked like it." Turner made a limp-wrist gesture. "Skinny. Leather jacket. Ponytail. Sissy."

"But he didn't say anything? Why he was there?"

Turner shook his head.

Frank pulled out the identikit drawing of the kid from the diner.

Turner nodded. "That's him. He stands up there, watches, I think he's gonna cry but he doesn't, and he leaves."

"You saw him leave the cemetery?" José asked.

"Yeah. Walked to the street, got in his car, drove off."

"What kind of car?"

"Rice rocket. Brown."

"Rice rocket—Toyota? Honda?"

Turner shrugged and pointed to the Harley. "I buy American. Don't pay much attention to Jap iron."

"No brown rice-rockets." Woody's voice came in hollow over the speaker phone.

José grimaced.

Frank, who'd been doodling on a legal pad, put his pencil down. "Well," he said a little too sharply, "I guess there's an answer?"

"Anything could have happened. The kid could have parked after the service started, and my guys missed him. Your guy could have been color-blind. Hell, Frank, you've been in this business. . . ."

"Yeah," Frank answered, after letting Woody wind down some. "Yeah, I know."

"I'm gonna work it, Frank."

"Yeah. I know, Woody. Thanks."

Frank jabbed a button on the phone, and the speaker went dead with an electronic *blip*. He leaned back in his chair, lacing his hands behind his head. José was slouched in his chair, chin on his chest in a way that made him look like James Earl Jones.

"What if?" José said.

"Okay, what if?"

This was an inside game between Frank and José. Early on as partners, they'd worked out the rules that would let each of them explore alternatives without getting into the kinds of personal arguments that had split up many a Homicide partner team.

José didn't say anything right away. He kept his chin on his chest and pushed his lips out, thinking. At last he cleared his throat: "What if our man Turner is right? That the kid is gay? That he and O'Brien had a relationship?"

Frank stiffened, then forced himself to relax. "What if?" rules put everything on the table. Everything was up for grabs. No protecting your pet theories, no sheltering sacred cows.

"Credibility. He's one source, and a redneck gravedigger," Frank replied.

"The clipping file is a second data point," José countered. "And while I'd nominate Bobby Neal Turner for honkie of the year, it's that kind who get a lot of practice putting people in boxes. Like I said, what if he's right?"

Frank felt trapped. "Leaves us with a queer priest."

"With half a million in cash that Simmons says could have been embezzled."

"*Could,*" Frank came back. "Simmons said *could.* He didn't say *was.*"

"*I'm* not saying it's possible, Frank. I'm saying we got an expert—a bean counter—saying it's possible. He said it on TV in front of a zillion people. Fact."

Frank rolled that over, then reluctantly nodded. "Yeah. Simmons did say it was possible. Yeah."

"So, my 'What if?' is this—what if O'Brien was gay and what if he did embezzle the money?"

Frank sat still, listening to the late-night sounds in the station. A vacuum cleaner, a radio or TV, footsteps and a door opening and closing. In his head, he moved the pieces around, trying to find a fit.

Finally he looked up at José. "Okay. Here it is: If O'Brien was gay, the killing could have been the result of some kind of emotional conflict. If he was embezzling, he could have gotten killed for the money—what he was doing with it or what he was going to do with it."

"And what if it was something to do with being gay that led to the embezzling?" José asked.

"Blackmail?"

"Wouldn't be the first time."

"Yeah."

"So we check it out?"

"We do it quiet, Hoser. See what the talk is."

"Yeah. If there is any."

Frank felt physically ground down, as if he'd just run a long way with a heavy load.

AT HOME THAT NIGHT, FRANK POURED HIMSELF A BEER, warmed up the last of the beef stew he'd made the week before, and sat down at the kitchen table to watch the tape of Worsham interviewing O'Brien. When he got to the part where Worsham asked O'Brien how many souls he'd saved, and O'Brien said, "You'd better ask God about that," Frank stopped the VCR. He studied O'Brien's eyes and the lines in the priest's laughing face.

"What did you know, Father Robert O'Brien?" he asked the frozen image. "What did you know?"

FOURTEEN

THE FOLLOWING MORNING, when Frank came into the office, José was at his desk.

Frank reached for the phone.

"I already called."

"Called who?" Frank said.

José got to his feet. He held his coffee mug in one hand and picked up Frank's with the other. "Called Prints to see if they've ID'd the Beamer Boy," he said, making for the door.

"Well?" Frank asked as José left for the coffee room.

"Maybe today, maybe not."

"*May*-be?" Frank called out to the empty doorway. "*May*-be," he said to himself, looking at his In box, stuffed with overdue reports, surveys, and queries from Internal Audit. "Maybe . . ." he muttered as he sat down and reached for the first file.

"THAT'S IT." FRANK SLAPPED A FOLDER INTO HIS OUT box and tossed his pencil on the desk. "That's absolutely it." By late afternoon the stack in the Out box had grown, but the In box was still winning. And Prints still hadn't come up with an ID.

"I'm tired of working for the clerks," he told José. "Let's go do something for the taxpayers."

José got up quickly and reached for his coat. "Work for the taxpayers? Where you get those crazy notions, boy?"

"Where you want to start?" Frank asked.

"Mister Charlie's?"

"Good as any."

HERMAN CHARLES HAD OPENED HIS BAR AND GRILL ON the corner of Southeast Pennsylvania Avenue and Eighth in the early sixties. Several blocks to the south, on Eye Street, stood the Marine barracks. Normally, the proximity would have made for a mutually beneficial relationship, except that Mister Charlie's was the flagship, so to speak, of Washington's gay businesses.

The first year, Mister Charlie's had been the scene of escalating violence. Sporadic fights between its gay customers and the Marines down the street had turned into regular brawls that increasingly grew into near-riots. When a smoke grenade rolled through the front door one night, Herman finally had had enough. He walked down Eighth to the barracks and knocked on the front door of the federal-style house that was home to the commandant of the Marine Corps. Herman told the four-star general that he'd had enough bad business, the general told Herman that he'd had enough Marines arrested, and the two shook hands. The truce didn't stop the occasional skirmish, but it did end the open warfare, and it established Herman as a village elder in Washington's gay community.

The after-work crowd had filled the bar when Frank and José walked in. Heads turned and conversations stopped midstream.

"Frank! José!"

From the back of the bar, Herman Charles cut through the crowd. Tall, bald, and deeply tanned, he looked to be in his forties. Frank knew he was closer to sixty. Herman shook hands with Frank, then with José, and the heads turned back and the conversations resumed.

"Got time to talk, Herman?" Frank asked.

"Heavy or light?"

"Heavy."

Herman pointed over his shoulder. Frank and José followed him past the bar and through a door leading into an office.

"Sit." Herman motioned to a pair of chairs and propped himself on the edge of the desk. "It's the O'Brien killing, isn't it?"

Frank tried not to show his surprise, but Herman picked up on it.

"You said heavy, Frank. And word is you and José got the O'Brien case. One and one adds up to that's what you want to talk about."

Frank got the feeling he sometimes had standing on a high place and looking down. He plunged in and asked, "Was O'Brien gay?"

Herman's eyes shifted to the floor for an instant. "You wouldn't be expecting me to answer that if it didn't have something to do with who killed him," he said.

Frank said nothing.

Herman shook his head. "Not that I know of," he answered. "I'd met him. We contribute to his center. But I'd never seen him here."

"Never heard any talk?" José asked.

Herman shook his head again. "One topic always batting around at the bar is who's in the closet. God! I've heard the wildest"—another emphatic shake of the head—"but never a word about O'Brien." He raised his eyebrows. "My turn?"

Frank nodded.

"Why? Why do you ask?"

Frank was about to deflect the question with a standard covering-the-bases response, then hesitated. Instead, he said, "José and I found some clippings." He went on to describe the file.

Herman listened, but when Frank finished, he said only, "Anything else?"

"And there's this." Frank handed him the identikit drawing. "There's some connection between O'Brien and this guy. A witness characterized the guy as looking gay."

Herman laughed. "Oh. And how does *that* look?"

"That's what the *witness* said, Herman," José told him.

"Of course. Sorry." Herman stared at the drawing. "Never seen him. Or anybody like that."

Frank stood. "You keep your ears open?" He pulled out his card case.

Herman waved the offered card aside. "I got your number. I hear anything, I'll call."

"And ah . . . we keep this quiet?"

Herman gave Frank an acid-tinged smile. "I grew up keeping things quiet."

Outside, José looked at Frank. "Feel better?"

Frank nodded. "Some. A little bit."

"That surprised me, you telling him about O'Brien's clippings."

"Yeah . . . well, hell, I surprised myself."

"Henry Eugene Brewington." Frank read the name aloud from the ID Section report. "Born nineteen seventy-five." He looked up at José. "'Seventy-five, Hoser."

"Just yesterday."

"Twenty-four years. A short lifetime."

Frank held Brewington's mug shot up against the photo from the scrapyard. "Nice-looking."

José flipped through his rap sheet. "Two counts petty larceny, one auto theft. While he was on probation, tested positive—PCP once, marijuana twice. Last residence of record, Benning Heights. Forty-four-hundred block, Clay Southeast. "

"Simple City," Frank said. The Heights had been known as Simple City for as long as Frank had been on the force. He'd tried to run down how it had gotten that name. He'd heard a lot of stories, but none of them held up. "Relatives?"

José ran a finger down the form. "Adult next-of-kin

here's given as Mrs. Sadie Wilson, same address. Relation not given."

Frank and José sat looking at each other for a long moment, both of them unhappy.

"Well," José said finally, "I guess we gotta."

Frank checked in with the watch commander, then got up and looked out the window. It was starting to snow, and even though it was only mid-morning, it was dark enough that cars had their lights on. He shouldered into his coat.

"Not a good day for it," he said.

"Never is," said José. "Never is."

BENNING HEIGHTS LAY JUST INSIDE THE DISTRICT LINE across from Prince George's County, Maryland. It had a Metro stop, a Safeway, a bank, and a town hall. It had a neighborhood recreation center. Every Wednesday the Benning Heights AME Church held Bible study for nearly a hundred teenagers. Benning Heights also had boarded-up houses, clusters of men on corners dealing crack, and convenience stores run by Koreans who sat behind bulletproof glass shields.

Forty-four twenty-six Clay Southeast was a brick bungalow in a row of other brick bungalows. José knocked at the front door and Frank stood back and off to one side. A muffled voice came from within.

"Police," José answered.

Frank imagined an eye on them through the door's peephole. José must have felt it, too, because he held his badge shoulder high. There was the clatter of locks unlatching, and the door opened.

The woman stood with one hand on the door as if ready to slam it shut. Tiny and precise, Frank thought. White apron over a faded floral-print dress, both starched and neatly ironed. Silver hair stood out against a dark brown oval face.

"Ma'am," José asked, "is this Henry Eugene Brewington's residence?"

The woman looked at José steadily before nodding. "He lives here." She said it firmly, but cautiously.

"And you are . . . ma'am?"

"I'm his grandmother," she answered in the same cautious voice. "I'm Sadie Wilson. What is it about Henry?"

They sort of know, but they don't know, Frank was thinking. You, a cop, standing there on their porch makes it almost so, but it really isn't so until you say the words. And when you say the words, time seems to stand still until they react. Some freeze, some scream, and some dissolve.

José didn't hesitate. "He's dead, ma'am."

Mrs. Wilson winced. Then she opened the screen door. "Come in," she said evenly.

José and Frank followed her into the living room. The house smelled of baking and furniture polish. Frank guessed that dust had a short half-life around Sadie Wilson. She pointed to two overstuffed armchairs. Both had lacy white things over the backs. His mother had had those. *Antimacassars?*

On a table next to the chairs was a large studio photograph of a handsome boy in a graduation cap and gown. Henry Brewington was smiling as if at someone off camera. No trace of the sullen hardness that the mug shots had captured.

On the wall above the chairs, a 1959 diploma from Spelman made out for Sadie Monroe Dorsey. Centered over the fireplace, a large ornately framed picture of Jesus standing on a hill, flanked by Lincoln, King, and the Kennedys. The five were wrapped in a golden light coming down from the sky.

"I've got coffee on the stove . . . ?" Mrs. Wilson offered.

José held up a hand. "Thank you, ma'am. My partner and I have reached our limit for the day. But if you want . . ."

She shook her head. "Please, sit." She motioned again to the two overstuffed chairs and stood until José and Frank were seated. Then she pulled up a straight wooden chair to face the two detectives.

"When did it happen?" she asked José.

"The best we can tell, last Wednesday night—maybe Thursday morning early."

"How?"

"He was shot, ma'am."

She shut her eyes, hugged herself, and rocked back and forth. Here it comes, Frank thought. But she straightened up and looked at José, and Frank, and back to José.

"Who did it?"

"We don't know," José said. "We don't know yet."

Mrs. Wilson pressed her lips together in disapproval. Frank connected the Spelman diploma and her expression. Teacher says that's not the right answer.

José soldiered on. "We came here to tell you, ma'am, about Henry. We just identified his . . . him. We're just starting the investigation. You could help us."

Mrs. Wilson sat quietly, then asked, "How?"

"Tell us about Henry's life," José said. "Tell us about his friends and associates. And tell us what he was doing the last days before . . . the days you saw him last."

"Three things," Mrs. Wilson said, as though getting the assignment down right.

Henry Brewington's basics were all too familiar. Father's whereabouts unknown. Mother had built a string of convictions by the time she was seventeen: prostitution, shoplifting, and minor drug peddling. The string ran out with an OD at eighteen. Sadie Wilson had taken Henry in when he was three. Did well through junior high school. After that, everything went to hell.

"It got so bad. It seemed like they were dying every day," Mrs. Wilson said. "The shootings. Day and night." She wrung her hands. "They overpowered us. Instead of rising up, we locked our doors."

" 'They'?" José asked.

Mrs. Wilson looked at José as if she found it strange that he had to ask. "Our children. Our own children," she said.

"It's getting some better," José replied.

"Some," she repeated without conviction. "I thought—

just the other day—Henry's lived through the worst of it. That's what I thought. I let myself hope he might have a chance. . . ." Her voice trailed off wistfully.

Frank gave her a moment, then said, "Henry had a record of . . . encounters with the police. But nothing recently."

Mrs. Wilson smiled. "Henry got a job. A regular job."

"A job?"

"Two years ago. Working for Mr. Jarvis."

"Solomon Jarvis? Jarvis Security?"

She nodded. "You know Mr. Jarvis?"

"Yes, ma'am. Tell me," Frank continued, "did Henry ever say where Jarvis had him working?"

"Places changed. Sometimes I'd ask him where he was working, it'd be here in the District. Other times over in Arlington, or up in Chevy Chase."

"Did you ever call him at work?" Frank asked.

"Not often. But once in a while. Ask him to stop by the Safeway or to pick up a prescription."

"He must have had different phone numbers," José said.

Mrs. Wilson shook her head. "No. One number. He had one of those cell phones."

"You have the number?" José asked.

"I remember it."

After Frank jotted the number down, José asked, "He have a car?"

"Yes."

"A Beamer?"

"I beg your pardon?"

"A BMW?"

"No. It was a Mercedes. A pretty car. Not flashy. Henry said he bought it used."

"Where is it?" José asked.

She shook her head and gestured toward the street. "I don't know. It's not out there where he usually parks . . . parked it."

"Ma'am?" Frank asked. "Would you mind showing us Henry's room?"

Henry Brewington's room was at the back, down a short hallway. It fit the rest of the house. Neat. Clean.

Mrs. Wilson looked around the room approvingly. "Henry always kept up after himself." She smiled ruefully. "One thing I was able to teach him."

Frank stepped toward a closet door where snapshots nearly covered a full-length mirror. A pretty girl, not more than a child, held a baby in her arms. Both were laughing. Mrs. Wilson noticed Frank looking at it. "My daughter, his mother," she explained. "She was fifteen."

"Who are these guys?" José asked, pointing to another picture. Three young men stood in front of a stretch limo. All three were dressed in black tie and tails. Henry Brewington's arm draped protectively over the shoulder of a smaller, darker-skinned companion. On Brewington's left stood a taller, lighter-skinned man.

Sadie Wilson gave a disapproving look. "Carlton Holmes and Lewis Strickland. If you want Henry's best friends, that was them. Senior dance night."

"They still around?"

"I suppose so. Carlton lives over on Eads. Lewis . . . Lewis, I'm not certain—"

"That's all right, we'll find him," Frank said. "Do you know if Henry kept any papers? Bills? That kind of thing?"

Mrs. Wilson opened the closet and pulled out an old-fashioned portfolio, with a string tie to keep it closed. She handed it to Frank.

"Can we sit and talk, ma'am?" José asked.

She nodded and went to the chair at the desk. Frank and José sat side by side on her grandson's bed.

Frank took notes for the next hour, as José led Sadie Wilson through her grandson's relationship with his friends and acquaintances, his life in the neighborhood. During lulls, Frank wrote up an evidence voucher for the things in the portfolio: receipts, ticket stubs, bills. All this would go into an investigator's first draft. He knew that when he and José worked up the story, they'd discover gaps and holes. Some of them you knew right away you'd have to go back and fill in, others you could let slide for a little longer.

Mrs. Wilson's answers started slowing, and Frank

caught José's questioning glance and nodded. José leaned across and patted the back of her hand. "We've got a good start, ma'am. I hope you don't mind if we come back?"

At the front door, José took out a contact card and handed it to Mrs. Wilson. "My home phone's on there. You call. Anytime." José opened the door.

"Mr. Phelps?"

José, one hand on the knob, turned to her.

"My Henry . . . when can he come home?"

Frank watched the unease flash across José's face. At the same time the image of the grinning skull on the crushed Beamer came back to him.

"I saved a suit for him," Sadie Wilson went on. "I hoped I'd never have to use it. But I saved it just in case. . . ."

José reached out and took her hand. "Mrs. Wilson. I'm afraid Henry's body . . . Henry isn't . . . I don't think you'd want to have a viewing, Mrs. Wilson."

The woman took it in, and the comprehension of what José said clouded her face. Frank thought that the break would come now, but it didn't. She gently pulled her hand from José's and tilted her head up.

"Thank you, gentlemen," she said evenly. She was standing straight-backed and dry-eyed when Frank and José shut the door.

On the porch, they stood shoulder to shoulder and looked down the street. José shook his head sadly. "God," he said, "what have we done to ourselves?"

FIFTEEN

STILL PARKED OUTSIDE Henry Brewington's home, José called in to get Carlton Holmes's record while Frank checked the portfolio with Brewington's papers. DMV registration for a 1996 Mercedes-Benz. An S500, Frank noted, $45,000 easy. Neatly sorted monthly phone bills, but not for a cell phone. Visa and American Express bills—clothes and entertainment—$3,000 for December alone. A well-fed clotheshorse.

Minutes later, they learned that Holmes had two convictions for petty larceny, one for possession of marijuana with intent to sell. Six months' juvenile detention, working off the second year of a three-year probation for the possession. Address 4504 Eads. Next-of-kin an aunt, Rose Perkins.

IT CAME FAST, NASTY, AND IRRITABLE: "CARLTON'S NOT here."

Rose Perkins filled the doorway. Massive in gray sweatpants and an old Redskins jersey. Frank pictured her in a head-down rhino charge. He noticed that, big as he was, José stood way back, to give her plenty of room.

"We'd like to talk to him, ma'am," José said.

Rose Perkins grew even more irritable. "What part of 'not here' don't you understand, Mr. Police?" Miz-tuh Poe-leese.

Frank stepped up even with José. "When did he leave, Mrs. Perkins?"

She looked at Frank as if she'd been suprised by something unpleasant. "Carlton's a grown man. I don't keep watch on him. He lives here because he's my nephew. He pays rent." Her eyes bulged. "You got something on Carlton? You got a suspicion?"

"No, ma'am," Frank said. "We just—"

"Well, if you don't got something on Carlton, if you don't got a suspicion, then get your police ass off my porch."

"WHAT ABOUT THAT?" FRANK SAID IN AWE. HE LOOKED out the car window at Rose Perkins's house. "That is one tough old broad."

José started the car. "Take a fool or a brave man to climb on top a that," he said. "Think she knows where Holmes is?"

"Hard to say." Frank kept staring at the house. "Either she knows and she just hates cops, or she doesn't know and she just hates cops. Take your choice. Either way, she hates cops." He looked at José. "Where next?"

"Solly?"

"Good as any," Frank said.

"How long's it been?"

"Five years? Six?"

JARVIS SECURITY WAS SEVERAL BLOCKS FROM MISTER Charlie's, on the third floor of a movie theater that had been converted to commercial office suites. A reputable building where you didn't have to pay an arm and a leg to get a Pennsylvania Avenue address. Jarvis's tastefully furnished offices looked out on the avenue through a wide window. Photographs on the walls traced the rise of

Solomon Jarvis. Frank recognized a thinner and younger Jarvis entering the police academy and, next to that, the standard graduation photo. Framed clippings about award ceremonies. Appreciation plaques from the FBI, the DEA, and state police from Maine to Oregon. A crystal bowl from the Defense Investigative Service.

"You doing good, Solly," Frank said.

"Body and soul holding together, Frank, body and soul." Jarvis chin pointed to the two detectives. "You and Hoser getting good ink. I look in the *Post* and there you two are. Looking like Hollywood. Glad somebody finally bagged that asshole Jimmy Foxworth."

"Emerson wasn't too happy."

Jarvis rolled his eyes. "Fucking Randolph. He oughta be teaching Sunday school, not running Homicide."

"We're working the O'Brien killing, Solly," José said.

Jarvis shook his head. "Damn drive-by. Good luck."

"We just ID'd a fella who might be connected."

"Oh?"

"Henry Brewington."

"Henry?"

"He's dead," Frank said.

"Oh." Jarvis's jaw dropped, and he swung his head from side to side, slowly, as if to the beat of a funeral drum. "Henry Brewington was a good man. Too bad. Too damn bad." He looked from Frank to José and back. "How?"

"The MacKenzie Salvage yard. They found—"

"Was that him?"

"He worked for you," Frank said.

Jarvis waited, then asked, "There's a question there?"

"Brewington in the salvage yard—was he on the job?"

Jarvis waved his hand. "We don't have any business with MacKenzie." He swiveled around to his desk and tapped a computer keyboard. He hunched forward to consult the screen, then turned back around. "And Henry wasn't on duty that night."

"What'd he do for you?" José asked.

"Henry? Started out on night patrol. Customers here in the District, over in Crystal City, Rosslyn. Malls, office buildings. Worked his way up to accounts managing."

"What does that involve," Frank asked, "accounts managing?"

"Making sure we meet the contract services with our customers. Filling shifts, getting substitutes when somebody calls in sick. Routine hiring, firing."

"Can we get a list of his accounts?" José handed Jarvis a contact card.

"Sure." Jarvis nodded, pocketing the card.

"When'd you last see him?"

"The morning before. Daily staff meeting."

"What about drugs?" Frank said.

Jarvis laughed. "I don't do them. Is that what you're asking?"

"I'm asking about your people."

"Look"—Jarvis leaned toward Frank—"I'm not my people's keeper, see? I'm just their employer. This isn't the department. I don't keep strings on them, on what they do when they're not working." He shook an index finger in warning. "But on the job, I catch them thieving, fucking off, doing drugs—buying, selling, or using—their ass is grass, and I'm the lawn mower. No second chances. First time—gone. They all know it."

"So you didn't have any trouble with Brewington?" José asked.

Jarvis put both hands on the arms of his chair and raised his chin. "Like I said, Hoser, their ass's gone if they're trouble," he rumbled. "Henry was still here." A pause. "Therefore I didn't have any trouble with him."

"You know he had a record?"

"Shit!" Jarvis waved a hand in dismissal. "If I only hired people with a clean sheet I'd be outta business."

"As far's you know he was keeping clean?" Frank asked.

"As far's I *know,* he was clean." He pointed at Frank's notebook. "And make sure you get that down exactly right."

Frank smiled back, enjoying having gotten under Jarvis's skin. "What was he making?"

"You mean, what was I paying?"

"You turned lawyer?" Frank needled.

"No. I'm just careful."

"Okay, how much were you paying him?"

"Fifteen an hour plus time-and-a-half overtime. Medical, dental. Even a 401(k)."

"Brewington—outside of work—you ever hear of any trouble?"

Jarvis shook his head. "Never heard of any. Like I say, I don't put up with any shit. You let shit get into the security business, your customers go somewhere else. My customers pay for quiet."

"And no shit," José put in.

Jarvis nodded. "And no shit."

"STILL YOUR BASIC NO-SHIT KIND OF GUY," JOSÉ SAID, shutting the car door.

"I guess."

"You pissed off at him?"

"No."

"Way you were sticking it to him there toward the last, I figured you might be."

"Oh, I guess. Sort of an attitude."

"His? Or yours?"

"Maybe a little a both," Frank acknowledged. "He quits the force and makes a bundle on the pick-and-choose stuff. We have to take all the shit that rolls downhill and—" He threw a hand up in exasperation. "Aw hell, just chalk it up to sour grapes."

"Yeah, I understand the grape business," José said. "So . . . who's next?"

Frank thumbed through his notebook. "Strickland."

"Record?"

"Pissant stuff."

"You sound like Emerson with that 'pissant.' "

"Meant to."

LEWIS STRICKLAND'S LAST ADDRESS WAS A RED-BRICK apartment project ten or so blocks south of the Marine barracks and Mister Charlie's. A girl who looked about nine answered the bell, then was yanked behind the door by a woman who stepped into the doorway.

"He ain't here." Right out of the box. *He ain't here.*

"We'd like to talk to Lewis Strickland," José said.

"I said he ain't here."

José frowned. "Ma'am, you didn't know who I was looking for, but right off you say he's not here."

The woman sighed. "Lewis be the only one you be lookin' for, an' he ain't here."

"He got a beeper?" Frank asked.

The woman gave him a flat stare. "What you want him for? He done something?"

"We just want to talk with him, ma'am," Frank said patiently. "We don't want him for anything except to talk to. If he's got a beeper, we'll call him. We'll be out of your way."

"THAT MUST BE HIM." JOSÉ POINTED TO THE FRONT OF Garrett's. A young black man had come in and was talking to Stanley at the bar. Stanley indicated where Frank and José were sitting.

Real English, Frank thought. Burberry trench coat, conservative wide-brimmed tan felt outback hat, tightly furled umbrella.

"You gentlemen call?" A gold-capped incisor jarred the Savile Row image.

"You Lewis Strickland?"

"You Phelps? Or Kearney?"

"Phelps," José answered, showing his badge and credentials.

"I'm Kearney," Frank said, doing the same.

"I . . . am Lewis Strickland." The theatrical way he said it, you expected a drum roll or trumpets from heaven.

Frank and José each gave him a fish eye and let him stand there long enough so it was clear there weren't going to be any drums or trumpets.

"Have a seat." Frank gestured. "You want coffee?"

Strickland sniffed. "I don't drink coffee." *Caw*-fee.

Frank shrugged. "Whatever." He reached into his coat and pulled out his notebook.

"I drink tea."

Frank looked up at Strickland. "That's good. They're saying too much coffee's bad for you." He leafed through his notebook, taking his time, knowing Strickland was setting up another play.

"I would like some tea."

Frank looked up again. He angled his head toward Stanley at the bar. "Go get your tea."

"I want that motherfucker to bring it to me." Strickland jabbed a space on the table in front of him. "Right here."

"You have lousy manners," José said.

Strickland sneered. "Good afternoon, gentlemen. See you around."

He pushed his chair back from the table and started to stand. He'd barely gotten off the chair when his body spasmed as if he'd stuck his finger in a light socket.

"My thumb!" he gasped.

"Sit down," Frank said quietly.

"Motherfu—"

"You've used up your quota of those here." Frank gently increased the pressure on the thumb hold.

Strickland sat. Frank held on to the thumb for a second more, then released it. Strickland stared at his thumb in disbelief, then at Frank.

"How'd you do that?" he asked with curiosity, his eyes half closed to slits.

"Lots of practice. You work somewhere? Or do you just live off the air?"

"Tower Records." Strickland motioned with his head toward downtown. He sat back in his chair and measured Frank. "You want to talk about John Henry, don't you?"

"I want to talk about Henry Eugene Brewington," Frank said.

"That's what I call him. John Henry was a steel-drivin' man."

"What kind of steel?" José asked. "A Beamer?"

"Naw. A Benz. S500. Silver. Black leather. Bose sound. Turn that fucker up, blow your eardrums."

Frank followed up fast. "How did you know we wanted to talk about Brewington?"

"Word is, he's dead. His grandma's pissin' and moanin' all over she can't bury him properly. What'd he do? Fall inna meat grinder?"

"How long did you know Brewington?"

Strickland looked at Frank, then at his wounded thumb, then again at Frank. "Nine, ten years. Since high school."

"The two of you got a fast start, dealing," José said.

Strickland grinned lazily. "Young entrepreneurs." Ahn-tray-pray-*nooers*.

"One-to-three," Frank jabbed.

Still grinning, Strickland parried effortlessly. "Out in six months."

"Brewington's batting record was better than yours," Frank said. "Was clean two years, driving a big Benz. Security business must pay off."

"Security business." Strickland said. "A growth in-*dus*-try."

"What *was* he into?" José asked.

Strickland eyed the two detectives.

"Come on, asshole," José said menacingly. "What was he into?"

Strickland didn't recoil. "I don't know."

Frank made a move toward Strickland's hand. Strickland snatched it off the table to the safety of his lap. "I don't know," he repeated.

"Where's Carlton Holmes?" Frank asked.

"Who?"

José leaned across the table so his face was an inch or two from Strickland's. "Lieutenant Kearney didn't stutter, you shitbird," he said. "Holmes, Carlton Holmes. Where is he?"

Strickland closed his eyes, taking time to get a reading on where he was and what around him could hurt most. It didn't take him long. He opened his eyes and said, "Carlton—I haven't seen him."

"When's the last time you saw him?" José asked. "Talked to him?"

Strickland squinted, made a show of thinking about it. "Week . . . ten days."

"Where is he?"

Strickland got a wise-guy look. "You mean you can't find him?"

"I just asked if you knew where he was."

Strickland shook his head. "Naw. Maybe I'll hear that later."

Frank stood up and tossed a contact card on the table in front of him. "You hear, you listen good, Lewis. And then you call José or me."

Strickland's lazy grin bordered on a sneer.

Frank smiled back. "I know some things to go along with the thumb trick, Lewis."

FRANK REACHED FOR THE PHONE. SINCE FIVE, HE AND José had been sorting out, getting down what they knew and what they didn't and where they might go from here. As he explained it to rookies at the academy, sorting out was an investigation's pit stop. Every so often you had to take time to sit down and pull things together.

Everybody did it differently. He and José had worked it out so that one of them would fire questions that needed answering while the other wrote them down. Then they'd switch. Frank had been taking the notes when Kate called.

"Anytime a lawyer in this town offers to buy dinner for a cop . . ." José shut his desk and started the closing routine. "This'll keep. What we don't know tonight we won't know tomorrow morning. Where she taking you?"

"Sam and Harry's."

José nodded approvingly. "She's got looks and she's got money."

"And she's got me."

"Well, two outta three ain't bad."

* * *

"SAME STORY ON BREWINGTON, EVERYBODY WE TALKED to—living good, no street action." Frank sipped his martini and felt the gin turn from ice to fire as it made its way down. "And nobody's seen one of his closest pals."

"So Holmes is getting to be a bigger dot?" Kate asked.

"Maybe. Problem is, guys like Holmes get mixed up in so many things they could be on the run for any one of them. Or any combination. Holmes could have everything to do with his buddy Brewington. Or nothing at all.

"We do know Holmes had connections to Brewington," Frank continued. "And Brewington's the only link in the chain to O'Brien, the red BMW, and the twenty-two-caliber slugs." He frowned in frustration. "And that's where the real questions start. Who's the guy in the trunk, what was his relationship to Brewington? Brewington had a Benz—where is it? His grandmother says he had a cell phone—where did he have an account?"

"And Jarvis Security—one of those rent-a-guard operations?"

"Yes and no. Most of these new outfits furnish foot patrols in the malls and guys in uniform to stand at the door at the Gap or Eddie Bauer. Jarvis does that. But they've been around longer, they do more than guard stores. Isaiah Jarvis started it back in the seventies. Had a reputation for being hired muscle. Grand jury targeted him, but he ended up in the Potomac wired to an engine block."

"Solomon?"

"Isaiah's nephew. Class behind José and me at the academy. Uncle Isaiah died, Solly left the force, took over the security business, ran off the crooks, made it legit, and started making pretty big bucks."

Frank finished the martini and let his mind float free.

"John Henry, the steel-drivin' man," he mused. "Two years ago he leaves the streets. Gets a Benz. Spending thirty, forty thousand a year on clothes and restaurants. Damn sure didn't make it on fifteen an hour."

"Maybe he won the lottery," Kate suggested.

Frank laughed and opened the menu. "Whatever our man John Henry was doing, I don't think he was playing the lottery."

SIXTEEN

A T EIGHT THE next morning, Frank and José knocked on the closed and shuttered door of Mister Charlie's. Frank heard nothing but the sound of traffic on Pennsylvania Avenue at first, but then from inside came the sound of bolts sliding back and the door opened. Herman Charles stood there in a pale blue silk robe.

He waved them in. "I didn't want to talk over the phone," he explained, and led them to the back of the bar, to a table set with a coffeepot and a basket of pastry. At the table sat a younger man: white, early twenties, short bleached-blond hair, and eye shadow. He watched Frank and José walk toward him the way someone might watch the approach of his executioners.

"This is Jamie," Herman introduced him, "Jamie Sutton. He's my best waiter. But he's also an up-and-coming actor. I have no doubt that I shall soon lose him to the stage." He turned to the young man. "Jamie, these men are my friends." He was obviously trying to reassure.

Sutton looked from José to Frank and nodded cautiously. The young man's tension was evident.

"Coffee? Croissant?" Herman offered.

Frank sat quietly while Herman poured coffee and

passed the pastry basket. For a while the four men sat immobile, as if frozen in amber.

Then Herman stirred sugar in his coffee, and the sound of the spoon against the cup snapped the spell. "Jamie waits late shift," he said, reaching over and patting the back of the young man's hand. "Tell Frank and José."

Sutton looked questioningly at Herman.

"Go ahead. It's okay. They're friends."

Sutton took a deep breath. "Last night a customer comes in. It was just after ten. I know because our kitchen closes at ten-thirty, you see." Sutton paused to make certain Frank and José understood.

Frank nodded and Sutton continued. "We started talking and . . . one thing led to another." Sutton glanced at Herman for reassurance. The older man smiled encouragingly.

"Well, we . . . uh, went to my place, and . . . and after, we were talking—"

Frank's impulse was to ask whether this guy had a name, but he held back.

"—and he started talking about the priest."

"O'Brien," Frank said, and he was suddenly aware of José's eyes on him.

Sutton froze at the interruption.

"Go ahead," Herman urged softly.

Sutton started again, this time in a measured, slightly dramatic tone. "He asked me if O'Brien had ever been in Mister Charlie's. I said no. Then he asked if there'd been any talk that O'Brien was gay. I said I hadn't heard of any. I asked him why, why he cared. He said he was just curious. We started . . . ah . . . well, later, we were talking some more. About people and things we liked and things we didn't. He got up and pulled a picture from his coat and asked me if I'd ever seen that person."

"A drawing?" Frank guessed.

Sutton nodded.

José searched through his notebook, found the identikit of the Kid, and unfolded it.

Sutton nodded again. "That's it. That's the drawing."

Frank didn't say anything until he decided Sutton was finished with his story.

"Did he say why he was looking for the guy in the drawing?"

"He just said he was interested in finding him, and I let it go at that." Sutton paused. "I didn't want to pry or get personal. People are always wanting to know about other people, aren't they?"

"This man you were with, Jamie . . . his name?"

"Hampton."

"First name, last name?"

Sutton shrugged. "Just Hampton."

José slipped into the conversation. "You said that when Hampton came here"—José glanced at his notes—"quote, 'We started talking.' Who started the conversation?"

Sutton smiled for the first time. "You mean who initiated the pick-up?"

"Yeah."

"He did."

"Do you know how to get in touch with him?" Frank asked.

Sutton nodded. "He gave me his box number."

"Box? Where?"

"One of those personals boxes. At the *Blade*."

"No phone number or anything?"

"No."

Frank hesitated. His stomach turned at what he was thinking about asking, but he asked it anyway. "Feel up to meeting Hampton again?"

Sutton got a sly smile. "*Up* to it, Lieutenant?"

Frank felt his face flush. "Comfortable meeting him again—"

Still smiling, Sutton nodded. "Sure."

"—under surveillance?"

"You mean recorded?" Sutton's eyes widened.

Frank nodded.

"Video?"

"If we can. Sound at a minimum."

Sutton kept smiling. "Oh, *yeah!* Sounds like fun. How do we do it?"

Frank handed him a contact card. "Write to Hampton. Try to arrange something at your place. When the meeting's set, call us."

FRANK AND JOSÉ WERE ON THE SIDEWALK OUTSIDE MISter Charlie's when Frank's cell phone rang. He answered, listened, and the only question he asked was, "When?" He punched the phone off and turned to José.

"Rose Perkins's neighbor," he said, picking up his pace toward the car at the curb. "Thinks something's bad."

"I ALWAYS GO BY. *ALWAYS.* EVER' MORNIN'. *ALWAYS.*"

Wrapped in a bright red man's parka, Frances Morrow stood on her front porch and gestured next door, to the house where Carlton Holmes lived with his aunt.

"And what happened this morning?" José asked.

Morrow gave José an irritated look. "I knocked on the door and she didn't answer," Morrow said, as if that made everything clear.

"How long have you known Mrs. Perkins?" Frank asked.

Morrow lifted her chin. "*Fif*-teen years, an' we've been having mornin' coffee ever' mornin' of the fifteen." Her look added, And that's that.

Frank saw the concern on her face. "We'll take a look," he said.

THEY BANGED ON THE FRONT DOOR. NOTHING. JOSÉ pressed his ear to the door.

"Music." He listened more. "Rapper shit."

Frank stood very still. He could hear it, too. "Music?" He looked next door. The Morrow woman stood on her porch, watching them. "Let's try around back."

Two steps led up to the back door. Frank knocked. The

rap music was louder. Frank knocked again, then opened
the outer storm door.

"Hoser." He pointed to the inner door.

José stepped up on the stoop to look over Frank's shoulder. Metal of what had once been a dead bolt glinted
through the splintered door jamb.

José was already calling for backup as Frank pushed the
door open. The rap reverberated through the house.

I'm movin' like the shark deep in the sea,
I'm killin' any niggaz who fuck with me.

A pungent coppery odor filled the kitchen. Within an instant, Frank had a two-hand grip on his Glock, business
end sweeping the right side of the room. Out of the corner
of his eye, he saw José covering the left.

Death becomes me, death becomes me,
Movin' like I do, like a shark in the sea.

Frank hesitated, then pushed through a swinging door
into the next room. "Hello, Mrs. Perkins," he whispered.

Rose Perkins lay spread-eagled, naked, over the top of
the dining room table. Her head hung off the edge, unseeing eyes staring at the ceiling. Her slashed throat opened
wide in an obscene toothless grin. Blood soaked the carpet
and had pooled on the polished hardwood floor.

"Jesus Christ," José muttered.

He sounded a long way away, down a nightmare's hall.
Then Frank heard him say, "Her fingers. They cut them off."

Frank felt it coming, the sour, slick swelling at the back
of his throat. Unable to move, he doubled over as his stomach heaved and knotted.

A stereo sat in a corner. It was covered in blood. And the
rap went on.

So what do you call me? Tell me my name.
Death becomes me, death becomes me,
Death is my game.

* * *

"Blood coagulation, body temp . . ." Upton pursed his lips, then checked his watch and looked at Frank. "Say four, five this morning."

Frank, José, and Upton stood in the dining room. Upstairs, Milton and his partner were going through Carlton Holmes's room with the forensic team.

Frank tried to concentrate on what Upton was saying. But he couldn't take his eyes off the obscene spectacle as two of Upton's techs struggled to put the large corpse in a body bag. The head, nearly severed from the neck, hung limply. One of the techs had to hold it like a basketball and steady it before the other tech could zip the bag. Finally, they got the bag onto the gurney and wheeled it out.

"A guess?" Upton asked.

Frank came back to focus on Upton.

"Her fingers. The shear wounds resembled those of our friend Trunkman. Just a guess. I'll be able to tell more at the morgue." Upton glanced around the room. Even the ceiling bore splashes of blood. He shook his head in wonder. "No matter how long I've been in the business, it always surprises me—the amount of blood in a human body."

After Upton left, Frank went to the backyard. The air outside was cold and clean, and he pulled at it greedily, trying to get the blood smell out of the bottom of his lungs.

"Think she told them where he was?" José's voice came from behind him.

"Could have—if she knew. Didn't matter one way or another for her. She was gonna be dead anyhow. The minute they started on her fingers, she was a dead woman."

Frank didn't turn to face José, but kept working at the breathing.

"I puked, too."

Frank said nothing.

"You hear me? I said I puked, too."

Frank took several more deep breaths. "Yeah," he said. "That was bad in there."

Frank nodded, almost automatically. Then he thought about it. He shook his head and turned to José. "No," he said. "We've seen worse, you and me. And we didn't puke."

José stared off, remembering. "Yeah." He was quiet for a long time. "You're right. We didn't puke back then."

"Frank, Hoser."

Milton was standing on Rose Perkins's back stoop. He held a sheaf of papers in one hand.

"Finished Holmes's room."

"And?"

"They tore it all to hell."

"What's that?"

"Phone bills." Milton waved the papers.

"Let's see."

"Out here?" Milton gestured toward the door behind him. "We can sit in the kitchen—"

"Out here," Frank said.

Milton got a puzzled look, then threw it off, and joined them outside. He gave the bills to Frank.

Frank held them out at arm's length. "Damn," he swore in frustration.

"Here." José handed over his reading glasses.

Frank looked at the first page and thumbed through the rest. He went back to the first page. "This all? All you found?" he asked Milton.

"Well, there's a buncha clothes, pocket trash on top a his dresser—"

"No." Frank felt the apprehension gnawing at him, sour in his belly. "Any more phone records?"

Milton shook his head. "That's what there is. All there is."

"What's the matter, Frank?" José asked.

Frank held out the bills. They'd been stapled together. Beneath the staple, the ragged corner of a torn page. "Last month's bill. It's not here."

SEVENTEEN

"**D**AMN." FRANK CHECKED the time.

"Your eyeballs wear that watch out, lookin' at it so hard." José shifted in the passenger seat. Frank had the motor running and the heat turned up high, and the air inside was getting bad.

"I could invent the damn telephone, the time it takes them to run a record check," Frank said. "Timmy's slowing down." Tim Haskill was a retired DC cop who now worked security for Bell Atlantic. He had always been willing to do a favor off-books, provided it wasn't too big or too often.

"Phone company lawyers," José grunted. "Gotta be careful with the customers' privacy."

"We don't get a move on, brother Holmes's privacy's gonna be a pine box."

It wasn't just Tim Haskill. Frank had headquarters running down Holmes's probation officer, as well as doing a records check through credit ratings, motor vehicles, public schools, taxes, and utilities—the works, even cable TV. Nothing had come back yet.

Frank glanced at the rearview mirror. In the car behind, Milton and his partner were waiting. Frank noticed that

Milton was reading the paper, which pissed him off and at the same time made him envious.

Two minutes later, Haskill phoned in. Frank and José copied the listing of Carlton Holmes's calls along with addresses.

"Tough luck, Milt. No calls to Paris," Frank said when he handed his copy of the phone list to Milton and his partner. Most of the addresses fell in a roughly oval cluster in the Benning Heights area. Frank penciled a north-south line through Simple City on a municipal map. He and José would take the eastern half, Milton and his partner the west.

"WHAT DO YOU WANT CARLTON FOR?" CHANDRA NELson stood behind the counter at Gibson's dry cleaners, obviously suspicious.

"We think he could be in trouble," Frank said.

"Your kind of trouble?"

José cut in. "You know about Henry Brewington, don't you? You've heard that word?"

The young woman stared at José for a moment, then nodded vaguely.

"That's the kind of trouble Carlton could be in," José said. Nelson's expression stayed distrustful. "You know Henry's grandmama didn't get enough of him back to bury."

Nelson's eyes darted to the door. If there had been a way to just walk out, she would have.

"I haven't seen Carlton for . . . two days." Chandra Nelson nodded, now emphatically. "Since Wednesday."

Frank dropped back to let José work Nelson.

"How'd he act?"

Nelson gave José a flirtatious grin. "How do you mean?"

José rolled his eyes. "I mean, was he worried? Scared?"

"No."

"He say anything about Henry Brewington?"

"No."

"He and Henry friends?"

Nelson eyed José, trying to uncover a hidden trap. She spoke carefully: "They were friends. Carlton's got a lot of friends."

"Lewis Strickland one of them?"

Nelson looked sour. "Lewis got a bad case of the bigs."

"How's that?"

"You know. Bossy. The bigs."

"Carlton," José said. "You know where he is?"

Nelson thought about it, then shook her head. "I haven't seen him since Wednesday."

"You told me that once, Miz Nelson. What I asked you was, do you know where he *is*?"

Nelson's mouth tightened. "No. I do not know where Carlton Holmes *is*."

José handed her a contact card. "You hear from him, you tell him he's got big trouble, Miz Nelson. But it's not from us."

"LYING LIKE A RUG," JOSÉ SAID, CLOSING HIS DOOR.

"Political talent there." Frank started the car.

José didn't respond. Frank looked over. José was studying the phone list.

"Something?"

José nodded. "How about our newest best friend, the Honorable Mr. Lewis Strickland?" He ran a finger under the entry. "See anything out of place?"

It took Frank a moment or two to catch it. "Lewis, you're just too much," he said as he eased the car out into the midday traffic.

STRICKLAND'S MANAGER AT TOWER RECORDS SAID HE had called in sick. Ten minutes before opening. The manager was unconvinced, and pissed.

Frank called Haskill. Fifteen minutes later, Haskill called back with two addresses for numbers that had called

Tower Records shortly before ten that morning. One was a residence in Potomac, Maryland, the other an Exxon station at the corner of Fourth and Pennsylvania Southeast.

"Come on," Frank told José. "We're gonna get a tiger in our tank."

"THAT'S HIS OVER THERE." A MAN WITH "KIRK" EMBROIdered on his work shirt pointed to a Lexus on the lube rack.

"When's he due back?" Frank asked.

"GOD DAMN! GOD DAMN! GOD DAMN!" STRICKLAND'S voice reached soprano as he danced on his toes, trying— and failing—to get away from the knifing pain in his shoulder.

"You son of a bitch," Frank said. He wrenched Strickland's wrist a notch or two higher.

Strickland had come in to get his car, and Kirk had led him to the lube rack. From there, Frank and José hustled the startled Strickland into a back storage room and shut the door as Kirk walked away.

"You lying sack of shit." Frank slammed Strickland up against a wall shelf. Cans of motor oil crashed to the floor.

Frank grabbed a fistful of Strickland's Burberry trench coat and shook him violently. "You think it's all something from a music video, don't you? Where tough dudes like you talk big about killing and cutting. Well, Lewis, we had some killing and cutting that you could have stopped."

Strickland looked desperately to José for relief. José crowded in and got his own fistful of the Burberry and jerked Strickland away from Frank. He lifted him so his toes barely touched the floor, and put his face in Strickland's.

"You hear of the good-cop, bad-cop routine, Mr. Strickland?" José asked, reasonable and smiling. "You think maybe Frank's the bad cop and I'm the good cop?"

Strickland, petrified, could only nod.

José lost the reasonable smile. "Well, asshole, you just

shit outta luck, 'cause you just drew two very bad cops."
For emphasis he bounced Strickland off the shelf again.

Strickland's eyes rolled between Frank and José. "What
the fuck do you *want*?"

"Where is he?" José shouted into his face.

"Where's who?" Strickland shouted back.

"Holmes. Where's Carlton Holmes?"

"Told you . . . I haven't—"

"We got Carlton Holmes's phone bills," Frank said.

Strickland picked up on that right away. "Oh," he said.
"Oh."

"Yeah—oh. Ma Bell says you and Holmes talked day
before yesterday. Then you tell José and me you don't
know where Holmes is."

Strickland deflated. "Yeah. We talked. It wasn't long.
An' he didn't say where he was."

"He knew about Brewington?"

"He knew. That's why he called."

"What was his reaction?" Frank asked.

"His shit was weak. Lots of 'Oh fuck' an 'Oh shit' . . .
that kinda thing. Wanted to know if anybody been lookin'
for him."

"And you told him . . . ?"

Strickland shrugged. "Told him I hadn't heard of nobody. But that doesn't mean nobody's out there."

"You said he didn't tell you where he was," José said.
"Where do you *think* he might be?"

Strickland got a look as if thinking was something hard
to do. "Well, he's got this woman, Chandra."

"Yeah. What else?"

"Got some relatives. That crazy old aunt over on Eads—"

"We know about her," Frank said. "He's not there."

"Well," Strickland said uncertainly, "he's got an uncle."

"Where?" José asked.

"PG County somewheres. I think a farm. In the sticks."

"Name? The uncle got a name?"

Strickland shook his head with a worried expression, as
though he expected the wall trick again. He said, "I don't
know," so softly they could hardly hear the words.

Frank and José looked at him, then at each other. Frank motioned toward the door. "Get out of here."

"NICE-LOOKING CAR," JOSÉ SAID AS THEY WATCHED Strickland drive away from the Exxon station.

Frank's cell phone rang. He answered and mouthed, "Milt," to José, then listened more. The conversation over, he turned to José, but before he could say anything, the phone rang again. "Damn," he muttered.

Less than a minute later, Frank put the phone away. He started the car. "Milt. He's at the dry cleaner's, at Gibson's. Two guys came in looking for Chandra Nelson. She couldn't ID either one. They wanted to know where Holmes was."

"Yeah?"

"She told them she didn't know."

José winced.

"Place was full of customers. Two guys said thank you and left."

"Young lady oughta thank those customers that she didn't get a manicure."

"For sure they're working down Holmes's billing record." Frank made a hard right on Pennsylvania and headed toward Maryland.

"Where we going?"

Frank handed José the list of Holmes's calls. "Name down toward the bottom? Winslow? Paul Winslow?"

José's eyes went down the list.

"Second call I just got was from Holmes's probation officer. Paul Winslow is Holmes's uncle. Has a farm just outside New Carrollton."

"THERE IT IS—'PAUL WINSLOW.' " JOSÉ POINTED TO THE rural mailbox. It was almost four and the dying winter sun hung just above the horizon.

From the main road, Frank could make out a house on a hill about half a mile away, pale white against the darker background of evergreens and surrounding gray fields. A plume of wood smoke angled lazily toward the south in a light breeze. The kind of house you'd find throughout the rural South: living room, bedroom, kitchen in one straight line. Fire a shotgun through the front door; it comes out the back.

As they got closer, Frank saw two cars parked down the hill from the house. "Bingo," he whispered.

One of the cars was a big silver Jimmy four-wheel-drive. The other, a Mercedes S500, crouched like a panther, gleaming black in the sun's last light.

Frank found an opening in the trees, and pulled off the narrow dirt road and cut the engine. José had retrieved the binoculars from under his seat and was scoping out the cars.

"Maryland plates on the Benz, DC on the Jimmy." He read the numbers, and Frank relayed them for a tag check.

José passed the binoculars to Frank. The way they were parked, they had a clear view of one side of the house and a partial view of the back.

"Anybody in there?" José asked.

"Can't tell," Frank said.

The tag check came back on the Jimmy—reported stolen four hours earlier from the Union Station lot.

"They didn't bother to change the tags," Frank said. "Probably aren't planning on keeping it long." He sat quietly for a moment, then turned to José. "Well?"

José's lower lip pushed out as he looked reflectively at the house on the hill. "Could be lots of bad shit up there."

There were open fields of fire around the house in every direction. Frank felt his stomach tighten, and he had to make breathing a conscious effort. He looked at the hill and remembered how he'd learned hills as a grunt in Vietnam. It was a quick lesson: he didn't know before his first hill; he knew afterward. He learned how it was to be climbing up a hill into someone's sights. And he looked at this hill and saw himself in those sights all the way up.

"Yeah," he said, nodding. After calling the D.C. watch office for backup from Prince George's County, he popped the trunk. He and José got out of the car. From the rack welded in the trunk Frank unlatched the stubby ArmaLite assault rifle with its bandolier of spare magazines, and the ten-gauge pump, which he handed to José. Both men strapped on their Kevlar vests and leaned against the car to wait.

Frank didn't like the waiting. He was wishing that he still smoked cigarettes, that the PG County backup guys were already there, when shots came from the direction of the house. At first a small pop. A sound like that, all by it-self, you'd hear and wonder what it was you'd heard. Then a man's shout, and then a deep, hammering *bam-bam-bam,* and you knew what it was.

"That was inside," José said.

"Oh, damn," Frank said, looking at the hill. "Oh, damn," he said again as he and José took off up the hill at a run.

Seconds later, Frank flattened against the house, just to the right of the back door. José was on the other side. Winded, he held his head against the wall and pulled for air, trying to keep quiet but hearing the roaring pound of his heart.

Frank looked down the hill. When he was running to the house, it had seemed it would go on forever. From here, it was nothing more than a gentle slope on a kids' playground.

Then more shots, this time more muffled, coming from the other side of the house.

Frank caught his breath. Ear pressed against the siding, he heard nothing from inside. He locked eyes with José and shook his head, then motioned to the interior.

José had been listening, too. He pointed the butt of the riot gun toward the door.

Frank nodded. He backed a step away from the house, then moved forward and kicked in the door. José spun into the opening, his gun sweeping a small kitchen. The house was laid out as Frank thought it would be: a door leading into a bedroom in line with another door leading into the living room. The living room door—the front door—was open, and a man was sprawled facedown over the thresh-old. And beyond the front door, Frank saw the woods.

José knelt beside the fallen man and felt for a pulse. "He's alive." José rolled him over gently. Gray hair, a nylon down jacket, denim overalls, worn high-top work shoes.

"Probably Winslow," Frank said.

"Whoever it is," José said, "he's bleeding." He opened the man's jacket. Blood formed a palm-sized stain at the belt line, and the man's breathing came quick and shallow.

The sound of a shot echoed from the woods. Frank squeezed José's shoulder. "You take care of him."

José looked up. "Where you going?"

Frank was already out the door and on the front porch. "Hunting," he called back as he made for the treeline.

FRANK SWITCHED THE ASSAULT RIFLE SELECTOR TO FULL auto. The shots he'd heard he judged to be nine-millimeters or thirty-eights. Probably a pistol, maybe a TEC or an Uzi—but most likely a pistol. Two, three guys from the city with pistols come out to whack Carlton Holmes.

He had tracked the sound of the shot. Sound, plus the fact that a panicked man usually ran downhill, gave Frank a rough cut at direction. He sprinted across an open space and entered the woods. Visibility was cut to a few yards by old-growth oaks and white cedars, wild holly, waist-high brambles, and stunted trash trees. He paused and listened. At first he heard nothing but the wind in the treetops, then, from off to his right, the slight whip of a pushed-aside limb springing back into place.

It was like opening a textbook used long before—old lessons came flooding back to him, fresh as the days he'd first learned them. You work the city primarily on visuals. City noise drowns single sounds. But in the woods—or in the jungle—where nature blocks lines of sight, you strain for sound, for the slightest splinter that tells you something is out of place, and out of place means danger.

The ground was still running downhill, and Frank pictured it meeting a stream or ravine within the next forty, fifty yards. Despite the fading light, he made out a dark spot on the silver-gray bark of a fallen sycamore. He touched it and brought his fingertips close to his face: fresh blood—there on the tree trunk where you might put a hand to steady yourself to get over. On the other side of the tree, the damp soil bore the imprint of a shoe heel.

Frank held the assault rifle close to his chest to keep from snagging the brush and took small steps, lifting his feet high, freezing often to listen. Now the out-of-place sounds came closer and more frequently: snapping twigs, the waxy rasp of holly leaves, and once, the tick of metal on metal—coins? car keys? Whoever they were, the hunters were city boys, and he was closing in on them.

Suddenly the world before him erupted into chaos.

Brush cracked, and Frank heard a body breaking free, crashing through the woods.

"Get him! Get him!"

Shots.

He sprinted toward a large oak at the edge of a drop-off, where the land fell into a steep gully. Some thirty yards down the gully, two men in parkas were scrambling after another man, who was now in the bottom of the gully. The man in front was rapidly losing ground, slowed by thick windfalls of brush on the gully floor.

One of the men in back fired twice.

The man in front staggered. He took a step or two, then fell.

The other two men made for him. They were no longer running. No longer chasing. They moved almost casually, men walking in to finish a job.

Frank stepped out from the shelter of the oak and swung the assault rifle toward the two men.

"Police."

It's as far as Frank gets.

The man who shot the runner spins toward Frank. His partner turns with him, perfectly choreographed. Both men hold their pistols in two-handed combat grips.

Frank fires low and to the left of them. He lets the rifle's natural climb carry the muzzle up and to the right. The hail of automatic fire stitches the two, throwing them into a convulsive, macabre dance, knees buckling, arms flailing overhead.

Time stands still. The shooting and the dancing seem to go on forever. Frank keeps firing, but he's detached, outside it all, watching it happen.

It is over in less than five seconds.

For an instant, the woods were frozen in the same petrified silence that follows the shattering of glass. Then Frank heard helicopter blades a long way off, slapping the heavy air of the winter sky.

EIGHTEEN

FRANK AND JOSÉ rode in the medevac chopper with Carlton Holmes and his uncle. The uncle died seconds after lift-off, and the paramedic turned his attention to Holmes, who gained consciousness toward the end of the short flight. His eyes darted between the paramedic hovering over him and José.

Out of Holmes's sight, the paramedic looked at José, then locked eyes with Frank and shook his head.

José gripped Holmes's hand. "You gonna be all right."

Holmes closed his eyes and drifted off.

Ten minutes later they landed on the roof helipad at Washington Hospital Center.

AFTER SURGERY, FRANK HAD HOLMES MOVED TO THE INtensive care ward on the hospital's security floor. Holmes could barely be seen through the machinery keeping him alive. Frank and José spelled each other at his bedside, while in the hall, two uniformed cops stood watch by the door. Both Frank and José happened to be there when Holmes came around eighteen hours later.

He opened his eyes and for a long moment stared bewildered at the two men. Frank reached over to the bedside table and switched on a tape recorder.

"Who're you?" Holmes asked.

Frank leaned close. "I'm Detective Kearney. José Phelps is my partner." Frank reached inside his coat for his badge case and flipped it open.

Bad off as he was, Holmes was able to put on the flat, sullen expression of street defiance that Frank had encountered from his first days walking beat. Frank understood it, but still it pissed him off. You ungrateful punk, he was thinking. But he asked, "You know who you are?"

"I'm . . ." Holmes hesitated, apparently trying to figure out whether a lie might help, and if so, what the lie would be. It must have been too hard a problem because he finally said, "I'm Carlton Holmes. My uncle . . . ?"

"They're dead. Your uncle died on the helicopter. They killed your aunt." Frank let it register. He watched Holmes's eyes narrow, as if the thought had momentarily tripped a switch inside his head, then the eyes went flat again.

José leaned in and brought his face close to Holmes's. "They're dead because somebody wanted you."

Holmes's eyes wandered, then came back to José. "I don't know who."

"They want you gone because you are a nuisance," José said. "You're a fly, Carlton, buzzing around. Something they just want to swat so they can go on doing what they were doing before."

Holmes didn't say anything for a while. Then he asked, "What happened to the two muthafuckers in the woods?"

"They're dead."

"You kill 'em?"

José head-motioned toward Frank. "He did."

Holmes gave Frank a long once-over. "They were two mean muthafuckers."

"They weren't your run-of-the-mill ball-busters off the street corner." Frank paused to raise Holmes's curiosity. "You know what we had to do to ID them?"

Holmes shook his head once, very weakly, as if the effort was too much for him.

"We had to run the prints through Interpol. You know what Interpol is, Carlton?"

"Foreigners," Holmes whispered.

"Imports," José said. "Interpol comes back in no time. Rafael Jiménez and Eduardo Escobar. Both Colombians. Two boys from Medellín. Both wanted for questioning in a string of hits in Europe, Miami, L.A., and points south."

José gave it time to sink in. Then he turned up the heat. "High-price talent for a guy like you, Carlton. They're dead, but there's a lot of those kinda guys out there. Whoever sent them to get you has more waiting."

"Doctors fix you up," Frank said. "You can walk outta here. But there'll be somebody waiting."

"I don't know who sent them."

José persisted. "They came because of something you were doing—or something you know."

"I wasn't doin' nothin' . . . an' I don't know shit."

"Okay." Frank shrugged as if it didn't matter one way or another whether Holmes talked. "Okay." He snapped off the recorder, slipped it into his briefcase, and picked up his overcoat. "Let's get outta here, José."

José rose from his chair, shaking his head at Holmes, whose mouth was still open in surprise.

At the door, Frank looked sadly at the man in the bed. "I thought you might be able to help. But if you weren't doing anything and you don't know anything, I guess that's it." He started out the door, then turned back. "We'll have you moved out of security. So you can have some visitors."

"Yeah," José said. "Have some of your friends drop by. You know, cheer you up." He half waved to Holmes and followed Frank out the door.

"What you want to know?"

The two detectives turned back into the room. Frank put the recorder on the bedside table, and like José placed his chair by the bed.

"Let's start with everything you've done that the law would be interested in." Frank said.

Holmes gave him a skeptical look. "I get immunity?"

"You tell us everything, we'll see about immunity."

"You don't tell us," said José, "your friends get visiting rights."

Holmes rolled his eyes around the room, then focused on the recorder. "Well, shee-*it*," he said in surrender. He glanced at Frank. "You got enough tape?"

"PUNK THINKS HE'S A ONE-MAN CRIME WAVE." JOSÉ pushed a tray in front of the cashier and paid for the two coffees and sweet rolls. When Holmes had drifted off to sleep, Frank and José took advantage of the break to go to the hospital cafeteria.

It was nearly empty, and they chose a table in a corner alcove.

José unloaded the tray. "Proud of himself, the little shit."

Frank slumped in the molded fiberglass chair and closed his eyes. Wearily, he opened them and regarded José.

"I don't feel too good, leading him on."

"If he's gonna die, he's gonna die," José said. "If you told him he was gonna die, he wouldn't have believed you. A cop bullshit trick to get him to talk. You did right. If he thinks he's gonna live, he knows he's gonna need protection, and that means he needs us."

"Still . . ." Frank began, then gave up.

They'd gotten through Holmes's history before he faded out. A depressing litany of beatings, pimping, break-ins, car thefts, street-corner drug sales, muggings, and shootings. What bothered Frank was how he himself now thought about it—nothing remarkable, just a kid growing up in the District.

They had let Holmes talk at random. He'd started out subdued, but once he began piling one misdemeanor or felony on top of another, weak as he was, he took on the swagger of a combat veteran boasting about his heroics on some long-forgotten battlefield.

Frank stared at his roll. A stale yellow slab topped with at least half an inch of cracked sugar-laden frosting.

"Want yours?" José asked.

Frank pushed the plate over. "Remember when we got out of the academy?" he asked.

The roll stopped on its way toward José's mouth. "Yeah?"

"Tell me . . . didn't we think that was a good time to be cops?"

"Well . . ." José hesitated. "Well, yes."

"I'm thinking it isn't a good time now, Hoser."

José put the roll back on the plate. "That what you been thinking?"

"Yeah. What do you think? Is it a good time to be a cop?"

José took a deep breath, held it, then let it out while he gazed off toward the lone cashier far away in the cavernous cafeteria. "No, Frank," he said finally, "it's a shitty time to be a cop."

"I've been trying to figure out when it turned bad. It wasn't just yesterday. Or the day before." Frank idly twisted his paper napkin and tossed it onto the tabletop. "But it *had* to start sometime."

He studied José's face. He'd learned to read that face, and he knew José could read his. What he saw was the look José got when he was turning over something he didn't want to deal with but knew he had to, and so he was.

"I think . . ." José began, then paused. "I think it was when they started calling cops pigs."

"Watts?"

"Not Watts."

"Oh?"

"My memory was, 'pigs' came outta Berkeley."

Frank thought back and nodded. "Rich white kids waving Mao's Little Red Book."

"Yeah. Won't call me nigger, but they don't mind calling me pig. Now they got kids of their own. They piss and moan about divorce, drugs, and kids shooting kids. They wonder how it all happened."

"Where's it going?"

José shrugged. "Beats the shit outta me."

Frank got up and put their table debris on the tray. "Me, too. Maybe it's better we don't know."

HALF AN HOUR AFTER THEY GOT BACK TO HIS ROOM, Holmes came to. The sleep hadn't rested him. He seemed thinner and his skin had an ashen tinge.

Frank pushed the Start button on the tape recorder and asked his first question. "How long've you known Henry Brewington?"

Holmes eyed the recorder, then José, then Frank. "All my life. We grew up together."

"And Lewis Strickland?"

"Lewis, too."

"You know Henry Brewington's dead," Frank said.

Holmes's eyes clouded. A curtain rolled down his face, top to bottom. "Yeah. Yeah." He dropped his eyes to the foot of his bed.

Frank pulled an eight-by-ten glossy color shot of the BMW out of his briefcase and held it in front of Holmes.

Holmes tried not to register on the photograph, turning his eyes away. But Frank could tell by the sidelong look of morbid curiosity that Holmes had taken it in.

"The way we figure it, Henry was up on the compactor watching the Beamer get crushed," José said softly.

Holmes's eyes turned toward the photograph.

"Somebody put two slugs in him," José continued, his voice quiet, calming, almost hypnotic, taking Holmes to the salvage yard, putting him on the platform beside Brewington. "Two slugs in his back. He fell onto the Beamer hood. The compactor crushed the car around him. Around every part but his head."

Now Holmes couldn't take his eyes off the photograph, with its reddish-white skull gleaming under the floodlights.

"What happened to his . . ." Holmes couldn't continue.

"Rats," Frank said. "They picked him clean."

Holmes shut his eyes and rolled his head away.

"You know who killed him?" José asked gently.

"No," Holmes answered, his eyes still closed.

José eye-signaled Frank, and Frank put the photograph back in his briefcase.

"Do you know who *might* have killed him?" José asked.

Holmes started to open his eyes, cautiously. When he saw that Frank no longer had the photograph, he opened them all the way.

"I don't got any idea," Holmes said. "That's no shit."

Frank glanced at José. He appeared to be buying it. Frank put on a gentler tone. "What were you and Brewington and Strickland in on, Carlton?"

Holmes muttered something, then gasped for breath.

José bent closer. "What?"

Holmes tried again. "I was helpin' him."

"Him? Brewington or Strickland?"

"Henry. Lewis had his own thing."

"How? How did you help Henry?"

"Deliverin'." Holmes's voice was barely audible.

"Delivering what, Carlton?"

"Packages."

"Packages of what, Carlton?" José asked.

"Don't know."

Frank shook his head. "Come on, Holmes. You expect us to buy that?"

"True!" Holmes whispered, his voice rough and croupy.

José patted his shoulder. "Describe the packages," he urged. "How big? Bags? Boxes?"

"Suitcases. They . . . suitcases."

"When did you begin?"

"June."

"This last June?"

"Year . . . last year June. Yeah, June." Holmes had to work hard at speaking.

"The packages," Frank said. "Where'd you get them, and where'd you take them to?"

"Different places. Get different place, deliver different place."

"Tell us about one," José said.

Holmes lay still for a while, his eyes closed. Frank was

beginning to wonder whether he'd slipped off, when Holmes opened his eyes. "Last package . . . fella hands key to me at parking lot, Adams Morgan . . . big lot on Eighteenth . . ."

"Know it," Frank said.

"Anyway, I got . . . key . . . plate number. Find car, open the trunk. There's a suitcase. I take suitcase. Leave key."

"Where'd you take it?" José asked.

"Locker. Union Station."

"And the locker key? What'd you do with the locker key?"

"Magnet box. Stuck key under a pay phone, walked away."

"Who told you where to go?"

"Henry."

"He sent you to the lot in Adams Morgan? Told you how to use the magnetic box?"

Holmes nodded.

"Give us the pick-up and drop-off points you remember," José said.

For the next several minutes Holmes gave addresses and landmarks. Frank scribbled notes as a backup to the recorder tape. When Holmes wound down, Frank resumed the questioning.

"You ever ask Henry what was in the packages? Where they went?"

"Wouldn't say."

"To you?" Frank asked skeptically. "He wouldn't tell his best friend?"

"Said, 'Better you not know,'" Holmes whispered.

Frank didn't know whether to believe him. His first reaction was not to. But something about Holmes's eye contact and tone of voice pulled him the other way.

"Those suitcases," Frank said, "you know they had to be worth a lot. You had to think about it. What did you guess was in the suitcases?"

Holmes mumbled something.

"What?" said Frank. "I didn't hear you."

"Dope?" Holmes said, barely audible.

"You ever get tempted to skim a little off the top? A little each time, you could step on it, wrap it up for retail, make some big money on your own."

"Glad I didn't."

Holmes's breathing was growing raspier. Frank noticed the respirator seemed to be speeding up.

"Why?"

"Henry . . . told me . . . somebody tried to trick-fuck them. Took . . . talked."

"Yeah?"

"Cut him up . . . little pieces . . . real slow."

Frank looked across the bed and saw José looking back at him. And he knew José was thinking the same thing he was, about Trunkman missing his fingers.

"Cut him up," Holmes was saying, drifty and vacant. "Little pieces. Slow. Real slow. Slow . . ."

Finally his eyes closed. The monitor beeps that had been part of the background stopped, flatlined. For an instant time stood still.

Frank reached over, punched the recorder off, then hit Rewind.

NINETEEN

"*C*UT HIM UP . . . *little pieces . . . real slow.*"

Silence for a moment, then the high-pitched flatline of the monitor.

"That's it." Frank snapped off the recorder.

"Transcript?" Eleanor asked.

"Getting it printed now," José answered. He and Frank sat at their desks facing each other, the recorder between them. Eleanor, seated on a folding metal chair next to José, had listened intently to the replay of the Holmes interrogation, taking notes on a steno pad.

"Well?" Frank asked her.

"You want impressions?"

"For now."

"Discipline."

"Discipline?"

"Yes. If you believe Holmes, he didn't know what he was carrying."

"That's easy," José said. "The boys from Medellín. Dope."

"Probably," Eleanor admitted. "But to run an operation like that and keep a guy like Holmes from hearing something, from nosing around . . . well, it gives me an impression of discipline. And then there's the secrecy about others."

Using the eraser end of her pencil, she pushed to a page in her steno pad. "Here it is. Question: 'Do you know who might have killed him?' Holmes's answer: 'I don't got any idea. That's no shit.' "

Eleanor tapped her pencil on the pad. "Killing's no longer an unusual crime—getting to be like spitting on the sidewalk. We had two shootings last week, one over a pair of Air Jordans, another in an argument over a parking spot. When punks shoot punks, everybody knows who did the shooting. The reasons may be stupid, but the reasons are known. For Holmes *not* to be able to finger a suspect is unusual."

"Brewington was keeping Holmes out of the big picture," José said. He thought about that, then nodded, buying it.

Eleanor looked at Frank. "What about you?"

"Impression?"

Eleanor nodded.

"Okay, here's my two cents: Holmes was a dangerous man—but he didn't know it." Frank pitched it like a riddle and let José and Eleanor play with it. Eleanor shrugged, and José was about to give up. Then Frank saw his "Gotcha" grin.

"Holmes could have been like a kid walking around with a kick-me sign on his ass that he didn't know about."

"A kick-me sign?" Frank asked.

"Yeah. If Holmes wasn't lying, if he *really* didn't know why somebody'd be after him, then it must have been because that somebody saw—or thought he saw—Holmes as a danger. And Holmes didn't realize he had this thing that worried somebody enough to bring in the Medellín twins."

"So what was Holmes's kick-me sign?" asked Eleanor.

"He may have already told us," Frank said.

"He damn sure ain't gonna tell us any more," said José.

The three sat in silence. From the hallway came the sounds of the shift change, and more distant, the drone of a television talk show. Frank contemplated the tape recorder, the overhead light shining dully along its stainless-steel casing. Slowly, without putting the thought into words, he fingered the Rewind and Play buttons until he got to the part he wanted, then turned up the volume.

"*Henry . . . told me . . . somebody tried to trick-fuck them. Took . . . talked.*"

"*Yeah?*"

"*Cut him up . . . little pieces . . . real slow.*"

Frank turned the recorder off.

"You think that coulda been the kick-me sign?' " José asked. "Knowing that, but not knowing how important it was?"

Still gazing at the recorder, Frank shrugged. "Could be. Could be something else on that tape. Or could be nothing we have."

"Might tell us how Trunkman got to be Trunkman. Was he the guy Brewington said talked too much? Who'd he talk to? What'd he say?" José looked from Frank to Eleanor and back.

Frank recalled Upton's postmortem photographs of the fingerless hands. "Did they cut him up as torture? Or was it punishment?"

"Result was the same, wasn't it?" Eleanor asked.

"Yeah." Frank worked it out for himself. "But getting there makes a difference."

"How?"

"If it was torture, it means they wanted to find out what Trunkman *knew.* If it was punishment, they were just pissed at what he *did.*"

"Play it again, Frank," José said.

Frank did the rewind-play-rewind exercise, then hit Play.

"*Henry . . . told me . . . somebody tried to trick-fuck them.*"

José shook his head. Eleanor looked at the recorder as if disappointed.

Frank hit the Stop button. He felt at sea. And José and Eleanor weren't any better off. Rub-a-dub-dub, three dummies in a tub. "Could be they were trying to find out who he told what," he said, "or Trunkman could have been caught in the cookie jar and they just wanted to make it real painful for him going out."

"We play 'What if?' " José raised an eyebrow.

"Yeah?"

"As a working theory, Frank, we say that Brewington's a Benning Heights success story. No more nickel, dime bags. Our steel-drivin' man's gone wholesale. Then he and a pal cross the wrong guy. He ends up as Beamer boy, and his buddy's Trunkman."

"And O'Brien?" Frank asked. "O'Brien's money? The same gun that killed Brewington killed O'Brien? How's that connection work?"

José looked at Frank sympathetically. "How do you think Worsham would spin it?"

"A priest dealing drugs. Is that it?"

"Easy, Frank." José held up a hand, palm out. "I'm not asking you to like it. You know it's a question that'll come up. So how do we answer it?"

Frank stared at José. Finally he sighed in resignation. "Hell, Hoser, it's a question we can't answer until we know more."

"Like?"

"Like how our Simple City boys got to the big time in two years." Frank turned away from José. "Eleanor?" he asked. "You mind spending a few hours tonight helping us on that computer of yours?"

THE NEXT MORNING, JOSÉ SHUFFLED THROUGH A STACK of projection slides, holding each one up to the light for a quick view.

Frank waited a second or two. "Well?"

José passed the slides to him. "It's a case. But Randolph ain't gonna like it one bit."

"We together?"

José nodded. "Always have been."

THEY GOT IN TO SEE EMERSON LATE THAT AFTERNOON. Emerson, in shirtsleeves, was at his plate-glass-topped desk. José sat to the side while Frank stood by a view-foil projector.

"We need Woody's help, Randolph," Frank began. He held up the slides. "We'll set the stage, then tell you what we want to do and why we want to do it."

Emerson sat with both hands protectively in his lap. "Go ahead," he muttered.

Frank switched on the projector, then stepped over to turn off the lights.

The first slide appeared on the screen.

"This is a map of the Benning Heights area. Because it's right on the Maryland line, the bad boys take advantage of coordination breakdowns between us and the Maryland police."

The second slide was the same map, this time peppered with red dots.

"Each red dot represents ten homicides. This is the total since 1960." Frank could tell from Emerson's tight lips that the Homicide chief wasn't enjoying this.

"Okay," Frank continued. "That's the map of total killings. What are the trends?" He advanced to the third slide. "This line graph shows the homicides from 1960 to 1999 by month."

The red ribbon ran relatively flat from 1960 through 1967. The climb began the next year. There were months when the number of killings dropped, but inevitably the next month or the next made up the deficit. In Benning Heights, the trend was up.

"Between 1968 and 1996," Frank said, "homicides reached a level more than eight times what they'd been in 1960. Taken as a percentage of population, violent deaths per hundred inhabitants, Benning Heights was one of the most dangerous places in the world." Frank paused for emphasis, then added, "Simple City was more dangerous than Beirut or Bosnia."

The next slide was the homicide graph with three additional lines, green, blue, and orange, running from 1960 through 1995—all going up, up, up. "The green line,"

Frank explained, "is the rate of single mothers giving birth in Benning Heights."

"How'd you get that?" Emerson asked.

"Zip code matches against birth certificates. Blue line shows arrests for theft and crimes against property. And the orange line—" This one, starting lower than the others in 1960, had crossed them all—homicide, births to single mothers, theft—by the mid-1970s. "The orange line," Frank repeated, "is arrests for drug sales and possession."

Emerson's lips had tightened over his teeth. "I suppose all this means something?" he grated.

"We're just setting the stage, Randolph." Frank tried to soothe without sounding like a suck-up. Emerson's running true to form, he was thinking. The clearer the reality, the greater the paranoia.

"The next slides are built on less complete data, because they're more recent—from 1996 to the present—but they show interesting trends."

Again a homicide chart. The red ribbon on this one started in 1996 and ended in January 1999. The precipitous downturn in killings later made it look as if the red ribbon had dropped off a cliff.

"Benning Heights no longer competes with Beirut," Frank said. "Now it's more like Brentwood . . . pre-O.J."

Frank noticed Emerson's small smile of relief. Wait a minute, Randolph. Wait just a minute. He put on the next slide.

"Same slide, and now we add the lines for single-mother birthrate, theft, and drugs."

While homicide almost dropped off the chart, theft and single-mother births continued their rate of growth. The orange line, drugs, was the shocker: it made a dizzying climb upward.

Emerson's smile spread. "Looks like Tyrone's got his work cut out for him."

Frank read Emerson's mind. Jesse Tyrone was head of Narcotics. He and Emerson were in unofficial but very real competition to head the department. Emerson was imagining the orange line rapidly rising straight up Tyrone's ass.

Frank let his boss enjoy himself for a moment, then said, "What we have is an organization that has a grip on Benning Heights, and it was able to get that grip by killing off any opposition."

"What are you saying?" Emerson asked.

"The drop in the homicide rate is an indicator of success," Frank said. "Not *our* success, though." He watched Emerson's mouth tighten. "I think it means the bad guys own Simple City. They own the Heights, and that's why the place is quiet."

Emerson's mouth got even tighter. "Then what explains Brewington and Holmes?"

"They were insiders. The organization needed to get rid of them."

"Why?"

"Why does General Motors fire folks? Survival. To keep on making money. This outfit has its own way of handing out pink slips. Holmes and Brewington point to leads that run through Benning Heights."

"And the leads are . . . ?"

"Next-to-last slide," Frank said, and flipped the slide on the projector. "We started with a map, we wrap up with one."

The first map had been of Benning Heights. This one showed Benning Heights as part of the Washington metropolitan area, with adjoining suburbs in Maryland and Virginia.

"Brewington gave Holmes pick-up and drop-off assignments every Monday. Brewington, or whoever *he* was working for, was smart enough to change the drops. Holmes didn't remember all his routes, but these lines show some of them."

Frank's last slide was of the same map, but now with a sunburst of bright yellow lines, all radiating from Benning Heights.

"Each line starts where Holmes picked up his package and ends where he dropped it off. He goes to Arlington, Alexandria, Chevy Chase, Bethesda, McLean—hell, several trips he goes out to Laurel and damn near to Baltimore." Frank rapped the center of the map. "But all the trips start here, Randolph. Here in Benning Heights."

Emerson looked at the map as if trying to find a catch somewhere. Then he turned the same suspicious expression toward Frank. "What do you want?" he asked cautiously.

"Eleanor. I want her to set up a war room. Restricted access. A secure place where we can lay out the timelines, the people, the evidence."

Emerson thought about it, and nodded.

"That's not all."

"What else?"

"Surveillance support."

Emerson looked at the map and back to Frank. "How much?"

"All of it. Woody and his whole division."

"Get real!" Emerson scoffed.

Frank stood impassively, with the expression of a long-suffering adult dealing with an obstinate child. He shook his head. "I *am* real, Randolph," he said, taking care with each word. "I want Woody and his people to blanket Benning Heights every Monday night."

"You said they changed the pick-up points," Emerson protested. "You could put a hundred surveillance teams in that neighborhood, and they could still move elephants without getting spotted."

"You're right, Randolph. They do change the delivery routes. But Holmes remembered some repeats."

Emerson persisted. "Brewington and Holmes are dead. What's there to find?"

"If you think it was a two-man operation, Randolph, you're right—we're wasting time and money."

"So you say it isn't."

"I say I don't *think* it is, Randolph. Those two guys were part of something bigger. Holmes was at the bottom of the totem pole." Frank took the map slide off and put back the graph showing the drop in homicides and the rise in drug traffic.

Emerson shook his head. "I don't like it. Putting all our eggs in one basket."

Frank placed both his hands on the glass desktop and leaned forward so his face was inches from Emerson's. "Maybe I'm wrong, Randolph. I hope I am." He paused, then asked, "But what if I'm right? And we don't go after this thing with everything we got? What then, Randolph? What do we tell the *Post* and Worsham and his buddies in the media when they come asking?"

"So HE DIDN'T APPROVE." KATE SAID.

"He didn't disapprove, either." Frank got up from the sofa and put another log on the fire. He turned to Kate and shrugged. "That's Emerson. Up-or-down situations bother him. The accountability's too clear. He likes fuzziness. That way, if things turn sour he's got cover." He refilled his snifter with brandy, checked Kate's glass, then sat down beside her.

"What was it about the drop in homicides?" she asked.

"All the indicators of a neighborhood out of control were there—the single-parent families, drugs, theft, street violence. Gangs going after each other over something as stupid as who walks on which street—'beefin' over turf.' All of a sudden, the killing gets focused—a few hits, but no more random gunplay. It means only one thing—"

"An enforcer's taken over."

Frank nodded. "And the competition's been run out, bought off, or killed."

"But Emerson doesn't buy it."

"He doesn't want to. As long as the number of homicides is down—whatever the reason—he's happy."

"But the rest of the stuff—the drugs . . ."

"Drugs? Theft? Birthrates? Not Emerson's worry. Those are other departments."

"But the sum of it—"

"The sum of it is that Emerson's only responsible for the homicides. If you connect a drop in homicides with anything, it better be that Emerson's doing a great job. You don't make points with him by connecting the drop in killings to the rise of organized crime. On the other hand, he has the problem that our request for surveillance is sitting in his in box, and if something nasty happens, that's the one place he doesn't want it."

"You've put him on the spot. He's got to pass it on."

Frank held the glass up and admired the burnished color of the cognac, highlighted by the fire. "I've got faith in Emerson. He'll find some way to push this onto somebody else's plate. His ingenuity knows no limits when his ass is at stake."

FRANK'S PHONE RANG AT FIVE-FIFTEEN A.M. IT WAS Emerson.

An hour later, at City Hall, Frank watched Malcolm Burridge struggle to control himself. The mayor stood leaning over his desk, hands on either side of a file folder. Burridge would look up at Frank, José, Emerson, then back at the contents of the folder. It was as if he couldn't connect what he was reading with the men standing in front of him.

Burridge's phone rang. He picked it up, listened, then spoke briefly: "Thank you, Gladys. Kindly tell him to get his butt in here."

Almost instantly, Charles Simmons came through the door. The look on his face said he expected it wouldn't be nice.

It wasn't.

Burridge glared at the District treasurer. "Thank you, Charles, for taking time out of your busy schedule to accommodate me," he said sarcastically. Simmons took a quick look around the office and walked over to avail himself of the protection offered by the other three men. Burridge looked down at the folder. He thumped it, then pointed a finger at the men before him.

"I got you all together to tell you what I told you once already." He gathered a deep breath. Slowly, punctuating each word with the shake of a finger, he gritted his teeth. "I . . . don't . . . like . . . surprises."

"What is—" Simmons began.

"Shut up, Charles," Burridge said in a near-shout. Then, more quietly, "All of you are in this goddamn mess with me"—he glanced right, then left—"and I want you all to know . . . that if I go down . . . you're all . . . going with me." He paused. "That understood?"

He looked around, shook his head. "I can see I'm not making myself clear. Another class in Politics One-oh-one, gentlemen. School's in session." Burridge sat down in his high-backed armchair. "Now, I already have *priests*—men of the cloth!—getting shot on every street corner! My police department can't solve that! My treasurer calls this saint an embezzler on TV—"

Simmons looked like he was going to shit. "Malcolm! I never—"

"Shut . . . *up,* Charles!" Burridge didn't raise his voice. That was more threatening than if he'd shouted. "This is *politics.*" He looked at the three other men to make certain they got at least that part right. Then he focused again on Simmons. "What you *really* said doesn't mean jack shit. It's what they *think* you said. It's what they tell each other. It's what they talk about in the bars. At the office.

"Now here . . . " Burridge held up the folder. "I have here today's *Post* lead story. Front page, right column, above the fold. The *Post* is telling the good citizens of the District of Columbia, of which I am the fucking mayor—at least until the November elections—the *Post* is telling them about a police report saying that Benning Heights is in the middle of a massive drug outbreak, and that the drug thing's connected to the priest thing."

Burridge dropped the folder to his desk. "Let me tell you what the water-cooler and coffee-break talk is gonna be. It's gonna be that the mayor—*me!*—is either stupid or covering up. See, I've been out telling anybody who'll listen: Crime's goin' down in the District! DC's safe for families! For business! I've been on *Today*! *Larry King*! Tellin' the whole world. The whole fucking world—the District of Columbia. And here I get blindsided by my own damn police department."

Frank shot a glance at José. José caught the look and

rolled his eyes toward Emerson. Frank expected to see Emerson's characteristic looking-for-cover twitching and shuffling. Instead, the Homicide chief was calm, poised.

And his execution was damn near perfect, Frank thought later: "Your Honor, I don't know how the *Post* got that"— Emerson pointed to the folder—"but what they're quoting isn't a department study."

"Oh? Oh? Well what the fuck is it, then?"

Emerson gestured toward Frank and José. "It's a proposal Detectives Kearney and Phelps briefed me on. Since it's their work, perhaps I should let them explain."

Burridge settled back in his chair. "An explanation? Oh? That'd be nice."

An hour and many questions later, a somber, reflective Burridge got up from his desk and stood at the big window that looked out on the buildings of the Smithsonian and the Washington Monument. He turned away from the window and back to the waiting men.

"Cover Simple City," he told Emerson. "Do what you gotta do. But for God's sake, don't let me read about it first in the fucking *Post*."

FRANK AND JOSÉ WALKED OUT OF CITY HALL TOGETHER. A light snow was falling.

"You gotta hand it to Emerson," José said.

Frank shook his head in wonder. "He leaks the Benning Heights stuff to the *Post*, gets Burridge between a rock and a hard place. Burridge doesn't have any choice but to approve the surveillance—"

"And Emerson leaves us and the mayor holding the bag," José finished.

Frank smiled. "That's why he gets the big bucks and glass desk, Hoser."

TWENTY

"WE GOT NIGHT-VISION coverage in this area." Woody tapped a computer key, and a pale blue segment highlighted the cluster of buildings along the southern rim of Benning Heights.

Frank glanced to the bank of video monitors lining one side of the large semi trailer van. The apartments stood out in a ghostly green. "Looks like CNN when we were bombing Baghdad," he said.

"Yeah," said José. "Only things missing are the surface-to-air missiles."

"Maybe in another couple of years . . ." Frank turned to another row of monitors showing the traffic, a blaze of headlights, taillights, and streetlights.

"Traffic monitor feeds," Woody explained. "All ramps to the freeway, major intersections on Pennsylvania and Independence, as well as Teddy Roosevelt, Memorial, and Fourteenth Street bridges."

"People?" José asked.

Woody tapped another key. The computer map morphed into a close-up of Benning Heights. Another key tap, and bright blue circles popped up on the map. Frank counted fifteen.

"Three convenience stores, four parking lots, six bars, a Popeye's, and a McDonald's."

José shook his head and looked at Frank. "You and I ever get stakeout duty in a bar?"

Frank got a small grin. "Every place we had stakeout had to be cold, wet, or bad-smelling, or all three." He asked Woody, "And they're looking for . . . ?"

"The profile we got from Holmes." Woody ran down the stakeout EEI—essential elements of information: "Males, one-on-one meetings, exchange of packages sized from shoebox to suitcase, males alone in cars, especially those obeying traffic laws—"

Obeys traffic laws, Frank said to himself, that'll narrow the field. He sat back in the command chair and gazed around the van with its monitors, computers, and switchboards. His duty station for the stakeout. That was the procedure; that was how things were done. He glanced at his watch. He and José had been there less than an hour. But it felt like a lifetime, and the hours to come stretched out to forever. The dry air in the van crackled with the steel-wool odor of electricity. The walls were closing in. His throat felt scratchy. His eyes drifted.

A phone rang once, twice, three times.

"That's you, Frank," Woody said.

The van snapped into focus and Frank found his cell phone. He listened, asked when, then pocketed the phone. He stood and stretched, feeling grateful, feeling he'd been rescued. "Adair," he told José. "Over at the diner. Says he has something for us."

"He left it here." Adair handed the book to Frank. "O'Brien?"

Adair nodded, but stopped as if he'd thought of something else. "O'Brien or the kid. They were"—he gestured toward a booth, then toward the book—"sitting there talking. Had this book between them. Talking about it, I guess."

"Where's it been?" José asked.

Adair looked down to the far end of the diner. "Hey, Toby," he called. A busboy clearing a booth looked up. Adair waved him over.

A slight young man stood before the two detectives, wiping his hands repeatedly on a dirty apron.

"Tell them about the book, Toby."

A straightforward story, Frank decided. Toby, mopping up before going off shift, had found the book in the booth O'Brien and the Kid had used. It had fallen between the booth and the wall. Adair had already left. Toby put the book in his locker, intending to turn it in the next night. Instead, he'd had a bout of the flu. Toby had found the book an hour before, turned it over to Adair, and that was that. José got Toby's address, Social Security, and date of birth, and Adair waved the boy back to work.

With his pen Frank nudged the book open.

"Fingerprints," Adair said, the light dawning. "Oh, shit."

"Don't worry," Frank told him. A thin scratch pad, blank, lay inside the cover. He came to the title page. *"Moving the Big Economy,"* he said. "By Nicholas Pasco, Ph.D., Georgetown University. Looks like it was well read." Someone had plastered yellow sticky notes throughout the book.

For the second time that night, Frank's phone sounded. He listened for a moment, then looked up to José. "Woody," he explained. "Fun times. Coming our way." He took the book and headed at a run toward the diner's exit.

FRANK STARTED THE CAR, THEN IMMEDIATELY DROPPED into gear and pulled away from the curb at full throttle. "Traffic monitors picked up a carjacking at Lincoln Park," he told José. "And get this—the victim is our pal Strickland."

"Dead?"

"No such luck. Two males stuck a gun up his nose, threw him out of the car, and drove off down D Street. Monitors tracked them passing the Monocle."

D Street Northeast ran east-west a block from the Senate

Office Building. The Monocle was an expense-account watering hole where facelifted lobbyists with two-hundred-dollar Christophe haircuts met with senators and legislative staffers to cut unobtrusive deals in the name of good government. From the Monocle, D Street ran downhill toward the Federal Courthouse.

Frank turned east onto D, falling behind a green Chevy van.

"There they are." José gestured through the windshield.

Frank saw headlights, three, four blocks away, weaving through the traffic, speeding toward them down D Street. Several blocks behind, the blue-and-red flashes from a patrol car in pursuit. One moment the headlights were there, then—click! Gone.

"They're down the tunnel!" José shouted.

The Third Street tunnel connected at D Street. Take the tunnel south and three-quarters of a mile away you got on an extension of Interstate 95. From there you headed south toward Miami or north for Boston. The tunnel itself was four to six lanes wide, one of the few places in the District where you could get up to a hundred without having to run a traffic light.

José radioed Woody at the same time the siren and lights kicked in.

Perhaps shocked by the sudden appearance of a police car behind him, the driver of the green Chevy van stopped abruptly instead of pulling over. Bumper-to-bumper traffic blocked the left lane.

"Son of a bitch!" Frank muttered. He tapped the brakes, jerked the wheel hard right, then jammed his foot on the accelerator. The car jumped the curb, crashing onto the sidewalk, shock absorbers screeching in protest. Frank got a lightning impression of metal-to-metal grinding as the van slipped past his window, stripping his sideview mirror. He spun the wheel left, bouncing back onto the street just as a parking meter sheared off his right fender. Inside the car the noise was horrific, like being in a steel drum with somebody beating on it with a baseball bat.

"Traffic's stopped!" he heard José shout. A block ahead,

the cars turning off D Street into the tunnel had come to a standstill. Frank got half a block before he became part of the gridlock. Angry drivers leaned on car horns and flashed their headlights. Some had left their cars and stood looking into the tunnel. Above the horns came a ripple of shots echoing from deep in the tunnel. People on the street ducked behind cars.

Frank's door was crumpled shut. He twisted in his seat and kicked with both feet. The door flew open with a popping, grinding protest. Dashing toward the tunnel, he caught a glimpse of José pulling the riot gun out from under the front seat.

Frank sprinted down the tunnel's pedestrian walkway, dodging panicked drivers as they fought their way back to the entrance, away from the shooting and the deadly slugs ricocheting off the walls and smashing through windshields.

As he rounded a slight curve where the feeder ramp met the main tunnel, the sounds of gunfire became deafeningly intense. In the yellow glow of mercury lamps, he saw a car on its side, maybe twenty yards away, skewed across the tunnel.

One man crouched by the car with a pistol, firing up the tunnel toward Frank. A second man was climbing out of the front passenger window. Frank saw that he had an assault rifle. Just as Frank recognized it as a Kalashnikov, the man got off a short burst of automatic fire toward the stopped traffic.

Kneeling beside a deserted black Saab, Frank took aim at the Kalashnikov gunner. "Police!" he shouted.

Unbidden, a flash of an old joke came to him: A flea with a hard-on floating down a river on his back, yelling, "Raise the drawbridge." Yelling "Police!" was just as crazy. You couldn't hear Gabriel's horn in this place. He was about to squeeze off a warning round when José's riot gun roared, a rolling, thundering fist-of-God sound. Tile and brick from the tunnel ceiling pelted down on the two gunmen.

The shooting stopped.

Frank gave it another try. He got "Police!" out, but that

was pretty much it before the two turned their fire on him and José.

A very big mistake.

Frank shot first. His target took a step toward him, then fell facedown on the pavement. The man with the Kalashnikov pulled the weapon down to his hip. The first burst hit ten feet in front of Frank. He felt the concrete splinters on his face, then brought his pistol around to line up on the Kalashnikov. Even as he did, he knew he wasn't going to make it. He could already feel how it would be, how the next rounds would slam into him, stitch him across the chest.

José's riot gun blasted, filling the tunnel with the roar of heavy artillery. The Kalashnikov and its owner disappeared in a red mist.

Frank shut his eyes. It was unreal to find himself still standing. Through the ringing in his ears, he heard an angry chorus of horns and shouting people, and above everything, the wail of sirens.

For a moment, it all seemed far away from the killing place in the tunnel. Then he heard himself saying to José, "Take a look?" And he and José walked slowly toward the dead men.

Frank's guy's eyes were still open, rolled back and staring unseeing at the tunnel ceiling. One slug had torn through his throat, and blood from a gut wound was still staining his shirt just above his belt.

"Nighty-night, pal," José said gently, nudging the gunman's body to make sure he was dead.

There was never any doubt about the guy with the Kalashnikov. The shot from José's riot gun had an optimum spread at thirty feet, and Kalashnikov must have been there within a tenth of an inch. More or less. Even so, José walked over to give him a look.

Frank rounded the car and stood looking at the trunk, which had sprung open.

José joined him.

"Lewis Strickland, our party animal, is going to be in the market for a new set of wheels."

José reached into the trunk and pulled out a wheeled suitcase, the kind that was supposed to fit into an airplane overhead luggage rack.

"Our Lewis planning on a vacation?" José guessed.

"Probably six, seven kilos in there."

"Locked." José worked at the zipper tab.

Frank flicked open the pimp's switchblade and handed it to José.

José jimmied the lock and handed the knife back to Frank. He worked the zipper and opened the suitcase, looked inside, then up at Frank.

"No kilos, Frank."

"Oh?"

Saying nothing, José tilted the suitcase to show Frank the neatly wrapped bundles of hundreds, fifties, and twenties.

LEWIS STRICKLAND WAS PACING BACK AND FORTH AT THE headquarters front desk when Frank and José finally returned from the chaotic scene in the Third Street tunnel.

"Where's my car?" he screeched as José came through the double doors.

"Being towed to impound," José said.

"*Towed?*" Strickland's voice rose.

Frank shrugged. "It's evidence in a felony. And besides, it's totaled. Nobody's going to drive that car again."

"You want to tell us how it happened, Lewis?" José asked.

Strickland, eyes wide, shook his head violently. "I already told half the fucking department what the fuck happened!"

Frank nodded. "We'll call you, Lewis, when you can get your car."

Strickland, uncertain what to do, stood for a moment, eyes darting around the room, then dashed out.

"Man with worries." José watched him disappear down the steps at a dead run.

"Strickland knows one thing for sure."

"Yeah?"

"The money was in the trunk when those guys took his car."

"Yeah. You could read that on his sweaty face."

"So what do we want Strickland to think?" Frank asked.

"Horses . . . or zebras?"

"Horses?"

"He thinks horses, then he's thinking we found the half-million."

"And zebras?" Frank asked.

"Zebras, Strickland thinks that it wasn't your basic carjacking, but somebody cutting themselves in on his action. Competition."

"I think zebras would be more fun," Frank said.

"How we do zebras?"

"Carefully, Hoser. Very carefully."

"THE MONEY?" KATE ASKED. "WAS IT GOING TO BUY drugs? Or was it from selling them?"

Frank slipped his hand into the warm hollow at the small of her back. "Everybody goes for the buying."

"Except you."

"Except I'm not too sure."

"Why?"

"That's the aggravating part of it. No real reason, I guess." Frank looked at the ceiling, at the parchment-and-gray abstracts made by streetlight shining through bare tree limbs. "Maybe it's just . . . consistency."

"Consistency?"

"Yeah." Frank hesitated. "Consistency" hadn't come to him in a flash of light, more like he'd stumbled on it in the dark. He thought about it, then said, "We didn't find dope in O'Brien's closet. We found money. The question hasn't been dope. It's been money. How'd O'Brien get the money? Now, how did Strickland get the money?"

"You're not saying anything about Strickland's money?"

"No."

"But the mayor called it a drug war."

"Yes, he certainly did, didn't he?"

Brokaw, Jennings, Rather led off the evening news with the tunnel shootings. Worsham was hounding Burridge for an interview, and the *Post* had run front-page color photos of sprawling bodies, smashed cars, even the massive hole José had blasted in the tunnel ceiling.

Malcolm Burridge was bouncing off the walls when Frank, José, and Emerson had answered his summons, Frank told Kate. Emerson, petrified, stood throughout Burridge's tirade with a pained look on his face, like he was trying to crap razor blades.

"José and I gave the mayor the drugs angle."

Burridge had worked himself up to a steady stream of unimaginative and repetitive profanity. It had taken him a moment or two to catch on to what Frank and José were saying, but once he did, he grabbed it like a life preserver.

"Hell of an actor," Frank said to Kate, still marveling at the mayor's press conference performance.

Malcolm Burridge had come out slugging—an embattled Churchill during the London blitz—wrapping all the old demands in his new theme of a brave mayor fighting federal "big government" indifference. He had pounded his lectern—home rule, bigger congressional appropriations, recognition of the District as a state. The tunnel shootings were evidence—*proof! proof pos-i-tive!*—that the White House and Congress were ignoring the politically powerless citizens of the District. Only the embattled Washington metropolitan police department stood against evil—underfunded, outgunned, but dauntless and determined.

"Our ... thin ... blue ... line," Burridge had concluded, a dramatic catch in his voice.

Frank, amazed, saw a real tear well in the mayor's eye and roll down his cheek. The camera crews had gone wild.

"Does it make any difference?" Kate asked. "I mean, whether it's money for buying or money from selling?"

"Yeah ... yeah, it does. The guys that carjacked Strickland. We haven't ID'd them yet. It could be a random carjacking. Or we could have a turf war over who's going to distribute where."

"And Burridge would be right."

Frank nuzzled Kate's shoulder. "Yeah, he would," he

said sleepily. "And we're going to start making him right tomorrow."

"How?"

"We're going to introduce Strickland to his competition."

TWENTY-ONE

T**ONY UPTON UNLATCHED** the two adjacent body-locker doors and rolled out the tray of the first corpse, then the second.

"Yeah," Lewis Strickland said, "that's them, the mother fuckers."

"Familiar faces?" Frank asked.

Strickland was still looking at the two dead men. "Never saw them before. Before they took my fucking car." He turned to Frank and José. "You know who they are?"

"John Doe, Richard Roe," José answered.

"Didn't they have ID? Driver's license?"

"Both had Virginia licenses," Frank said. "Both phony."

Strickland got a squinty, questioning look. "Finger-prints? Don't they have fingerprints?"

José searched Strickland's face. "We appreciate citizen interest," he said with mock enthusiasm. "Maybe you oughta be a cop."

"I just want to know who robbed me, is all."

Frank pushed one of the drawers and John Doe's body rolled back into the refrigerator. "Well, whatever their names, they're dead and your car's junk."

Strickland pouted. "That was a *nice* car. Very nice." He

waited a beat. "Those guys—Doe and Roe—they . . . they, ah, leave anything in the car?"

"You can check it down at impound," José said. "You worried about missing anything, Lewis?"

"Me?" Strickland drew himself up. "Naw—I'm just pissed about that car."

"You gotta get your car outta impound," Frank said. "Get it towed or whatever."

"What do you mean?"

"I mean that storage is seventy-five a day."

Strickland had an incredulous look. "You mean . . . *my* car gets stolen, shot up by the police, an' *I* gotta pay storage to the police?"

"Cash, Lewis," José said. "You got any cash?"

JUST AS FRANK AND JOSÉ WERE ABOUT TO LEAVE FOR lunch, a clerk brought in a folder. José signed for it, then looked it over. "Strickland's employment record. Tower Records." José dragged it out, giving it an air of mystery. Teasingly he added, "Employment application."

"You're screwing with me, Hoser."

José got a lazy grin. "Seems bro' Strickland had previous employment . . . Jarvis Security."

"I KNOW LEWIS." JARVIS TILTED BACK IN HIS CHAIR.

"He's been in some excitement, Solly," Frank said.

"Oh?" Jarvis asked cautiously, as if he knew Frank had another line to drop.

"Third Street tunnel—"

"He was in that shit? The *Post* didn't give any names."

"Two guys took his car. We're working on a theory that these two guys were somebody's soldiers."

"Burridge said drug war. How do you make a drug war out of a carjacking?"

"An educated guess."

"What you got that makes it educated?"

"Strickland's associates. Some of them were dealing."

Jarvis laughed cynically. "Shit, Frank, find some a those guys who *aren't* dealing. That all? Burridge sounded awfully certain."

"Burridge has a talent."

"You ID'd the guys who hit Strickland?"

"Not yet."

Frank waited until he thought Jarvis would be wondering what the next question would be. "Strickland worked for you," he said.

"I *said* I knew him." Jarvis leaned heavily on the word, as though he wanted Frank to know he was being up-front. "That's how I knew Strickland. He worked for me. Once in a while. Part-time. Two years back, we were expanding. Needed extra help."

"Strickland worked for you. Brewington worked for you. Brewington's gotten real dead, Strickland's a target for some very bad guys."

Jarvis squinted. "You going somewhere, Frank?"

"Basic question—is there a connection? Or is it coincidence?"

"Whatever," Jarvis threw his hands up and settled back in his chair. "It had nothing to do with their working here. Like I told you before, they screw up on the job or get in trouble with the law off the job—either way, they're outta here."

"Well, they're both outta here."

Jarvis shook his head. "Violence," he said sadly. "On the other hand, I can't complain."

He stood and walked to the window, then beckoned Frank over. Together the two looked down on Pennsylvania Avenue. It was raining. All Frank could see of the people below were umbrellas bobbing along the sidewalk.

"Sometime today, every one of them's scared," Jarvis said, gesturing to the umbrellas. "Oh, maybe not right this second. But they've been scared—or they will be. Scared of a bum on the street. Maybe scared tonight going home on the Metro. Scared somebody's gonna take something away from them. Or hurt them. Or hurt somebody they care about."

"And you make money off them being scared."

Jarvis faced Frank. "Yeah. I do. And more all the time. And do you know why?"

"Tell me."

"Because the umbrellas don't trust you."

"Me?"

"Not you personally, Frank Kearney—you in general, the cops. And it's not just cops they don't trust—it's government. The umbrellas don't trust City Hall. They don't trust the clowns in Congress. Or the liars in the White House. The umbrellas want security. They pay for security, but you don't deliver. You tax the shit out of them, then you give their money to the Jews in Israel and to the bums on the street. You bomb Arabs. You bomb Serbs. But you don't stop a bunch of punks shooting up the Third Street tunnel."

"We stopped them."

Jarvis gave Frank a look of admiration. "Yeah. You and Hoser. And you probably got your asses chewed insteada getting a medal. Wrong image for the city. You done a lotta that in your lifetime, haven't you?"

"We're cops."

"How many years, now, Frank? Twenty-five? Six?"

"Twenty-eight."

"Twenty-eight." Jarvis paused, as if trying to get his head around such a number. He looked at Frank and asked, "And before that was Vietnam, wasn't it?"

"Yeah."

Jarvis's eyes shifted away in thought. Then they came back to Frank.

"I was on the force when you were shot."

"Yeah."

Jarvis nodded. "Isn't it about your turn?"

"Meaning?"

"Meaning you been hanging your ass out for everybody except yourself."

"I like doing what I'm doing."

Jarvis bored in. "What you goin' to do when they say, 'Thank you, Mr. Kearney, for hanging your ass out for us, but we don't need you anymore'? What are you going to do then?"

Frank looked at him for a long moment, then asked, "I suppose you've got some ideas?"

Jarvis nodded. "You're a smart man, Frank. You got loyalty *up*. But you're in a system that's got no loyalty *down*. I know pussy Randolph Emerson. I know Malcolm Burridge, that fucking gasbag. You think they'd stand up for *you*? For one second, they'd stand up for you?"

Frank knew from the way Jarvis's eyes narrowed that he had read the answer on his face.

Jarvis turned and again motioned down to the sidewalk.

"And you think any of the umbrellas would stand up for you? Only time they come face to face with a cop, it's something bad. Traffic ticket. Their kids getting in trouble. Hassle in a crowd, that kind of shit."

"So we get rid of all the cops," Frank said. "What do the umbrellas do when things go bump in the night? Dial nine-one-one for Oprah? Alan Dershowitz?" And then, because he couldn't resist, he added, "Call for Jarvis Security?"

Jarvis put a hand on Frank's shoulder. "We're talking about two different things."

"How different?"

"Simple. You're talking about how to make all this"— Jarvis pointed to the sidewalk—"a perfect world for *those* folks. I'm saying that world down there's always gonna be fucked up. I'm saying the politicians will always be screwing cops. And the umbrellas will always be hating cops. In *that* world, I'm asking how a smart man like Frank Kearney can take care of *himself*."

Frank felt the room closing in. "I'm not talking about making anything perfect, Solly. Just better."

Jarvis shook his head sadly. He put his hand back on Frank's shoulder. "And you've been trying for half your life. Vietnam and here in the District. You lost in Vietnam. An' you're losing here."

He squeezed Frank's shoulder. "It's not your fault, Vietnam and the District—they screwed them up beyond repair, Lyndon Johnson and Malcolm Burridge. Question is,

Mr. Franklin Delano Kearney, what do you do for yourself with what's left of your life?"

Frank took a deep breath, felt it hit the bottom of his lungs. He felt himself going under and, like a drowning man, reaching out. Desperately, he grabbed at a hand-hold.

"But none of that's got anything to do with Strickland and what happened in the tunnel."

Frank saw Jarvis smile, as though he knew how much he'd gotten through.

"You want me to find out?" he asked, the smile growing. "The city can't afford my fee."

Frank smiled back. "I thought you might come across a little information about Brewington and Strickland. Volunteer a little help. You know . . . be a good citizen."

Jarvis laughed, big and loud. "I vote. I pay taxes. I stop at red lights in the middle of the night, even when there's no traffic. But I don't volunteer. Not anymore, Frank." He waved him off with both hands. "*Nev*-er volunteer."

JOSÉ WAS LEANING BACK IN HIS CHAIR, FEET ON HIS DESK, reading the Pasco book when Frank got back to the office.

"You talk with Solly?"

"Yeah. I did."

Umbrellas on the sidewalk. *Isn't it about your turn?* Frank looked around the cramped, dingy office with its battered institutional furniture, the chipped paint, the scarred floor, the smell of disinfectant.

"Anything?"

"What?"

"Solly say anything?"

Frank shrugged, tossed his notebook onto his desk, and hung up his overcoat. The seam was parting where the right sleeve joined the shoulder. Bought on sale at Joe Banks, what—five, six years ago?

"Strickland did some part-time work for him. Dates he gave matched Strickland's application at Tower. Far's Solly knew, Strickland was clean."

"They trouble, they out?"

"Yeah, that." Frank nodded toward the Pasco book. "Forensics finished?"

"Forensics finished it." José closed the book over a thin manila folder and pushed the package across to Frank.

The manila folder held three pages. The first page was Forensics' standard report form: date of request, name of requesting officer, name of forensics tech conducting analysis, then the summary of findings.

"They got some unknown partials," José said as Frank looked over the findings.

Forensics had identified Frank's prints on the cover, as well as those of Adair and Toby, the busboy. Inside, O'Brien's prints on every page. The unknown partials showed up on three pages in the last section of the book. In carefully couched wording, the forensics tech described the partials as likely thumb and index prints, left hand.

"There was a scratch pad in the book."

José peered into the manila routing pouch. "Not here."

Frank turned to the section of the book where Forensics had found the partials. Blocks of text had been highlighted in yellow, and the margins of several pages were filled with notes in ballpoint pen.

"They say it's O'Brien's handwriting, they don't say what it means." Frank flipped through his Rolodex to find Nicholas Pasco's number.

Pasco wasn't in. Frank identified himself to his secretary, told her he was sending the book over by messenger, and said he'd like to see Pasco soon. Then he dialed Forensics. There had been a scratch pad with the book, he explained to a tech. The tech put him on hold. A delay; then the tech came back on the line. "Nobody knows nothing about no scratch pad," the tech said, obviously wanting to get rid of Frank. "What did it look like?" Frank asked for Renfro Calkins, the senior evidence specialist. Calkins came on after another delay, listened and said he'd look for the pad. Frank knew Calkins would. He hung up just as José was finishing a call.

"Manny Dale," José said. "Brewington's Benz *was* stolen."

"I thought it was okay. Registration checked out."

"All the same." José shrugged. "Manny says it's hot."

TWENTY-TWO

"IN BRIEF, HOTTER'N hell," Manny Dale said, taking a sip of his beer.

"How come it didn't come through first time?" Frank asked. "Registration check?"

"Ever hear of a tag man?" Dale looked at Frank and José, sighed, and shook his head. "You guys in Homicide live in a different world."

"Yeah, Manny," José said. "We hate killers, but you love thieves."

Dale, a chubby bald man, threw his head back and laughed, his thick bifocals catching the light from the street. "A good thief is a challenge. Most of my bad boys exercise a little more finesse than your delinquents. Besides, I can't stand the sight of blood. If I could, I'd have been a doctor."

"Tag man?" Frank said.

"Okay, here's how it goes. Let's call our tag man Horatio." Dale paused—a storyteller making certain everybody was lined up at the start. "Your man Brewington takes a fancy to Mercedes S-class. Brewington goes to Horatio. Horatio might take a down payment from Brewington . . . but anyway, Horatio starts looking for a wrecked or junked Benz—abandoned."

"Not many of those," José said.

Dale nodded. "But all he needs is one, and he's got a lot of time. And if Brewington wants the car bad enough, Horatio will take the Metroliner up to New York, or get one of those cheapie airline tickets to Chicago. Anyway, Horatio strikes oil. He goes to the guy who has the junker and offers him a hundred or so for the car. The junker guy, happy to get anything, turns over the title to Horatio."

"So now Horatio has a junker Benz that won't run." Frank tapped a finger on Dale's empty mug. "Another?" Without waiting for an answer, he waved to Stanley for another round. ·

"Thank you," Dale said. He smacked his lips and tilted the mug to peer at the bottom, then, satisfied it was empty, put it down. "Horatio has what he needs—the title and the VIN tag, the vehicle identification number tag— that little doohickey cars have where the dashboard meets the windshield.

"Now Horatio swipes a same-model Benz, but one that's in good shape. Switches VIN tags, turns the title over to Brewington, and makes some good change."

"Sounds like a lotta work," said José.

Dale made a ring on the table with his mug. "Do two, three deals a month and you can clear a couple hundred thousand a year—and no IRS bite."

Stanley arrived with the new round, and Dale raised his mug to Frank and José.

"So how'd you find out Brewington's Benz was hot?" José asked.

"Department procedure is to check an impounded car's VIN tag against registration. Guy at the impound lot does that. Brewington's Benz looked okay. But any big-ticket car, I got a policy we go down to the lot and double-check. You see, every automobile with a VIN tag has the same number engraved in the frame. It's purposely hard to get to, so it can't be stamped out or ground down."

"And Brewington's Benz frame number didn't match the VIN tag on the dashboard," Frank guessed.

"You got it," Dale said. "An orthodontist out in Potomac reported it stolen last year."

Garrett's was beginning to fill up for afternoon happy hour. A loud peal of laughter up front momentarily caught Frank's attention. As he saw Stanley wave in a new customer, a thought struck Frank. "You check out wrecks?" he asked Dale.

"Not usually."

"Do me a favor?"

"Ask."

"Look at a Lexus?"

Over the top of his raised mug, Dale looked at Frank. He put the mug down. "The tunnel fracas?"

Frank nodded.

"While you're at it," José added, "you might's well look at a Beamer, too."

"You've got mail," José mimicked in his best AOL voice.

The voice-mail light on Frank's phone glowed irritably. He hung his coat and stood looking at the phone.

"Damn thing's pissed off," he said.

"Voice mail," José groaned, settling into his chair and reaching for a weekly time card. "Used to be if you weren't here, only people who'd call back were the ones who really wanted you. Now you got to listen to every salesman or wrong number who leaves a message on the machine."

"Yeah. And the ones with the least to say leave the longest messages."

Frank's first call was from a roofing contractor about an estimate. He jotted the number down. The roofer was important—he'd been chasing the guy for two months. Easier to get a brain surgeon than a good roofer.

Nicholas Pasco had called next. He had gotten the book. Give him a couple of days to look at it?

Randolph Emerson was the third caller. Frank listened, replayed the message, and hung up.

"Johnny Sam deposition's day after tomorrow," he told José.

"Son of a bitch."

Johnny Sam. Frank's stomach cramped at the prospect of a grilling by Sam's attorneys. The goddamn legal profession—if you could call it a profession—at war with the DC police department. Everybody wins: nobody dares go after Johnny Sam, for fear of bringing down more trouble on the department; Sam's lawyers get a third of any damages; and the ACLU gets to nail another cop's hide to the wall. Everybody wins—except the cops.

Frank shook off a momentary flash of self-pity, then turned off his desk lamp. Time to call it a day.

TWENTY-THREE

WHEN FRANK SWITCHED on his desk lamp the next morning, the first thing he saw was a thick folder with a red-and-white "Urgent" cover filling his In box.

"Never stops, does it?"

"Coffee." José held a quarter between his index finger and thumb.

"Heads."

"You always call heads."

"That's because I win with heads."

"That's what I mean."

"Okay, then," said Frank. "Tails."

The quarter traced a silver arc, up and back into José's palm.

José stared at it disbelievingly. "Shit."

"Maybe you oughta change quarters, Hoser."

"Two outta three?"

"Don't think so."

José sighed. "Decaf?"

"High-test," Frank said, sitting at his desk and reaching for the folder.

The legal format of the one-page memorandum inside gave Frank a rising hope that the mailroom had screwed up on distribution. Hope rose even higher when he saw that His Honor Malcolm Burridge was the first on the list of addressees. Then hope deflated when he saw, farther down, his name and José's.

He read the memorandum, then, reluctantly, its tabbed attachments. Despite the stilted legal jargon, he was being pulled back into a once familiar room, through a door he had closed a long time before. Once again, Terry Quinn—last of the department's old-time Irish Homicide detectives, silver hair, golden tenor, iron courage. And Frank, running down the ramp of the dark garage, knowing that as fast as he could run, he'd never be fast enough, and that Terry Quinn was going to pay.

"Frank?"

José's voice came from far away.

"Frank!"

He shook himself. José was standing in front of his desk, a coffee mug in each hand.

"Yeah?"

José pointed one of the mugs toward the folder.

"I said, 'What's that?' "

Frank closed the folder. He reached for the mug. "Deposition tomorrow," he said. "U.S. Attorney sent over the Cliffs notes."

José sat at his desk, hunched forward, hands wrapped around his coffee mug, eyes on Frank. "Johnny Sam." He said the name with a trace of yearning.

"Used to be the wages of sin were death," Frank said. He thumbed to the Q&A section, the hypothetical questions and answers the U.S. Attorney's Office had put together. *Hypothetical.* Not a script for Frank's testimony, the lawyers would carefully disclaim, merely a guide to sharpen the mind, to recharge tired memory banks.

Q: Did you properly identify yourself as a police officer when arresting Mr. Sam?

A: Yes.

A good answer, Frank thought. Simple. Declarative. But it never was that simple. It could be simple only for a lawyer who'd never been a cop, angry and afraid and alone in a dark garage with a Lincoln Town Car bearing down on him.

"I'm supposed to talk to you about discovery," San-ford Lyles told Frank and José the next day. Lyles was a large-gutted lawyer from the U.S. Attorney's Office. Decades of government legal campaigning had rewarded him with a duodenal ulcer, thinning gray hair, and a musty office that looked out on a brick airshaft.

The two hours Frank had slept last night might as well have been nothing at all. Fatigue dragged everything out as he listened to Lyles. He felt he was in one of those satellite phone conversations with the disconcerting time lag between callers, only here the lag was between what he heard and what he understood.

Despite his fatigue, a synapse tripped somewhere in Frank's memory, and out came the legal definition of discovery. In a classroom manner he recited: "Discovery allows the plaintiff—in this case the asshole Johnny Sam—to question José and me under oath before a trial."

Lyles's heavy-lidded eyes put Frank in mind of an old turtle. "Very lawyerly, Lieutenant. And the purpose of discovery is?"

Still on autopilot, Frank answered, "The purpose of discovery is to assess the strength or weakness of an opponent's case."

"And another?" Lyles stacked the papers scattered on his desktop.

"To gather information to use at trial."

Lyles studied Frank, then held up the sheaf of papers. "Lieutenant, this is the complaint Mr. Johnny Sam has filed against the city." He waved the offending papers. "Mr. Sam says that you and Mr. Phelps have abused his civil rights. He is filing similar charges against your colleague Mr. Bouchard at the Bureau."

José flared. "I'd like to abuse more than that bastard's civil rights."

"He killed—" Frank started.

Lyles held up his hand. "I know the background of this case."

Frank shook his head. "No, Mr. Lyles. You were appointed to handle this. You read the files. You know the facts. But you weren't there when Johnny Sam blew Terry Quinn's brains out. You think you know what it was *like*, but you'll never know how it really *was*."

Lyles began to say something, but Frank wouldn't have it.

"Terry was lying helpless. Gut shot. Johnny Sam stuck a chrome-plated Beretta up against his head and pulled the trigger."

Lyles's face tightened. "That's . . . enough." He chopped out each word and leaned forward in his chair, and wagged a warning index finger at the two men. "What you *saw* was a man in a trench coat with a shiny pistol in a dark underground garage. You saw this man at a distance of over forty yards in this dark underground garage. You never saw the man's face. You only knew it was a Beretta after the fact, from the autopsy and ballistics."

Lyles paused. "You never saw the man's face," he repeated coldly, shaking his finger to emphasize each word. "You couldn't identify the pistol. *Those* are facts. *That* was your sworn testimony at the trial. And *that's* what the court sees as the truth."

"All the same," Frank said, "it was Johnny Sam and it was a Beretta."

Lyles stared at Frank stone-faced. Then his face softened and he nodded. "Okay, Lieutenant, okay. It was Johnny Sam. But you . . . the District . . . didn't make a case that convinced the jury. Johnny Sam's trial is over. That's done. And now Johnny Sam is bringing this charge against the two of you and the city." Lyles was silent, then asked sympathetically, "Now what do we do?"

Frank got up and gathered his coat. "Well, José and I know what discovery is, Mr. Lyles. Let's get on with making Johnny Sam and his lawyer rich men."

* * *

"THREE BLACK. TWO REGULAR, ONE DECAF?" A TALL, elegantly dressed ash-blonde made eye contact in turn with Frank, José, and Lyles. She got three nods and left the reception area.

"Mayor would like that ass," José commented, watching the woman disappear.

Lyles glanced up from his notes. "Our mayor's taste is rather catholic," he said, and went back to his reading.

Frank took in the room. Whether or not you're a lawyer, you live long enough in Washington and you get to know it as a lawyers' town. And you come to picture its premier law firms the way baseball fans in other cities characterize their teams. Frank always thought of Williams & Connolly as bold, bare-knuckled. Arnold & Porter, quiet, competent. So far Trumbull & Herbert was coming across as smooth, assured. Hushed atmosphere, antique chairs, lavish Oriental carpets, heavy brass table lamps, glowing English woodwork and paneling.

Frank watched the receptionist reappear with three coffees in china cups on a silver tray.

"Looks like you're doing your lawyering on the wrong side of the tracks, Mr. Lyles," he whispered.

Lyles raised his chin. "Government service has its own rewards, Lieutenant."

José raised his eyebrows, thinking Lyles was joking. "You find out what they are, Counselor," he said, "you give us a call."

The three men drank their coffee in silence. Frank felt exhaustion creeping back. His shoulders sagged, surrendering to gravity. He took a deep breath. That didn't work. He was tempted to shut his eyes and doze off. He was giving the coffee and deep breathing one more shot when a door into the reception area opened. A stocky man with a thick head of silver hair combed into a modest pompadour entered.

"I'm Manson Herbert," the man said in a creamy bass voice. A Washington insider voice, one that could be heard at the Burning Tree bar ordering Courvoisier after golf with a Supreme Court justice and two senators.

Lyles and the two detectives introduced themselves. Herbert shook each hand.

Confident, Frank thought, a man used to making things happen.

Herbert pointed to a door. "We've got everything set up. Shall we go in, gentlemen?"

He led the way into the room. As Frank stepped inside, clashing images hit him like a burst of machine-gun fire. A stark, white, windowless room . . . a wooden chair behind a plain table . . . a videocamera on a leggy tripod that looked like a malignant insect . . . a heavyset man sitting at another table off to the side.

"What's *that* doing here?" José asked.

Herbert turned to Frank and José, a smile on his lips. "You gentlemen have met." Herbert waved a manicured hand from Lyles toward the heavyset man. "Mr. Lyles, Mr. John Sam."

Sam nodded and flashed an ugly grin.

Frank looked at Herbert angrily, then at Lyles.

Lyles, obviously caught short, was uncomfortably eye-balling the floor.

"What the hell?" Frank asked him.

Lyles shrugged and turned both palms up. *What can you do?* "The plaintiff has a right to sit in on a deposition, Lieutenant."

Johnny Sam's grin widened.

A tall, slender woman entered the room. She wore a severe dark gray business suit and carried a bulky attaché case.

"Our court reporter," Herbert explained. He gave a name, but Frank, staring at Johnny Sam, didn't catch it. The woman went to a side table and began setting up her recorder. She flipped a few switches, spoke a few words into the recorder's facemask, then looked up to Herbert with a curt nod.

"Shall we get started?" Herbert motioned to the armchair on the platform. "We would like to depose you first, Lieutenant Kearney."

The reporter produced a Bible from her attaché case. As she approached Frank, she stopped by the videocamera control box to press a series of buttons. A red light blinked on over the camera lens.

"Do you swear to tell the truth . . ."

The adrenaline rush faded, and Frank's weariness returned. He felt unsteady, as if he were on the deck of a rolling ship. The reporter finished the oath. Through a fog of fatigue, Frank heard himself say, "I do." Then he sat, the relief of getting off his feet almost sensual. Lyles and José were to his right front, Herbert and Johnny Sam to his left. Directly ahead were the staring eye of the videocamera and the bulb-shaped microphone pick-up, looking like the business end of a clenched boxing glove coming toward his jaw.

Herbert studied a folder open before him on the table. Then he pushed back, and rose and walked toward Frank. He stopped beside the videocamera.

"Lieutenant Kearney. April 3, 1997, was a Wednesday—"

"Thursday," said Frank.

"Pardon?" Herbert asked, his voice silken soft.

"April third was a Thursday."

Herbert looked up and flashed Frank a smile of apparent gratitude. "Quite so, Lieutenant. Thank you. On that Thursday, you met Mr. Sam, the plaintiff. Please tell us how that meeting came about."

"I saw him kill a helpless man."

Herbert shook his head sadly. "No, Lieutenant. No you didn't. You were unable to prove you saw anything of the sort. Now, without the dramatics, tell us about your meeting with Mr. Sam on April third, almost three years ago."

Frank took a deep breath. The fatigue was replaced now by a cold anger. He glanced at the court reporter and saw her eyes, expectant, watching him over the rim of the facemask.

"After I saw someone in a tan trench coat kill a helpless man," Frank began, "I met Mr. Johnny Sam as he was driving his car at a high speed out of an underground parking garage near Twenty-second and K Streets Northwest."

"Did you stop Mr. Sam?"

"Yes."

"How?"

"I attempted to wave him down. When it appeared he wasn't going to stop, I stepped aside and shot out his tires."

Herbert nodded like a teacher approving an answer from a chronically slow pupil. "Did Mr. Sam have any way of knowing that this person trying to stop him as he left a public parking garage was a police officer?"

"I don't know what he knew or didn't know."

"Were you in uniform?"

"No."

"Were uniformed officers with you?"

"No."

"Were you prominently displaying your badge?"

"No. I had an officer dead and a car coming at me. I—"

"That was not my question," Herbert interrupted. *Let's try again.* "Were you prominently—"

"No. I was not prominently displaying my badge."

"After you shot at Mr. Sam—"

"After I shot at his tires."

"What happened then?"

"Mr. Sam got out of his car and began to run away. My partner, José Phelps, had just come into the garage with FBI agent Robin Bouchard, who was working with us. We chased Mr. Sam on foot."

"Chased him." Herbert made it sound like an accusation. "Did either you, Mr. Phelps, or Mr. Bouchard identify yourselves as law enforcement officers?"

"He knew José and I were police."

"How? You weren't in uniform. You weren't displaying badges. You could have been anyone. Mr. Sam had reasonable cause to fear for his safety, given the level of personal violence in this city."

Frank looked at Lyles. The attorney was gazing off into the distance. With a flush of anger, Frank shot back at Herbert.

"You want an answer? Or do you want to give a sermon?"

Herbert bowed slightly. "An answer, please, Lieutenant."

"Johnny Sam knows José and me," Frank replied. "We've busted him before."

"Lieutenant. The garage was dark. So dark you couldn't make a positive identification of the killer of Detective Quinn. Isn't it possible that those same conditions prevented Mr. Sam from recognizing you?"

"Anything's possible," Frank said, angered that he had to say it.

"So Mr. Sam ran. You caught him. Both you and your partner, Mr. Phelps? And the FBI agent, Bouchard?"

"Me."

"Why just you?"

"I was faster than Mr. Phelps. Agent Bouchard was farther back in the garage when the shooting happened."

Herbert glanced to the table where José and Lyles sat. "I see. So after you caught Mr. Sam, what happened?"

"I stopped him from leaving the garage."

"How did you stop him?"

Frank looked past Herbert to Johnny Sam. Sam had a smirk on his face.

"I cold-cocked him."

"Cold-cocked." Herbert's lips pursed primly as if Frank had uttered something totally foreign. Alien. Out of this world. Or at least out of Herbert's world. "Explain, please, what that means—cold-cocking."

"I hit him with my fist," Frank said.

"You hit him with your fist," Herbert intoned in his rich bass, sounding again like a teacher. "Once or twice?"

"Yes."

"More than once or twice?"

"Yes."

"Three times? Four times? More?"

"I wasn't exactly counting."

"How many times did you hit Mr. Sam with your fist, Lieutenant Kearney?"

Frank suddenly felt very, very tired. Washed out. "I don't remember."

"You . . . don't . . . remember." Standing beside the videocamera, Herbert shook his head. The camera wouldn't see it, of course. But the microphone would catch the way he rolled out the words. Herbert paused, then asked briskly: "Did Mr. Sam resist? Fight back?"

Frank locked eyes with Lyles. His mouth was slightly open and his eyes seemed to have a prayer in them. A prayer that wasn't going to be answered.

"No," said Frank.

"Once you caught up with him, Mr. Sam didn't resist?"

"No."

"Was Mr. Sam conscious when you stopped hitting him?"

"He didn't appear to be." *I really wanted to keep on hitting the sonofabitch. Forever. Pound his head into a pulp on the concrete floor.*

Herbert gave Frank a superior, pitying look. "A last question, Lieutenant." It was something he didn't want to ask, you understand, but had to. "Lieutenant . . . what caused you to stop hitting Mr. Sam?"

Again, Lyles had that "Oh Jesus, please" look in his eyes.

And again Frank delivered. "My partner and Agent Bouchard."

Herbert didn't say anything for a long time. The video-camera stared unblinkingly at Frank, and he stared back, trying to keep his chin up, his eyes at ease, his mouth from drooping into a frown.

Finally Herbert nodded. "Thank you, Lieutenant Kearney. That's all we need." He turned to Lyles and José.

"Lieutenant Phelps?"

"A FUN DAY." FRANK WATCHED STANLEY MAKE HIS WAY down the bar with the two drafts.

"You talk to Robin?"

"Yeah. They deposed him down at the Bureau."

"Bureau pissed?"

"Not too. He's still running their Johnny Sam task force."

"Bouchard's a good man, even if he is Bureau."

"He'll get by."

"Think we'll go to court?" José asked.

Frank shook his head. "No. Lyles will lay out what we have, what they have, and Burridge will decide to settle. Election year's no time to have a police brutality case in court." Frank peeled off a five as Stanley pushed the two mugs across the bar.

"And Johnny Sam walks, with a million or two."

"Maybe not that much. Maybe just what it'd cost to re-open that pool down in Anacostia. Hire a couple of teachers." Frank sipped his beer and caught his reflection in the mirror behind the bar. "I feel like hell," he said.

"Sam'll get his," José said, hustling to the rescue. "Some way. Someday."

Frank thought more about it, about how he was feeling. "It's not so much him getting his. It's just that if I'd collared the bastard according to procedure—"

"He'd still be walking."

"Yeah, but he wouldn't have been gaffing us in a civil suit. If . . ."

José worked his mug around on the slick surface of the bar. "Shit, Frank. If my uncle hadn'a died in the poor house, I'd a been a rich man."

"I've heard that a few times, Hoser."

José raised his mug. "To righteous anger."

Frank raised his. "To playing it smart."

TWENTY-FOUR

"FATHER O'BRIEN SHOULD have been taking my course for credit. He'd have set the curve." Nicholas Pasco handed the slender book over to Frank. Pasco's office looked southeast across the Potomac. A bright winter sun glittered off the Washington Monument's metal scaffolding, and the white marble of the Kennedy Center glowed like mother-of-pearl.

"He was particularly interested in some parts of this." Frank opened the book to the pages O'Brien had worked over with the yellow highlighter.

"Yes. Computer networks—especially the banking networks." Pasco looked puzzled. "I didn't develop that section to any great depth. I intended it to be a layman's technical foundation for my more theoretical discussion of the advanced dynamics of a globally integrated economy."

"But if Father O'Brien had done his homework on networks, he could have come up with a more detailed picture?"

Pasco nodded. "Oh, yes. There are authorities that specialize in the field—Kurtzman at Harvard, Van Slyke at Brooklyn Poly . . . any number of bright young minds at Microsoft and in Silicon Valley."

"Tell me about networks."

Pasco got up from his chair and walked over to a white-board that covered much of one wall. With a felt-tip marker, he drew a handful of circles randomly across the board.

"Imagine a nervous system," he said, tapping one of the circles with the marker. "It's made up of computers of all sorts, mainframes, PCs, specialized trading devices."

"Like the Internet?"

Pasco smiled. "As vast as the Internet is, it is but one of several thousand networks."

He sketched dotted lines between several of the circles. "And these networks are connected by wires, fiber-optic cables, microwaves, satellite dishes—at work twenty-four hours a day, constantly crunching numbers, constantly calculating, constantly exchanging information. Talking to each other. And the calculating gets faster. Now the networks measure time in *billionths* of a second, and they're gaining speed every day."

Pasco gained momentum as his enthusiasm shifted to high gear. "At the same time they're calculating and getting faster, the networks are engaging more people. These networks cover the West like a blanket, and they're damn near everywhere in Asia. They've already got a foothold in the Third World—in less than ten years, places like Bhutan and Zanzibar will be as wired in as we are today. Spreading like wildfire."

"Or like AIDS," Frank said.

That rocked Pasco back. Momentarily at a loss, he rolled the marker back and forth in his hand. Then he nodded, apparently catching on to Frank's analogy. Slowly at first, then faster. "There's a point there, inexorable advance," he admitted. "Irreversible consequences. You've got something, Lieutenant. But"—he shook a qualifying finger at Frank—"but not without its benefits." He stopped as if he'd found out a new fact about Frank. "You're not a computer enthusiast, are you, Lieutenant?"

"Not exactly. I know they're here. They damn sure aren't going away. And I know we can't get along without them. But that sort of makes me uneasy—that we can't get along without them." Getting back to the subject, Frank pointed to the board with its circles and lines. "Banks—how do they use networks?"

"A lot of ways. One you're most familiar with is settling checking-account balances—yours, mine, our friends', the checks of companies and corporations. On a normal day, American banks handle two billion checks. To balance accounts between banks that get the checks and banks that issue the checks, the American banking system must transfer more than two *trillion* dollars over the networks—every day." Pasco paused and asked, "You know how much two trillion is?"

"Boggles my mind, Professor."

"Two trillion would pay the salaries of all Americans now working for a whole year. It would cover the Pentagon's spending, four-hundred-dollar toilet seats and all, for seven years.

"Now"—Pasco paused again, to make sure Frank understood the importance of what he was about to say—"that two trillion is just money transferred to cover checks. There are other networks shooting money around. All over America. All over the world."

"Credit cards," Frank guessed.

"Yes. Plastic money. MasterCard, for example, operates Cirrus, a check-cashing network through which you can draw money from your account at eighty thousand ATMs here and abroad. And it gets even more complicated. Cirrus talks to other networks—MAC in New York, STAR in California, Yankee in New England, and even Plus—and Plus is operated by Visa, MasterCard's competitor."

"International?" Frank asked.

Pasco nodded. "An example: When my wife and I go on vacation, I never convert dollars to pounds or francs at a money-changer's. I get better exchange rates with my American Express card at an ATM just about anywhere in Europe, Asia, or Latin America. If for any reason I have to write a check in Spain, the SWIFT network in Switzerland clears it"—Pasco snapped his fingers—"like *that,* and instantly transfers money from my bank here in the District to the Banco Nacional in Madrid."

"All the networks talk to each other? The network I use for my ATM hooks into the SWIFT network in Switzerland?"

"You go to the Exxon station down the street," Pasco said, gesturing in the general direction of M Street, "you fill up your tank at a self-service pump and pay with a credit card. The electrons that transaction creates can go anywhere in the net and from that net to any other net, anywhere in the world. The ten or fifteen dollars you give Exxon can end up within minutes as part of a payoff of a Barclays Bank debt in Hong Kong."

Frank looked out the window. Down on the Potomac, someone in a single scull. Whoever it was would be working hard, sweating despite the chill. Frank found himself envying the solitary rower. No brain-warping complexity—you pull on the oars, the scull goes. You stop pulling, the scull stops.

Frank shifted back to Pasco. "Remember what Willie Sutton said when somebody asked him why he was always robbing banks?"

"Because that's where the money is?"

Frank gestured toward the board, with its circles and connecting lines.

"Suppose I can get into that net? Suppose I figure some way to skim off some of those electrons from the Exxon station down the street?"

Pasco bounced the felt-tip in the palm of his hand. "You wouldn't be alone, Lieutenant. There're thousands of hackers out there at this moment. They're playing with random-number programs, trying to get around the PIN numbers, passwords, and access codes that protect the networks. And there're thousands of people on the other side, grinding away to keep the networks secure. It's a seesaw war."

"Offense, defense."

Pasco nodded.

"Seems to me the hacker has a big advantage."

"That's . . . ?"

"The guy playing defense—keeping the hacker out—has to be successful all the time."

Pasco looked owlishly at Frank. "So?"

"The hacker has to be successful only once."

"YOU THINK O'BRIEN AND THE KID HACKED THEIR WAY into a bank?" Kate asked. The cold night air turned her breath to frost.

Frank walked beside her, their shoulders touching, their hands together in the pocket of his overcoat. They had the path along the Reflecting Pool to themselves. Just ahead, the Lincoln Memorial. Behind them, farther away, the Washington Monument.

"What else?" Frank had been circling the idea all day since talking to Pasco. "It's a reasonable assumption."

"All those hoofbeats . . . horses? No zebras?"

Frank sighed. "Looking that way. O'Brien . . . a priest with half a million in his closet. The Kid . . . a hacker. The two of them together, thicker than—"

"Thieves?" Kate stopped and turned to face Frank. "Is that what you think?"

Frank got a trapped feeling. It was sour and burning in his chest. "It's a logical conclusion, Kate," he said, not wanting to say it even as he did. "Reasonable. What do you think Worsham and all the rest will think? And what am I supposed to think?"

"Maybe Worsham and all the rest will think O'Brien was a thief. And maybe that explains the money. And maybe that explains the killing." Her eyes searched his face. "What do you really think . . . down inside? Not what you're *supposed* to think . . . but what do you *really* think?"

Frank stood for a long time looking at the Lincoln Memorial, a white glow in the winter night. "I want to think," he finally said, "that there might be a zebra still on the loose."

BEFORE EIGHT THE NEXT MORNING, TONY UPTON CALLED from the morgue. Fifteen minutes later, he sat at the table in the Homicide conference room with Frank, José, and Eleanor.

Frank motioned to Upton. "Tony's got an ID on the two tunnel rats."

The medical examiner passed two photos around the conference table. "The brothers Godcharles, Terrance and Maurice." The photos showed two bodies laid out on Upton's stainless-steel tables.

José opened a folder. "Terrance has . . . had . . . priors for manslaughter, armed robbery, and grand theft auto. Maurice—he was the gunner with the Kalashnikov—murder two, extortion, assault, grand theft auto." He looked around the table. "They'd been a team for four, five years. Carjackings. They were probably after Strickland for the Lexus—unless they'd branched out."

"Connections?" Frank asked.

José shook his head. "Just each other. Independents. Lived together. Had an apartment over in Southwest."

It's never so simple, Frank thought. Last night he was sure it was either/or. Either it was a turf thing, or somebody was after Strickland's suitcase. Sun comes up and it's neither—it's Butch Cassidy and Sundance out to swipe a Lexus.

Frank looked at the wall behind Upton. Individual plastic sleeves for investigation notes and background files hung beneath framed eight-by-ten photos of the case's major players. An empty frame represented Trunkman, the body in the Beamer trunk; another held the identikit drawing of the Kid.

The adjacent wall displayed a timeline. Days, hours, and minutes made a horizontal scale. Various colored lines, each representing an individual's activities and locations, ran left to right above the time scale. Robert O'Brien's line— green—ended abruptly at one on the morning of January 3.

There were similar lines for known characters—Lewis Strickland, Carlton Holmes, Henry Brewington, the two Colombians, Nicholas Pasco at Georgetown University, Adair at the diner, Solly Jarvis, and most recently, the Godcharles brothers.

Then there were dotted lines for the unknowns, three of them. One for Trunkman, one for the Kid, and one for Hampton, the guy who'd been nosing around Mister Charlie's looking for the Kid.

Frank wondered what the chart would tell him if the lines could be pushed far enough back in time. And what they'd look like if they showed the future.

He turned to José. "Let's keep the ID of the Godcharles boys close-hold."

"Close-hold," José repeated.

Upton gave Frank a sidelong glance, and Eleanor's eyebrows raised a fraction, but neither said anything.

"Yeah," Frank said, circling the table with his hand. "Just here."

MINUTES LATER, FRANK AND JOSÉ SAT ALONE IN THE WAR room.

"Okay. Want to let me in on the close-hold business?"

Frank slouched deep in his chair, chin on his chest, staring at the conference table. "Don't know, exactly, Hoser. Just a feeling."

"A feeling like what?"

"Putting myself in the place of O'Brien's killer. How he—or she—might be seeing this." Frank sat still, trying to pull bits and pieces of thoughts together into something that would make sense.

"Burridge has already spun it as a drug war. And the media's running with it."

Frank paused, like a mason selecting the next stone to fit into a wall. "Now, we know brother Strickland was—is— in the delivery business. But if the Godcharles brothers *didn't know* about the money in the trunk . . . if they were just out for the car . . . and if Strickland's boss—whoever that is— *doesn't know* they were out for the car . . ." Frank eyeballed the thought to José.

José smiled. "Gives us room to screw over some minds. My second-favorite indoor sport."

Frank went off focus, as if something else had come up over his mental horizon, then locked eyes with José. "Let's go see Woody."

"About?"

"About our friend Mr. Sam."

TWENTY-FIVE

WOODY STOOD BEFORE a whiteboard juggling a felt-tip marker in one hand. "You asked how tight a cover we could throw over Johnny Sam."

Frank nodded.

"You want the short answer?" Woody asked.

Frank nodded again.

"Depends."

Frank and José waited for more, and it took no longer than a second or two for Frank to realize there wouldn't be any more.

"Depends?" José asked.

"Depends is a little *too* short, Woody."

"I wanted to make a point." Woody drew a bull's-eye on the whiteboard. "Johnny Sam—our target. We want to cover him so tight he can't fart without us knowing what kind of beans he had for dinner."

Down the side of the board, he scribbled a short list. "Taps . . . bugs . . . trackers . . . monitors . . . human assets." He dashed an arrow from the list toward the bull's-eye. "These are the tools I have to do the job you want me to do." Woody hesitated. "Got a second for a couple of show-and-tells?" he asked casually.

Frank said yes. Whatever Woody's show-and-tell was, it

was more important to him than he was letting on. Armchair cops like Emerson always described policing as a science. It wasn't. It was an art, like playing the violin. And Woody was like a violinist with a Stradivarius he took pride in trotting out when he got the chance.

He opened a drawer, and out came a plastic container about the size of a ring box.

"TV camera," he said, thumbing the lid open. Inside, a flat silicon chip. "Lens the size of the head of a pin." He held it up for inspection. "Self-contained power. Hide it in the leaves of an office plant. Tuck it in the folds of a curtain. Broadcasts to a pick-up half a mile away. In color."

Woody put the camera back inside and held out something that looked like a black box with knobs and a tiny satellite dish.

"Sends a high-frequency beam into a room. Think of that beam as a conveyor belt. But this conveyor belt can even go through brick walls. It finds a hollow object like a vase, coffee cup, lightbulb—anything that the sound of the human voice causes to vibrate. The beam bounces off the hollow object, and when it does, it picks up the voice vibrations and carries everything back to junior here"—Woody pointed to the antenna—"and he strips out the high-frequency beam and gives us the conversation."

Woody put the gizmo away and returned to the whiteboard. He stared at the bull's-eye with his head to one side as if the target were whispering something to him, then turned to Frank and José.

"All the gee-whiz stuff, and I got to give you a 'depends' answer. You know why?"

Frank shook his head.

Woody reached out and rapped the bull's-eye with a knuckle. "Because what I can do for you depends on Johnny Sam. You see, he's not sitting still all the time, giving orders to his soldiers, making phone calls. He's on the move. There're places I can use the high-tech stuff, other places I can't. I gotta know whether to put an induction tap on his phone or use an old-fashioned direct wire."

"We can give you a starting point," Frank said.

José handed Woody a folder. "Copy of his rap sheet and file background. Johnny runs a front business—a commercial janitorial and sanitation service—down on E Street. Address's in there."

"How long'll it take, Woody?" Frank asked.

"That depends. The more time we have, the better we can cover him."

Frank stared at the bull's-eye, then told Woody, "Let's get as much as we can, as fast as we can."

LATER THAT AFTERNOON, MANNY DALE WALKED INTO the office carrying a stack of papers. "Strickland's Lexus was stolen," he said without a hello or how are you.

José looked up. "Why'm I not surprised?"

Manny handed the top two pages of the stack to Frank. "A copy of Strickland's Lexus registration and title. Among other things, they give you the name of the owner of the junk car that furnished the VIN tag and registration."

Manny handed over two more pages. "And here's the paperwork for Brewington's Benz."

Frank read the documents, then, sliding them across his desk toward José's, looked at Manny. "So we know the owners of the two junked cars that fronted for the two stolen cars? Is there anything else this tells us?"

"Told us enough to check the owners."

"And?"

"The Benz owner's dead. Killed in the crash that totaled his car."

José looked up from the papers. "The Lexus?"

"He's alive. Car totaled, but he made it out."

"There's more, isn't there, Manny?" Frank knew it was a pretty safe bet.

"Well, yes." Manny smiled modestly. "The insurance companies covering the cars reported that the Benz and Lexus were sold for scrap . . . standard procedure." He shrugged slightly, then leaned forward as though revealing a deep family secret. "But both insurance companies sold the cars to the same junkyard—MacKenzie Salvage." He paused. "I think you guys know where that is."

EARL GRUBBS ROLLED A FAT QUID FROM HIS LEFT CHEEK to his right and aimed a foul-looking stream of brown tobacco juice toward a Buick hubcap. He frowned at his marksmanship before turning to Frank and José. "GEICO and USAA say they sent their junks here, I guess they did."

Junkyard dog, Frank was thinking. Complete with three-day salt-and-pepper beard and grease-stained mackinaw. Right down to the scarred industrial safety shoes.

"You guess?" José said. "Don't you have records?"

"Yeah. But we're behind in posting."

"You show us?" Frank motioned toward the shack that served as an office, where a plume of smoke promised relief from the cutting wind. Over the scrap piles, Frank made out the rusted superstructure of the compactor. The night they'd found Brewington and the BMW seemed another lifetime.

Grubbs must have been reading his mind. As they got to the shack, he turned to Frank. "This have anything to do with that shit over at the compactor?"

"How about just showing us your records?" Frank asked.

"DAMN, I THOUGHT *MY* PAPERWORK WAS LOUSY." José, his half-moon reading glasses propped on his nose, sat at a desk jury-rigged from a sheet of plywood and two file cabinets. In front of him was a large ledger book, surrounded by a rats' nest of loose papers stuffed in a bank of pigeon-holes and spilling over into cardboard boxes on the floor.

"Paper," Grubbs said, as if it were a dirty word. "I do paperwork, the junk piles up. I do junk, the paperwork piles up. Paper and junk . . . they never stop making the stuff."

As Frank watched over his shoulder, José worked through the ledger. Something caught his eye when he turned a page. He went back to the previous page and ran his finger down to an entry near the bottom. "Here's the Benz," he said, dog-earing the page. Three pages later, he pointed out the Lexus to Frank.

Grubbs looked alternately curious and worried. "What's up?" he finally asked.

"This column"—Frank pointed—"says 'Received by.' Whose initials are these?"

Grubbs bent over the ledger, then looked up. "Kenny Dee."

"His name's Kenny Dee?" José asked.

"Actually Deane. Everbody calls him Kenny Dee, though."

"The Beamer," Frank said, "what year was it?"

José began leafing through the pages again. "A ninety-seven, Five-two-five."

Four more pages and Frank pointed to another entry. "'Ninety-seven Beamer. 'Received by . . .' "

"Our friend Kenny Dee."

Frank turned to Grubbs. "Tell me—what does Kenny Dee do when he takes in a junker?"

"He puts down the VIN, like there, for the Lexus. Then he puts the title number in the next column." Grubbs passed a grease-blackened fingernail under a string of numbers and letters.

"And what does he do with the title?" Frank asked.

"He nullifies it."

"How?"

"He fills out a DMV form sayin' the vehicle's scrap, staples the title to it, I sign the form, and he mails it in."

"Where is he?" José asked.

Grubbs hawked, pushed the door open, and cut loose another stream of tobacco juice into the chill air. He wiped his mouth with the back of his hand. "This's one of his gone times."

"Gone times?" José echoed.

Grubbs rolled the quid around. "Fucker just skies up sometimes. Goes off a week, maybe two. Comes back, gets this paper mess straightened out, stays awhile, then gone time rolls around again."

"Why you keep him around?"

Grubbs shrugged. "He's good when he's here."

"You got an address? Phone number?" Frank asked.

Grubbs shook his head.

"You got him on your payroll and you don't have an address?"

"He works part-time," Grubbs replied. "He doesn't take a check. I pay him cash. His call."

"He works at this desk?"

"Yeah."

"Mind if we take a look?"

"Go ahead." Grubbs waved a hand. His forehead wrinkled. "I'm not gonna get in any trouble, am I? Payin' him in cash, I mean."

Frank opened the top drawer. "That's between you and the IRS, fella."

Half an hour later, Frank was sinking in quicksand. It wasn't that there was a lot of wrinkled, dusty paper, which there was; it was the variety that made for slow going—bills, invoices, labor bulletins, environmental reports, employment applications, even a two-year-old pizza carry-out menu. Trying to understand each piece of paper, figuring out what it was he was looking at, and then figuring out whether it was something useful or not, that's what was making him feel claustrophobic.

Frank glanced at a work order, and tossed it on the growing pile of discarded paper. In mid-reach into the drawer, he stopped and retrieved the work order. A business card was stapled to one corner. He handed the document to Grubbs.

"Due out from a print shop," Frank said. "But it's made out to K. Deane, not to MacKenzie Salvage."

Grubbs studied the work order and business card suspiciously, then slowly shook his head and handed them back to Frank. "Never heard of them. What print work I need, my brother does it up in Laurel."

"I keep this?"

Grubbs nodded.

Frank folded the work order and put it in his pocket. He stepped outside and phoned Manny Dale, gave him Kenny Deane's name. Manny laughed, and gave Frank chapter and verse on Deane. Frank made another call, to Eleanor, for Deane's rap sheet. He went back into the office, stood looking murderously at the stack of paper waiting for him, then sighed and dove in.

BRAXTON PRINTING WAS A DARK TWO-ROOM SHOP OFF AN alley in Petworth. It had a metallic ink-and-grease smell, accented with a touch of coriander from the kitchen exhaust fan of the Ethiopian restaurant next door.

Joseph Braxton, gaunt and stoop-shouldered, with thinning gray hair and cracked black fingernails, kept looking at the work order, until Frank asked, "Well, is it yours?"

"Yeah." The man's voice was tentative and reedy, and his eyes darted between Frank and José, and the door.

"Is it ready?"

"That's a work order for a customer."

"That wasn't my question," Frank said. "Is it ready?"

"You don't have—"

"We can call and get a search warrant."

Braxton wiped his hands on his ink-stained apron while he weighed cops with a warrant versus cops without a warrant. He pointed toward a doorway to a back room filled with an offset press. "It's running now."

In the noisy room, Braxton pulled a page from the press run and handed it to Frank.

Frank looked at the paper, gave it to José, and grinned at Braxton. "What do you know . . . blank automobile titles, for the Virginia DMV."

Braxton said nothing, just stood there looking very unhappy.

"Those Virginia guys," José said with an ironic smile, "so good of them to send their work to the District."

"I print what the customer wants," Braxton finally got out.

"While you're at it," José said, "why don't you run off a batch of hundreds for Frank and me?"

Braxton looked even more unhappy. "Look—"

"You got Kenny's address?"

Braxton shook his head emphatically. "I was gonna meet him tonight. . . . Whitey's."

"Tell you what," Frank said. "We'll wait here while you finish doing this work for the state of Virginia and we'll deliver it to Kenny for you."

"I don't want any trouble," Braxton whined.

"You already got trouble, partner," José said. "What you got to work at now is getting rid of it."

FRANK HAD ALWAYS LIKED WHITEY'S, A SOFT-CASE RED-neck joint in Arlington, just off the Shirley Highway. Cash only, with Patsy Cline on the jukebox and big hair on the waitresses. Wooden booths with Formica tables down the length of the floor, bar along the other wall, ladies' and gents' in the back. Neon bar signs pushing Rolling Rock and the house specialty, a mystery called broasted chicken.

From a booth at the back, Frank watched the door. He'd ordered the chicken, José the country-fried steak. The NASCAR clock over the cash register said six-fifteen, and the early crowd of construction workers was giving way to Lands' End–casual couples, soldiers from Fort Myer, and clusters of bikers heavy with tattoos and leather.

"That's Kenny. Just came in. Blue ski jacket." Frank and José's waitress materialized at their booth with a Silex, bending forward to freshen Frank's coffee.

Kenny Deane looked younger than his mug shots, Frank decided. Then again, most people did. Something about getting booked that put shadows under the eyes, wrinkles around the mouth.

José didn't turn around, but watched Frank's eyes. Kenny worked his way down the bar, slapping backs and squeezing shoulders, and as he neared their booth, Frank stood up and closed in. Kenny brushed by, and Frank touched his elbow. Kenny turned, his pleasant smile showing a row of white, even teeth.

"Hi," he said. "Do I know you?"

"No," Frank replied. "We're friends of Manny Dale. He sends his regards." He discreetly flashed his badge.

Kenny's smile faded as he eyed Frank, then José, still sitting in the booth. Then he smiled again. "How's Manny . . . his ulcer and all?"

"He's good. He says you're on probation."

Kenny looked questioningly at Frank. "You guys aren't Auto Theft."

"Homicide." Frank pointed at the booth where he'd been sitting. "Join us?"

"Sure." Kenny slid in and Frank followed.

Frank signaled for the waitress. Kenny ordered a Rolling Rock.

"I haven't killed anybody," he said after the waitress left.

"We want to talk about restoring cars," Frank said. "Manny tells us you're good at that. Raising them from the dead, so to speak."

"Manny's too kind," Kenny said easily. "I'm outta that racket."

José leaned forward. "We're not really interested in what you're doin' now, Kenny. Like Frank said, we're Homicide, and like you said, you haven't killed anybody."

"What we're curious about," Frank cut in, "are three cars. A Benz, a Lexus, and a Beamer."

Kenny stiffened. "I think I better get a lawyer."

Frank shook his head wonderingly at José. "Why is it? You want an innocent conversation and everybody starts yelling for a lawyer."

José nodded sagely. "One of these days a lawyer is gonna want to talk to somebody and somebody will yell for a cop."

Frank laughed. "That'll be the day, Hoser." He turned to Kenny, sitting beside him. "You're not being charged with anything. Matter of fact, you call a lawyer, that might start Manny Dale looking into your record-keeping at MacKenzie."

Kenny got a look like he tasted something sour.

Frank upped the ante. "By the way, Kenny, your printer finished your job," he said, handing him the packet of automobile titles Braxton had printed. "Hoser and I thought we'd deliver them. Didn't know you worked for Virginia DMV. You're a busy boy."

Kenny took a long sip of his beer, then put the bottle down and sighed. "Okay, Lieutenant, okay."

Frank laid copies of pages from the junk register on the table.

"You recognize these?"

"Yeah."

Frank pointed to an entry. "This Benz listed here . . . you took its VIN tag and title, and they showed up on the Benz that Brewington had. The real VIN, the one on the frame, has it belonging to a guy out in Potomac."

"Henry wanted a Benz."

"And you got it for him," José said, leading Kenny on.

"Yeah."

"The Lexus, here," Frank pointed to another entry again. "Who got that?"

"Strickland."

Frank watched Kenny take another pull at his beer. "And how about the Five series 'ninety-seven BMW? Who'd you get that for?"

Kenny coughed beer onto the back of his hand.

"You know the car, Kenny," Frank said it hard. "The one that ended up in the compactor with Brewington as the hood ornament."

Kenny drew a deep breath and looked as if he was going to get very sick. After a long moment, he said in a whisper, "Alvarez."

"Alvarez," José repeated. "He's got a first name?"

"Angel. I think it was a nickname."

"Where's he live?"

Kenny shrugged.

"Come on, Kenny," José frowned. "You get the guy a car and you don't know where he lives?"

"I don't exactly run a door-to-door service." Kenny tried

a suck-up smile. José came back with an iced-snot look.
Kenny dropped the suck-up and added quickly, "I figured
he lived somewhere near Mexican Corner."

Frank knew Mexican Corner—a double misnomer. The
place wasn't particularly Mexican and it wasn't really a corner. It was a vacant lot in northern Alexandria, a neighborhood of weekly rental apartments for Latino immigrants.
Weekday mornings, the men smoked cigarettes and waited
for contractors who came in their trucks from Sterling or
Manassas to hire day laborers for work in the District.

"How'd you get that impression?"

Kenny bobbed his chin as the light came on. "He wanted
an Alexandria address on the Beamer paperwork. Strickland and Brewington listed theirs in the District. When Angel said Alexandria, I guessed it was the Mexican Corner
area."

"How was he connected to Strickland and Brewington?"
Frank asked.

"I'm not sure. I knew Strickland best. Sold him the
Lexus. Then he brought Brewington around, and then Angel. I figured they had some kind of deal going, maybe Angel and Brewington worked for Strickland, but you don't
ask about those things."

"When was this . . . that you made the sale to Alvarez?"

"Just before Christmas."

"Last month?"

"No. Christmas 'ninety-eight."

"Let me guess," José said, "he paid cash."

"Yeah." Kenny's smirk said that he was surprised José
would even ask.

"You opened the yard the night they put the Beamer in
the compactor, didn't you?"

Kenny recoiled as though José had stuck a snake in his
face. His breath caught and his eyes flicked back and forth
between Frank and José.

Frank watched Kenny attempting to make up his mind.
You're in a hole, kid, Frank tried to send the thought over.
You can either keep digging or come along with us. When
he saw that the chemistry between Kenny and José was

starting to work, he sat back to watch his partner play Dale Carnegie.

José reached across and put his hand on Kenny's forearm. "Look," he said sincerely, "you been around. You know how the system works. Property crime's one thing. Killing people's another. You get tagged for a few cars"— he shrugged—"you get a couple of years. Jail's crowded, you serve maybe a few months. But," he said, squeezing Kenny's arm for emphasis, "you get mixed up in multiple homicide . . ." José shook his head regretfully. "Look at it this way, Kenny—you want to deal with Frank and me? Or with a sweet guy like Manny Dale?" He let that sink in, then whispered, "What's it gonna be?"

Kenny looked at Frank, and back at José. Then he looked longingly around the boisterous crowd as if reminding himself why he wanted to stay out of jail. His eyes returned to José.

"Strickland came to me. Said he wanted to get rid of a car. I didn't like it. I'll sell, but I don't want to get into the disposal business. Too many chickens coming home, you know what I mean."

He paused, and José nodded his encouragement.

"We went back and forth. Finally I told him for a price I'd get him a key to the yard. What he did when I wasn't there, I didn't give a shit, long as it didn't come back to me."

"When was this?" José asked.

"The Sunday before, before the Beamer showed up in the compactor."

"He tell you what kind of car he wanted to get rid of?"

"No. Just he wanted to get rid of a car."

José glanced at Frank with the look that meant, Over to you.

"Kenny," Frank said, "Strickland . . . his Lexus got totaled."

Kenny nodded.

"He put in an order for a replacement?"

Kenny hesitated, then nodded again.

"You filled it yet?"

"No," Kenny said, knowing Frank was going somewhere, he didn't know where, but he knew he was not going to like it.

"What does he want?"

"Asked for another Lexus."

José laughed low and short. "Customer loyalty."

Kenny shrugged. "Long's the price is right."

"S'pose we find you something for Mr. Strickland? Right price?"

Kenny got a guarded look. "You two in the car business, too?"

Frank picked up the check. "We do a little bit of everything, Kenny. Regular Renaissance men."

TWENTY-SIX

AT TEN-THIRTY THE next morning, Frank pulled over to the curb halfway down the block. He and José sat quietly for several minutes, scanning the suburban neighborhood. They had started the search for Angel Alvarez with the Virginia Division of Motor Vehicles. DMV had looked for an Alvarez in the Alexandria zip codes who had registered a 1997 BMW. In minutes, the DMV computers had produced the address of a Raymond Cervantes Alvarez, Jr.

Alvarez Jr., in turn, had a file at the National Crime Information Center. NCIC reported that he had been born in Balboa Heights, Canal Zone, August 14, 1964. His parents, Maria and Raymond, had moved to Alexandria twelve years later. Five years after that, Alvarez Jr. had been found guilty of car theft and gotten two years on probation. The next year, 1982, he'd violated probation with a convenience store burglary, for which he'd gotten four years as an adult offender. He served two years at Petersburg before being paroled. Alvarez's last entry was 1987, cocaine possession, intent to sell. Crucial witnesses for the prosecution had changed their stories and the charges had been dropped.

After they'd reviewed Alvarez's file, it had taken Frank

and José two and a half hours to coordinate with the Alexandria police department and get a search warrant from the district judge.

"Not bad," José said, eyeballing the Alvarez address.

The Los Serranos Apartments perched halfway up Arlington Ridge, above the weekly rentals surrounding Mexican Corner—a way station to the neat single-family homes along the top of the ridge. Fresh paint and neat landscaping, Frank noted. No trash, no cars on blocks in the parking lot. He slipped his hand inside his coat and adjusted his shoulder holster.

"Ready?" he asked José. They got out of the car and started for the building entrance.

Inside the vestibule, José checked the directory and buzzed Alvarez's apartment. The two men waited.

"Zip," said Frank. José pressed the button opposite the plate engraved "Manager."

"Haven't seen him in two, maybe three weeks."

Thelma Tompkins, a heavyset woman wearing a pink cardigan over gray sweatpants, led them down a corridor laced with the faint odors of cooking.

"That usual?" José asked.

Tompkins shook her head. "No. Usually run into him couple a times a week."

"Behind on his rent?"

"No. Always been good about that."

"He with anybody?"

Thelma Tompkins came to a stop in front of a door and began sorting through keys on a large ring. "By himself most times. Had a girlfriend I'd see once in a while. *Did* have," she corrected herself. "She dropped outta sight two, three months ago." She found a key and pushed the door open, did a proprietary sniffing of the air and a look-around of the living room, then turned to Frank and José. "Here you are. Pull the door shut when you leave?"

* * *

THEY STOOD FOR A MOMENT, TAKING IN THE LIVING room.

"Look at *that*," José said under his breath.

A massive Sony dominated the room. Even blank, the huge screen was hypnotic. To the right of the Sony, a Bose sound system was flanked by compact discs stacked on teak shelves behind smoked glass. Similar shelves on the other side of the TV held videocassettes. Leather covered anything you could sit or lie on—a vast sofa, two lounge chairs with hassocks. A garish bar, complete with tinted mirrors and brass rail.

José shook his head in wonder. "Everything but Elvis on black velvet."

"We haven't seen the rest," Frank said, motioning down a short hallway. At the end of the hall he nudged open the first of two doors. "No Elvis."

"Holy shit," José said.

Frank glanced around. "Looks like a storeroom for Sharper Image."

In one corner, boxes of cigars stacked on crates of cognac. In another, a matched set of Callaway Big Bertha golf clubs in a richly hand-tooled leather bag. An English raincoat had been carelessly slung over the handlebars of a sleek racing bike that looked like it'd been machined from a solid block of titanium. A partially unpacked exercise treadmill with a built-in computer that could run the space shuttle. Yet another Bose stereo.

Frank opened a cigar box. Cuban Cohibas. He pressed one with his index finger and shook his head. "Guy spends four, five hundred bucks a box but doesn't know enough to put them in a humidor." He sighed, thinking about the hours of good smoking shot to hell.

The other door led to a bedroom.

"Why am I not surprised?" Frank asked, catching his reflection in the mirrored ceiling.

"No trapeze." José took in the large round bed, a twin of

the monster Sony in the living room, and a videocamera on a tall tripod peering down over the bed.

The night table drawers yielded pretty much what Frank expected—condoms, videocassettes, amyl nitrite poppers, ready-rolled joints, a glass vial of what he was certain was nose candy, and several dozen assorted sex toys, hand-powered and battery-driven. Clues to a personality, but nothing about the person.

Frank examined the videos. There were four: three commercial porn flicks—the *Debbie Does* series—and the other one unmarked. Frank slipped this one into the VCR and punched buttons until the screen blossomed. He sat with José on the edge of the bed to watch.

The scene opened with a pull-back shot of the round bed and a man and a woman fucking. No preamble, no buildup, no foreplay. Not making love. Not having sex. Fucking. They went at it mechanically, as though constantly aware of the bug-eyed camera and the need to keep everything in view.

"Suppose that's the girlfriend," José said. "Look at those tits."

"Twin peaks of silicone valley," Frank said. "Like to get a look at his face."

"Well," José smirked, "I'd recognize his ass anywhere."

As if obliging José, the woman rolled on top.

"There he is," José said.

Frank froze the frame.

The Alvarez on his back was the Alvarez in the mug shots.

"Want to see any more?" Frank asked.

José gave him a bored look. "Doesn't look like they're having much fun."

"Least he's not wearing black socks." Frank shut off the Sony.

José got up and started searching his side of the room. "Always wondered why they did that," he said, opening a large walk-in closet.

"What?" Frank went into the adjoining bathroom, took out several Ziploc evidence bags from his coat pocket, put them on the counter, and began going through the medicine cabinet. "Wear black socks?"

"Yeah," came José's voice from the bedroom. "First skin flick I ever saw had a skinny guy wearing black socks."

The medicine cabinet held the usual—mouthwash, men's cologne, over-the-counter painkillers, a tube of hemorrhoid cream. Frank took a sterile cotton swab from an evidence bag, ran it over the hemorrhoid cream applicator, and sealed it in the bag. "Maybe it was to give them a head start getting dressed and getting out."

"My theory was peer pressure," José said.

An electric razor stood in its recharging cradle. Frank put the razor into another evidence bag and tapped the shaver head. He held the bag up to the light, gave a satisfied nod at the small collection of whiskers, and put the razor back in the cradle. With the bag sealed he returned to the bedroom.

"Peer pressure?" he asked.

"Yeah," José's voice floated out of the closet. "You know, the first guy happened to wear black socks and that sorta set the tone. I wonder if . . ." There was a pause, then, "Oh, yes." José came out of the closet with a file box.

He set it on the chest of drawers and pulled a pocketknife from his trouser pocket. The two blades had been ground to the thickness of a toothpick. Both had an L-shaped hook at the tip. José slipped the larger hook into the file box's built-in lock. It was too big, so he tried the smaller one, worked it around, then pressed the latch and opened the lid.

He and Frank stood side by side, José going into the box one item at a time, reading it, then passing it to Frank to read. Frank saw personal papers as a particular challenge. On the one hand, you might come across something special that would pay off the jackpot. On the other hand, the realization that you had that something special didn't always jump out at you. So Frank sorted the stuff into two piles—one for things he knew right off *were* important, and the other for things that *could* be. He never made a throwaway pile.

The "could be" pile grew: bills, canceled checks, credit card receipts and bills, telephone records. When José gave him a Delta Airlines ID—a plastic card with Alvarez's picture—he saw that it had expired. He started the "important" pile with that.

"Here we are," José announced, handing over an official-looking form.

It was a Virginia motor vehicle title. A 1997 BMW. Four-door. Red. Frank had no doubt that the VIN on the title would match the VIN on the BMW that Kenny Dee had listed earlier as being junked at MacKenzie Salvage.

"Alvarez's passport," José said, passing the blue-covered booklet over.

Frank flipped through the pages. Visa for Colombia. Entry and departure stamps at customs. He laid the passport on top of the BMW title.

"And here's Miss Silicone." José passed Frank an eight-by-ten glossy in a cardboard protective sleeve. Alvarez's partner in the video, posed in a G-string on a photographer's street-corner set, back arched, legs astraddle, crotch nuzzling a lamppost, breasts pointing skyward, long black hair flowing over her shoulders. On the cardboard sleeve, a brush-script logo—"Cheshire's." A goofy cartoon cat leered out of the opening in the C, and a word balloon gave an address in the 1800 block of M Street Northwest.

BUGGY CHRISTOPHER SNIFFED TWICE—TWO QUICK, sharp snuffles that Frank figured had nothing to do with a cold. "That's Crystal." He nodded at the eight-by-ten glossy from Alvarez's file box. "Had a way about her."

"Looks like she had a couple," Frank said.

Buggy's lip curled. "It's not the tits. Anybody can get 'em if they can't grow 'em." He nodded toward the stage, where a weary redhead was grinding for a sparse lunchtime crowd. "I seen Rhonda go from D to E to double E. She can't see her toes for those things now, but she still doesn't do squat for the business the way Crystal did."

"Did?" Frank asked.

Buggy half turned to look at Rhonda, who was now trying to tease a few bills into the top of her G-string. Nobody in her audience seemed interested. "No-showed one day, and never saw her again," Buggy said sadly, shaking his head at Rhonda. "Had a way about her, Crystal did."

"How long ago?"

Buggy thought for a moment. "It was . . . yeah, just after New Year's. Crystal did that night, maybe the night or two after, then . . ." Buggy did a palm-up, palm-down hand roll.

"Where'd she live?"

Buggy got a look like it never occurred to him that strippers lived anywhere. "Around, I guess. They float from guy to guy . . . or gal to gal. Some of them are that way—"

"You paid her?" José asked.

"Yes," Buggy said slowly, knowing it was a hook and there wasn't anything he could do about it.

"Withholding taxes?"

Buggy nodded.

"She pay taxes in the District?"

"I don't remember. That was—"

Frank cupped Buggy's elbow in his hand. "Let's go check. I'm sure a businessman like you keeps good books."

Buggy KEPT SURPRISINGLY GOOD BOOKS. CRYSTAL, known to his bookkeeper as Mary Lou Livingston, claimed D.C. residency and had a valid Social Security number. By two-thirty in the afternoon, the District Office of Tax and Revenue had reported a Corcoran Street address for Livingston. It was just off Dupont Circle, a rambling three-story red-brick rowhouse that had been cut into apartments in the early forties, when single women had flooded the city, coming to work in wartime Washington.

Livingston's apartment was on the third floor. Frank and José stood quietly outside the hallway door. From inside, Frank heard muffled bits of a conversation and the sporadic sound of footsteps. José stepped to one side of the door, while Frank pressed the buzzer beneath a loudspeaker. The conversation continued, but the footsteps stopped. He knocked insistently. He and José exchanged glances.

He was about to knock again, when the loudspeaker sputtered.

"Yes?"

The voice was flat and metallic, and Frank thought it sounded female. He waved his badge in front of the peephole. "Police," he said into the loudspeaker.

The door cracked open with the clanking of a heavy chain lock.

"Yes?" The voice came again, this time direct and this time definitely female. In the background Frank heard the canned laughter of a sitcom rerun.

"Police," he said again, and again held up his badge. "We'd like to talk to Ms. Livingston."

For a long moment, nothing. Frank imagined a pair of eyes searching, considering. The door closed shut. He heard the rattling of chains, and then the door swung open.

The woman of the voice and the eyes wore jeans and a large green Notre Dame sweatshirt, and had short blond hair. Not much like the Crystal in the promo photos, though women became blondes every day and a baggy sweatshirt could hide a lot. Frank glanced past her into the living room, which was filled with cardboard packing boxes. An open can of diet Coke stood beside a roll of brown paper tape on the mantel. A stack of china wrapping paper shared a tabletop with glasses, mugs, and stacks of dishes.

"What do you want?"

The woman's voice was level and controlled, but Frank picked up a faint tension, a quaver of fear.

"Like I said, we want to talk with Mary Lou Livingston." He paused. "You her?"

The woman's lips compressed; then she sighed and shrugged. "Yeah. I'm her. And you want to talk about Angel." She invited them in with a lift of her chin, and locked the door behind them.

She waved toward the sofa. "Push those boxes out of the

way. You want something to drink? I got no booze. Diet Coke?" She held up her can.

"No, thanks," Frank said. "Let me ask you, why do you think we want to talk about Angel?"

Livingston settled into a large armchair. "Because Angel was the only trouble I knew. He was into shit up to his eyeballs."

"Tell us from the start," Frank suggested, "like how you met him?"

Livingston curled her feet beneath her. "Like I met most men—at Cheshire's. Angel came in about a year ago. It was around Valentine's. Good-looking guy, big tipper." She smiled almost innocently. "What wasn't there to like?"

"You said he was in over his head. . . ." José prompted.

"He was skimming," Livingston said matter-of-factly.

"From who?"

"People he worked for."

"Names?"

"No."

"You meet any of his friends?"

"Henry. Henry Brewington."

"When was this?" Frank asked.

"He was with Angel first time he came to the Cheshire. We'd go out together, four of us. Henry knew lots of women."

"How'd he know Angel?"

"They were in prison together."

"Where was this?" Frank asked.

"Didn't ask, didn't want to know."

José asked, "Angel and Brewington worked together?"

"Again, I didn't ask, because I didn't want to know. But I got the impression they were both a small part of something big."

"What gave you that impression?" Frank asked.

"I've been around." Livingston flashed a knowing smile. "I know punks and I know big guys. Angel and Henry weren't punks. But they weren't big guys, either."

"But they had money," Frank said. "Drugs?"

Livingston glanced from Frank to José and back. "I don't think they were stealing out of collection plates."

"But Angel was stealing from Brewington," Frank said. "How'd you know?"

Livingston shut her eyes, then opened them and took a deep breath, psyching herself up.

"One night Angel and me are at his place. We're both flyin' real high. Anyway, he got to talking trash. How he's a big man—all that. I'm pushin' his buttons real hard. Tell him big men don't talk, they show." Livingston's eyes sparkled at the memory of her own bravado. "Angel's really pissed. Goes out, comes back. Carries a suitcase. Opens it. Dumps it all over me. It's cash. 'Half a million,' he says."

She stopped with a wistful smile, rerunning how it felt, rolling in money.

"And then?" said José.

"Oh." Livingston returned to the room full of packing boxes and shabby furniture. "I ask him how he got it. He tells me he and Henry are in business. Then he gets giggly and says, 'This's a little off the top.' "

"Did he say—" Frank began.

Livingston shook her head. "Nothing after that. He zonks out. Cold. He sleeps all night on that cash. The shit happens the next morning when he wakes up."

She paused and did the Frank-to-José-to-Frank bit again. She's scared but enjoying it, Frank thought. A fright high. Like a roller-coaster ride.

"He sees the money," Livingston continued, "and that's where I make my mistake." She paused dramatically. "I tell him what he told me—about the skimming."

"And?"

"He loses it. Goes absolutely batshit. Mad at first. The man's scared. Scared shitless. Curls up in a little ball in all that cash and starts crying. I get dressed and I get out."

"What happened then?"

"I broke it off. Never saw him again."

"Oh?"

"Look," Livingston said. "You didn't see him that morning. He was a basket case. I was there for a good time. Not for that kind of shit."

"When was this?"

"November. First weekend, I think."

"You see him after that?" José asked. "Did he come by the Cheshire?"

Livingston shook her head.

"You heard anything about him?" Frank tried.

"No. Just that Henry ended up dead."

"You have any idea where Angel is?" José asked.

"No." Her voice wobbled. "But I don't feel good about it, wherever it is."

Frank closed his notebook and looked around the room. "You going somewhere?"

"Karma's turning bad here." She ruffled her short hair. "I thought I'd try life over as a blonde."

Frank got up, followed by José. "Good luck," he told her, "but I don't think karma or hair color has a helluva lot to do with it."

TWENTY-SEVEN

BIG JOE'S WAS a two-bay garage next to a Dunkin' Donuts, just off Georgia Avenue. Tires waiting for repair leaned against the office side of the building. A Malcolm Burridge campaign poster hid part of a rusting Quaker State sign. A combative Burridge stood hands on hips, tie loosened, sleeves rolled. Behind him a montage of the White House, the Capitol, and the Washington Monument, all bathed in a golden light. The caption read "Malcolm Fights to Make Washington Work for You." At the bottom, in small print, "Charles Simmons, Campaign Manager." A corner of the poster had come loose and was flapping in a stiff northwest wind.

"Pull up here." Woody pointed to the bay on the left.

He had been waiting for Frank and José when they got back from interviewing Mary Lou Livingston. The car was ready. Did Frank want to look it over?

Woody clicked a remote and the door rolled up. Frank eased the car in, and Woody lowered the door. The three men got out of the car.

In the adjoining bay, floodlights bathed a glistening silver Lexus LS400 sedan. Cables strung from the trunk, the interior, and under the hood ran to a large computer terminal, where a pair of men in white coveralls flicked switches and watched lines squiggle on the monitor. The men looked up as the three men entered. One nodded to Woody, then turned back to the monitor.

Woody led Frank and José to the car. All four doors were open. Frank leaned in on the driver's side and ran a hand over the butter-soft leather upholstery. The odometer showed just over two thousand miles.

"Slinky," Frank said.

"IRS confiscated it off a dealer in Baltimore who was doing business for cash and forgetting to report it," Woody explained.

José pointed to the cables. "This spaghetti go with the car?"

"Some of it, but nobody's gonna see it when we get it all buttoned up."

"When we get it all buttoned up," Frank asked, "what're we going to have?"

Woody looked like a proud parent. "We're gonna have an instantaneous, stereophonic, multimedia extravaganza in full color of everything that happens in and around that car." He pulled on a pair of white cotton evidence gloves before opening the back door wider. He leaned into the passenger compartment and waved a hand to encompass the headliner: "Audio and video pick-ups."

He touched a burled walnut compartment between the front bucket seats. A panel slid noiselessly open to reveal a cell phone. "Bugged."

After lifting the trunk lid, he peeled back the carpet and rapped the floor. "GPS transmitter. We'll know where this car is within forty feet anywhere in the world." Woody looked at his companions, inviting questions. He got none and, with a slightly disappointed air, shut the trunk and moved around to the engine.

"A remote cutoff chip in the computer that controls engine operation. We can bring the car to a screeching stop inside of three seconds."

"Cuts the engine off?" José asked.

"That, and we can also jam on the brakes." Woody tapped the hood. "What we got here, we can do damn near everything with this car except steer it." He gave Frank a conspirator's squinting glance. "Sure you don't want the blue plate special?"

"What's that?"

"We wire a half-pound of plastic to the gas tank. Makes for some nice fireworks if you want."

Frank studied Woody's face. "You're only half kidding."

Woody only half smiled.

"How we doing on Johnny Sam?"

"Got his phones covered. Home in McLean, personal and car cells, office. Put a bug in his office."

Frank motioned to his car. "We're going back to the station."

Woody pointed to where the men in coveralls were unfastening test cables from the car. "I'm gonna stay here," he said. "Make sure we haven't left any telltales in the car."

He stood there, on the edge of saying something, but holding back.

"Anything bothering you, Woody?" Frank asked.

He shook his head a couple of times, then stopped and nodded once. "Ah, yeah." He walked Frank and José a few steps away from the men working on the car. He looked at them, searched their eyes. "I'm assuming, Frank, you guys got the court orders for"—he head-gestured back to the Lexus—"this little deal and the Johnny Sam operation."

Frank looked at Woody long enough to read a splinter of concern in his eyes. Skilled as Woody was, there weren't too many jobs for him on the outside that could pay tuition and medical insurance and let him put something away for retirement. Frank reached out and squeezed his shoulder. "I got it taken care of, Woody. All taken care of."

"WHAT WAS THAT?" JOSÉ ASKED AS FRANK BACKED THE car out of the garage.

"What was what?"

"What you told Woody."

"I don't want Woody's ass in a sling if this all heads south."

"Giving him a way out."

"Yeah."

"Giving me one, too? *I* got it taken care of?" José paused. "*I* got it taken care of," he repeated. "*We* got it taken care of, Frank," he said. "*We.*"

"That how you want it?"

"Never has been any other way."

BACK AT THE STATION, FRANK FOUND A SEALED FORENsics evidence bag in the middle of his desk.

"Tooth Fairy?" José asked as Frank opened the bag.

Inside, a scratch pad in a Ziploc and an interdepartment buck slip from Calkins asking whether this was the tablet Frank had been looking for.

Frank sat at his desk and examined the pad. About four by six inches, gummed binding, cheap unlined white paper. He leafed through it. Blank. Ten, fifteen pages. He angled it under the overhead lights, tilted it back and forth, then reached for the phone and punched in Calkins's direct line.

"Your guys go over this, Renfro?"

"Not yet," Calkins answered. "Wanted you to know we weren't totally fucked up down here. Prints? Fibers?"

"The works. And look at the impressions. . . ."

"Priority?"

"The usual."

"Like yesterday?"

"Isn't that the usual?" Frank said, and hung up.

Frank was rerouting the evidence bag with the scratch pad to Calkins when Tony Upton came in without knocking. Melted snow made tiny pearls down the front of his overcoat. He offered Frank a folder. "DNA analysis from Alvarez's apartment. He's Trunkman."

TWENTY-EIGHT

RAYMOND ALVAREZ'S MOTHER answered the door, a slender, dark-haired woman who looked to be in her mid-fifties. The home, Frank figured, would go for six, seven hundred thousand, easy—a wooded acre on the Potomac a couple of miles north of Mount Vernon.

Maria Alvarez glanced at Frank's badge, and José's. She looked up into Frank's eyes with a steady, direct gaze. "My son's dead, isn't he?" She said it quietly, evenly.

"Yes. Yes, he is."

She continued looking into Frank's eyes. Then she turned. "Come in," she said over her shoulder, and led them into the living room.

"You can see the river," Maria Alvarez said. She stared out the large picture window toward the river. The Potomac was a slate-gray ribbon through the white of snow and the black trunks of trees. "At least in the winter. That's why my husband bought it." She turned, looking slightly startled. As if she had forgotten Frank and José standing there. "Please sit."

She took an upholstered armchair near the window. A side table with a large gooseneck reading lamp stood by the chair. Two books lay on the table, three more on the floor beneath.

Frank waited for her to sit. He noticed scraps of paper marking places in the books. He saw the title only of the top one.

"*Crossing to Safety*," Frank said.

"You've read Stegner?"

"Last I read was *The Spectator Bird*."

"He wrote it a long time ago."

"It has a different meaning. Each time you read it. As you grow older."

She gave Frank a more careful look and pointed to a nearby chair. A less worn twin of hers. José sat down on the sofa facing them.

"Raymond," she said.

"There was an unidentified body. We know now it was Raymond."

"Where was this? When?"

"Three weeks ago. In a salvage yard near Bolling Air Force Base. We found a car—"

"I remember reading . . . Raymond was one of the bodies in the car?"

Frank nodded.

"It was three weeks ago?"

"We had to identify him by DNA, Mrs. Alvarez."

Maria Alvarez searched Frank's face. Behind her eyes he could see she was filling in for herself what it meant that it had taken three weeks to ID her son, and then it had to be by DNA and not by his fingerprints or even his teeth. She finally nodded. "How did it happen?"

"I don't know." Frank waited, then asked, "Please tell us about Raymond."

"Raymond," Maria Alvarez repeated, and looked out the window at the river. Then she turned back to Frank. "We were *zonistas*, Lieutenant. You know what *zonistas* are?"

"Americans who lived in the Panama Canal Zone."

"That and much more. It was a special culture. Our own schools, our own stores, our own churches and theaters. We were a little country. It was a place of . . . of *confidence*. A good place. Generations of us were born and buried in the Zone." She cut a glance at the river. "But we knew it was going away with the treaty. So Raymond . . . my husband, Raymond Senior . . . we decided to come here. We came here. Built this house. And Raymond Junior . . ." Her mouth tightened. "Raymond Junior went to hell with himself."

"We have his record, ma'am," José said.

She finally nodded. "They don't go away, ever, do they . . . our records."

"Last arrest in 'eighty-seven, but the charges were dropped," Frank said. "After that there's nothing."

"His *police* record, you mean. Do you have children, Lieutenant?"

"Yes. Two. Son and a daughter. They're grown now."

"Did they ever cause you trouble?"

Frank wondered why she'd asked this, and what she wanted as an answer. "They were better kids than I was. They got in the usual kid kind of trouble. But nothing like what I did."

"That's not what I asked. I asked if they caused you trouble—*caused*. Getting in trouble is different from causing trouble."

"Oh?"

"There is a difference. It was hard when Raymond went to the prison. But his father and I, we saw it as getting in trouble. The years after the prison, the years your records don't record, those were the years he caused trouble. He brought the trouble home."

"This was 1988?" Frank asked.

"The First Alvarez War." She said the words in a way that capitalized them, and her eyes went flat and bitter. "In stages, Raymond Junior degraded himself. First it was drinking. Then drugs. Sleeping on heating grates. Living in his own filth and the filth of others. Every step along the way he'd show up. To rub our noses in it. He wanted us to see his failures as ours."

"He's got a nice apartment," José said.

"Wars don't last forever. Even family wars. Raymond went through rehabilitation. Two years. It was like he was climbing up the stairs he'd gone down. He and his father started talking again." She shook her head.

"But . . . ?"

"The Second Alvarez War."

"Drugs and booze again?"

"Money. Raymond Junior suddenly began throwing it around. Raymond Senior and I got suspicious."

"Any new friends?"

"Not that I met. But when the fighting started again, Raymond Junior stopped coming around. Before, when he was on drugs, on the street, he'd show up so we could see. This time he stayed away. He didn't want us to see."

"When did the money start showing up?" Frank asked.

"Two years ago. I remember thinking, I shouldn't have hoped so much."

"You mean after the rehab?"

Maria Alvarez nodded.

"Did your son offer any explanation?"

She shook her head. "That's what the fighting was about."

Her face sagged as if the muscles and tendons had been severed. Frank glanced at José, who gave him a barely perceptible head-shake. Frank looked over his notes. He had one question left. "The rehab program," he asked, "where was it?"

"Here," Maria Alvarez replied. "Well, not really *here* in Alexandria, but in Washington. The man who got Raymond to commit himself was a saint." She crossed herself. "Father O'Brien. The one who was killed."

FATHER DASH SKATED THE MOUSE AROUND UNTIL HE found an entry on the spreadsheet.

"Ray Alvarez," he said, his eyes picking over the screen. "Meadows, drug rehabilitation in September 'ninety-three."

"You don't do rehab here?" José asked.

"No. There're others who are better. Father O'Brien always liked the Meadows people." Dash referred to the screen. "Alvarez came back here in early 'ninety-four. Stayed thirteen months. Left here for a job with Delta."

"You mean the airline?"

"Yes. Ground operations at National."

Frank asked, "Did you know him?"

"He'd already left when I got here."

"He ever show up again? Did Father O'Brien ever see him that you know of?"

Dash hesitated.

Was he trying to remember, Frank wondered, or was he thinking about how much to tell?

"He kept up with what he called his 'old boys.' "

Frank nodded.

"It was late July, last year. One evening Father Robert and I were having dinner. Outdoors at a place on the Hill. La Brasserie. On Mass Avenue—"

"I know it," Frank said.

"We were finishing. A car pulls up out front. An expensive German car. Two couples get out. One white, one African-American. Expensive clothes. A lot of gold. On the men as well as the women. They took a table on the other side of the terrace. They didn't notice us. Father Robert said, 'Let's stay awhile.' He was intent on the two couples and didn't say anything at first. Then he told me that the white man was Ray Alvarez and he'd been in our program. I said it looked like he was doing pretty well. Father Robert just shook his head. He was deeply bothered."

"The glitz?" Frank said.

"They . . . Everything about them said drugs." Dash glanced warily at Frank, as if trying to judge whether he thought he was nuts or not. What he saw assured him.

"There's an aura around drug people," the priest continued. "How they dress. How they walk. The arrogant edge. The swagger. Sad thing, Lieutenant, the drugs—it's nothing unusual anymore."

"It's illegal," Frank said.

"You and I both work the streets, Lieutenant. We both know what happens when the law says no but the culture says yes. Drugs are an epidemic. They've infected everybody in this city, one way or another."

"What'd you do?" José asked.

"We had another coffee. Halfway through that, Alvarez got up to go to the men's room inside. Father Robert waited a second or two, then followed him in."

"You waited?"

Dash nodded.

"I sat there. They were both gone some time. After a while, the people at Alvarez's table started looking around. The black man finally got up, and I knew he was going to check on Alvarez. Just then Father Robert comes out. He's flushed. Obviously upset. He tells me he's paid the bill and says let's go. So we go.

"He doesn't say anything else until we're almost back at the Center. He has that absentminded manner he gets when he's thinking. He comes to a stop right in the middle of the block, turns to me, and says, 'I guess when you sign on as shepherd, you have to round up the occasional stray.' I ask him if the man at the restaurant was a stray. He just smiled and said, 'Not for long.' "

"After that?" José asked.

"After that, he pretty much stayed on Alvarez's case. One-on-one counseling. Jawboning. Arm-twisting."

"Did Alvarez move back into the Center?"

"No. Father Robert would meet him here, but he didn't live here."

"Did he—Father O'Brien—tell you about their meetings? What it was that Alvarez was doing?"

"No."

"Didn't you find that unusual?" Frank asked.

"No. Follow-ups are part of the job. Father Robert, our lay volunteers, me—we stayed pretty busy, post-program counseling."

CALKINS CLICKED THE REMOTE. "A BLOW-UP OF THE scratch-pad impressions."

Frank tried to make sense of the picture on the screen, and gave up. "I see why they call it a scratch pad."

Calkins leaned against a lectern. "The anatomy of a scratch pad. You start with, say, thirty pages on a pad. You write on the top sheet. These days most likely with a ball-point pen. The impressions of what you write get passed onto the second sheet."

José frowned. "Yeah?"

"And the third sheet and the fourth sheet as well. The average adult handwriting goes down through fourteen, fifteen sheets of twenty-weight paper."

Frank pointed to the indecipherable tangle on the screen. "The result?"

Calkins nodded. "The pad you gave us was blank. We estimate ten pages had been written on and torn off. What you see are the collected impressions from ten pages of writing—"

"All laid on top of page eleven," Frank said. "There's a way to sort them out?"

"A way to try." Calkins clicked the remote again. The screen swirled and settled.

"You're now looking at page eleven—the top page of the pad—from the edge on. This is a cross section from the middle of the page, where the layers of impressions are most dense."

"Looks like a bunch of potholes," José said.

"Those are the impressions from pages one through ten."

"Deepest ones come from page ten?" Frank asked.

"Give the man an A," Calkins said. "And the most shallow ones are from page one. At least that's what we tell the computer. Then we tell the computer to trace just the heaviest impressions and to give us a picture of that tracing."

Calkins clicked the remote once more. The end-on view of page eleven tilted the paper around so that it lay flat on the screen's imaginary desktop. As if penned by an invisible hand, writing appeared on the upper half of the page.

"Two numbers?" Frank said. "That's it?"

"That's what was on page ten."

Frank copied the numbers in his notebook. 12359 and
0—12359 on one line, the 0 beneath. He looked up at
Calkins. "How accurately did the computer figure these
out?"

"Ninety-seven point four percent accurate."

"Point four makes it sound like real science."

Calkins nodded. "Supposed to."

José asked, "Handwriting?"

"O'Brien's."

"Fingerprints?" Frank asked.

"Yours. O'Brien's. The busboy at the diner who found
the book the pad was in."

"Nobody else?"

"No."

"So O'Brien could have torn off page ten and given it to
somebody?" José asked.

"Or he could have torn it off and torn it up. But whatever, nobody but Frank, O'Brien, and the busboy touched
page eleven."

"Page nine?"

"Still working on that," Calkins said. "The going gets
tougher the further we move toward the top page. There're
fewer impressions, but they get fainter. Harder for the computer to read. Stuff from page nine we might read at
eighty-something percent. Page eight would drop to somewhere in the sixtieth percentile."

Frank looked at the two numbers on the screen. "How
soon?" He got up to leave, José a split second after him.

Calkins shrugged. "We might have page nine tonight
sometime. After that . . . like I say, everything gets pro-
gressively tougher."

"What doesn't?" Frank asked.

"ONE, TWO, THREE, FIVE, NINE," FRANK SAID TO HIMSELF
as he and José walked out of Forensics.

"Coffee?"

"What?"

"Coffee?" José repeated.

"None of that mud here."

"Garrett's. I'll drive."

FRANK WATCHED JOSÉ SPOON SUGAR INTO HIS COFFEE, then half-and-half until it turned a light chocolate. Down at the far end of the bar, Stanley was inventorying stock. Two jocks were nursing drafts and watching soccer reruns on the big screen.

"Connects a lot of dots," José said. "Alvarez gets in on a deal through Brewington. O'Brien puts the squeeze on Alvarez. Who confesses to O'Brien. Then Alvarez gets caught skimming, fingers O'Brien—"

"And they both end up dead," Frank finished.

"Loose ends?"

"What?"

"Like why didn't O'Brien go to the law?"

"Why do you think?" Frank asked.

"You know how Worsham would play it, don't you?"

"The good father as Godfather?"

José leaned back in his chair, raised both hands above his head, and stretched. "We're asking each other questions, Frank. Get back to mine. Why didn't O'Brien go to the law?"

Frank glanced up front again. Stanley was drawing fresh drafts for the two jocks. A car horn blared irritably somewhere out on the street.

"Maybe . . . " Frank began, "maybe he thought he didn't know enough."

"How much would that be?"

"Enough so the people and the system he didn't trust would have to do the right thing."

"And what do we know?"

"Not much more. Probably less."

Both men sat quietly. Down the bar, Stanley was back at his inventory. On the big screen, Italy scored and the two jocks cheered.

"What we know now," José said, "we might be able to catch Strickland with another Samsonite full of cash."

Frank finished his coffee. "We need more than Strickland and another suitcase. What we need," he said as he stood up, "is to draw this out into the open."

José stood, too, and shouldered into his overcoat.

At the bar the two jocks cheered again.

"A little bait?" José asked.

Stanley looked down the bar in their direction, waved good-bye, and returned to his inventory.

"Maybe we got the bait. We just got to figure out how to put him on a hook."

TWENTY-NINE

THE NEXT MORNING, still working out the bait trick, Frank punched his voice-mail button. Halfway through the first message, he realized he hadn't been listening. He cleared his head and replayed the message.

"Here we go," he muttered.

José glanced up.

"Jamie Sutton."

"Jamie? Sutton?" José looked baffled.

"The waiter from Mister Charlie's. He just got a call from Hampton, the guy nosing around O'Brien."

"Yeah?"

"Hampton and Sutton are getting together."

"Oh?"

"Tonight."

Frank forgot about the bait business as he put in a call to Woody in Surveillance.

"WHERE'RE YOU MEETING HIM?" FRANK ASKED.

"Here," Jamie Sutton said. He and Herman Charles stood with Frank, José, and Woody on the balcony over-looking Mister Charlie's bar. The room was already two deep with a happy-hour crowd. "Meet here seven-thirty, then dinner someplace."

"Dinner . . . he didn't say where?" José asked.

"No. Meet here, then . . ." Sutton shrugged. "Just . . . someplace."

"Woody?" Frank said.

"How many entrances?"

"Just the one coming in off Pennsylvania," Herman said. "Fire doors on Eighth and in the alley are alarmed."

Woody made a note on his clipboard. "We'll put a van across the street. Here, we'll have two guys at a back table," he told Frank. Then to Herman: "You put one of our guys behind the bar?"

"He can mix?"

Woody nodded. "With the best."

"What do you want me to do? To say?" Sutton asked eagerly. "Am I going to wear a wire?"

Frank shook his head. He didn't like using civilians. Things went wrong even with professionals. But at least most professionals knew to get out of the way when pretty plans turned to shit.

"No. No wire," Frank told him. "We've got a very limited objective, Jamie," Frank said slowly, making sure he understood. "We just want to talk to this guy. Find out why he's interested in O'Brien. He comes to Mister Charlie's, we take him in for questioning. So what I want you to do is be careful. You're just meeting this guy for drinks, dinner, and . . . whatever. That's what *you* do."

"Okay."

"You still willing to do this?"

"Yes."

"You sure you understand?"

"Sure, sure."

"Something wrong?"

Sutton shrugged again. "Nothing wrong. Just isn't a very big role, is all."

"Look at it this way, Jamie. Tonight's New Haven. Do good here, maybe you get a chance to play New York."

* * *

"SUTTON'S AT THE BAR, WAITING." THE VOICE CAME IN soft and clear over the radio speaker. Reynolds was working the bar, a two-way radio wired to his back, a buttonhole camera in a harness beneath his flowered vest. Frank and José were covering Mister Charlie's from their car, parked across Pennsylvania Avenue. Forty yards away, in the step van, Woody and a cameraman with a long-lens Canon were picking off the customers entering Mister Charlie's.

It was six forty-five. Frank poured a cup of coffee from a Thermos and settled back in his seat to wait.

"EIGHT-FIFTEEN," FRANK MURMURED.

Sprawled in the driver's seat, his head back, his eyes fixed on Mister Charlie's front door, José grunted an acknowledgement.

"Busted play?"

José nodded. "Busted play."

Frank shifted, trying to ease the knot forming in his right buttock. He reached for the Maalox bottle in the glove compartment, shook out a couple of tablets, and chewed them slowly, thinking about busted plays. The toughest thing about a no-show was deciding how long to stay before packing it in.

"Forty-five minutes?" Frank tossed up for grabs.

"Fifteen," José came back. "My ass's killin' me."

Frank was about to offer a compromise of thirty when Reynolds called in.

"Sutton got a phone call from Hampton."

José picked up the mike. "Go? No go?"

"No go here," Reynolds answered. "He called from Metro Center station. Wants Sutton to meet him there."

"Wait one," José turned to Frank "What do you think?"

"Let's check Woody."

Woody, who'd been monitoring the radio conversation, was set up for a meeting in Mister Charlie's. Metro Center was a different game. But if he had to . . .

"Back to us," José told Frank.

Frank gestured for the mike and José handed it over. "Reynolds?"

"Yeah, Frank?"

"Can you put Sutton on?"

"Wait."

Frank was turning over in his mind how he'd lay the situation out, when the loudspeaker clicked and Sutton came on. "Meeting Hampton at Metro Center changes things," Frank began.

"I understand that."

"I want to be sure you do."

"Covering your ass, Lieutenant?" Sutton teased.

"Being sure, Jamie. Being sure." Frank paused. "We can put a tail on you to Metro Center. But we weren't planning on working through a crowd. There's a chance we could lose you."

"So?"

"So it's up to you. We can shut this down or we can improvise."

Silence. Frank and José exchanged looks. "He's gonna take it," Frank said.

"Lieutenant?"

"Yeah, Jamie?"

"If you can't improvise, you shouldn't be onstage." Sutton's voice had a chip-on-the-shoulder tone.

"Meaning you're comfortable with this?"

"Meaning we improvise."

Minutes later, José gestured through the windshield. "There he is."

Sutton stood outside, under Mister Charlie's awning. He glanced across the street toward Frank and José, then headed down the block.

Frank heard Woody radio the foot surveillance team at the back table in Mister Charlie's.

Sutton was halfway to the Metro station when Woody's team, two guys, one white, one black, both in leather jackets, came out of Mister Charlie's and fell in behind him. Frank watched as the three disappeared down the escalator.

* * *

TWENTY MINUTES LATER, WOODY RADIOED IN.

"They lost them. The crowd . . ."

Frank slumped. Woody didn't have to draw any pictures. At Metro Center, you could transfer to the Red Line, taking a train toward Shady Grove or one in the opposite direction to Glenmont. Or you could use the maze of escalators, stairs, and elevators to go topside, where you'd have access to dozens of bars, theaters, restaurants, and hotels.

"We got his apartment covered," José said. "We might as well wait back at the office."

THE INSTANT HE SAT DOWN AT HIS DESK, FRANK FELT very weary. He thought about how many hours, days, months—hell, *years*—he'd spent just waiting. Waiting like the pigeon in a snipe hunt, waiting for something that wasn't going to happen. Or if it did happen, it'd come about in a totally surprising way that later everybody would say should have been foreseen.

Frank looked at his watch again, wondering where Sutton was. It was going to be a long night.

Just before ten, the phone rang.

"I'll get it," José told Frank. He listened for a moment, then hung up. "Sutton," he said. "Obelisk. Dupont Circle."

THE WAITER AT OBELISK HANDED JAMIE SUTTON'S photograph back to Frank. Table eight, the two-top in the corner, had come in just before nine. Two beers—Menebrea—calamari salads, one linguine with white clam sauce, one veal Milanese. A bottle of Castellari. No dessert.

The waiter glanced at his watch. "They left . . . oh, ten minutes ago. Not more than fifteen."

"Any idea where they might have gone from here?"

The waiter shrugged.

"They have coffee after dinner? Drinks?"

The waiter shook his head.

"Who paid?"

The waiter motioned toward the photograph. "His friend."

"Credit card?" Frank asked, without much hope.

The waiter didn't surprise him. "Cash."

FRANK AND JOSÉ STOOD AT THE TOP OF THE STEPS LEADing up from the sidewalk outside the restaurant. Frank surveyed P Street. A neon-lit string of bars, restaurants, hotels, and video stores leading up to Dupont Circle.

"He called in once, maybe he'll try again," José said.

Frank phoned the team watching Sutton's apartment. "Nothing," he told José.

He was putting his phone away, when across the street and halfway down the block, the door of a bar crashed open. Glass exploded into the street, followed by two men locked together, rolling on the sidewalk. More men spilled out of the bar, some running away, others fighting.

José pointed to the two men down on the sidewalk. "Sutton!"

Frank was already on the steps when he heard José's shout. Sutton's assailant, a heavyset man in a red parka, had pulled Sutton to his feet. He appeared unconscious, his arms hanging limp at his sides. The attacker was beating the helpless Sutton, roundhousing great hammering blows to his face.

Frank twisted through the narrow space of two parked cars and dashed into the street toward the bar. A car, turning the corner, caught him in the glare of its headlights. Tires and brakes screeching, the car went into a drifting skid as the driver tried to avoid him.

When the car slipped by, Frank felt a grazing hip-high blow—more of a heavy push than a direct hit. He bounced across the hood of a parked car and tumbled onto the sidewalk. Somewhere behind him, he heard José yelling and sirens wailing.

Frank scrambled to his feet, looking around for Sutton. He heard the noise at the same time he saw Sutton: a cascading, almost slippery sound, like a spilling of silver dollars, as Sutton crashed through the bar's plate-glass window.

Sutton's assailant stood at the window, as if surveying his work. Then, turning to see Frank coming toward him, he took off at a dead run toward Dupont Circle.

José pulled up just as Frank got to the window. Sutton lay crumpled facedown inside the bar, surrounded by large glass splinters and broken furniture.

"I got Sutton," José said, squeezing Frank's shoulder.

Frank hesitated only momentarily, giving José a nod, then started in pursuit. A man twenty years younger with a head start of half a block—you'd run down somebody like that about as often as you'd catch the Easter Bunny. But it was something cops were supposed to do, and you did it.

Word of the fight spread up P Street. Bars emptied onto the sidewalk. Sutton's assailant plowed into a crowd blocking his way. Frank lost sight of the red parka. Then shouts and confusion from inside the crowd, and Frank caught a flash of red on the pavement. The man huddled in a ball, basically getting the crap stomped out of him by a circle of very enthusiastic drunks. Frank stopped running and took his time getting to the red parka.

"YOU'RE LUCKY," FRANK SAID.

"This's luck?" Sutton asked. Thick bandages hid most of his lower face, and the wired jaw made him come down hard on his *s*'s. An oxygen feed snaked into his nose to ease breathing against two broken ribs.

"You could be dead. All that glass around you, you looked like a target in a knife-throwing act."

"How'd it start, the fight?" José asked.

"He went to the john. Left his jacket hanging over his chair. I thought I could sneak a look at his wallet—"

"—and he came back and caught you," Frank said.

"He caught me," Sutton confirmed.

"Didn't we tell you, no Mod Squad shit?" José asked.

"Yeah, yeah." Sutton's eyes rolled to Frank. "You got him?"

"Yeah. New York driver's license says Ronald Hampton."

"Told me Thomas Hampton."

José shook his head. "People you meet in bars . . ."

Frank looked Sutton over. "You going to press charges?"

"I have to?"

"No. We can hold him without. Just makes it easier."

"Bastard broke my face."

"He did a pretty good job," José agreed.

Outside Sutton's room, Frank checked his watch. Almost three A.M. "I suppose we better see to booking him."

He started toward the elevators, but José stopped him with a grip on the shoulder. "That coulda been done already, Frank. Why'd you have them wait for us? Get our ass in a sling, holding without booking."

"We're gonna book, Hoser. I just want to have an informal discussion with Mr. Hampton before."

Frank surveyed the tiny room. The plain wooden table at which he sat had been battered and burn-scarred by countless cigarettes during thousands of interrogations. An empty straight-backed chair faced him across the table. Behind the chair, a sturdy solid door, the only door in the room. To his left, a one-way window filled most of the wall.

The interrogation rooms reflected a rough history of the department, in the way that the rings in a stump tell the story of a tree's life. Changes to the rooms marked the seesaw battles the department had waged with the courts over the years. With each ruling that gave a criminal—an *alleged* criminal—another layer of protection, another rock to hide under, generations of District cops had modified the interrogation rooms in an attempt to keep the home court advantage. If you could no longer work over some obviously guilty bastard with your fists or a rubber hose, you could screw up his head another way. Dimmer lights and darker, more forbidding paint to impart a mood of helplessness and depression. Ceilings dropped and walls brought closer to kindle claustrophobia. Extensive but hidden soundproofing to heighten isolation. Frank looked around the room again and idly wished he hadn't given up smoking. How good a cigarette would taste now.

Because of the soundproofing, he heard nothing from the hall. The door swung open and Ronald Hampton entered, manacled hands in front of him.

"I want my lawyer."

O'Leary, the booking sergeant, removed Hampton's cuffs, then stood behind him.

Hampton was bigger than Frank remembered from the brief encounter on P Street. Six-one, six-two. Two-fifty. Mid-thirties and big-handsome: blue eyes, blond hair cut short and neat, only the slightest hint of a gut.

"I want my lawyer," he repeated.

Frank pointed to the chair. "Sit down . . . we'll talk about it." He said this reasonably, as if Hampton had walked in for a loan, or to plan a vacation.

"I'm not sitting—"

Smoothly O'Leary pushed the chair into the back of Hampton's knees with one hand and with the other pressed down his shoulder. Hampton sat.

"Coffee?" Frank asked, still reasonable.

The legs of Hampton's chair had been shortened. As a refined touch, one leg had been sawed off an inch more than the other three. So, big as he was, not only did Hampton have to look up at Frank, he was distracted by having to keep his balance when the chair shifted with his every movement.

"No. I want my lawyer."

Frank gave Hampton an indulgent smile, then looked up at O'Leary. "Al, a coffee for me and call our guest's lawyer."

O'Leary started to turn.

"Oh . . . Al?"

"Yeah?"

"Take your time."

Frank watched as O'Leary closed the door. He paused, then looked at Hampton.

"Mr. Sutton is at George Washington University trauma center."

"Fucker was trying to lift my wallet."

"Lifting a wallet isn't grounds for homicide."

Hampton's eyes crossed Frank's face in quick, nervous motions. "Homicide?"

"That's what it could be if Sutton dies," Frank said, laying it on heavy. "You shoved him through a plate-glass window, Mr. Hampton. Slivers of glass a foot long . . . needle-sharp . . . we have witnesses."

Hampton took a deep breath and ran his tongue over his lips. He leaned away from Frank. The chair wobbled. Hampton corrected by swaying forward. "I'm not talking until my lawyer gets here."

"Your constitutional right." Frank smiled reassuringly. "You mind if I do?"

"Do?" Hampton asked. "Do what?"

"Talk," Frank said, keeping the smile. "Thanks." Hampton still looked puzzled. "Here's what I have to say, Mr. Hampton. I want you to think about it. Think—that's all I want you to do. If you still don't want to talk after I say my piece, after you think about it, that's up to you. Okay?"

Hampton nodded cautiously.

"Good," Frank said. "Now think about this. If Mr. Sutton dies from his wounds, there could be a wide range of charges against you. Worst could be murder one. No death penalty here in the District, but you'd be up for a long, long time. You might set up house at Lorton—find yourself a young honey to be your girl—but I just don't think you'd have much fun. On the other hand, you could get as light as a suspended sentence."

Frank paused. Hampton's eyes narrowed. He's nosing

the bait, Frank thought. He didn't say anything else, waiting for Hampton to set the hook.

Hampton nibbled. "Suspended sentence?"

"We haven't booked you, Mr. Hampton. Not yet." Frank wanted him to see there was no fine print, no smoke, no mirrors. "And Mr. Sutton hasn't pressed charges—not yet. What I book you for and whether Sutton files charges could have a lot to do with what happens to you." Frank smiled. "Those are just facts of life. I'm sure your lawyer would agree."

Frank sat back and did the body language that spelled relaxed. Then he added the kicker. "And what I want to know has nothing to do with you throwing Mr. Sutton through that window."

Hampton bit. "What do you want?"

Frank smiled again. "I want to talk about a priest." And with his right knee, he pushed the button that signaled José to start the video recorder in the observation room.

HUGH WORSHAM LIVED ONLY TWO BLOCKS AWAY FROM Frank's house on Olive Street. The big difference in real estate, though, Frank figured, was a couple of thousand square feet and about two million bucks. Somewhere in the depths of the massive federal-style house, chimes were ringing, but as he leaned on the doorbell, Frank couldn't hear them. He stayed on the bell. It took almost five minutes, but finally a loudspeaker squawked and a voice Frank recognized as Worsham's demanded to know who the hell was there.

Frank identified himself to the voice.

"It's four-fifteen! What the hell . . ."

"I think you'd prefer to talk here than at your office," Frank said. "Or down at the station."

Silence. Then the sounds of bolts sliding back and chains dropping. And the door opened. Hugh Worsham wore a green flannel shirt over striped pajamas. "This's about?" he asked.

"The murder of Father Robert O'Brien."

Worsham stood back to let Frank in. He followed Worsham down a narrow hallway hung with eighteenth-century flower prints that Frank guessed went for at least two or three thousand each. Worsham turned the lights on in the library and waved Frank to a pair of leather morris chairs facing each other across a Chippendale gaming table.

"Okay, Detective," Worsham said. He took a dark Turkish cigarillo out of a lacquer box and lit it with a gold lighter. Already, Frank was thinking, I've walked by, sat in, and had blown in my face a couple of months' pay. Before taxes. Worsham conspicuously wasn't offering a smoke or a cup of coffee. But then, Frank had to admit, at this hour, he wouldn't, either.

"Okay, Detective," Worsham repeated.

"I've got a proposition."

"Proposition?" Worsham asked. "What the fuck is this? Cops knock on my door at four in the morning? With a *proposition*?"

"I think you'd better listen."

"Is that a threat?"

"No." Frank waited to let Worsham realize there wouldn't be any more than that no.

It took Worsham a second or two. "What is it?"

"Simple." Frank smiled. "You lay off peddling this crap that O'Brien was crooked or gay, or both. In return I'll make sure you get an exclusive when I nail his murderer."

"That's a proposition?" The way Worsham said it, Frank might as well have offered him a case of hemorrhoids. "You don't know how the media works."

"I guess I don't . . . know how the media works, that is. But I do know how you work."

"What do you mean by that?"

"I mean," Frank said, "a New York investigator scumbag named Ronald Hampton."

Worsham opened and shut his mouth, looking like a fish

out of water, then managed, "I don't know what you're talking about."

Frank reached into his coat pocket and pulled out a video cassette. "Mr. Hampton says he works for you. All here in living color, expletives not deleted."

"It's a lie."

Frank put the cassette on the gaming table and pushed it across. Worsham looked at it as if Frank had pulled a gun on him.

"Hampton says he's been digging up dirt for you for years. Who's sleeping around. Who's doing a little nose candy. Who's in the closet. Hampton comes to you. You have one of your dinner parties, you sidle up to your target and subtly or not so subtly let him or her know you got some nasties on them. By the time you're serving coffee and cognac, you've got another source in your pocket who'll tell you what's happening in Cabinet meetings or with the Joint Chiefs of Staff so you'll keep your little secret about them. That sounds like blackmail to me."

"There's no proof," Worsham said.

Frank nodded. "Doesn't have to be, Mr. Worsham. This's the media, remember? You know how that works. I send a copy of this tape to the *National Enquirer.* It bounces off the supermarket news rack to the Internet— maybe the Drudge Report? Then Imus gets a hold of it. Finally, Jennings or one of the other network lips has to air it because after all, everybody's talking about you, and what everybody's talking about—isn't that the news? Isn't that how the media works?"

Worsham wiped the corner of his mouth with the back of his hand. He looked at Frank, then at the cassette lying in front of him on the Chippendale table. "Hampton goes away," he said. "And you get me an exclusive?"

"That's the deal."

"And the tape?"

"You get it when it's over."

"The original?"

"The original."

"How do I know I can trust you?"

"You don't," Frank said.

HALF AN HOUR LATER, STANDING UNDER THE SHOWER, Frank scrubbed himself until his skin reddened. He thought about how he would give Worsham his exclusive.

THIRTY

Kenny Dee shut the driver's door. It made a solid, chunking sound that echoed in the near-empty garage. He stepped back and gave the Lexus a long once-over.

"Nice," he said, still looking at the car.

Frank didn't detect any enthusiasm.

Kenny turned to Frank and José. "Papers?"

Frank handed him a heavy brown envelope.

He opened the envelope and spread the documents on the hood. With the care of a diamond cutter faced with a new stone, he examined the title, then the registration.

"Nice." Real flat.

"Glad you think so," Frank said. "When're you meeting Strickland?"

"Tonight."

"There's a time? A place?"

Kenny mumbled something.

"What'd you say?" José asked.

"Ten-thirty. The Bar Nun."

"Up on U Street?"

Kenny nodded, shifting his feet nervously, looking seasick.

"Something bothering you?" José said.

Kenny nodded toward the Lexus. "This. What's the deal? Why're you giving me this car to give to Strickland?"

"We're not giving it to you to *give* to Strickland," José said. "We're giving it to you to *sell* to Strickland."

"That's the deal, as far as you're concerned," Frank said. "You sell it to him like any other car you've sold."

"I don't like it. I don't like a deal where shit's going on I don't know about."

Frank took a long look at Kenny Dee. "There's deals every day where people don't know all that's going on," he told him. "The basic thing you need to know is, you do this, you're square with Detective Phelps and me. You don't, and we guarantee you, there's things you'd like a lot less."

FRANK BOLTED UPRIGHT IN BED TO THE RATTLING OF windows. The clock said four forty-five. He remembered last night's TV weather report: a Canadian front was supposed to be passing through. He listened to make certain it was the wind, then lay back down and stared into the darkness. He thought about how it'd be with Johnny Sam. And Strickland. What he'd say and how convincing he'd have to be. And about Bouchard and Bouchard's source. And then Emerson, and how Emerson would try to cover his ass. And how, even if it all worked, the fickle finger of fate could still fuck you. Then he thought about all the other times he'd stared into the dark and conjured up disasters and somehow things had turned out okay, maybe not the way they'd been planned, but at least okay enough, and as he did that, he drifted off to sleep again.

"HE JUST LOOKS PISSED, DOESN'T HE?" JOSÉ SMILED.

Frank watched Sanchez and Gabriel guide Johnny Sam over the snow slush in the parking lot. Sam wore an expensive-looking black wool coat. Probably cashmere. And a black fedora and an even blacker scowl.

"Cheesy elegant," Frank said.

The trio disappeared momentarily as they entered the walkway to the medical examiner's offices, then reappeared as Sanchez pushed open the door.

"What the fuck is this, Kearney?" Sam swore as he came through the door.

"A request for information is what it is." Frank kept to the script he'd built during the night. "The police do have a right to ask citizens for information."

Sam shook his head. "I don't mean that. I mean these two goons." He waved a hand at Sanchez and Gabriel. "You wanted to talk to me, you coulda walked in and asked me. You didn't have to send two uniforms and a car to my place, pick me up in the middle a business, and haul my ass down here."

"We couldn't carry two stiffs to your office, Johnny," José said.

Frank motioned to a set of double doors. "We got a couple of guys we want you to look at."

José pushed the doors open, and Sanchez and Gabriel came up from behind. With Frank at his shoulder, the crowd pressure gave Johnny Sam no choice but to go into the dissection suite.

His eyes widened as the implications sank in of the rows of stainless-steel tables and the scales hanging empty and waiting above each. He gave an involuntary gasp, pulling in the thick, sweet odors of formalin and rotting flesh. Frank guessed it was Johnny Sam's first time in a morgue.

Tony Upton stood by the two farthest tables, dressed in black jeans and T-shirt under his white lab coat, looking like Dr. Death himself. The Godcharles brothers had been laid out. Their scalps, which had been pulled over the tops of their skulls, were stitched back into place. But the Y-shaped body incisions remained gaping open, and the whitish ribs in the enormous cavities of their chests made the empty bodies look like two ship hulls under construction.

"We've already cremated the internal organs," Upton said matter-of-factly.

Frank and José closed in on Sam, pressing him nearer to the gutted corpses.

"Jesus," Sam said. His face looked oily and slick.

Upton smiled. "Lucky it isn't summer," he said. "July, August, the AC can't handle it."

"I'm supposed to know these?" Sam asked, his voice tight.

"You don't have to know them, Johnny," Frank said. "Just recognize them. Seen them around?"

"These the guys from the tunnel?"

Frank nodded. "You get around, Johnny."

"I saw their pictures. In the papers. Mayor says a drug war. These guys part of it? They do something more than lift a car?"

"You fishing, Johnny?" José asked.

"José and I figure they were into something for big money," Frank said, "and you're a guy who knows what money's moving in the District."

Sam ignored him. "I don't know these guys from shit." He struggled to get his stomach and voice back.

"Oh? Okay." Frank shrugged. "Sanchez will take you back."

Johnny Sam stared suspiciously at Frank. There had to be more. He did another take. Then, apparently having decided this was indeed all there was, he sneered and made for the double doors and the parking lot, and never looked back. Sanchez and Gabriel followed.

Frank, José, and Upton said nothing until they heard car doors slam and an engine start.

"We do okay, Frank?" Upton asked.

"You get an Oscar for Best Actor, Tony," Frank said. He patted the shoulder of the nearer Godcharles brother. "And you guys get Best Supporting."

Two hours later, Frank stood in front of the Hope Diamond. The great blue-white stone always struck him as a ridiculous exaggeration. Now, it wasn't that it was too much of a good thing. Frank hadn't seen many examples of that. No, the Hope was more like a good thing that you wouldn't turn down, but you knew you'd have a tough time figuring out what to do with all of it. Sort of like Dolly Parton's tits.

"Every time I see it, I wonder how to steal it." The voice came from behind, off his right shoulder.

"Ever figure it out?" Frank asked, his eyes not leaving the diamond.

"It's still there, isn't it?"

Frank turned to a stocky man with a smooth olive complexion and the angle-seeking eyes of a pool hustler.

"Get you away from anything?"

"A miserable-ass budget meeting," Robin Bouchard said. "FBI really means Fuss Budgets International. Good to see you again. Hear our pal Johnny's been putting you guys over the hurdles."

"Got to protect murderers' civil rights."

Bouchard shrugged. "Victims don't need them. Terry Quinn's widow moved to Georgia somewhere?"

"Macon. She and their daughter. Son's at Virginia Tech."

"A shame." Bouchard glanced around. A tour was approaching down a corridor. He gestured toward the Paleolithic exhibit down another corridor. "A damn shame." The two men's footsteps rang hollow on the polished marble floor, and they walked until they were out of earshot of the tour group. "You and José working that drive-by on the priest?"

"It wasn't a drive-by. It was a hit."

"Is that close-hold?"

"Yeah, graveyard. Plus he had over half a million in cash. Stashed in his closet."

"I don't guess he was speculating in cattle futures."

"Lots of money's moving, Robin."

"Dope?"

"Safe bet. Only dope generates that much cash. A guy named Alvarez, a graduate of O'Brien's academy, got him involved. And somebody killed them both for it."

They were in the Dinosaur Hall. A *Tyrannosaurus rex*

loomed over them, with its dinky little forearms and its daggers for teeth. On *T. rex*'s far side, a father pointed out the prehistoric killer and his young son stood transfixed, mouth open. Frank imagined the kid would probably be hearing frightening noises tonight, after the lights were turned out.

"Who's the somebody?" Bouchard asked.

"A guy named Strickland is who we know."

"You don't sound too certain."

"I'm not," Frank said. "We could probably build a case against him now. But if we did, I don't know that it'd lead to who killed the priest."

"Would that be enough for the politicians?"

Frank paused. "Probably. Get the heat off the mayor. Let him declare victory and move on."

"Yeah. Moving on's popular. A good thing. Everybody likes moving on. Anything on the street?"

"Nada. Zip. Zilch."

"So you're thinking about smoking them out."

"Uh-huh."

"And that's why we're here. Not to figure out how to lift the Hope."

Frank nodded. "For a fed, you're very sensitive, Robin."

"It's our training." Bouchard examined a display label, then turned to Frank. "What do you need?"

"You had a snitch with access to Johnny Sam."

Bouchard gave Frank a heavy-lidded look. "I did."

"You still got him?" Frank knew it was a big question.

"Or her," Bouchard tacked on. He didn't say yes, but he didn't say no. "What do you want to do?"

"I want to show Johnny how he can earn a half-million or so. Tax free."

"Meaning you want to dangle him."

"You might say that."

"A scam."

"Sort of."

"Risky. Those things rarely work out according to plan."

"What does?"

"I suppose there're details?"

"There's always details." Frank took Bouchard's elbow and pointed toward the oceanographic exhibit. "Let's go look at some sharks."

On the map, East Potomac Park resembles a swollen appendix hanging down into the river. The Jefferson Memorial anchors the northern end of the park. A half-buried statue, *The Awakening,* holds down the southern tip, which is called Hains Point.

At three-thirty, Frank stood at the railing at Hains Point, looking down the Potomac. The river was a dirty brown, flecked with whitecaps as a north wind cut down the valley. Across the river, planes from Reagan National climbed to altitude and disappeared into the low-lying clouds, their engines jackhammering the thick winter air. At three forty-five, a silver Lexus pulled in next to Frank's car in a nearly empty row of parking spaces thirty or so yards away. Frank recognized the tan felt hat and the Burberry trench coat as Lewis Strickland got out. Strickland walked clumsily over the winter-browned grass. A street man, Frank thought. Real flat-earth kind of guy.

As Strickland came nearer, Frank picked up on the yellow do-rag under the hat. It matched Strickland's tight leather gloves. Despite the gloves, he rubbed his hands together.

"Freeze my ass off out here." Strickland looked past Frank, upriver into the wind, as if searching for a window some fool had left open.

"Fresh air's good for you, Lewis."

"What you want?"

"You said you wanted to know who robbed you. Who took your car."

Frank suddenly had Strickland's full attention.

"Who . . . who were they?"

Frank shrugged and pointed to the pathway along the river. "Let's walk," he said. Strickland fell in beside him.

"You got some names?"

"They were out-of-towners, Lewis. And they're dead.

The name you want, and the name I want, is who they were working for."

"Well, who's that?"

"I thought you might know. Have some idea."

"Why'd I know?"

"You can do better than that."

"What the fuck do you mean?"

"Figure it my way," Frank said. "A couple of goons come to town because somebody's paying them. I figure they're getting paid to do more than boost a car. That's kid shit."

"I don't understand."

"Sure you do, Lewis. I think those guys got more than a car. They were trying to muscle in on something, and you're in that same something. Up to your ass in it."

"I'm not part a nothing."

Frank sighed. "You're just a guy making a buck selling records."

"That's me."

"Well, whoever hired those two goons still has you in his sights. Word is he's making another run on you."

Strickland got a sly, inquisitive look. "Word on the street's you been hassling Johnny Sam. He have something to do with this?"

Frank frowned and shook his head. "Lewis, the police don't hassle citizens. And our business with Mr. Sam is between Mr. Sam and us."

Frank stopped walking. Strickland stopped, too, and turned to face him. "You got something on tap for Monday night?"

Strickland sneered. "Where *do* you hear that shit?"

"That'd be telling. And why should you worry? You don't need my help. You're not part a nothin'. . . . You're just making a buck sellin' records." Frank paused a beat, then turned back toward his car.

Strickland caught up with him. Most of the way, neither spoke. When they had almost reached the parking area, Strickland said, "You know how this town is. You can get in the way of something without knowing it."

At his car, Frank unlocked his door and opened it before speaking. "Yeah, that's the way this town is, all right. You can get in the way of something just like that." He snapped his fingers and smiled pleasantly. "Good-bye, Lewis." Frank got in and started to close his door.

Strickland held on to the door. "That's it?"

"Yeah, that's it. I've done everything I can do," Frank said. "You want to do something, you know how to reach me."

EMERSON WAS WEARING HIS SUIT COAT. "YOU TWO PUT me in a box," he said. He sat behind his glass-topped desk, hands in his lap, shoulders narrowed forward, elbows tight into the waist.

"How's that, Randolph?" Frank asked.

"You get things moving, then you"—Emerson pointed an accusatory finger at Frank, then at José—"then you tell me, when it's too late to do anything about it."

José managed to look offended and uncomprehending at the same time. "I don't know what you mean, Randolph."

"The hell you don't," Emerson said in a near-whisper. He tilted forward, and both hands came up to grasp the edge of the desk. He swung his head from José to Frank. "Let me review. Correct me if I'm wrong. Or if I leave anything out."

Frank nodded and tried a little smile to work the needle a bit further into Emerson.

"What we have here," Emerson began, "is a hypothetical operation that deals in large amounts of money. Probably related to drugs—but that's yet another supposition. And we have this suspect, Strickland, who's alleged to be part of your hypothetical operation—"

"He *is* part," Frank put in.

Emerson sighed. "You *say* he's part. You don't have any evidence, Frank. Evidence is something that somehow you and Phelps here believe is below you. You two are legends. You two are above grubbing around for evidence."

"Shit!" José exploded. He sprang to his feet. "Half a million in the trunk of his car . . . that's not evidence?"

"Sit down!" Emerson's voice cracked. His knuckles whitened as he tightened his grip on the desk.

José shot a glance at Frank, who gave him a barely perceptible nod. José continued standing, glowering at Emerson, then sat.

"The dumbest public defender would cut our legs out from under us," Emerson said, more confident of his ground. "There's no proof Strickland had possession of that money. The people who did have possession, you two shot."

"Let's get on with it, Randolph," Frank said.

"Okay. Now Strickland may . . . or may not . . . believe Johnny Sam is out to muscle in on this operation . . . this hypothetical operation . . . right?"

Frank nodded.

"And Johnny Sam may . . . or may not . . . believe he can make a few bucks knocking over a deal involving Strickland . . . right?"

"Yeah," Frank said, getting very tired of Randolph Emerson.

Emerson put on a thank-you smile, tilting his head ever so slightly. "So what we have," he gloated, "*all* we have, is a couple of maybes. It only works out if this hypothetical organization sets up a trap and if Johnny Sam walks into it."

"Good for you, Randolph. I knew you'd get it." José leaned heavy on the sarcasm.

"I don't like it."

"What's not to like?" Frank asked.

Emerson pulled his elbows in closer to his sides. "There're too many uncertainties."

"There's always uncertainties. But if Strickland and Johnny don't play it out, nothing happens."

"Nobody's embarrassed," José added, heavy again with the sarcasm.

Emerson shook his head. "But if they *do* play it out . . . we don't know how or where . . . it could get messy."

"Yeah, it could," Frank admitted.

"This's nothing but a scam," Emerson said. "Something goes wrong, we could be accused of setting this whole thing up."

Frank put on an incredulous look. "So we're not supposed to scam these rats? We should sit on our hands because something *might* go haywire? That what you're saying, Randolph?"

Emerson sat without saying anything, just holding on to the edge of the desk. Then he tilted his chin up and leaned back in his chair, and skated his fingertips across the glass desktop.

"We're going ahead with this, Kearney. But the slightest screwup, and the next sound you hear will be the two of you being flushed down the shitter."

FRANK WAS GETTING READY TO MEET ROBIN BOUCHARD when Calkins phoned.

"I'm sending page nine up to you."

Frank took a second to connect. "What's on it?" He picked up a pencil and held it poised over a pad.

"Looks like the word 'onion,' three indistinguishable characters, and the numbers eight, three, three, zero," Calkins said.

"Onion?"

"Maybe we got the priest's shopping list?"

"Could the three characters also be numbers? Could we have a phone number with the last four eight, three, three, zero?"

"Could be."

"Could you check it out?"

Silence. "Frank," Calkins protested, "you can't be serious. Eight, three, three, zero—any four numbers—is bound to be part of *somebody's* telephone number . . . hell, a whole bunch of somebodies' numbers. Lot of phones in the world."

"Let's start with the District."

"Just the District?"

"That first, then the metro area. And don't forget cell phones."

"Oh shit, Frank. Okay."

Frank hung up and sat staring at his own scratch pad,

trying to make sense of it. "Onion, onion, onion." After a few moments he gave up. He tore the page off the pad, put it in his shirt pocket, and went out to meet Bouchard.

"There he is." Bouchard nodded toward the corner of Fourteenth and Pennsylvania as he edged into the curbside lane.

In the flashes of passing car headlights Frank saw a dark figure standing at the curb ahead.

"He's going to be antsy," Bouchard said.

"He's got a right," Frank said.

As Bouchard drew closer, Frank saw that the man wore a heavy ski jacket and a knit watch cap. Bouchard flicked the high beams three times and pulled up to the curb so the man could easily reach out and open the back door. Which he did.

"Who the fuck is this?" The voice behind Frank rasped, carrying with it the growl of a New York City cabdriver.

"Get in," Bouchard said.

Frank heard the door slam, and Bouchard pulled back out into traffic.

For several blocks, no one spoke.

When Bouchard turned right onto Independence, Backseat Guy sounded off again. "Who the fuck is this?"

"He and I work together," Bouchard explained. Then he added, "We go back a long way."

"I don't care who you are or what you look like," Frank said, keeping his eyes fixed on the traffic ahead.

The silence seemed to soften, and Bouchard asked, "What's going on?"

"He bought it."

"What's next?"

"It's tomorrow night. Nine-thirty."

"Where?"

"Simple City."

Frank edged in carefully. "Pretty big place."

"Buyer . . . this Strickland punk . . . and the dealer . . . one of the cartel guys . . . agree on a meet time. Place . . .

Dealer calls Strickland half-hour before. Strickland gives the dealer the address. Johnny thinks it's gonna be in the projects."

"Sounds like Johnny's got somebody inside," Frank said.

"I don't know. I don't ask. But Johnny wouldn't be in business if he didn't have ways."

"Yeah, Johnny's got ways. How's it going to happen?"

"There's four a them," Backseat said. "Strickland an' his gun, the Colombian an' his gun. We're going in with eight."

"Artillery?" Bouchard asked.

"Two shotguns, couple of Uzis, AK's."

"Backup?"

"War wagon an' a garbage truck."

"A . . . garbage truck?" This struck Frank as comical. Something out of a Jimmy Breslin column. "For picking up what's left?"

"Don't know. Didn't ask." Backseat sounded offended. "Johnny says garbage truck, there's gonna be a garbage truck."

They were now passing beneath the Memorial Bridge in sparse traffic.

"That's all I got," Backseat said. "Anywhere here's good."

Bouchard pulled over. Before the car had fully stopped, Backseat was out and taking the Watergate steps two at a time. Frank watched him disappear.

"Wheels starting to turn." Frank's eyes were fixed on the emptiness at the top of the steps.

"Yeah," said Bouchard, "but what is it? Does Johnny have the drop on Strickland? Or is Strickland setting Johnny up?"

Frank looked at him. "Tomorrow night, we'll know."

THIRTY-ONE

"FRANK, YOU'RE ONE evil-looking fucker."

Frank glanced down. Scuffed combat boots, loose-fitting black fatigues, and Kevlar vest with pockets for a radio, a first aid pouch, and extra magazines for his stubby assault rifle. José's variation on the theme included the ten-gauge riot gun and bandoliers of shot shells crisscrossing his chest.

"And you look like a regular Captain Hook."

Frank glanced across the cavernous garage. Groups of cops similarly dressed in combat gear bantered in the adrenaline-drenched atmosphere. Pregame locker room high. Lungs sucking in oxygen reserves. Electricity playing over the skin.

"How you feeling?"

"Kate and I went to mass tonight."

José didn't look surprised, didn't raise an eyebrow.

"Confession?"

"No. Just candles. Lit one for O'Brien. One for Terry Quinn."

"What'd you pray?"

"That it works out right," Frank said. He was struck, looking around the garage, by how young the cops were.

José followed Frank's eyes. "They know why they're

here. They wouldn't want to be anyplace else. You tell them to go home now, they'd be pissed off."

Frank kept looking at the young cops. "It's like slop-shooting in pool," he said, watching the shucking and jiving. "You can't figure all the angles, so you shoot hard. Get all the balls rolling. Hope you drop a couple of the right ones."

As if on a silent signal, the two SWAT teams stopped the grab-assing and began loading into their war wagons. The uniform cops paired off to their cars. The back door of the nearby step van swung open. Woody leaned out.

"All aboard."

THE VAN BORE THE FADED LOGO OF A TWENTY-FOUR-hour plumbing service. Two coveralled cops in the front took care of driving and security, while the back was Woody's: radios, computers, video screens, and racks of black boxes. Two screens covered the scenery outside the van. Another showed a street map of the District.

Within the van, the tingling odor of ozone flashed through intermingled layers of oil and grease smells, exhaust fumes, and the indelible essence of feeding Surveillance—leftovers from countless burgers and fries, and pop-top cans of chili and beef stew eaten cold with plastic spoons while they waited and watched.

"That's us," Woody said. A winking blue light showed up on the video map of southeast Washington near Eads and Fiftieth. Out of mainstream, but close enough to get anywhere in Simple City within a couple of minutes. "Red light is Strickland." The red shone steadily, a few miles away across the Anacostia River. "Or rather, it's the Lexus. He's had it parked there all day." The three men sat back to wait.

Frank looked at the digital clock. 20:55:34.2.

"Hope he uses the Lexus." José said to nobody in particular.

Frank didn't feel like talking. A thin sheen of perspiration on José's and Woody's faces glowed in the light of the video screens, and Frank knew they could see him sweating, too. The clock now said 20:56:47.8.

"I fucking hate fucking waiting," José ranted. Again to nobody in particular.

A mousy chirp from the electronics. Woody pressed his fingertips to his earphone.

"Strickland's getting a phone call."

"Trace?" Frank asked.

Woody shook his head. "Lasted just a few seconds— wait—now he's making a call." The computer screen flipped over several times. "To a pay phone. A 7-Eleven in Anacostia."

"Meet's on." José's voice was husky with anticipation.

"Anything on Johnny Sam?" Frank said.

"No."

The waiting started again. 21:02:47.7. Time froze. A lifetime later, it was 21:03:19.6. Frank listened to his heart, and watched a bead of perspiration gather on José's temple. The sweat finally achieved critical mass and rolled down his cheek.

José swung his head wearily from side to side. "Fucking waiting."

Another electronic chirp. Woody pushed a button, acknowledged the call, then listened.

He turned and gave Frank and José a thumbs up. "Johnny Sam's on the move." He listened more. "Johnny's blue Caddy, a white 'seventy-four Lincoln four-door, a black Bronco —"

"Regular convoy," José muttered.

"—garbage truck." Woody paused to get clear what he was hearing.

Frank watched a yellow light blink on the video street map. "Coming down Benning Road." Bouchard's snitch was right about the garbage truck, but he'd missed the Bronco. A mistake, or an omen for disaster? The red light that was Strickland's Lexus blinked and started moving. The digital clock said 21:04:02.8.

"Both headed for Simple City," José said.

"Where'll they meet, Woody?" asked Frank.

Woody's hand flicked across the keyboard. Luminous lines shot out from the blinking lights, intersected.

José leaned close to the video map and traced the streets with his index finger. The finger stopped. He tapped the screen. "Forty-fifth, Forty-sixth. The projects."

FIVE MINUTES LATER, THE POLICE VAN DROVE SLOWLY down Forty-fifth toward Blaine. A solitary mercury-vapor streetlamp highlighted hulks of abandoned cars and a five-story brick building that ran the length of the block.

"Condemned," Frank said, hunching close to the video screen, studying the building.

Graffiti outshouted the housing authority's No Trespassing signs. Thieves, vandals, and addicts had cut holes in the chain-link fence. Smashed windows and dark doorways stood open where plywood panels had been ripped away.

"Can't say Strickland goes for the high-rent district," José said.

"Woody," Frank asked, "can you get the floor plan?"

Woody was already on the phone to the District operations center. On the street map, Strickland's red light rounded the corner of Forty-fifth. Frank and José watched the Lexus appear on one of the video screens, its headlights approaching the van. The lights flared in the hidden camera lens and Frank felt the van rock as the car passed. It reappeared as the other camera picked it up, and slowed and parked in front of the condemned building.

"It's Strickland and some other guy." José watched the men get out.

Strickland, complete with Great White Hunter hat and Burberry trench coat, took a long, unhurried look up and down the street, then made for a darkened doorway, his back watcher a few paces behind.

"Gunner's carrying a long piece," José said. "Right side, under his coat. See the way he's got his shoulder hunched."

Frank was thinking about the next ten, twenty minutes. With Strickland setting the place for the meet only a half-hour before, Johnny'd have to go with your basic smash-

and-grab. Go in front and back, kill Strickland and his gunner. Grab the cash. Haul ass. The money was the draw. If Johnny could bag the Colombian and his gun and take the drugs, too, so much the better. In, out. Five minutes max, Johnny'd be thinking.

But if Strickland played his cards right, he would slam the trap shut once Johnny got inside. Several hours before, Strickland would have had his troops scattered through the building, left there to wait quietly. Intending to catch Johnny Sam and his soldiers on a stairwell or landing.

"Where's SWAT?" Frank asked.

Woody clicked his mouse and a blue oval materialized over the Potomac between the Memorial and Fourteenth Street bridges. "Chopper's here," he said. Another mouse click and two stationary lights blinked a block away. "The war wagons."

"And here's Johnny," José said in an Ed McMahon voice. He tapped the video map and the blinking yellow light. "Right around the corner." Suddenly Woody was busy, rogering calls from the uniform cars.

Now video was picking up Johnny Sam's convoy speeding down Blaine: Johnny's Caddy, the Lincoln, and the Bronco. And a garbage truck.

Frank touched Woody's shoulder. "Start bringing in the SWAT war wagons. Make sure they don't spook Johnny."

"Call in the chopper?"

"Not now. Not yet."

On the screen, Johnny Sam's Caddy and the Lincoln were pulling over to the curb. The garbage truck continued on, then turned the corner, followed by the Bronco.

"Going in the back." José whispered as if he were watching through a keyhole. Doors on Johnny Sam's car and the Lincoln swung open. "Four . . . six guys going up the front stairs."

Frank squeezed Woody's shoulder. "Okay, bring them in, war wagons, uniform cars. And the chopper."

He checked his radio and jacked a round into the chamber of his assault rifle. When he looked at José, he didn't have to ask. José worked the pump action of his riot gun and nodded. Frank unlatched the back door of the van and stepped out into the street.

The first shots came from inside the tenement just as the war wagons were pulling up. Another round of gunfire, and uniform cars had filled in between the SWAT vehicles. Floodlights were flicking on and playing across the scarred front of the building. More uniform cars arrived farther down Blaine and down Forty-fifth as the gunfire in the building swelled, a rattling crescendo.

"Must be really shooting the shit outta each other," José said. His eyes were fixed on the flashes from inside the building, and he was smiling excitedly like a kid on the Fourth of July.

Frank tried to imagine what was going on inside. From the sound of the shooting, he thought Strickland had sprung his trap but Johnny wasn't about to roll over. "Well," Frank said, "I guess every good thing has to come to an end." He raised the bullhorn and gave the orders to stop shooting and come out. Gunfire increased inside the building. The windshield of a uniform car disintegrated and several tires exploded with a gusting blast. From behind their cars, the police opened fire.

Frank switched on his radio and gave the order to prepare for tear gas. Around the cordon, tear gas gunners picked out windows and doors for targets.

He was about to give the command to fire when a thin scream slipped through a lull in the gunfire. At the same time, he caught a movement at a fifth-floor window.

"Cease firing," Frank called into the bullhorn. "Cease firing."

José, with his back to the building, was talking with Dayhuff, the SWAT commander. He turned to Frank in surprise.

"People up there." Frank pointed to the upper floors. Leaning from a window, a woman screamed and waved a cloth. Other people appeared at other windows, more waving, more screaming.

"What the hell?" said José.

"Squatters." Again Frank went to the bullhorn and called to cease fire.

Without warning, the air around the building shuddered, lashed by a hollow thrashing roar that drowned out Frank's bullhorn.

He caught the flash of the SWAT helicopter coming in at treetop level.

"Dropping gas," a flat metallic voice announced over the radio.

"No!" Frank managed.

Even as he said this, a large shape separated from the helicopter. Glittering in its fall through the crisscrossing floodlight, the tear gas bomb traced a short arc to the tenement roof. There was a large crash as shingles and lumber flew.

"Went through the roof," said José.

A fraction of a second later, the dispersing charge in the bomb exploded. Plywood panels over windows blew out while clouds of tear gas drove through the upper floors.

The sounds of shooting intensified inside the building. More uniform cars were now taking hits.

"Fire!" someone shouted.

Frank saw it too: flames tonguing through top-floor windows.

Dayhuff's radio squawked. He turned to Frank. "Public Works says three, four families been squatting there."

Frank saw the flames gaining headway. "We're going in."

Dayhuff grinned. "That's our job. One team up front here. The other'll be coming in the back."

Frank glanced overhead. The helicopter that had screwed this all up was making another run. He was tempted to cut loose with a few rounds at the stupid bastards. "I'm going with you," he told Dayhuff.

"We both are," said José.

Dayhuff was busy on his radio. Getting his people together. He shrugged. "No skin off my ass. Just don't get in our way."

Frank smiled at the younger man. "I'll try not to," he said.

FRANK HEARD DAYHUFF'S WHISTLE SIGNAL THE ASSAULT. It seemed to him that he was frozen in place, crouching behind the safety of the van. Then he was out in the middle of the street, running hard. Cops behind him were spraying the lower floors of the building, the bullets snapping and whining around him. The street was a thousand miles wide. He was running as fast as he could, but felt he was standing still and every gun in the tenement was lining up on him.

He was in the alcove of the main stairwell. Only two men from the SWAT team were ahead of him.

Dayhuff ran up, squeezed in beside him. "You run pretty good for a Homicide dick."

"Getting shot at helps my time." Frank looked around for José but didn't see him. He figured he'd gone on into the building with the rest of the SWAT team.

He peered down the darkened hallway. Great jagged holes through the walls created a twisting warren between apartments. Gangs, crack pushers, and vagrants had stripped doors, plumbing, wiring, anything that could be sold, traded, or used elsewhere. All that was left was graffiti, trash, and the stench of urine and feces, now joined by smoke and the first tickling hints of tear gas.

Dayhuff dashed into the stairwell and flattened himself against the wall by the entry to an apartment. Frank followed, taking up a position on the other side. He'd intended to stay with José. Assumed they'd be together. But in the way that combat rolls the dice, he and Dayhuff had ended up together, and that was how it'd work until they wrapped up the operation.

At a crouch, Dayhuff spun into the living room of the apartment. Frank covered his left flank. The room was dim, light coming through holes in the wall and splintered gaps in the plywood over the windows. The room was empty. Frank heard his own breathing, hard and rasping, and Dayhuff's breathing, too. And he realized that the sustained roar of gunfire had tapered off to an occasional shot or short burst. He could hear the sirens of fire engines somewhere in the distance.

From the shooting and the shouts, Frank guessed Dayhuff's guys were working up the stairwell. Standard operating procedure said you cleared each room before you moved on. You did that to keep from getting back-shot by somebody you'd bypassed. SOP also said you cleared buildings from the top down, but the idiots in the helicopter had foreclosed that option by setting the building on fire.

He and Dayhuff were moving toward the bedrooms when two quick-snapping pistol shots, and then the heavy crumping roar of José's riot gun, sounded behind them.

"What the hell?" said Dayhuff.

"Hoser . . . in the hall."

Frank was almost at the door when a third pistol shot rang out.

He ran through the doorway.

Dark hall . . . empty. Stairwell . . . José sprawled on the landing, struggling to get up.

Johnny Sam stood on the next landing, his mouth stretched in a crazy silent laugh as he swung his pistol toward José.

And Frank saw Terry Quinn looking up the instant before dying in the garage.

He also saw a shimmering red light from the stairway above—a pinpoint—that touched Johnny Sam's head.

Johnny's head jerked. For an instant, Frank thought he had sneezed.

The crazy silent laugh stayed on Johnny's face as he fell.

José struggled into a sitting position.

"My shoulder."

Frank found the bullet hole in José's fatigues and ripped his shirt open. He pulled the battle bandage out of José's vest pocket, and José grabbed it.

"I can take care of this," José said. He motioned up the stairs with his free hand. "He's . . . going for the roof."

Frank heard the sounds of footsteps scrambling up the stairs. He hesitated. José wasn't bleeding heavily, and now Dayhuff was there, helping him with the bandage.

Running up the stairs, Frank passed Johnny Sam. He lay facedown in the filth of the third-floor landing, dribbling dark blood from his temple. As he kicked Johnny's nickel-plated Beretta down the steps, Frank thought about pumping a few rounds into Johnny. Just to make sure. By the time he finished the thought, he was already on the next flight of stairs.

Squatters shoved their way down the narrow staircase. Crying, screaming. Mostly men, a few women, one little girl. Plastic garbage bags of possessions slung over shoulders, clutched to breasts. Frank fought upward against battering waves of feet, knees, and elbows.

Behind him, down below, two shots. Then a single shot. Men shouting.

As if an invisible hand had turned a switch to Stop, the squatters froze.

A sudden downdraft carried a choking cloud of smoke and tear gas from above.

The collective brain weighed its choices: Uncertainty below? Certainty above? The hand turned the switch back to Action. Voices roared and the squatters surged down the stairs in a renewed frenzy.

At the fourth-floor landing, Frank was alone. He took the steps two at a time toward the fifth floor. Smoke and tear gas tore at his lungs and eyes. He thought about the gas mask in its carrier under his left arm, and then he thought about the time he'd lose putting it on.

Coming off the fifth-floor landing, Frank ran down the hallway at a low crouch to avoid the thickest smoke. Ahead, he heard a racking cough, then the sound of splintering wood. Several yards down the hall, a door hung off one hinge. Through the doorway, a short hall, and at the end of it metal rungs set in a concrete wall. The ladder led to an open trap door through which Frank saw the winter sky.

He scrambled up and tumbled out onto the roof. He lay belly down, lungs pulling at the fresh air. On his left, flames from inside the building licked at the crater made by the tear gas bomb. To his right, the floodlights from the street below cast a deep shadow over the rooftop. In the shadow, even darker shadows, a maze of chimneys, ventilator shafts, and wrecking-crew junk. And the grating sound of feet moving across gravel.

Running at a low crouch, Frank covered the ten or so yards to a ventilator. He strained to listen, to hear over the blood roaring in his ears. Again, the slight crunching of gravel. This time ahead, to his right. From two large brick chimneys, twenty, maybe twenty-five feet away.

He had made it halfway to the chimneys when fireworks exploded behind his eyes. At the same time, a hammer blow in the center of his chest. Through a silver rain of dying fireworks, a searching eye, a ruby-bright spot fluttered, wavered, and turned toward him. Falling, he swung his assault rifle toward the light and held the trigger down until the magazine emptied.

Overhead, a beating of rotor blades as the SWAT chopper made a low pass, its xenon floodlights scorching the rooftop in a sunburst of brilliance. Frank raised his head and saw a dark form crumpled at the base of a chimney.

The pistol lay a foot or two from where the man had fallen. A Colt Woodsman .22 with a laser sight. Frank went and knelt beside the man.

"Hello, Frank."

"Solly." Jarvis's breathing was ragged, and flecks of foamy blood gathered on his lips. Frank loosened his shirt to search for the lung wound.

"Knew you were wearing a vest, Frank. Coulda made it a head shot."

"I know, Solly. Take it easy."

Frank reached for his radio.

"Don't bother."

Frank called for medics on the roof, then turned to Jarvis. "Thanks for taking care of Hoser, Solly."

"You shoulda done Johnny Sam a long time ago."

"You did the priest, didn't you, Solly?"

"He knew too much. And he was gonna know more."

"Never thought you'd be running drugs."

"Didn't. Wasn't." Jarvis's voice was now a whisper, and Frank had to bend close to make out the words.

"The money, Solly, what was it for?"

"Wasn't selling," Jarvis said. He coughed up heavy, blood-laced phlegm. "Just banking. O'Brien was going to shut us down."

"Us? Who's us?"

Jarvis's eyes clouded as he looked past Frank. "Umbrellas," he said. "Fucking umbrellas." And he died.

FRANK STOOD AT THE OPEN END OF THE AMBULANCE. THE DCFD was putting out the tenement fire. Cops clustered nearby, drinking coffee and talking, the postmortem on the field before heading back to the locker room. They had all gone into the same building. But each had done something different, seen something different. These were things to talk about. Talk about now, talk about later, talk about forever. Each telling would be different, the now-telling the most basic. The closest to some of the most important things that might never be talked about again.

"Solly Jarvis." José, sat on the hood of a car, getting seen to by a medic.

Attendants wheeled a gurney by. José glanced down at the wounded man, heavily bandaged and with an IV drip started. "Get well soon, Lewis," he said.

Frank watched as they loaded Strickland into the ambulance. "Wasn't buying or selling," he said, thinking about Solly Jarvis. "Just running the laundry."

Twenty yards away, the SWAT helicopter hovered several feet off the ground, blowing trash over everybody. TV klieg lights glinted off the Plexiglas canopy. The chopper landed and cut its engines. While the rotor blades were still windmilling, a figure in combat gear jumped from the aircraft and strode toward the waiting cameras. Actually, *strutted* toward the cameras.

"John Wayne," said José.

"Audie Murphy," Frank came back. "H. Norman Schwarzkopf, Junior. Look at that." He got a big grin, in awe of the audacity of it.

"Randolph Bomber Emerson," José said in wonder.

"That's why they didn't land until the shooting was over," Frank said.

It would be an interview for network coverage. And the guy with the microphone was, of course, Hugh Worsham. From another direction, a tall figure stepped out of a limousine and walked to join Randolph Emerson.

"And Malcolm Burridge," said José.

Frank smiled. He was enjoying himself. "Fighting to make Washington work for me."

WHAT WITH CLEANUP AND FILING INITIAL AFTER-ACTION reports, Frank didn't get home until past two. Waiting on his machine was a message.

"We got a phone number and address you might be interested in," said Renfro Calkins from Forensics.

THIRTY-TWO

THE ADDRESS THAT Calkins had traced to the phone
number on O'Brien's scratch pad was a walkup in
Friendship Heights. The name on the mailbox in the lobby
was Hunter Elliott. Frank heard faint strains of music
through the scarred metal door of the apartment. He
knocked and waited.

The door opened to a room crammed with computer
screens.

Frank recognized the music. It was Handel's *Music for
the Royal Fireworks*. And he recognized the young man
who stood in the door. Tall, skinny, ponytail. Bottle-bottom
glasses. For once a good match to an identikit drawing.

"Hello, Kid," Frank said.

WHEN HE OPENED HIS OFFICE DOOR, A MONTH TO THE
day after the O'Brien murder, the first thing Charles Simmons saw was Frank Kearney looking out the window, sipping coffee from a foam cup.

"Janitor let me in, Mr. Simmons."

Simmons stared at Frank. "Why?"

"I asked him."

"No. Why are you here?"

"To tell you a story."

Simmons did a double take, then frowned. "I don't have time for stories, Lieutenant."

"It's short. It won't take long."

Simmons stood motionless in the doorway, his hand on the knob. Frank stepped over to a side table, where a computer screen glowed. He sat down in an armless swivel chair, set his coffee by the keyboard, and turned to face Simmons. He motioned toward the big leather chair behind the city treasurer's desk.

"You might as well sit down," Frank said.

Simmons looked Frank over, then walked to his desk, threw his briefcase on top, and sat. He leaned back and made a tent of his hands.

"Okay. Your story."

Frank leaned forward. He and Simmons were now less than two feet apart. "It begins when Father Robert J. O'Brien runs into one of his alumni. A man named Raymond Alvarez. O'Brien sees that Raymond Alvarez is doing okay. Better than okay. Alvarez is driving a very expensive set of wheels. A BMW. Red—"

Simmons sighed heavily. "There's a point here?"

"Getting there," Frank said, nodding, "getting there. Anyway, O'Brien puts the arm on Alvarez. Got him down and put the heat on him big time. Where'd the car come from, O'Brien probably asked. Maybe even threatened Alvarez with a long vacation in hell. You know, eternal damnation."

"Come on, Kearney." Simmons's voice was deadly. "You're already endangering your career. You want to start on your retirement, too?"

Frank ignored him. "Anyway, Raymond Alvarez comes clean. He's working for Solomon Jarvis. He runs money. Cash. Lots of cash. You see, Solly's a laundryman. Money laundry. Took the contacts he'd made in the department and set himself up for the drug lords on the East Coast."

"Jarvis, Jarvis," Simmons said, trying to place the name. "Ah, yeah. He's dead—that thing in the projects . . ."

"Yeah. Solly's dead. But you see, Solly wasn't *the* laundryman. He was just part of the operation—the collection agent. I figure the deal worked like this: Solly's customers—the wholesale drug dealers—dropped their cash at prearranged pick-up points. Then mules like Alvarez would pick up the stuff and carry it to a drop-off point. Both ends of the deal were what the boys at CIA call dead drops—Alvarez would go to a spot, the money'd already be there. He'd carry it to another spot, drop it and leave. It'd be picked up for laundering—a chain where no link knew who the other link was."

"Oh. What's to stop the mules from skimming cash off the top? Or running off with the whole bundle?"

Frank massaged his knee. "I wondered about that, too, Mr. Simmons. Try this on for size: The laundry route had a tight accounting system. A customer arranges for a pick-up by putting an ad in a newspaper. A personal ad with a simple code. Pick-up point and amount of cash. When the stuff got to the laundry, another ad would go in the paper, acknowledging receipt."

"That's ridiculous, Detective. Why should any of your imaginary wholesalers trust such a setup?"

Frank shrugged. "There's good news and bad news for dealers. Good news is, business is booming. Bad news is that the feds are making it harder to bank the profits. Sell a hundred kilos of coke and you have to do something with a ton of cash. A lot of wholesalers would risk a week's take to find a secure way to move their cash into a bank without jingling the feds."

Simmons got a lazy grin, but his eyes weren't smiling. "Okay, so Solly Jarvis had a courier route *from* the dealers. To where?"

"To you, Mr. Simmons," Frank said. "To you."

The silence froze the room. Then Simmons laughed. A deep rolling laugh, a man genuinely enjoying a great joke. Frank sat motionless, his face expressionless.

Simmons finally stopped laughing, but sat smiling big at Frank. "Okay, Detective, what puts the priest on my tail?"

"Probably happened like this, Mr. Simmons. O'Brien sweats it out of Alvarez, what he's up to. He also finds out from Alvarez there's a newspaper ad code. O'Brien collects enough ads to figure out the codes for the other drops. He stakes out the drops. Finally, he hits it. He's able to follow the pick-up man and traces him to you."

Simmons grinned more. "Oh, Jesus," he muttered in feigned disbelief, "this just gets wilder. They're gonna come after you with the butterfly net, Kearney. You're certifiable." He leaned forward, his bushy eyebrows arched. "But tell me, what did I do with these sacks of money?"

"O'Brien went to one of his buddies, a banking guru over at Georgetown University. O'Brien picked up a lot about banking, especially electronic fund transfers."

"And?"

"From public records, he got the listing of city accounts. Accounts that your office handled. Computer accounts."

"Yeah. Computer accounts," Simmons said, as if instructing a backward child. "I don't deal in cash."

"Oh, but you do. Large amounts. Every week."

Simmons sat without moving, but imperceptibly he seemed to sag.

Frank pressed on. "The lottery, Mr. Simmons—the District lottery. Powerball, Pick Four, all that. O'Brien likely figured that somebody—you—could mingle the dope money with the weekly lottery take. Every Monday, the lottery take's collected. That computer trick turns the cash into a legitimate bunch of electrons. Another computer trick, and the money's in the cartel's accounts. Minus your percentage, of course."

Simmons's eyes darted. "All you have's your little story. A bullshit story, Lieutenant. You've got a bunch of probables and maybes. But no evidence."

Deadpan, Frank stared at Simmons. Then he nodded. "You're right, Mr. Simmons. I don't have any evidence. Just a story."

It took a second for Simmons to register. Frank saw relief run through the man's body, the shoulders lift, the back straighten.

"Get out," he said. "Get the fuck out."

Frank stood, walked to the door, then turned. "There's just one more little bit to the story, Mr. Simmons."

Whatever was in Frank's voice made Simmons's face freeze. "Yeah?"

"O'Brien knew he wouldn't get anything solid, either. All he'd have would be a story. And besides, he didn't trust government."

"So?"

"So O'Brien called on another friend. A friend who put him in contact with a kid with the working alias Orion."

Simmons's anger flared. "God damn it—"

Frank held up his hand. "Orion's a hacker, Mr. Simmons. And when O'Brien was killed, Orion was working on a computer program for him."

"A computer program?" Simmons was still angry, but a note of wariness had crept into his voice.

"Yeah. Orion got the program finished. He was working on how to get it into your system when O'Brien was killed." Frank motioned to the glowing computer screen. "Once into the system, the program would search the entire network. It would ignore all the legal accounts. But if it found a secret account, it would send in a virus."

Simmons's face drained of color. "Virus?" his voice cracked. "Virus?"

"Yeah. The virus would do two things. Señor X, let's say, down in Medellín, would open his account. He'd find that all that untraceable electronic money was gone. Zeroed out. But the account wouldn't be entirely empty." Frank smiled. "No. In place of the money would be a little message that told Señor X where the virus had come from." Frank gestured toward the computer stand by Simmons's desk.

Comprehension, then disbelief and finally fear swept across Simmons's face. "You mean—"

Frank nodded. "Orion's program." Frank reached into his coat pocket and came out with a floppy disk. "I just put the virus in your computer." Frank checked his watch. "According to Orion, the virus should be all the way through the system by now."

He took in Simmons's stricken face. "Look at it this way, Mr. Simmons. If there aren't any illegal accounts, you've got nothing to worry about."

Then Frank smiled again. "On the other hand, if Señor X's checks start bouncing, you've got plenty to worry about."

International Herald Tribune

AMERICAN VICTIM OF HIT-AND-RUN

GENEVA, Feb 6—Charles Taylor Simmons, a Washington, D.C., official, died this afternoon of injuries sustained when he was struck by an unidentified vehicle. Mr. Simmons was reportedly in Geneva on government business, the nature of which was not disclosed.

The Washington Post

BURRIDGE CALLS IT QUITS
Rumors of Campaign Finance Collapse

By Charles Babcock
WASHINGTON POST STAFF WRITER

Washington mayor Malcolm Burridge sent shock waves through political circles across America when he announced suddenly that he will drop his run for reelection. Burridge, a seemingly invincible politician whose seesaw career has been marked by felony convictions and presidential awards, was widely seen as unbeatable. Even critics dubbed him Washington's "Mayor for Life."

Rumors are that the status of Burridge's campaign finances caused him to quit the race. The untimely death in Switzerland of Charles Simmons, city treasurer and Burridge's campaign manager, is said by some to be a major factor in his withdrawal.

Turn the page for a special preview of

A MURDER OF PROMISE

Available in hardcover March 2002
from G. P. Putnam's Sons!

MONDAY MORNING, OCTOBER 16, 2000. LILITH Hoagland burrowed deeper under the comforter to get away from Figaro, who was nuzzling her neck.

His tongue grazed her cheek.

She sat up.

"All right, damnit," she said.

Twenty minutes later, Figaro cocked his right leg, urinated on the Eisler's boxwood next door, scratched at the brick sidewalk, then leaned into his leash, eager for his morning walk.

Sunrise in the Georgetown enclave of Washington, D.C. Last night's front had brought an invigorating chill and the promise of a clear, blue autumn sky. Hoagland held Figaro's leash in one hand, and in the other an insulated coffee mug. She felt like a long walk. And Figaro, an English pug, hadn't seen his pal Blackberry, a Portuguese water dog, in some time. So, she decided, they would go to the park.

Figaro sniffed and peed his way up the hill toward R Street, while Hoagland sipped her coffee and enjoyed the early morning luxury of thinking about nothing in particular. Suddenly, a violent tugging on the leash snapped

Hoagland out of her reverie. The small dog had disappeared into a tall hedge.

"Come here." She yanked at the leash.

Figaro whined and struggled farther into the hedge.

A cat or a squirrel, Hoagland thought.

Until she saw the blood on Figaro's muzzle.

ONE

FRANKLIN DELANO KEARNEY and Josephus Adams Phelps looked down at the dead woman. Ten yards away, the woman who'd found the body stood on the sidewalk with the two uniformed officers who'd secured the scene. Forty-five minutes ago, just after daybreak, her dog had followed a blood trail to the base of a giant sycamore, at the edge of the small park.

"Used a big blade," José said. He pointed. "Look here."

Frank walked around to stand by José. He bent closer to look at the woman's right hand. A victim's hands frequently got cut up, trying to fend off a knife assault. Bone-deep gashes had laid the palm open. The little finger was missing.

Frank stared at the body, ticking over cases in his mind. Like a roulette ball, the names dropped into place. *Coleman and Janowitz.*

"Coleman and Janowitz? Didn't they . . . ?"

"Greek in the Creek," José said.

"Boukedes . . . Sarah . . . no, Susan," Frank corrected himself. Coleman and Janowitz had gotten the case two months ago. White female. Hacked to death in Rock Creek Park. Defensive wounds to both hands. He got a tightening in his throat.

"Wasn't she missing a finger?" he heard José asking. He

pulled air deep into his lungs and tried to shut out everything but here and now. He looked at the dead woman's face.

"Sort of familiar."

"Don't see how you can tell," José said.

Twenty-five years ago, there hadn't been many white-black partners on the District force. When Frank and José teamed up, everybody called them Salt and Pepper. Today it was unremarkable, and besides, no one dared talk that way anymore. Both were tall men, over six feet. Frank's dark auburn hair had grayed along the temples and José's close-cut nappy curls had turned a rich silver. Otherwise, both looked pretty much like their academy graduation photos: Frank the lean cross-country runner, José the heavyweight boxer. Both now were the most senior homicide detectives in Washington, D.C.'s Metropolitan Police Department.

Frank squatted low, taking care to avoid the blood-splattered leaves. The victim lay partially over her purse. He lifted the body enough to free the purse. Snapping it open, he found a key ring: two Schlage house keys and Volvo car keys. Then a billfold: three twenties, a ten, a five, and several ones. Behind a plastic window in the billfold, a District driver's license.

He looked up at José. "Mary Keegan," he said.

A nod of recognition. "Oh."

Frank looked back at the dead woman and tried to find a resemblance to the face he remembered. A regular on the Sunday talk shows. One of the best of the *Washington Post*'s legendary investigative reporters. Mary Keegan, the scourge of shady dealmakers in the White House and on Capitol Hill, winner of a Pulitzer for her exposés of government malfeasance and corporate corruption. Good-looking in an honest, straightforward way. High cheekbones, subtle makeup, ash-blond shoulder-length hair. Frank checked the date of birth. September 3, 1958. Forty-two years old. Moderately famous and probably moderately well-off. At least she had been. Now she was just dead.

"Sixteen seventy-three Thirty-second," he read the address off the license. He placed the address. East of Wisconsin Avenue—Georgetown's East Village. A block down from Dumbarton Oaks. Six, seven blocks from his home on Olive. He recalled seeing her occasionally, the inevitable crossings in a small town. Joking with Steve at Potomac Wines and Spirits. Picking up dry-cleaning at Uptown Valet. Buying stamps at the post office. Walking on late summer evenings.

"Stabbed her first near the sidewalk," Frank said, looking back to where the woman and her dog stood with the officers. "She got away. . . ."

"She got here," José continued. "He catches up with her. Stabs her in the back. She turns . . ."

". . . and he finishes the job."

"Last night sometime."

Frank studied the ruined face, trying to imagine it without the gaping wound below the left eye, the slashed throat. Trying to see her as she'd been yesterday this time. Maybe at church. Or a Sunday brunch with friends. A drive in the country. But alive. No idea of what was to come. Who she'd meet here.

"You know how this's going to go, don't you?" José asked.

Frank nodded. Mary Keegan might not be a household name, but she was known by a lot of people who were.

Early in his career, Frank had learned that Washington politics, like an overhead fan, was always turning. He imagined the fan picking up speed. Who was it, he wondered, who'd come up with the image of crap hitting the fan?

"Emerson's going to shit a brick."

"No doubt." Frank got a sour taste on the flat of his tongue, as if he'd bitten a penny. What got him about a high-profile case wasn't the pressure—the incessant phone calls, starting with Randolph Emerson, homicide commander, and running all the way up the so-called chain of command—it was the time you had to waste hand holding, answering the calls, sending up reports you'd already sent up before. Time you could be spending doing the job you were paid for, the job you signed on to do. He stood up, took a deep breath, and let his eyes wander over the park, searching out a world where there wasn't a dead woman on the ground and leaves covered with her blood.

Half an hour later, Tony Upton, the medical examiner, arrived at the same time as Renfro Calkins and his forensics team. An hour after that, Frank released the body to Upton. The two detectives waited until they were satisfied forensics was on track, then walked to the curb where they'd parked the car.

"You want to walk?" Frank asked. "Only a couple of blocks."

"Couple of blocks?" José frowned. "We walk a couple over, we got to walk a couple back. Couple blocks here, couple blocks there—"

"—and they begin to add up to some real distance," Frank finished.

The two detectives walked down Q Street and crossed Wisconsin, where the morning traffic from the Maryland suburbs was already beginning to clog the avenue.

"You still bringing him home tomorrow?" José asked.

"Yeah."

"How's he taking it, coming in to stay with you?"

"What do you think?"

"It's only for a little while."

"He suspects it's the first step to moving him into town."

"He's what . . . seventy-five? -six . . . ?"

"Seventy-eight."

José shook his head. "Not good, living out there by himself."

"Too old to be alone . . . stubborn man."

"Something about 'like father like son,' " José said.

"I think I've heard that."

"He looked good last month."

Last month had been a hundred years ago. Before the call at two in the morning. His father's voice, choking over words that wouldn't come out right.

"It was a warning. He might not be so lucky next time."

* * *

Mary Keegan's home on 32nd Street and scores of others like it made Georgetown Georgetown—a two-story red-brick Federal town house, white ornamental detailing around windows with rippling glass panes that had looked out on cobblestone streets two hundred years ago.

Georgetown's years as a major colonial port still shape the village's geography. Shops and businesses line M Street and run down to the waterfront. The residential area begins with modest row houses just above M. It crests on R Street with Montrose Park, Dumbarton Oaks estate, and the homes of Washington's power elite and the B-list pilot fish slipstreaming in their wake.

Frank lived just a block off M Street. Fifteen years ago, coming out of the divorce, he'd bought "as is" a crumbling little house on Olive Street. He'd stayed longer than he'd intended. He'd gotten attached to Georgetown. He felt more at home in the quirky, human-scale village than in downtown monumental Washington. Now the place on Olive had a dry basement, a sound roof, and fifteen years of sweat labor invested in plumbing, wiring, and plastering, not to mention refinishing floors, revamping AC and heating, and stripping layers of paint from wood paneling.

Now, standing in front of Mary Keegan's house, the brick walls glowed in the autumn sun's slanting light, and October's yellows and reds flared against a sky so blue it seemed to go into forever.

"Nice place," José said.

"Yeah."

"Washington does fall good," José said as they climbed the steps to the front door.

"Too bad it doesn't last longer." Frank rapped sharply with the heavy brass door knocker.

Down the street a painter rattled an extension ladder into place against a house front.

"Nothing going on inside," José said.

Frank knocked again, and waited.

After a moment, José shook his head. "Nobody home."

Both men snapped on latex gloves. Frank fished Mary Keegan's key from a Ziploc. The key turned smoothly as the heavy deadbolt fell back. Frank eased the door open. The two men stepped inside and stood motionless in the entryway, as if trying to get a sense of the house through the pores in their skin.

Frank identified the acid tang of tomato and under it the licorice of fennel and the solid blue-collar richness of garlic. Soft sounds of a flute solo came from somewhere in the depths of the house.

José touched Frank's shoulder. "Alarm," he said, nodding toward a keypad panel on the wall. A red light glowed steadily, accompanied by a low buzzing sound.

Frank flicked open his cell phone and dialed the security service number on the panel. The phone rang once, twice, three times.

"Somebody's still asleep," Frank said.

The red light now blinked angrily. Somewhere in the house above, a siren opened up with a howl. Finally, a dull voice answered. Frank gave the shut down code that the District-licensed commercial security companies supposedly recognized. The voice at the other end sounded confused and put Frank on hold. The siren now switched to a braying Klaxon.

Through the open door, Frank watched a patrol car pull up to the curb, its light bar blazing blue and red. A woman darted from a home across the street to the car and pointed to Mary Keegan's house.

José, flashing his badge, met the uniformed officers at the door. At that moment the alarm shut off.

"Thank God," Frank said, looking over José's shoulder.

The woman who'd run out into the street stood on the sidewalk at the foot of the Keegan house steps, hands on hips. Slender, with short, well-cut gray hair. Camel hair jacket, white silk blouse, red patterned silk scarf, dark gray flannel pants. Very neat. Very Georgetown. Mid-sixties, Frank guessed. She turned to leave. Frank edged past José and the uniformed cops.

"A minute, ma'am?" Frank called out.

"Me?"

Frank walked closer. He opened his badge case. "I'm Lieutenant Kearney, and this's my partner, Lieutenant Phelps."

"I've seen you," the woman said, looking at him as if trying to place him somewhere else.

"I live down on Olive, ma'am."

"They had a fire down there several weeks back."

"Two doors up."

"You have any damage?"

Frank shook his head. "Smell of smoke. Lucky, I guess. You live over there?" He pointed across the street to the white-brick duplex.

"Fifty years." She tilted her chin up. "Husband came here with Harry Truman."

Seventies, Frank thought, adjusting his estimate of her age.

She extended a delicate hand. A large diamond flared blue-white in the sun. "I'm Judith Barnes. Is there trouble?"

"We have an emergency involving Ms. Keegan," Frank said.

Barnes searched Frank's face. "She's in trouble."

"We need some information. Can we step inside?" Frank asked, nodding toward Mary Keegan's open door.

Barnes hesitated, then nodded. Frank stood aside. Judith Barnes entered the house and led the way into the living room. José closed the door and joined Frank and Barnes across the room.

Barnes looked around the room, started to sit, then changed her mind. She looked sternly at Frank and José.

Frank began. "Mrs.—"

"Just a damned minute, officer." Barnes held up a hand. "*You* tell *me* just what's happened."

A moment's hesitation, then Frank said, "She's dead."

Barnes's hand flew to her throat.

"How?" she asked in a strangled voice.

"We can't say yet, ma'am."

"Murdered?" Barnes's eyes widened. "But it *was* murder?"

"It looks like it."

Barnes sagged into a chair, shut her eyes, and hugged herself. "Murder," she repeated in a disbelieving whisper. She silently shook her head, then looked up to Frank and José. "You need information," she said, her voice picking up strength.

"Did you see Ms. Keegan yesterday?" José asked.

"Yes. I'm the block's nosey old maid, gentlemen," Barnes said. "I see a lot."

"Tell us when you last saw Ms. Keegan yesterday," Frank said.

"When she came back from her run. She went out just after four in the afternoon. She came back around five."

"Her running," Frank asked, "a regular thing?"

"You could set your watch by her. She was a disciplined woman. If her alarm hadn't gone off, I would have come over this morning, anyway."

"Why?"

"It's Monday. She's usually up and out by now. But her car's still there." Barnes made a head motion toward the cars parked along the street.

José made a note. "She drove it yesterday?"

"Grocery shopping. Two, two thirty. I'd just come back from a friend's. We waved to each other. Didn't say anything, though. I saw her through my kitchen window when she went out to run. As I said, that was just after four."

"Do you know of any relatives?" Frank asked.

"There's Damien, her brother. He lives in Boston."

"Parents?"

"Both dead."

"She was single?"

Barnes fell silent. As if hit by the second wave of realization of Mary Keegan's death.

"Married once," Barnes picked up. "I never met him. They lived up Wisconsin, near the cathedral. She bought this place after his death. That's when I met her, ten years ago."

"You've met the brother?"

"Oh yes. Mary introduced us several years ago. A splendid young man. I have his phone number. When Mary travels, she leaves the key with me and asks that I call Damien if anything happens."

"Has anything ever happened?" José asked.

"Not until now."

"How about when Ms. Keegan was here? Anything unusual happen?"

Barnes frowned at Frank for a moment, then shook her head. "She was a good neighbor. No parties. Perhaps some people over for dinner occasionally. She wasn't terribly social. I saw the light on in her study,"—Barnes pointed to the ceiling—"she worked late at night quite frequently. I've read all her articles, books. She wrote well. It's hard to find young people these days who can write a simple declarative sentence."

"Any regular visitors?" José asked.

"*Men*, you mean?"

"Men will do."

Barnes shook her head. "Nobody in particular. I mean, it wasn't as if there were a lot of . . . that there was *any* . . . promiscuity. She had some men friends." Barnes pursed her lips as if she'd stepped in something disagreeable and wanted to get away from it. "Mary Keegan was very much her own woman."

"You'd know," Frank asked, "if there was any one man in particular?"

"I'd *know*, Lieutenant. Despite our age differential, we had gotten quite close."

"Any recent men visitors?" José asked.

"Well . . ." Barnes seemed to be weighing her response. "Yes. One gentleman."

"Did you know him?"

"No."

"Did you and Ms. Keegan talk about him?" Frank asked.

"No."

Frank keyed in on Barnes's guarded tone. He glanced at José. José had picked up on it, too.

"What did he look like?" José asked.

Barnes hesitated. Her look said she realized she'd said

too much and had been left with nowhere to go but forward.

"Ma'am," José said softly, "she's dead and we have to find who killed her."

Barnes drew herself up.

"He was black." She blurted, eyes straight ahead. Then she looked at José and blushed, raising a hand to her mouth. "I mean," she stammered, "African-American."

"A black male African-American," José said, keeping a straight face.

"Tall. Well dressed," Barnes added.

"How often did he come calling?"

Barnes's mouth tightened. "I wouldn't describe it as *calling*."

"How often did you see him?" Frank asked.

"Several times."

"When was the last time you saw him?"

"Last month, sometime."

"Any specific date stick in your mind?

Barnes frowned in concentration, then shook her head. "I'm sorry . . ."

"Car?"

Barnes thought. "A Buick, I think. Gray. Very conservative."

"Did Ms. Keegan ever mention him?"

"No."

"You never asked her?"

Barnes frowned. "Of course not."

"Did she ever talk about enemies?"

Barnes frowned at Frank. "Enemies? That sounds rather melodramatic, Lieutenant."

"People difficulties, then."

"There were people who didn't like what she wrote. But they had only themselves to blame."

"How do you mean?"

"I mean that Mary Keegan discovered the truth and wrote about it. There are people in this town who have a congenital aversion to the truth."

José asked, "She ever mention any of them as problems?"

"No. None that I can recall. It was as if she kept those kinds of matters in another room. Another compartment. Separate from her personal life."

Frank glanced at the mantel clock. It was nine forty-five. It felt later. "You said you have Ms. Keegan's brother's phone number?"

Barnes stood. "I'll fetch it."

Frank and José walked her to the door and watched her cross the street. Frank turned and looked back into the house. He knew the house's layout. Not this particular house. But enough of ones like it. Straight back from the entry, the hallway would run toward a rear courtyard with living room, dining room, and kitchen off to the right. To Frank's immediate left the stairway to the second floor. Upstairs he'd find a bedroom at the back, looking down on the courtyard, a bathroom, and a second bedroom at the front, overlooking the street.

Frank glanced appreciatively around the orderly kitchen. Mary Keegan hadn't scrimped on the renovation. Sub-Zero fridge, Viking range, Miele dishwasher. A small fortune on English cabinets. Lustrous terra-cotta tile floors and creamy soapstone countertops. A small wine rack held a merlot and a shiraz Frank recognized and several Chiantis he didn't.

Upstairs, the front bedroom had been turned into a study. Bookcases and cabinets built into three walls. A stereo was tuned to WGMS. Something by Bach replaced the flute solo they'd heard on entering. One of the Brandenburg concertos, Frank thought, but he wasn't sure which one. An easy chair with a floor lamp faced a small fireplace. A large antique walnut desk paired off with a credenza that ran under the windows. On the credenza, a computer. Keegan had left it on, and as Frank watched, a rendering of Monet's water lilies morphed into a scene of a town on a river. Frank nudged the mouse. The screensaver vanished, its place taken by several columns of numbers.

José glanced over Frank's shoulder. "Refugees," he read.

"Looks like a research paper of some kind," Frank said.

Index cards had been neatly laid out on the credenza next to the computer keyboard. He glanced at the top card. "German," he said.

Frank turned away from the credenza. Mary Keegan had kept a neat desk. A brass banker's lamp, a leather-edged blotter, and an appointment calendar.

Only one entry for Sunday, the fifteenth. At seven P.M., a handwritten annotation, "1789."

"Seven o'clock last night," Frank read. "1789."

"Meaning?" José asked.

"Down on Thirty-sixth and Prospect, the restaurant."

"Walking distance."

And the park where Mary Keegan had been murdered lay halfway between her house and the restaurant.

A gleam of silver behind a stack of books caught Frank's eye. He held up an antique picture frame. Keegan stood beside a man. She wore a summer dress. She was smiling and looking at ease. For an instant, a screen flickered behind Frank's eyes, a TV clip—Keegan in talk-show banter, then the Keegan in the park. He switched focus to the man in the photo. He was dark-haired, ten, fifteen years older than Keegan. He had the fine bones of good breeding offset by a thickening along the jawline. Beneath the smile, Frank detected a world weariness; a man who'd seen a lot and wasn't eager to see more. In the background, the Eiffel Tower.

"That's her."

"Probably her husband," José said.

Frank put the picture back. He worked through the desk drawers. The expected home office supplies. In the large bottom drawer on the right side of the desk, file folders neatly tabbed with cryptic notations.

He walked around the room, scanning the books and mementos on the floor-to-ceiling shelves. Keegan had been a serious reader, he concluded. The Romans—Juvenal, Seneca, the Plinys Elder and Younger—nestled against Freud, Schopenhauer, Marx, and Engels. Two shelves filled with Churchill's works and a bronze bust of the bulldog prime minister. Government Printing Office collec-

tions of presidential papers, reports on world trade, United
Nations references on population, food, and energy. Fiction, too. Her taste ran from Elmore Leonard through Cor-
mac McCarthy to Thomas Hardy and Henry James.

By the window, a framed photograph caught Frank's
eye. Richard Nixon stood in the Oval Office, handing a
book to a young girl. Frank recognized the girl's smile.
Nixon wore a shifty look, as if caught at the border of a
forbidden act. Mary Keegan looked like she owned the office and Nixon was her visitor. The inscription across the
photo was standard Washington boilerplate: a best regards,
a signature, and a date: "June, 1971."

Frank looked out the window, down onto the street. A
nanny pushed a stroller along the sidewalk. Where'd he
been in '71? Returning to College Park, Maryland, a
twenty-two-year-old sophomore. Coming back to UMD
after a year in Vietnam and a year getting over Vietnam.
And Mary Frances Keegan had been thirty miles away in
the White House getting a book from Richard Nixon. And
now she was dead and he was standing in her house looking out the window. On the opposite sidewalk, a big black
Lab strained at its leash, pulling its human, a slender,
white-haired man, from tree to tree. Who owned who,
Frank wondered.

Frank glanced at his watch. By now, Tony Upton would
be checking the body into the morgue.

The thought came to him that, outside this house, people
were going about their lives, lives shaped and influenced
by their connection to Mary Keegan. Her brother. Friends
and maybe lovers. And, despite what Judith Barnes
thought, enemies: this was Washington and Mary Keegan
hadn't been a person to spare the pen.

Tony would photograph the corpse, take DNA samples,
and lift a set of prints. And then the woman who'd lived in
this house yesterday would never return here but would be
laid out on a tray and rolled into a locker in the body
cooler.

And the word would spread of Mary Keegan's death.
And Washington's network would buzz. And then the con-

nections would bypass the void. And people would re-adjust their lives and move on. And leave Mary Keegan in a fast-receding past.

Down below, the street was empty. The nanny with her stroller and the Lab with his white-haired man had disap-peared.

Suddenly, like a camera shutter closing and opening, Frank was no longer thinking about Mary Keegan. Now he was looking at a mental picture of the dark outlines of the killer. Like the silhouette target at a pistol range. He heard recorded voices. He turned around. José was making notes of calls left on the answering machine. He waited until José had finished.

José closed his notebook and put it in his pocket. "1789?"

"1789."

FRANK KNOCKED ON THE LOCKED DOOR. HE WAITED AND knocked again.

"They keep pretty good hours," José said. "Maybe we ought to go into the restaurant business."

"Policing's safer," Frank said. He knocked again.

Finally a pale face materialized out of the dark interior of the restaurant and mouthed the word "closed." A small stocky man in a shirt and tie shook his head and started to turn away.

Frank held up his badge.

"MARY KEEGAN?" MARCEL DUBOIS, 1789'S MANAGER, nodded. "She's a regular."

"Was she here last night?" Frank asked.

"I wasn't," Dubois said. "We can check the reserva-tions." He led them back to the maître d's station and opened a leather-bound ledger.

"Around seven o'clock," José prompted.

"I hope there's no trouble," Dubois said, trolling while running his finger down the Sunday dinner page. He looked up, and when Frank and José didn't say anything, he turned his attention back to the reservations.

Dubois shook his head. "No reservation in Ms. Keegan's name." Before Frank could say anything, Dubois raised a manicured hand. "But . . . she is listed as an expected guest."

"Whose guest?" Frank asked.

"The Honorable David Trevor." Dubois said it with the lofty majesty of a DAR dowager. As if to make certain Frank and José appreciated the importance of David Trevor and the glory his presence reflected on his restaurant, Dubois added, "He is deputy secretary of state." And as if that weren't enough, "He is Madeleine Albright's deputy."

"Thank you for telling us who the Honorable David Trevor is, Mr. Dubois," Frank said dryly. "Now, can you tell me if he was here with Ms. Keegan?"

Dubois examined the ledger. "There's a line through his name. We do that to show that the guest arrived. He claimed his reservation shortly before seven." He bent closer to the book. "But there's no line through her name."

"Trevor," José said, "can you tell when he left?"

Dubois thought for a moment, then snapped his fingers. "Last night's checks are in the office."

Ten minutes later, Dubois handed Frank a restaurant check. Stapled to it, a credit card charge slip. David S. Trevor had been billed for a bottle of San Pelligrino and a glass of chardonnay. He had paid with an American Express card, leaving a three-dollar tip on the twelve-dollar charge. The check had been closed out at 7:43 P.M.

It struck Frank that standing outside 1789 was like standing outside an eighteenth-century tavern. But then, look across the Potomac at Rosslyn and the glass-and-aluminum towers of *USA Today* and you fast-forward a couple of centuries. He turned away from Rosslyn to José.

"If we want to cover our asses, we'll sit down with Randolph before we go talk with the Honorable David Trevor," Frank said.

"On the other hand," José said, "we drop that in Randolph's lap, we'll have to sit there while he agonizes about you and me pissing off the establishment. And we end up talking to the Honorable Mr. Trevor, anyway."

Frank nodded. "Yeah," he said. "Let's save poor Randolph the agony."

About the Author

Before turning to crime fiction, **Robert Andrews** published four thrillers that drew on his own experiences as a Green Beret, a CIA operative and senior liaison officer with the White House and the Departments of State and Defense, and a national security advisor to a senior U.S. senator. An expert on intelligence and defense matters who holds an advanced degree in Asian history, he has lived and worked in Washington, D.C., for many years, and his intimate knowledge of the city, its people, and its politics permeates *A Murder of Honor,* enriching what is already a superb, action-packed tale.

ROBERT ANDREWS

A MURDER OF PROMISE

A NOVEL

PUTNAM

A GAME OF SPIES

A NOVEL

JOHN ALTMAN

author of A GATHERING OF SPIES

PUTNAM